Philip G. Williamson is thirty-six years old. His formal education ceased at the age of fifteen and he spent the next ten years in intensive study at the University of Life. He lives in north London with his wife and young daughter. Under the pseudonym Philip First he has written two novels, *The Great Pervader* and *Dark Night*, and one story collection, *Paper-thin and Other Stories* – all published in Paladin.

# PHILIP G. WILLIAMSON

# The Firstworld Chronicles

## 2: The Legend of Shadd's Torment

Grafton

*An Imprint of* HarperCollins*Publishers*

Grafton
An Imprint of HarperCollins*Publishers*,
77-85 Fulham Palace Road
Hammersmith, London W6 8JB

A Grafton Original 1993
9 8 7 6 5 4 3 2 1

Copyright © Philip Williamson 1993

The Author asserts the moral right to
be identified as the author of this work

A catalogue record for this book is
available from the British Library

ISBN 0 586 20906 9

Set in Trump Mediaeval

Printed in Great Britain by
HarperCollinsManufacturing Glasgow

For Elizabeth.

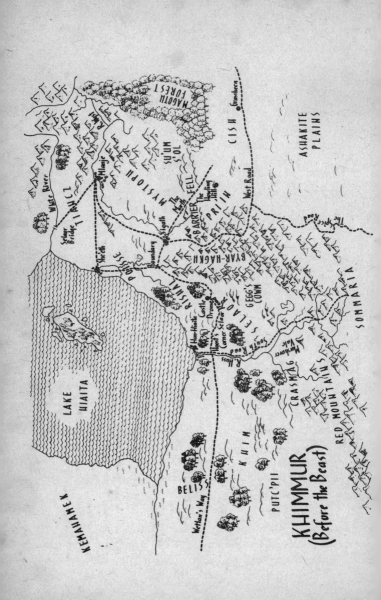

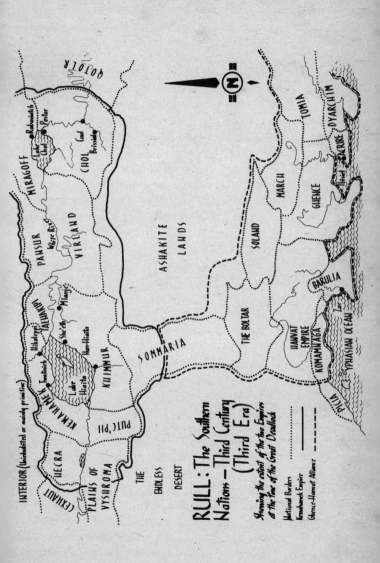

RULL: The Southern
Nations — Third Century
(Third Era)

Showing the extent of the two Empires
at the Time of the Great Deadlock

National Borders ————
Kewharek Empire
Ghence-Hamat Alliance - - - - - -

# PROLOGUE

*(A brief note on the genesis of a humble tome.)*

'Summoned, as I was one winter's morning four months past to attend upon Her Majesty, our Holy Queen Serhlin, Sage-Empress and Benefactress of all Rull, I found the august personage in a state of high excitement not wholly consonant with one of her dignity and stature. It has been my privilege, I will say, to share acquaintance on recent occasions with aspects of the Holy Queen-Empress's personality not revealed to the populace at large. This I take to be a great compliment, a gracious acknowledgement on her part of my low person in respect of the meagre talents I possess. In short, a confidence. She has seen fit, in my presence, to dispense with certain lofty mannerisms and regal deliveries that befit her exalted status when dealing with members of the lower orders. I believe I have been granted admittance to the most outer chamber of a privileged Inner Circle.

'Lest my words be wrongly construed, I hasten to add that there has never been anything undignified in her comportment. Nothing in the least improper. No, I believe the Holy Majesty simply revealed herself as she felt herself to be, without the usual constraints that such elevated office and her extraordinary descent place upon her. I saw her capable of gaiety, of almost girlish ebullience, of bright humour and emotion. I caught glimpses not only of the strength we all know her to possess, but of frailty and vulnerability too. Upon reflection I saw for the first time not a deity, not a queen, not an object of worship and devotion, but a woman, fair and lovely. I saw her as human, and I cherish those moments.

'"Parvislopis," cried she upon my entrance, "we are to rewrite history!"

'I took mental note of her casting of the first person. I was not without an inkling of what was to come. Inasmuch as the physical performance of the task involved was concerned I suspected that the "we" translated more precisely as "you" – that is to say, I. "We" might well take credit for the finished product, though that too was improbable: if my work, upon completion, met with the hoped-for Holy Majestic approval, I had little doubt that I, as its true author, would have to content myself with a most secondary place when plaudits resounded. Some reference to my efforts might somewhere, perhaps, grace a page, in small and undistinguished fount. But recognition would belong to our Sage-Empress, who commissioned the work, after all. Her name it is which will be recalled in history.

'Which is as it should be, for Serhlin *is* our Revered Queen-Empress, and I am but a worthless instrument in the Holy Royal Design.

'She paced her chamber, the fingers of both hands playing distractedly with a small jewelled talisman of abstract configuration and inestimable value. To one side a huge log fire threw out its warmth, holding at bay the chill of winter which seemed embedded in the old stone walls and floors of the palace. Her maids-in-waiting and a couple of expressionless pages stood respectfully close by, and I recognised one or two ladies and a gentleman of noble extract who served in the capacity of advisors to the Holy Royal Personage.

10

'Close before the hearth I saw to my satisfaction a small reading desk upon which rested, open, a large book bound in blue doeskin. This was the rough of the newly translated second volume of the Dinbig Manuscript, that vital set of historical documents recovered four years or so earlier from the ruins of the city of Rabaviatch in the land once called Miragoff.

'Queen-Empress Serhlin gazed shiningly upon me. Her august lips had formed into a quivering smile. Her eyes were bright with the reflections of the flames, and her cheeks, I saw, were touched with twin highpoints of colour.

'"It is marvellous," quoth she. "I have read it, and it is marvellous."

'She extended her arms towards me. "Come now, Parvislopis. Have you nothing to say? I am pleased. It is a wonderful translation. So remove that sheepish expression from your face and come forward. I want to hear what you have to say."

'"You are most gracious, Holy Majesty," I replied, stepping forward, relieved, for it is I who have headed the team charged with the translation of those nine hefty tomes that comprise the Manuscript in its entirety. The first volume had already seen the light of day, receiving instant royal approval, and gone immediately to print. This second volume, despite the most difficult aspect (the actual translation of the old Kemahamek language in which it was written) having been overcome, had yet posed particular problems of its own which had proved almost equally taxing.

'Holding my hands, palms up, the statutory six inches below those of the Holy Queen-Empress, I bowed from the waist to touch my lips to her sacred aura, an inch above the curved, ivory-toned wrists. "I am indeed honoured."

11

'"Yes. Now, come. We are to be candid and informal. Have wine. Have ale. Have biscuits. Be at your ease."

'I straightened. The two pages came forward bearing platters supporting pitchers of both wine and ale and various small confections. I declined the biscuits but indicated my choice of beverage; the rich, fragrant ruby wine of the Queen's own vineyards was poured with a musical sound into a golden goblet. I took it and sipped with a degree of circumspection.

'"I am excited," resumed the Queen-Empress, "as indeed you indicated I might be when you delivered the work to me yesterday. I have not slept, so rapt was I by what I read. The candles in my chamber burned constantly throughout the night, for I could not take my eyes from the pages of this wonderful book. I feel that I have travelled. I have been back in time, to a world that the centuries have swallowed. He lived! Yes, of course, we knew that; Dinbig told us so in his first volume. But now, what a picture we have! Shadd lived, and the legend too is now revealed to be based firmly in truth! Oh, marvel of marvels. How this will resonate when it is made known to the public!"

'I nodded, already knowing the answer to the question I now posed. "Then it is your intention to have the work reproduced for public consumption?"

'"For public *education*, Parvislopis. Public *education*. Of course it is. Of course it is. This is far too great a treasure to be kept hidden from the eyes of the world." She gave a little joyful laugh. "It belongs to the people, and they shall have it, in its full and proper form. And you, it goes without saying, will be its executor. Now, how long do you estimate you will need?"

'I pondered a moment, for effect rather than out of necessity, for in my mind I had lived through this moment many times. "Four to five months, Holy

Majesty, provided I am able to devote my time solely to this task and no other."

'"Done!" declared Queen-Empress Serhlin, clapping her hands together. "Be away with you this instant, Parvislopis, and return to me when your work is complete."

'The honour of re-writing the famed Legend of Shadd's Torment so as to place it in its true historical context was immense, but not without risks. Folklore, legends, myths, have always played an important role in our culture, and Shadd's Torment was one of the best loved and most oft-told tales in all Rull. Now Dinbig's great historical journal had revealed hitherto unknown facts about the legend, its setting, its characters and its time.

'The challenge before me was to reintegrate the popular elements of the legend with the simple historical data previously known plus those facts now revealed to us in Dinbig's writings. The legend had to remain intact; to tamper with it in a manner that did not find favour could lead to unhappy consequences. Reprobation, perhaps demotion, would follow in the natural course. The glimpse I had been favoured with, the initial small step out of commonality into the outermost of the elevated Inner Circles, would certainly be my last.

'A successful re-writing, on the other hand, would open doors beyond reckoning.

'The legend unfolded in the beginning of the period known as The Hiatus, the years of the Beast of Rull, between the Third and Fourth Eras of our history. Prior to the Dinbig Manuscript little existed in the form of reliable documentation of this time. Now, quite suddenly, we had a first hand account. But could history and legend be made to merge — both being effectively altered – without creating suspicion or resentment? I had a mighty task before me.

'Then there was the problem of the actual telling. The legend, handed down over generations, has always been told in the third person. Dinbig, on the other hand, narrated his work in the first person. He told Shadd's story alongside his own, with an insight into the character not only of Shadd himself, but of those other characters and events which are now seen to make up the tale in its entirety. Other favoured Rullian fables, such as "Yshcopthe's Ruse", "The Tale of the Good Vhazz", and "The Wanderer and the Mage" are seen, thanks to Dinbig's account, to be inseparable both from history and from the Legend of Shadd's Torment itself. Consequently I had to somehow incorporate these into the work, again making adjustments in order to establish historical fact.

'A mammoth undertaking. But I believed I could do it. I hoped I could. No matter the risks, there was nothing I desired more than to work upon this magnificent find.

'The weeks and months have now passed. My task is complete. I have worked unstintingly, my neck rarely straightening in all this time as I sat at my desk, surrounded by works of fact, of fiction and fable, of simple speculation. I resolved, as I considered the task I had set myself, that mine would not be a conventional approach. The two originals upon which I worked commanded respect: for one such as I to attempt to alter their individual characters would be deplorable. Thus Dinbig unfolds his own personal history as Shadd's compelling tale is told – with the bonus of Dinbig's experience and observations – in unadulterated form. I have kept my own interpolations to a minimum, merely inserting

14

explanatory notes and comments where I deemed necessary.

'Now I wait. The Holy Queen-Empress, her Sage and August Majesty Serhlin, Benign Ruler of all Rull, Hope of the People, Benefactress of the Poor and Needy, Supporter of the Oppressed, Vanquisher of Oppressors, Bride of Wisdom and Light, Defender of the Good and Righteous, Foe of Ignorance, Terror of Malefactors, Illuminator of the Past, Exemplar of the Present, Mother of the Future, Just and Mighty Leader, has been informed. The manuscript has been delivered into her hands.

'What do I feel? It is hard to describe. Pride and trepidation, anxiety and hope, and, well, resignation. I have done my best. No man can hope to do more.

'My future even now is being decided. Promotion, esteem, a thousand new possibilities, will surely be mine if my work meets with the approval first of the Sage-Empress and her advisors, and then the people. Should the opposite be the case, well, it will be my end. Perhaps a modest clerical post in some forgotten backwater, if I am lucky. It is better not to dwell on it. I have staked my career and reputation on The Legend of Shadd's Torment. You who read what follows are perhaps the most able judges of my endeavour.'

Parvis Parvislopis

Archivist

# 1

I

The Enchanter Wars of the First Era of Firstworld's fractured history are inaccurately named. Magic in various modes and forms was utilised almost randomly by practitioners with awesome abilities. It is true that specialisations and individual styles and methods were beginning to make themselves apparent as the search for knowledge developed, but these could not yet properly be termed disciplines. The word suggests a direction or control which was plainly lacking at this juncture. Under the probings of the obsessed minds of its manipulators magic was revealing much of its profound and apparently illimitable scope, as well as its unpredictable nature. But systems and rules were as yet barely formulated, and no schools of learning existed by which knowledge might be passed down.

The term 'Enchanter' was therefore broadly used to describe any of the magic-wielding beings that existed during the First Era. It was taken from the common parlance of peoples who had no means of distinguishing between the forms of magic being utilised, but who found themselves hapless witnesses to, and victims of, their oft-times monstrous and devastating effects.

The 'Enchanters' were of non-human origin and, it would appear, immortal unless their existence was interrupted by unnatural means. It is widely held that they were not of Firstworld, or were of some ancient godlike race now all but vanished. Frequently, however, they chose to appear in human semblance in order to mingle in human society for study or simple amusement.

What little is known of the history of the time records that twenty-four of these beings made their homes in Rull. With them they brought strife and terrible discord as they contested, each against the others, for ultimate power.

Decades of struggle saw the very face of Rull altered due to the sheer volume and strength of magical forces unleashed. No dominant being emerged, nor seemed likely to, but the wars continued. The Enchanters strove ever harder to streamline and perfect their arts in order to find some means of achieving supremacy over their adversaries.

The enchantress, Yshcopthe, was percipient of the havoc wreaked as a consequence of the ambitions of herself and her kind. She saw too the cruel suffering endured by the various races of Rull. She devised a ruse intended to bring about an end to the strife.

Yshcopthe appealed for a truce, an idea that was initially not well received. Every magic-wielder suspected every other of subterfuge and underhandedness in their efforts to gain ascendancy. But Yshcopthe was acknowledged by most as being among the cleverest and most potent of the twenty magicians still active (four having perished during the course of the war). She had attracted several lesser mages as allies (though admittedly with differing degrees of enthusiasm and questionable motives). Thus when she spoke she was paid some heed.

A simple truce could not endure without the inclusion of strong incentive in some form, proposed in such a manner as to emphasise advantages to each and every participant. Yshcopthe despatched a missive to each of the nineteen combatants:

*Brothers and Sisters of the Arcane Reach, Worthy Opponents, Most-Honoured and Potent Friends and Adversaries,*

It has surely come to the attention of you all that the contest we wage against each other has in the years of its persistence brought no favourable result to any particular individual. Nor is a favourable result foreseeable. We struggle, we compete, we wage war and we achieve nothing of worth, but in our self-centred striving we give little heed to the devastation we are wreaking upon this place that we have made our domain.

I have taken note of what we have done, and predict that if we continue we will cause irreversible harm. The world we now behold may soon cease to exist in the form we know it.

'What is this to us?', I hear you mutter. 'There exist worlds aplenty. When this one is done, we will away to another.'

But I ask, to what end? To amuse ourselves further with strife and discord when logic surely informs any of us still possessed of wits that there can be no satisfactory conclusion? For my part I find this a wearisome exercise, fit only for those intent upon exploring the bounds of futility in all its forms.

I have applied long deliberation to this matter. I asked myself, What is it that drives us on in our course? The answer came: It is the desire for power. Each of you, I believe, will agree that this is so.

But power is an effect, derived from knowledge, understanding and judicious application. A full and comprehensive knowledge of the principles which govern the profound arcana in which we have immersed ourselves may well be impossible, but there is yet much which can be mastered. And each one of us, we will surely admit, desires everything it is possible to have.

*Therefore I have arrived at an alternative. I propose hereby a convocation of all parties who seek to learn everything it is presently possible to learn. Let us assemble at some location of mutual consensus, there to pool the cryptic knowledge that we have gained as the fruits of the endeavours of years. And let it be done in such a way that as we give so do we receive.*

*Our spells, our chants, the methods and modes of our respective fields will be entered and recorded in a great secret repository. All who attend and give of their knowledge shall have the opportunity to draw from the repository and thus learn the secrets of others. Thereby shall we each gain new potentials which will surely be sufficient to engage us for years to come, without further recourse to unnecessary and destructive conduct. And equally, though each will gain immensities, none will emerge more powerful than the others.*

*Those who perceive advantage in this course, apply to me forthwith,*

> *Yshcopthe,*

> – *at my home, Ance Arb, in the mountains of the Harsh Maiden, in Qotolr.*

Simple in nature but deft in its understanding of the motives that underlie strife, the missive offered too great a challenge to be wholly disregarded. The greatest immortal foes of its writer, tempted initially to scoff, could not but acknowledge the possibilities embraced by her proposal.

Of the nineteen, the majority waited to view the responses of others. Yshcopthe's four most loyal (or perhaps opportunist) allies were the first to pledge support. Almost immediately three more gave their approval, among them, surprisingly, Urch-Malmain the

Diabolist, a morose and foul-tempered creature, not normally given to keeping company of any kind.

Then Blelac the Arch-Enchanter joined the growing band, and with him two of his own supporters, the naturomancer Krimlinnic of Blone, and Tchouchourezzin, an illusionist. The necromancer, Vaclad the Grim, a dark and saturnine fellow of peculiar habits and perverse temperament, next sent word of his support. Another followed, then another, and those that remained were quick to perceive the disadvantages of their position – for surely Yshcopthe now had enough support to press ahead, with or without unanimity?

And so the full complement of magic-wielders was gained, and the first phase of Yshcopthe's Ruse was complete.

Next to be agreed upon was the venue. Reluctant to impose her own opinions, for fear of appearing to be angling for personal advantage, Yshcopthe arranged a tour. Setting out from Ance Arb, the twenty commenced a survey of the surrounding lands in order to choose a suitable location. After several days of squabbles and disagreements Yshcopthe took them past the mountain called M'nag dro'b'Ggos, or 'The Blade which Enters the Belly of Heaven'.

Here, unbeknown to the others, she had earlier cast a veiled enchantment of such a nature as to impress with its stature and magnificence any who beheld M'nag dro'b'Ggos, and draw them to investigate more closely a plateau lying some distance below its summit, where stood a palace of immense grandeur and charm.

Krimlinnic it was who first spotted the mountain, and veered immediately towards it. The others followed, each perceiving in his or her own manner something which appealed most subtly and irresistibly to their aesthetic senses.

As the twenty descended to the plateau Yshcopthe, to safeguard her ploy, introduced an element of authentic discord. She carefully Opened the Enchanted Eyes of both Vaclad the Grim and the sorceress, Blue Pessilia, such that they, gazing upon the place, saw not a picturesque plateau and magnificent palace, but the reality that had existed prior to the enchantment: a couple of dilapidated goatsheds on a rainswept glacial meadow.

Pessilia and Vaclad immediately protested at the inappropriateness of the site, but were shouted down by the others who were already adding touches of their own to the charmed landscape they perceived. Yshcopthe had chosen her stooges carefully: Blue Pessilia was considered something of a dilettante by the majority. Her petulance tested the patience of many; she was somewhat hideous to the naked eye – even the eyes of Enchanters, who employed the ghastly and grotesque as a matter of routine – and was unmoved by petitions to modify her appearance so that others might gain pleasure from the sight and experience of her. Thus her opinions carried no weight. And Vaclad, potent and so accorded a certain respect, was universally despised.

Yshcopthe herself pointed out one or two small failings in the chosen site, but again, to her secret pleasure, was overruled.

The venue then was agreed upon. And all voiced the opinion that now was as good a time as any to commence the Great Pooling.

They entered the palace, assured in their own convictions that this superior site had been of their spontaneous choosing. As they passed through the illusory chambers and galleries each, in accordance with his or her own preferences, effected alterations to the environment, to the extent that where in fact there had previously existed little at all of true substance there now came into being a most wonderful confection which bore an uncanny resemblance to the palace Yshcopthe had conjured via her enchantment.

Yshcopthe walked among them, her satisfaction well-concealed. The second phase of her ruse was accomplished, but there remained much to be achieved before she could begin to count herself successful.

The twenty took up residence in their temporary new abode. Each moved into apartments of his or her own choosing and refashioned them as they pleased. Yshcopthe prepared the chamber, high in the northernmost tower of the palace, into which all would come to give up their secrets. Here she called upon the assistance of beings rarely encountered in the confluence of dimensions that together composed the reality of which Firstworld and its universe were a part. With these helpers and the aid of much magic she constructed the great Crystal Repository, a living artefact whose components were drawn from many different worlds and dimensions, which would one day bring forth the book known as Yshcopthe's Pandect.

And here is another term wanting of precision. For though the Crystal had the potential to absorb all that could be placed within it, and subsequently transcribe into the Pandect everything that was currently known of the magical arts, Yshcopthe was wise enough to realise at the outset that this would never come to be. Suspicions would at all times run high among the magicians gathered in the palace. The process of yielding up their knowledge would be slow and weighed with great caution. Few, if any, would be willing to give up all of their secrets.

The Great Pooling held an aspect that Yshcopthe had not disclosed when proposing her plan. The success of her Ruse depended upon this aspect remaining a secret from the other nineteen for the longest possible duration. Yshcopthe had placed numerous powerful enchantments in and about the chamber which contained the Crystal Repository. Into the sensorium of the Crystal itself she had cast a command of Memory Theft. This had the effect of accepting, from the mind of the magician yielding his or her knowledge, not only the specific spell offered but the very memory of that spell. Thus, having yielded a spell, its donor would retain no recollection of it.

Supplementing this command was a spell of Theft of the Memory of Memory. This was a complex and crucial addition which robbed the magician of the very recollection of ever having possessed that particular item of knowledge.

Here then was the essence of Yshcopthe's Ruse. As each of the magic-wielders gave up their knowledge, they would, unbeknown to themselves, be unwittingly deprived of that knowledge forever.

Various enchantments of Magic Concealing were placed upon the Crystal and about the chamber, disguising all trace of the spells within the Crystal. As a further safeguard spells of No Magic and Reveal Other Magic were cast upon those of Magic Concealing. Monitors of one form or another were hidden within the shadows of rafters and cupboards to observe and report all comings and goings inside the chamber. The Crystal Repository was garbed with numerous spells of protection to guard against attempts to directly interfere with its intricate and delicate processes.

Even so, Yshcopthe knew that skulduggery of one sort or another would be afoot. Each of the nineteen would come armed with magical defences and tricks of their own. It could only be a matter of time before one or the other of them found a way around her protective spells, upon which her deception would be promptly brought to light. With the realisation of the memory theft would come the grand reckoning.

Yshcopthe's primary hope was that it might come later rather than sooner. With every secret given up to the Crystal the magical power of its former possessor would be commensurately reduced. The longer Yshcopthe's duplicity remained undiscovered the greater would be the Crystal's store of secret knowledge. When revelation became imminent, if she could transcribe that greater knowledge from the Crystal Repository into the Pandect, then make her escape, she would possess the key to immensities untold. The remaining nineteen magic-wielders would suffer significant diminutions of their powers, and Firstworld would have become a safer place.

II

The Great Pooling was slow to begin. On the morning after the Repository was completed, the nineteen assembled with Yshcopthe before the great Crystal, but none was willing to volunteer to initiate the process. Yshcopthe was obliged to give up one of her own secrets in order to demonstrate the safety and simplicity of the operation. Unable to negate the command of Memory Theft, she chose a minor spell, the loss of which would be of no great consequence, and prayed that none would interrogate her afterwards in regard to the nature of her offering.

The others observed with murmurings and dark glances, and when Yshcopthe rose smiling from before the Crystal, fired various questions at her. Eventually satisfied they made off to a more spacious chamber within the palace, there to decide who would go first.

Yshcopthe waited. The morning passed and no one showed. Eventually, with the sun outside the palace well beyond its zenith, the door to the chamber of the Repository opened and in stepped Manomin the Wizard. He wore the guise he most frequently favoured, one which would much later be commonly employed by magic users who focused upon the fields of wizardry: that of an elderly man with flowing white locks and beard, draped in a long, midnight-blue cloak adorned with yellow stars and a tall conical hat of similar decoration. He stood beside the door, casting an habitual wily grin, as if somehow cognisant of being the progenitor of a fashion.

Manomin's eyes, however, held little amusement. They shifted restlessly around the chamber, and were drawn again and again to the great Crystal in its centre, which glowed with a pale, unearthly pink lucence. Yshcopthe detected the aura of powerful raptures. She tensed somewhat. Would Manomin see straight through her ploy? Was she to be discovered so early?

'Well, Yshcopthe,' smiled Manomin in a voice both reedy and glottal, 'I am here. The first.'

'By free choice?' enquired the enchantress.

'Ah, indeed not. Rather, by lot. We drew straws. One did not like the result and declared it null and void. So we cast dice, to similar result. We devised tests: of stamina, patience, wit and intellect. Still we failed to reach agreement. So we fell back again upon the straws. This time it was I who drew the shortest. I would have protested but for the knowledge that to do so would merely set the whole tedious process into motion again from its beginning. I lack the patience to endure such an ordeal a second time. So, I have agreed to be your sacrificial beast.'

25

'There is no sacrifice required, Manomin, be assured. And remember that when all is done and the Pandect complete, you will gain far more than you have given.'

Manomin sniffed the air. 'This chamber is replete with magical effectuation!'

'I do not deny it. The Repository itself is magical in nature, and I have of necessity placed protections of my own about it. It is unique and has cost me greatly. If it were damaged or destroyed I do not believe I could create another.'

Manomin inspected the Crystal. 'It is indeed a curious device. I once witnessed something of its kind on Fallipticotia, one of the far moons of the planet Hase in the constellation of Argus. That, however, had a quite different purpose. Tell me, what form of Crystal is this?'

'That I cannot say,' Yshcopthe replied, perceiving the direction of his enquiries. 'I employed a variety of entities who supplied me with the raw materials and components. Even the device's final construction was performed by sentient agencies more knowledgeable than I.'

Manomin gave a stiff waggle of his jaw, tugging at his beard, and said peevishly, 'Let us proceed, then.'

Yshcopthe guided him to a chair placed before the glowing Crystal. 'Be seated. Remove your splendid hat. Now place your head within this aperture, as you saw me do earlier, so that your venerable chin rests upon the knobbed plate. Good. Now, the helmet here will descend to cover the forepart of your crown, so. Allow the membrane within the aperture to float forward and lightly cover your face. You will experience a light but not unpleasant tingling sensation as sensorial probes of an energetic nature penetrate your outer cortex. Now simply concentrate upon the

26

knowledge you wish to yield. The probes will perceive your thought patterns and relay them into the Crystal itself. There they will be decrypted and transcribed into the Pandect for retrieval at a later stage.'

The wizard made himself comfortable. Yshcopthe retired to an adjacent chamber. The Crystal throbbed and emitted a low hum, indiscernible to a human ear. Manomin sat quietly, absorbed in the process. Yshcopthe waited, and her monitors observed and reported all that transpired within the chamber during her absence.

Within three minutes all was done. Manomin rose from the Crystal with a smile and declared himself quite invigorated, then departed. Yshcopthe re-entered the chamber to gaze into the Crystal. As she had suspected Manomin had yielded little: a single minor spell of scant use to anyone. She gave a sigh, though she'd expected no more. The process was going to be of long duration, and every minute that passed increased the chances of her being undone.

A week went by. Each of the twenty gave a little, then a little more. Gradually their reticence was overcome, for they found the process pleasant and remained unaware of their losses. Suspicion, though, still ran high. Requests to Yshcopthe to view the uncompleted Pandect were frequent, and denied. She explained, with some prevarication, 'The transcription is an ongoing process. To interrupt it at any stage, as must be done to view the contents of the Pandect, is to bring the entire process to an end. I beseech you all, have patience.'

One morning while inspecting the Repository Yshcopthe was shocked to discover that a certain minor mage, Feluthagast by name, had yielded up his entire stock of arcane knowledge. This threw her immediately into a dilemma. On the one hand it was a measure of Feluthagast's confidence in her, coupled perhaps with a foolhardy impatience, that he had felt himself able to do so. It might be hoped that others would follow suit. On the other, it meant that Feluthagast was now reduced to the state of a mere man (assuming that male human guise was what he had adopted at the instant at which he yielded his magic), dispossessed of all power.

A happy development, for Yshcopthe and for First-world itself, if all had done likewise. But Yshcopthe knew that her enchantments of Memory Theft could not hope to deceive one who had lost everything. The loss, though perhaps not immediately understood, would soon become evident to some degree or other. And the others would be equally quick to perceive.

She flew to Feluthagast's apartment to find the erstwhile mage in a state of befuddlement reminiscent of one who has smoked one too many pipes of shugweed. No recourse suggested itself other than to render him wholly insensible, then secure his apartment so that no one might enter or leave. This she did, taking some comfort in the knowledge that the nineteen magicians seldom mingled by choice in one another's company; some time would pass before anyone noticed or thought to remark upon Feluthagast's absence.

Over the next few days four others similarly yielded their total knowledge to the Crystal. Yshcopthe responded with similar dispatch. Each was confined to his or her apartment, in a state of uninterrupted stupor, with entities in the Enchantress's employ set to attend upon their needs.

It is written in Firstworld lore that these five, upon their release from Yshcopthe's enchanted palace, descended in bewilderment into the surrounding lands. Four became eventual leaders of the foremost tribes of men. The fifth, Quirde, a former summoner, was condemned, due to the unorthodox and now permanent guise he had adopted at the time of yielding his knowledge, to seek the company of dogs and canine-like beasts. Many attribute the evolution of the vhazz, those reviled and savage creatures, part-dog part-human, to Quirde's influence.

Yshcopthe, meanwhile, understood that her time was growing shorter.

### III

Three nights later Yshcopthe was awakened in her bed by a voice urgently sibilant in her ear.

'Someone tampers with the Crystal!'

'What do they do?'

'I told you, they tamper.'

'What is their motive?'

'I am a Monitor,' hissed the Monitor. 'I monitor and report and can do nothing other. Neither my instructions nor capabilities embrace the possibility of reading minds.'

'Then what is the identity of the intruder?'

'He is the diabolist, Urch-Malmain.'

Yshcopthe immediately dispatched an Enquiring Wisp to the chamber of the Crystal.

Urch-Malmain, who was bent over the silently glowing, strangely configured Crystal, absorbed in the mysteries of its complex workings, straightened and glanced about him. 'Ah, I perceive I am discovered. I know not by whom, though I suspect it is you, Yshcopthe, the engineer of all that has come to pass in this strange and unnatural place.'

Via the wisp Yshcopthe spoke. 'What do you do here, Urch-Malmain? This chamber is barred to all.'

'All, I suspect, save yourself.'

'Even I do not enter at night, when the Crystal is busy decrypting all that it has absorbed during the previous hours. Stand back, Urch-Malmain. To touch it now – even to pass close to it – may disturb it, causing fluctuations and vitiation, rendering unfaithful its transcriptions. Such is its sensitivity.'

'Hmph!' retorted the diabolist with a scowl, plainly unconvinced, though he retreated a step from the Crystal.

Yshcopthe spoke with firm authority. 'I would advise you to leave. Or would you undo all that we have achieved?'

'Certain things cause me to wonder,' said Urch-Malmain.

'What things?'

'Oh, for instance, I have noticed in recent days that there has been little or no sign of certain members of our party. Namely, Dazdun of Bright Mountain; Ghismile the Proud; the beautiful Olecte; Quirde the Summoner, and the little warlock, Feluthagast. Having detected and confirmed to my own satisfaction their apparent reclusiveness, I dispatched a Vigilant Daemon to each of their apartments, only to find them inaccessible, with all means of entry well-guarded by potent magical forces.'

'You are concerned by their absence? You, Urch-Malmain, whose love of solitude is so great it is rumoured that not even birds are permitted to alight within the grounds of his manse.'

'I am merely observant. This is not my abode and I cannot rest easily in it. Certain precautions I deem necessary in the interest of preserving my well-being. Who is the owner of this unnatural place, Yshcopthe? What is its history? Do you know? Will you say?'

'It is unnatural, I will grant you that. But beyond

this I have no knowledge. You chose it, Urch-Malmain, in disregard of my own sentiments.'

'Perhaps.' The diabolist cast cold glances around him, then fixed the wisp with a gimlet stare. 'What of the five, then?'

'As you have so perceptively observed, all among us must take reasonable precautions. If these five have prevented access to their private apartments, it is no doubt because they wish to deter intrusions from others such as yourself.'

Urch-Malmain made an angry sound. 'I could destroy this "device". I could tear down this palace now and be done with this whole business.'

'As could any one of us,' replied Yshcopthe, 'but to what useful end? The Pooling is more than half complete. We have all yielded much and can gain nothing until the Pandect has been delivered.'

Urch-Malmain stretched his purplish lips across two rows of clenched, discoloured teeth. His eyes burned. He ground a heel upon the wooden floor as if crushing a beetle. 'Beware, Yshcopthe, I am watching you. Something is afoot, and I shall know of it. If you are fooling with us you do not know with what or whom you meddle. We will destroy you. You cannot escape us all.'

He wheeled, uttering a dark curse, and stamped from the chamber.

Yshcopthe lay back in her bed. Was this the end? Now was a time for quick decisions.

Hastily donning a robe she went next door to the chamber where the Crystal did its near-silent work. First she examined the Crystal and its internal weft for signs of corruption in the delicate organic tissue caused by Urch-Malmain's presence. Nothing was apparent. She assessed the condition of its volatile non-world essences. Again, nothing seemed to have been harmed.

31

Yshcopthe seated herself before the aperture where the participants in the Great Pooling positioned themselves to yield their knowledge. She placed her head within the aperture and laid a hand upon a glyph engraved upon the Crystal to her side.

Within the depths of the Repository a membrane stretched, then folded and puckered, to form itself into a mouth. 'Who disturbs me?'

'It is I, Yshcopthe.'

'Yshcopthe. Yes, I perceive it is you and none other. I will respond. You require something?'

'Have you decrypted all that has been passed to you this day?'

'I have.'

'And is the transcription completed within the Pandect?'

'It is.'

'So all that has thus far been given to you is now contained within the Pandect?'

'That is so.'

'Then I command you, produce the Pandect.'

'But it is incomplete. My probings indicate that much remains to be yielded from the minds of at least thirteen of the subjects, yourself included.'

'Nothing more will be forthcoming. Your task is done, and I thank you most sincerely. Now, produce the Pandect, please.'

The Crystal emitted a soft breathlike sound and the mouth within it pouted, then spoke again in tones of disquiet: 'It will be a solecism, an aberration! A Pandect which contains less than all that is known of what it was created to contain? It is a contradiction!'

'Nonetheless, deliver it to me, now, in its present form.'

The mouth made agitated "pupping" motions. 'It will not be a Pandect!'

'Call it what you will,' cried Yshcopthe impatiently, her own agitation mounting. 'Pandect – thandect, I care not. I simply wish you to give it up to me now in accordance with the instructions I bound you to when setting you this task.'

'But I will have failed in the task,' drooped the mouth. 'I am a perfect device, set to create a book of consummate artistry. If I deliver it now, in an imperfect form, I will suffer swelling pangs of conscience and a subsequent diminishment of confidence and self-esteem.'

'I absolve you of all blame. Circumstances have changed. Your task is now complete. You will deliver to me the Pandect–'

'It is not a–'

'The book! The book!' screamed Yshcopthe. She composed herself. 'Give it to me now. You will then be reduced to your constituent elements and essences, each of which will be returned to the environment and situation from which it was drawn. You will suffer nothing, you will retain no memory of any failing. And indeed, there is no failing. I am more than satisfied with what you have achieved.'

'You are?'

'Indeed I am. I offer you my heartfelt and unreserved gratitude.'

'And you will not breathe a word of what has passed between us here?'

'Nothing.'

'I am relieved.'

'Now, please,' said Yshcopthe. 'The Pand–, the book.'

The mouth formed itself into a wistful pout. 'I have enjoyed being me.'

Yshcopthe's eyes rolled upwards. 'I am pleased.'

'Yshcopthe?'

'Yes.'

'I cannot help but wonder: what will I be when I no longer am?'

'You will be what you were before. That is to say, your essences will exist within many things, their qualities and characters contributing to the overall nature of everything in which they are. But with the added benefit of the experiences and memories gained as a result of your sojourn here.'

'I see. And will I be aware of this?'

'You will have no direct recollection, for you will not be you as you are now. But being in many things, you will create harmonic resonances between them, perhaps forming correlations that were previously absent. Eventual understanding will be yours, and that is a treasure to be nurtured.'

'I see.'

'Now,' sighed Yshcopthe, 'if you please, the book.'

The mouth hung open in a moment's contemplation. 'Yes, very well, it is not within my power to disobey you, who created the I that is recognisably myself – at least, myself for the present. You shall have it, then. Please withdraw your head, unless you wish it transformed into something other than that which it is now, and wait seven minutes.'

Yshcopthe withdrew. While waiting she summoned various entities and sentient agents from a number of locations, both upon Firstworld and from worlds and realities beyond. These she gave appropriate instructions involving the dismantling of the Crystal Repository immediately upon its delivery of the Pandect, and the returning of its component essences to their original loci.

There came a sound like a distant wind from the Crystal. It glowed deepest vermilion, then faded to dull ochre. The aperture, which had vanished while

Yshcopthe waited, now reappeared. It jettisoned a large object onto the chair before it.

Yshcopthe leapt forward and seized the object: a great book bound in a gleaming rubescent leather-like material, with golden spine and web of some unfamiliar substance. She looked within: the pages were formed of vellum, of a leaf-like, but soft and resilient texture unlike any she had known. Upon them was inscribed the arcane wisdom of many great and immortal minds. Yshcopthe clutched the great book to her bosom.

'Do your work!' she commanded the sentient agents, and hurriedly departed the chamber.

Outside in the passageway Yshcopthe was confronted by another of the nineteen, Strymnia, a powerful enchantress with dark predilections, known for her delight in arousing the lustful attentions of human males whilst in the guise of a beautiful maiden. Luring them to her bedchamber and exciting them to feats of ardour, she would, at the moment of coition, reveal herself in her true, most shocking and loathsome form. The stricken victim would then be slaughtered and consumed, or turned into a slavering thing, bound to Strymnia's service. She was believed to have a small army of such creatures at her command.

Strymnia came forward so as to block Yshcopthe's path. 'Hold, Yshcopthe. I wish to speak with you.'

'Then speak quickly, for I am in haste,' Yshcopthe replied.

Strymnia's eyes lit upon the great red-hued book. 'What is this?'

Yshcopthe spoke quickly. 'An enchiridion. Tonight someone has unlawfully entered the chamber of the Crystal Repository. I have therefore had to consult these texts, which provide precise instructions for the Crystal's maintenance, in order to ascertain whether wanton vandalism or sabotage had been perpetrated, or damage caused by simple doltish lack of care.' In the gloom further along the corridor Yshcopthe discerned the shadowy figure of Urch-Malmain. 'Your lurking companion can corroborate this.'

Strymnia glanced over her shoulder. 'I was not aware of his presence.' She scrutinized Yshcopthe's face. 'You are flushed, somewhat on edge.'

'Angered. Such reckless irresponsibility might have ruined everything we have striven to achieve.'

Strymnia extended a hand. 'I will see the book please.'

At the same moment Urch-Malmain strode forward, pushing rudely past the two of them, and swung open the door of the chamber of the Crystal Repository. Upon the threshold he froze and uttered a sharp cry. 'What treachery is this?'

Yshcopthe moved. Strymnia, distracted by Urch-Malmain's outburst, had glanced his way to try to see into the chamber where the Crystal Repository was being reduced. Yshcopthe summoned an Invisible Protector, which thrust Strymnia forcefully in the flank so that she was propelled into Urch-Malmain. Both tumbled sprawling to the floor.

Yshcopthe fled to her apartment. Inside she uttered words to call down an Encystment of Ethereal Walls, then ran to her workroom. The Encystment would serve as a temporary barrier against her enemies, but fourteen wrathful magic-wielders could not be held at bay for long. She estimated she had scarcely minutes before the means to negate her spell was discovered.

But Yshcopthe had long prepared for this moment. Her choice of location for the Great Pooling had been deliberate. Here, in the atmosphere some one hundred and fifty feet above the ground, at precisely the position, in fact, occupied by Yshcopthe's workroom within the northern tower of her palace, there existed a Variwhere Convergence. This was an evanescent condition of temporal and spatial flux, undetectable within the range of normal human sensoria, though it might exert bizarre effects upon any unfortunate enough to stray unwittingly into its field. To one with the correct training, knowledgeable of precise metaphysical formulae, however, the Convergence provided a gateway to a variable number of worlds or possible realities of consciousness beyond Firstworld.

Holding fast to the uncompleted Pandect, Yshcopthe performed a set of gesticulations with her free hand and uttered numerous resonant phrases in an unfamiliar tongue, for the most part designed to provide protection against the forces she was to encounter as she entered the Convergence. Voices clamoured outside her door. She climbed upon her workbench.

Had any stood by as witness, they would have seen then a shimmering of pale spectral light distorting the atmosphere around the figure of the enchantress. She appeared to merge with the distortion. She faded, seemed to diminish, and was gone.

Yshcopthe's adventures beyond Firstworld are not relevant within the context of this tale. Suffice to say that she was pursued, for her enemies, once they had penetrated her apartment and discovered the Convergence, were not slow nor without the means to follow. But their pursuit at this time was little more than a token and emotional response, for they had no way of knowing which of perhaps a thousand or more realities she had entered. Even had they by chance chosen the correct one, her precise whereabouts within that world would still be unknown.

Yshcopthe, then, became custodian of the great book of secrets, which from that day on was known as

Yshcopthe's Pandect, despite the inappropriateness of the title. The Pandect held the secrets of twenty approaches to mastery of magic. And though Yshcopthe might have used it to increase her own powers, this was not her design.

By her Ruse, and the creation of the Pandect, the remaining magic-wielders were rendered far less powerful. By ordinary human standards they remained awesome, but much of the terrible destructive power they had formerly possessed was lost.

These events marked the beginning of the end of the Enchanter Wars. The nineteen were forced to specialise ever more in order to capitalise on the powers they still possessed. From them came the numerous magical disciplines of later generations of mortal beings.

The magicians remained for the most part within or about Qotolr, hoping that it was to Ance Arb that Yshcopthe would eventually return. They squabbled continually. Some were slain. Others succumbed to ennui and departed Firstworld altogether.

Yshcopthe, with Pandect intact, returned after many decades' absence. The remaining magicians sought her out. Great battles ensued and in time Yshcopthe was outwitted, and perished in a magical conflagration set against her in her abode within Qotolr. Had she utilised the knowledge secreted within her Pandect, none could ever have destroyed her, but this she had vowed never to do.

Of the Pandect: the magicians, said now to number only five, sought high and low. In a secret recess within a locked library high in a turret of Ance Arb the charred remains of a massive tome were found. But the tome was so badly damaged as to defy identification, and its remains were of no use to anyone.

Rumours later came to circulate. The burnt tome

was not the Pandect; the Pandect was hidden some-where on Firstworld; the Pandect remained within an Otherwhere; a magician (variably named) had discovered its whereabouts in Variwhere/on Firstworld; the burnt tome *was* the Pandect, but certain pages had escaped the flames; scraps had in fact been found, but no one knew how to decipher their contents . . . And so on.

Perhaps the truth would never be known, but history is testament to the fact that the immortal magic-wielders who remained in Rull did not regain their former powers.

This then is the story of Yshcopthe's Ruse, in the form that it has been handed down over the millennia. Remote it may at first appear from the Legend of Shadd's Torment, but its subtle resonances were to pass barely perceived down through the centuries, to have fateful consequences upon both individuals and nations during that period known as The Hiatus, when Rull fell under the sway of the Khimmurian Beast.

# 2

## I

Dinbig.
  I am . . .
  I am . . .
  Ronbas Dinbig.
  Of Khimmur.
  I was . . .
  I died.

. . . Dreaming . . . No longer . . . anything.

I was he.
  I am . . .
  . . . that which I am.
  Not he. Ronbas Dinbig.
  Of Khimmur.

I died.
  And yet . . . *I am*.
  Not he. Not I. Something other.
  But existing. Knowing. Not knowing what.
  I was he. I am he . . . and I am not.

I died, but I have not gone.
  There comes . . . a knowledge. A knowing. A recalling. Passing . . . out of grasp. Returning. Washed back.
That is all that I now am.
  *But I am not gone!*

The fortress of Drurn March, set above a deep valley pass in the Chol-Qotolr borderlands, was the largest of several Chol strongholds dotted about that remote region. It guarded a rough mountain road which wound east out of Chol and disappeared into the cragged reaches of mysterious Qotolr. The fortress was basic in its amenities but well fortified, of durable construction and inspired design, utilising as far as possible the natural protection of the rocky hill upon which it sat.

Drurn March had stood intact for centuries, testament to the resilience of its character. Though it had from time to time changed ownership, this was due more to the fickle nature of its defenders, or the ingenuity of those who sought to occupy it, rather than any inherent failing in its defences.

It had been set originally as a Chol outpost to keep in check the bandits and unruly barons of the region, to discourage foreign incursions and exact tolls from travellers using the road. Its gatehouse straddled the road itself at its highest point. Two squat stone towers blocked the way, facing east and west. They were constructed so as to fuse on the inner side with the cliff face and with the overhanging rock above, and ascended flush on the outer with the sheer cliff below.

A massive double-rung wooden door was set in the base of each. Any wayfarer with hopes of passing Drurn March was obliged to enter through one of the doors into the outer fortress itself, and exit through the second. By this facility tolls were not easily avoided, but few people these days had the need or inclination to travel this route.

The fortress had been designed to withstand siege. From the gatehouse in both directions the road was steep, narrow and tortuous, providing a major hindrance to any large company intent on assault. Artillery weapons could find no elevated platform on the rocky slopes below, nor uninterrupted line of sight to hurl their missiles against the towers or the main fortress above. The view from the fortress' battlements commanded wide vistas of the pass and nearby hills in all directions, which negated the possibility of a surprise attack.

Within the gatehouse a third fortification guarded the main entrance to the upper fort. A tunnel at the rear ascended through the rock via some thirty steps to open onto a walled path which connected by short traverses to the main fortress. Here was the keep, a three-storey stone construction with two walls rising, as with the gate-towers below, from the lip of the cliff face. Its position was such that in times of strife missiles could be rained from the keep and fortress walls upon the roadway beneath. Double ramparts ringed a large enclosure containing numerous outhouses: barracks, stores, infirmary, gaol, common rooms and living quarters for officers and essential staff and labourers.

The Drurn March garrison at this time consisted of a motley band of soldiers, twenty-two strong, though the fortress was capable of housing many more. Their commander was a man named Odus, a large, coarse-humoured soldier, now firmly into middle-age. Though loyal to Chol and its ruling Regent Prince, Odus, in his remote outpost, held himself somewhat outside the law. On occasion, through boredom or overspending, he was not above supplementing his income by sudden bursts of banditry against the inhabitants of the eastern marches.

Today the bleak sun of early spring rose to reveal activity within the walls of Drurn March. A party of eight armed troopers, Odus at their head, descended the steep footpath from keep to inner gatehouse. Here were situated the stables, for the upper stronghold was not easily reached by horse. Nine mounts waited in the gatehouse court, saddled and provisioned, restlessly snorting vapour into the cold air.

Odus was garbed in dark fustian trousers stuffed into goatskin boots, with a goatskin overjacket and leather brigandine over a mail shirt. A broadsword and knife hung at his belt, shield and bow and arrows were strapped to his horse, and upon his head was a tarnished steel basinet from beneath which his long grey hair protruded. Odus, not yet fully awake, was in an impatient mood. He swung himself onto his animal's back, his belly bulging over his belt, and turned to address his second-in-command.

'Lead the way, Dade. And this time be right. For, by the devils, if you've led me on a goose-chase I'll rip away your gonads with my bare hands and have them braised and served to you with a garnish of sheep's currants in axle grease.'

Dade, a young lieutenant of slighter build, with a crooked nose and pockmarked cheeks, produced a smile of no great amusement. 'I am right, there is no mistake. There is but one entrance to the lair. Our nets are slung across it and my men wait outside with weapons drawn. The creature can't escape.'

Odus grunted and leaned to one side to eject a jet of brownish spittle onto the hard earth. He wiped his mouth and thick grey beard with his sleeve, scratched at a flea-bite beneath his jacket and rubbed his eyes to clear the tears that the frosty morning air had induced. Raising his hand he called a command to the gatekeeper. With a grinding and clanking of metal the portcullis was raised, the double-door swung open and the troop departed Drurn March.

43

Through the long shadows of trees and rock they made their way slowly down the winding road. The hills and forest of Chol's eastern march rose around them. Hoar-frost glazed the road, grass and rocks, glittering where touched by sunlight. In the valleys and hollows wraiths of dense white mist had materialised, to hang motionless and ghostly quiet.

The troop passed a cluster of peasants' huts situated near the foot of the hill beneath the fortress. No one had yet risen from their beds and the soldiers were gone before any could remark upon it. A half-hour's ride brought them to a hamlet of some thirty or so cottages. Here the road, such as it was, forked. The market town Coul lay a day-and-a-half's ride to the southwest; Brissial, southern Chol and the Ashakite Lands beyond it. Northwards the way meandered seemingly without purpose, to link eventually with other roads leading west towards Postor, the capital on the shores of Lake Chol, or further north towards the Miragoff border.

One or two villagers were astir, and as the troop rode in they paused to watch. Odus pulled to a halt outside the single inn, called the Broken Tusk. A portly, red-cheeked man emerged, wearing a long apron and drying a wooden mug with a rag.

Odus nodded in greeting. ' 'morrow, Hidgad. What news?'

The innkeeper pulled a face. 'Little. A merchant carrying wool passed through two nights ago on his way to Coul. He said the Beast of Rull drives on into Chol. Now that Miragoff has fallen the way is clear for assault from the north. He said our army lost a great battle close to the border only weeks past and has retreated to defend the capital. But the man was befuddled. He claimed Fhir Oube had been killed, then that he was on the run.' Hidgad shrugged. 'Perhaps we

44

already have a new Khimmurian ruler. But what of it? It is all the same.'

Odus spat. 'Be thankful that the March is of little consequence. With luck the war will pass us by.'

'I have never been a lucky man,' observed Hidgad, and examined his mug.

Odus laughed. 'Hah! You should complain! Would you not far rather that your common room rang to the clamour of drunken soldiers, of whatever nationality? A canny innkeeper can grow rich overnight in times such as these.'

'Aye, and he can with far greater ease find himself ruined. Foreign soldiers on campaign are wont to expect the best of everything without payment in return. And woebetide the landlord who demands their coin! He may quickly experience the delights of dangling by his neck from his own sign. But speaking of the common room, will you and your men not step inside out of the cold, to quench your thirst and fill your bellies? It is early yet, but there is ale aplenty, and jugged hare is all prepared. I can quickly heat it. Or if you prefer to wait awhile I will have quails turning on the spit with a good garlic and rosemary basting, and turnips in butter, with bread and potatoes.'

'You tempt me, Hidgad. But another time. I have urgent business elsewhere and would hope to be back at Drurn March before nightfall.'

Odus waved his troop on. They rode from the village, taking the southwestern fork.

An hour later Dade directed them from the road and into the forest. From here on he led the way. They climbed and descended beneath pine, cedar and spruce, following a trackless course. The sun glinted slantwise between the topmost branches, dappling the earth with a filigree of bright gold. The mists were dispersing, the frost beginning to lose its grip. The air held the tang of the trees and the smell of earth and mouldering vegetation.

The troop broke cover, emerging onto the rocky brow of a low green hill. Before them lay a shallow, boulder-strewn vale, beyond which rose a tall limestone bluff, lit by the sun and streaked with browns and greys, heralding a line of high rugged hills and mountains beyond.

Dade pointed. 'The man-thing's lair overlooks the bluff. We would be wise to lead the horses from here. The way is not easy.'

They descended into the vale, following the uneven lip of the rise, and picking their way with care, for the path was slippery, strewn with loose rock, and given to sudden pits and gulleys. Close to the foot of the bluff they came upon a soldier from Drurn March, one of Dade's original party. He was seated before a campfire, guarding five horses which were tethered to bushes nearby. Odus and his men relinquished their own mounts to his care and Dade led them up the steep incline towards the head of the bluff.

The way grew more demanding. They followed rough animal tracks, using hands as much as feet, clambered over great boulders and outcrops of rock, and at one point were obliged to climb a near-vertical section of the cliff face itself. Arriving at length at the crest of the bluff they paused to regain their wind. Odus red-faced and breathing heavily, stood with his hands on his hips, bending forward a little from the waist, his features bathed in sweat.

When they had recovered Dade motioned silence and led them further beneath close-growing firs, through clumps of gorse and brambles, to the perimeter of a small grassy glade. Here he halted, crouching, and with Odus beside him, pointed.

46

A small stream cut across the glade, tumbling down from the heights above, and disappeared into the woods to continue on over the bluff. The area was ringed by trees and dense scrub, and directly opposite them, about twenty paces away, the land rose steeply again. Following the direction of Dade's finger Odus discerned a narrow opening within the rocky face, almost hidden by the branches of a thick clump of hazel. Rope netting was stretched across the opening, secured to scrub and boulders overhead.

Dade glanced about him. He cupped his hands to his mouth and gave the call of a screech owl. Some ten yards away the bushes trembled and a man rose, a Drurn March soldier, and raised a hand. Another, with bow and arrow, appeared nearby. Out of the trees just yards away from where they crouched came a third. With heedless stride he approached them and saluted. Odus signalled his men to spread out.

Dade addressed the newcomer in a low voice. 'How goes it, Gharst?'

'We have watched all night,' the man replied. 'The creature is still inside.'

'It has made no attempt to escape?'

'None. Nor has it shown itself since we covered the entrance.'

Odus spoke. 'I would look more closely at this cave. How safe is it to approach?'

Gharst shrugged. 'We have moved about openly this morning. The thing has arrows and perhaps slingshot but has made no attempt to engage us, though we know it to be skilled with both.'

'Aye, we know it well,' growled Odus, and spat upon the damp grass. 'Let's not provide it with a clear line of fire. We will approach from the side.'

They moved towards the incline. Odus and Dade kept low, but the soldier Gharst walked brazenly erect

47

between the trees. Odus noted this. In the light of what they had learned of their quarry it was a foolish show. The man-thing had eluded them for months, frustrating all attempts to capture it. In three separate incidents it had wounded five of Odus' troopers. When they'd believed they'd had it cornered it had simply 'disappeared', once escaping quite literally from beneath their noses. It had shown itself capable of formidable martial skills, it scaled cliffs with astonishing agility, and utilised its natural terrain like no hunter – human or animal – that Odus had encountered.

Plainly their quarry was not without intelligence, so if it had chosen this morning not to attack, one could assume there was a reason. A foe such as this, still unidentified beyond its basic mannish form, should not be underestimated, least of all treated with contempt. To present oneself openly as a target, as Gharst was doing, was irresponsible lunacy.

Punishment awaited Gharst upon the company's return to Drurn March. But for now his swanking at least served to divert from Odus' person any shaft that might speed from the cave's interior.

Reaching the rocky face they moved with greater caution to within a few paces of the cave entrance, kneeling to conceal themselves off to one side behind a jutting boulder. Here they had a clear view of the exterior of the cave and the nets spread across it, and were equally well hidden by the deep shade and soft hanging curtains of an ancient blue juniper.

Odus peered forward in an attempt to see inside the cave mouth, but could make out nothing more than a patch of dark featureless earth and a few inches of rock walls merging into blackness. He spoke aside in a gruff whisper to Dade.

'Has it occurred to anyone to try communicating with it?'

Dade looked surprised. He quickly signalled in the negative and turned questioningly to Gharst. He too had obviously failed to consider the possibility, and mumbled words to that effect.

Odus smiled inwardly. The idea had just occurred to him, but it did no harm for his subordinates to take the question as a reproach. They grew slack far too easily. He slightly raised himself and leaned forward across the rock. With a hand at his mouth he called out in a loud voice.

'Ho! Man-creature! You are trapped within your lair. My men guard the entrance. You cannot escape. If you can understand me, come out now. Do not fight us and you will suffer no harm.'

They waited. A bird called from down in the valley. A breath of a breeze stirred the foliage on the trees. The little stream burbled unobtrusively. The cave entrance yawned, mute and still. Ordinarily this was a tranquil place.

Odus called again, enunciating his words with care. 'Do you un-der-stand? I am plac-ing you un-der ar-rest for your past of-fenc-es ag-ainst my men. You will be just-ly trea-ted.'

Still there was neither sound nor movement from within.

'It is uncommonly quiet,' said Odus at length, with annoyance. 'Are you sure the creature is in there?'

'There is no other exit,' replied Dade.

'How do you know? Have you been inside?'

'When we found the cave it was unoccupied. Within we discovered food, a bed of grass and leaves, clothing, weapons, basic utensils, so knew it to be the man-thing's lair. We searched and found no other way out. Then we established watch from a safe distance, and when the creature returned at dusk threw the nets across the entrance. We expected a

49

fight, or at least some sign, but it has been like this all night.'

Adopting something of Gharst's attitude, and to ease a stiffness in back and knees, Odus straightened. He eyed the cave entrance darkly. It presented an uneasy prospect for assault, being wide enough to permit access in single file only.

'How far back does the passage extend?'

'Perhaps fifteen paces.'

'In a straight line?'

'Veering somewhat to the left, and with a natural recess at the rear, where the sleeping area is.'

'Easily defended from within, then?'

Dade nodded. 'We removed the weapons we discovered. But upon its return the creature carried a bow and quiver full of shafts, and there are doubtless pebbles for a sling.'

Odus considered. 'Plainly it does not understand human speech. It is therefore either primitive or animal.'

'Or of some other race,' said Gharst.

Odus ignored him, becoming irked. He tested the breeze with a dampened finger. 'There is dry wood and tinder beneath the trees. We'll build a fire at the entrance and smoke it out.'

From behind them a voice spoke, so close and unexpected that all three jumped. 'There is no need.'

They wheeled. Confronting them, barely an arm's length away, was a man, tall, gaunt, dark-skinned, spare and sinewy of build, and yet of powerful mien. He was clad in furs. His skin appeared somewhat mottled, in shades of reddish earthen brown. His hair was long, unkempt and matted, dark in colour. A sparse, untrimmed beard covered his lower face.

'It is he!' cried Dade. He stepped back and drew his sword, calling: '*Guards!*'

Odus too drew his sword, as did Gharst, but the man carried no visible weapons and made no threatening movements. He simply stood, calmly observing them from within the deep shade of the juniper. Soldiers came running.

The men of Drum March surrounded the gaunt figure. A net was thrown over him. Odus called for shackles, which were brought and quickly clamped around wrists and ankles. Still the man made no attempt to resist. It was as if all this were of little or no relevance to him.

Sheathing his sword Odus folded his arms across his broad chest and widened his stance to convey an air of confident authority. Sizing up his captive he tilted his head and spat. 'You speak, then.'

The man, who it could be seen now was young, perhaps no more than twenty or so, nodded. 'I speak.'

His voice was soft – cultured, Odus noted with some surprise – but somewhat flat. There seemed a weariness about it.

'Then why did you not answer my call?'

'My interest was in observing you. I was intrigued by your method.'

Odus' eyes widened. 'You are in no position to offer insolence!'

'I intended no offence.'

Again the leaden voice. Indeed, a quality of listless-ness, dejection, characterised the man's posture: the slight hang of his head and droop of his shoulders, the weight of his limber body supported mainly upon one leg. He seemed indifferent to his predicament. And yet he did not lack self-command or presence. And there emanated from him, in some intangible way, a sense of subtle energy or strength which affected and somehow discomfited Odus.

Odus frowned curiously. 'You speak well, with some refinement, but with an accent I can't place.'

'Indeed, your earlier summation was incorrect. I am, as you can see, neither primitive nor animal.'

Now, for the first time, Odus discerned a disconcerting strangeness in the man's features. He peered forward. There! It was the eyes! They were extraordinary! He looked closer. They seemed to be entirely white, lacking both iris and pupil.

Odus took a step towards his captive and pushed his face even closer. In the shadowy light beneath the tree the man's eyes, contrasted against his brown skin, seemed almost to emit a soft glow. But upon closer inspection it was evident that the iris and pupil were not actually absent. They were merely pale, almost white. And a delicate and intricate tracery, deep blue in colour, could be seen to criss-cross their surface. Odus drew back, somewhat unnerved.

'Maybe,' he growled, 'but neither are you entirely human.'

The tall man made no response. He tossed back his head to remove a hank of dark hair that obscured his vision.

Odus grew suddenly animated, glancing about him. 'How are you here? My men had you in the cave!'

'Your men perform with the ability of domesticated apes,' said the prisoner. A quiver of amusement hovered momentarily on his lips, though it was impossible to read the expression his eyes conveyed. 'I have watched them from the beginning. Had I been of the inclination I could have killed them, one by one, as they waited here. You too, Commander, as you brought your soldiers here this morning. I could have killed you many times over. You came like drunks to a cockfight.'

'Impossible!' Odus' cheeks glowed abruptly crimson, but he was prevented from finding adequate vent for his anger. The evidence of the prisoner's presence here among them when he should by all accounts have been trapped inside the cave had the effect upon him of a vigorous slap to the face. 'How did you escape? There must be a hidden entrance!'

The prisoner shrugged. 'A blind man could have searched that cave more thoroughly.'

'Bah!' Odus turned away. He tugged hard at his beard and glared at the soldiers standing in a nervous circle around him.

'You have caused me much trouble,' he said, re-addressing his captive.

'And you I.'

'You have wounded five of my men.'

'Not by choice. I did not initiate any form of communication with you or your soldiers. You chose to hunt me, for sport, and I was obliged to defend myself. And again take note: those men would now be dead had that been my intention.'

'You ran when we sought to apprehend you!'

The prisoner uttered a hollow chuckle. 'Indeed so! I desired neither imprisonment nor death.'

'Then you have something to hide?'

'Your reasoning advances in great skips and leaps. I merely wished to preserve my freedom.'

'Then why have you surrendered to me now?'

The prisoner sighed. 'It is not freedom to be hunted like a fox or a deer. I came here to these hills a long time ago, seeking something. I have not found it. And last night and this morning, observing you and your soldiers, I understood that I would not now find it. Not in the way I had chosen.' He lifted his wrists so that the chains jangled. 'Truly, there is no need for these, Commander. I have given myself voluntarily into your custody and will not seek to escape.'

'Nevertheless, they will remain.'

Odus gave himself to thought. Having the man-thing

53

in his custody at last, he now found himself wondering what to do with him. This was not the beast or savage he had expected, whose head he had planned to exhibit as a trophy upon the wall of Drurn March hall. And it was true, the man-thing had committed no real crime – at least, none known to Odus. His actions had quite genuinely been in self-defence, and resisting arrest when no formal warrant had been issued and no known misdemeanour perpetrated did not qualify as a criminal action. But who, or what, was he? And what was he doing, alone in these wild lands?

A new thought came to Odus: Could there be others like him? Odus cast his eyes swiftly around the glade in sudden apprehension, into the woods and up, to the rocky incline over the cave.

'By what name or title do you call yourself?'

The prisoner responded matter-of-factly. 'I use neither.'

Odus clenched his teeth and spat. He turned to stomp back along the perimeter of the glade towards the edge of the bluff and the route by which they had ascended. He issued curt orders. 'Bring him. Bring everything that's in the cave. And search properly this time if you would avoid a flogging! I will question him further at Drurn March.'


III


Back at the fortress the fur-clad, strange-eyed wildsman was given food and water before being brought before Odus once more. Still to Odus' questions he gave only the sparsest answers. Of his origins Odus could learn nothing. He persisted in his refusal to reveal any name by which he was known, and in response to repeated questions as to his purpose in these remote hills replied only that he had chosen to live away from the company of men.

Were there others of his kind? Odus enquired. He smiled with rueful irony and said that he believed not.

Finding these limited responses ever more irksome Odus at length had the prisoner taken away. He was consigned to the Hole, a cell shaped like an inverted funnel set eighty feet beneath the surface of Drurn March's compound. The cell could only be reached or exited by a rope lowered into a circular shaft, some five feet in diameter. With the rope removed the bottom of the shaft was too high to be gained from within the cell. Even so, ever mindful of talents previously displayed, Odus did not permit the prisoner's shackles to be removed. He did, however, have the iron rings bound with cloth to help prevent chafing of the skin.

Now Odus pondered further on what to do with his new charge. He had found nothing to personally dislike about the prisoner. Though his lack of words was an irritant, he was not actually troublesome, nor disagreeable or offensive in any way. The contrary, in fact. The prisoner possessed a calm dignity and authoritative presence which was quite unaffected and which prompted not merely curiosity, but respect and a degree of deference.

From the outset Odus had been most conscious of this. Odus was moreover a touch cowed by the quiet energy and somewhat disturbing force of personality which he sensed in the captive. Thus the Drurn March commander was loath at present to resort to torture, though it would have been the swiftest and most efficient way of eliciting the information he sought. As a further acknowledgement he ordered a tarpaulin canopy to be erected over the opening of the shaft so that rain would not fall directly into the Hole.

That night Odus communed with his woman of the moment, Este, as they lay upon his palliasse. 'He troubles me. I don't know what to make of him.'

'He is a strange one, there's no denying,' Este replied, her head on Odus' chest. 'Gaunt and wild-looking for one so young, but not unhandsome. From the tone of his skin I'd reckon him a Southerner. But those eyes . . .'

'Aye, I have never seen their like. Southerner . . . I don't know. But the men fear him. They consider him a *weird*. Finding him here, so close to Qotolr, suspicion runs high that he is an Enchanter, or the minion of one.'

'If that was so you could never have apprehended him, or held him,' Este declared, then added, lifting her face to look into his, 'Could you?' She had not been informed of the precise circumstances surrounding the prisoner's 'capture', and Odus chose not to enlighten her.

'Unless he has some other design,' he muttered questioningly. 'Why will he not talk?'

'He will, if you truly wish it,' said Este. Having that afternoon witnessed the spectacle of Gharst's naked flesh being made to quiver and bleed under the three harsh lashes applied to his glistening back, she had found her appetites aroused.

'And if he is an Enchanter, or of their ilk?' exclaimed Odus. 'What visitation might I then expect? But no; he has refinement, education. I suspect him to be of high birth. He is not one for the crude exactions of torture.'

'Then pass him over to the authorities?'

Odus scratched at his groin and snorted. 'What authorities? If the news is to be believed I *am* the authority for this region. At least until Khimmurian troops arrive.'

'Will they come here?' There was concern in her voice.

'If Chol has fallen someone will come, sooner or later.'

'Then give him to Khimmur.'

'Perhaps. But there is a mystery here I would sorely like to solve.'

After a moment's silence Este pushed herself up and slid one leg over his hips to sit astride him, smiling, her hands upon his chest. 'You bother yourself too much with mysteries, my love. It strikes me that you are working too eagerly with your brain and neglecting your ample body, which after all is always the more able of the two.'

'Is that so!' Odus rose to flip her onto her back and pin her down.

She laughed. 'Ah, now that's better! Talk no more. I will clear all thoughts of this otherworldly prisoner from your troubled head.'

IV

As it happened the matter was removed from Odus' authority the very next day.

The prisoner had been brought to the hall to take breakfast with Odus, who once more endeavoured to lure him into conversation. Odus ordered the shackles removed. Overnight he had come to a decision of sorts, not in regard to the precise fate of the prisoner, but more as to his treatment whilst in Odus' custody.

*A wise leader does nothing that will redound to his personal disadvantage or that of his troops, which are in effect one and the same.* So reasoned Odus, recalling lessons from the officer training of his youth. *And in uncertain circumstances caution is best applied until the lay of the land is known and the enemy's precise disposition ascertained.*

Thus the wise custodian of a prisoner such as this would treat him at all times with courteousness and respect. If the prisoner were indeed an Enchanter, or in an Enchanter's employ, then it would be unutterably foolish to risk incurring his displeasure. Deep within Qotolr five Enchanters were still believed to reside. The extent of their powers was unknown. In Odus' lifetime, and for years before, they had not mingled directly in human affairs, at least not beyond Qotol borders. But strange events were coming to pass on the continent of Rull. Things were not as they had been. If an Enchanter had chosen to investigate and perhaps operate beyond its usual boundaries it would certainly not be in Odus' interests to be perceived as an adversary.

And if the prisoner was not of Qotolr? Well, he could be a spy; but what was there to spy on in Drurn March?

Whatever the case, he was undeniably of a social stratum well above Odus' own. Courtesy, common decency, a certain regard for the prisoner's general welfare, all kept well in hand by the firm assertion of authority, could surely in no way impair Odus' future prospects, whichever way they might incline?

Other factors, tales recounted in recent months by local villagers, had come to Odus' mind in the night. He hoped that an answer might at least be forthcoming in regard to these.

'Will you give me your word that you will attempt no escape?' he asked as the shackles were taken away.

The prisoner massaged his wrists and manipulated his feet and ankles, first one then the other. 'I gave you that assurance yesterday. To give myself up simply to escape again? Where is the sense in that?'

58

Odus stretched his jaw and passed his hand across his bearded chin. 'Then sit and join me. Here is ale, hot cornbread and honey, sizzling bacon. Eat your fill and we will talk.'

The stranger sat, pushing his lank brown hair behind his ears. Odus watched as he ate, intrigued by those enormous unearthly eyes. He cleared his throat uncomfortably. 'I regret, er, the discomforts of last night. I have today passed orders for a more suitable chamber to be prepared for you. You remain my prisoner, of course, and I must for the present hold you under lock and key.'

The young man shrugged. 'I was comfortable enough in your underground cell. There are far worse accommodations.'

'Nevertheless, I would not inflict undue suffering.'

'You are most kind.'

Odus paused, searching for irony, but the young man's expression was impenetrable.

'There are still questions we have to resolve. How am I to call you, for instance? Do you still insist on giving me no name?'

'Call me as you see fit. It's all one to me.'

'Must I take it, then, that you remain adamant in your refusal to tell me anything about yourself or your purpose here?'

'I have told you everything about myself that it is sufficient for you to know. I intend no disrespect, but that is the fact of it. As for purpose, I have none.'

Odus was not a man slow to temper. His anger rose and he fought it down with difficulty. Endeavouring to keep an even voice he said, 'Then at least tell me this: during the harshest months of winter, both this year and last, the poor folk of Drurn March have known bitter hardship. Some have come close to starvation

– and indeed, in winters past there have been deaths aplenty among the weak, the aged and infirm. But tales have reached my ears of poor families in direst need opening their doors in the freezing snows to find upon the threshold the carcass of a freshly slaughtered doe, a brace of wild geese, or rabbits, half a dozen fish, or some other inexplicable "gift". Have you knowledge of this?'

The young man at first said nothing, then looked up with a distant, disconsolate expression. 'I am aware of such tales.'

'Were you the benefactor?'

'I understand no indication was given of who had left these things.'

'That's so.'

'Then who can say who the benefactor was?'

'Blast you!' Odus' emotion got the better of him. He smashed his fist upon the table. 'Must you always answer in vaguenesses and riddles? Will you tell me nothing at all?'

He breathed deeply and struggled to regain his temper.

The prisoner spoke in a mild voice. 'Commander Odus, I am sorry, I truly have nothing to tell.'

Odus was unaccustomed to rebuffs, above all from a prisoner in his charge. He had been polite, he had been respectful. He had demonstrated unusual largesse in difficult circumstances. And this was his reward.

He rose to his feet, his appetite gone, and made vague motions with his hands.

'Eat and drink your fill. When you have done the guard will take you to your cell. I have other business to attend to.'

The young man stood. 'I thank you for your hospitality.'

The Drurn March commander faced him, appraising

60

the gaunt features. He shook his head in bafflement and strode quickly from the hall.

Late that afternoon as the sun, in a crimson, gilt and violet splendour, began its descent behind the western hills of the March, a company of soldiers, more than one hundred strong, was spotted approaching the fortress along the steep winding road that came up out of the pass. In the fading light it was impossible to discern any identifying emblem. The company halted a half mile or so from the fort and a single horseman egged his mount on up the slope towards the gatehouse.

Within Drurn March's compound the tocsin was rung. Odus himself came out onto the battlements to peer down into the deepening gloom. The soldiers below had lit no campfires and he could make out little, though the snorts and whinnies of horses and the vague sounds of men's voices drifted up out of the still valley.

The rider had reached the gatehouse. Odus waited at the top of the walled path. At length a Drurn March soldier, torch in hand, came running, breathless, from below.

'Sir, the Prince Regent is here!'

'What?'

'A captain of his personal guard is at the gate. He delivers this word.' The soldier thrust a tube of parchment bound with a fillet of scarlet ribbon into Odus' hands. In the light of the torch Odus studied the words inscribed:

*Good Commander of my fortress, Drurn March,*

*Would you grant ingress to your Prince Regent and his loyal but tired company? We have travelled long and would hope to pass the night within the safety of your walls.*

The message bore the unmistakable signature of the Prince Regent of Chol, Fhir Oube, and alongside this was impressed in red wax the mark of the Royal Seal of Chol.

'It could yet be a trick,' muttered Odus to himself. He called for Dade. 'You once met Prince Fhir Oube face to face.'

'Four years ago I saw him when he passed through the city of Brissial where I was then in service to Sir Dancet.'

'And if you saw his face now would you know him?'

'I would.'

'Then go, and identify the man who waits below.'

Dade departed. Odus watched as he rode slowly from the gatehouse in company with the officer who had delivered the message. Within a minute they were lost to sight, though the faint sounds of their horses' hooves as they picked their way down the rough road continued a while longer. Odus waited tensely upon the parapet. Minutes passed, and there came new, unmistakable sounds from below.

The soldiers waiting there were on the move again, resuming their ascent to Drurn March

V

The Prince Regent* Fhir Oube of Chol was a youthful-looking man of no great stature, standing well under

* Under mysterious circumstances some generations earlier the then King of Chol, Obardist III, had disappeared. He was never located, nor any clues discovered as to his fate. The Chol royal line was maintained, but in honour of the king who it was held would one day return, no heir had since been crowned king sovereign.

six feet tall and tending to stoutness. With a manner decisive if a trifle diffident, he was, at the age of thirty-seven, a popular, just and demonstrably capable ruler. He had acceded to rule some three years earlier following the abdication of his ageing father, Fhir Despirian. Since that day he had worked devotedly, displaying foresight and a keen administrative talent, to develop his nation and improve the lot of its citizens. Lake Chol, with its numerous ports and cities, had long been a centre of trade and an important source of food. Fhir Oube had seized upon this to exploit ever further the natural bounty of the lake and the wealth-building potential of its shores and rivers. He improved docks and warehouse facilities, poured money into bigger fishing and trading fleets, developing export and encouraging foreign investment.

Already, within Fhir Oube's short reign, the results had begun to manifest. Chol had become the dominant commercial centre on Lake Chol, outclassing its neighbour and rival, Miragoff. New roads were under construction, more land being cleared for farming, and a strong standing army established, superseding to a great extent the traditional and somewhat fickle clan-system of defence, which was subject to breakdown at crucial moments.

Now it seemed the army had been crushed at its first confrontation. The new wealth had gone to Khimmur, an erstwhile friend and ally.

'I thank you, Commander,' said Fhir Oube to Odus as they sat at the main table set before the fireplace within Drurn March's hall. 'The repast is excellent, the entertainment compelling. I thank your cooks, your musicians and dancers. And I commend your guard. Their response to the arrival of my company under the cloak of evening was proper and fitting.'

Odus nodded, not yet comfortably adjusted to the

arrival of his liege, nor well-apprised of what it might impend. That Chol had suffered a major defeat was evident, but the full extent of the loss had still to be made clear.

There was no disguising the air of despondency carried by the one hundred and twenty-four soldiers and the retainers and followers that accompanied the Prince Regent. Their mood upon arrival had been one almost of despair. Many were wounded, one or two beyond help. All were tired and travel-soiled from long days of retreat.

Fhir Oube himself had been lightly wounded, an arrow having pierced his armour and entered the flesh high on his left breast. He had been tended by a physician well-versed in herbal lore, but the injury, combined with circumstance and the long ride to Drurn March, had robbed him of vigour nonetheless. He made attempts at light-heartedness, but his features were grey, and he lapsed easily into brooding introspection.

Odus and Dade shared the main table with the Prince Regent and several of his officers and close advisors. Others of Fhir Oube's retinue occupied lesser tables, or were upon the floor. The troops for whom there was no space in the hall were within the Drurn March barracks, or in tents set up in the compound – apart from the wounded who had been taken directly to the infirmary.

Odus had ordered the slaughter of pigs and lambs, which had then been roasted. From the stores had come various dried and jellied meats, fish, preserved goose, meal and grain, vegetables and fruit, along with copious amounts of ale and wine.

To further aid in lifting the spirits of these, his most important guests, Odus had called in young female dancers from the nearest villages. They were peasant girls, wooden-footed and wanting of grace, but their performances had been well-received. No doubt as the night grew older they would be called upon to render additional services, but they would return to their homes tired but with pockets heavier than they had ever known, whilst the demoralised and battle-weary men of Chol would have found at least some small comfort on this otherwise cheerless night.

Musicians of sorts had also been brought from the villages. Their talents were comparable with those of the dancing wenches, but a couple of youths had shown themselves adept at the high-step. The piper from the Drurn March garrison was summoned to embellish the musical provisions, and several of the Prince Regent's soldiers turned out to possess skills of some degree or other on various instruments. As the food, ale and wine did their work most rediscovered vestiges of their love of banter and song, and the evening did not pass without life.

Fhir Oube's words of appreciation, then, were not mere blandishments. A small transformation had been achieved, and its value was not lost upon him.

Odus' eyes fell, not for the first time, upon a young woman seated at the neighbouring table. She had arrived with the Prince Regent's entourage, and no introduction had been made. She was exceedingly attractive: her hair long and lustrous russet in colour, confined by a thin band of silver set with sapphires and turquoise. Her eyes were large and deep blue, almost violet, her skin ivory-toned and blemish free. Her cheekbones were high and well-formed, her mouth generous and wide. She was slender and shapely, wearing a long clinging red velvet dress, cut low over a full bosom, embroidered with a complex design in blue and silver, with deep tapering sleeves.

Odus wondered as to her identity. She appeared to

be unchaperoned, which was unusual in itself. A par-
amour of the Prince Regent, perhaps? But then why did
she occupy a separate table? Was theirs a clandestine
liaison? Odus had gathered that Fhir Oube's spouse,
the Princess Blensetha, had been safely removed from
the capital, Postor, some weeks earlier, and along
with their two children taken out of the country to
a place of greater security. This slender beauty had
been exchanging meaningful glances with the Prince
Regent as they ate and drank. Fhir Oube's eyes in fact
were rarely off her. But no words had actually passed
between them.

A companion such as this, thought Odus to himself,
could do much to dispel any man's gloom. Was she
highly-placed? A lady of Chol, or of a neighbouring
country? Was her reputation, as well as Fhir Oube's,
to be safeguarded? Perhaps this was the reason they
acted like strangers.

A pity I cannot make polite enquiry, continued the
train of Odus' thoughts. For if in fact there exists no
amorous connection between this lady and my lord
Prince Regent then perhaps, just perhaps, she might
cast a favourable eye in the direction of her host.

Indeed, the young creature had returned Odus' gaze
once or twice during the evening, with a lowering of
the eyelids and a smile so full of possible meanings as
to quicken a poignant yearning within his breast and
send the blood surging to his loins.

But no! Odus blinked and shook his head. He was of
mature years and experienced enough to recognise the
voice that directed his thoughts. He clamped a hand
around the mug of wine before him. I know you well,
he told the sultry liquid glimmering there. A good and
welcome companion you may be, but given full rein
you become a treacherous friend. Aye, I recognise your
temptings, even if you disguise your words as my own.

He glanced across again to the next table. The lady was engaged in muted conversation with a young officer. Odus suppressed a throb of envy and gave himself to other matters.

A short while later the Prince Regent voiced a desire that they might talk with a little less distraction. Odus had the entertainers dismissed to the compound, where flames were touched to a great bonfire around which any who wished might dance or sing long into the night. The soldiers and retainers followed. The garrison commander, along with Dade, remained in the hall with Fhir Oube and perhaps fifteen or so of his entourage, including the russet-haired beauty.

They waited expectantly as the sounds of revelry, albeit chastened, continued outside. The Prince Regent stretched his short legs beneath the table, touching his fingertips together above the table's surface as he considered what he was about to say.

At length he spoke to Odus. 'Again, my thanks, Commander. We could have asked for nothing better than the service you have rendered us this evening. I am burdened now with the task of revealing to you and your men what has come to pass in recent weeks. I can see no point in misleading you as to the sad plight of our nation.'

He rose and crossed with heavy steps to the fireplace. 'The simple truth is that Chol has fallen. Our First and Third Armies in the north, along with the contingent of Miragoff troops who joined us after their own nation fell, were defeated in a great battle two weeks ago. This is not the time or place to go into detail, but suffice to say that we were forced to withdraw towards Postor to attempt to regroup. But there we were met by a second Khimmurian army advancing from the west. Our troops fought bravely, but the enemy have gained much from their campaigns of the last two years. They were superior in number, in tactical skills, and – I will confess it – in leadership ability. Their battlefield tactics are masterful. They fight with a ruthless savagery with seemingly little thought for individual survival. In addition, they have monsters in their ranks which we do not know how to combat. Attacked on two flanks, with the odds so overwhelmingly in the enemy's favour, we had little hope.'

He fell silent. Odus and Dade absorbed the news, which was not entirely a surprise. It followed a familiar pattern which had spread over much of Rull within a mere two years or so. Nations had fallen one by one; armies shattered; prisoners in their thousands taken as slaves; towns had been razed, raping and looting widespread. Khimmur under the Beast seemed invincible.

'Then where are our forces now?' Odus asked.

Fhir Oube's grey features, lit by the flames, were drawn briefly into an expression of hopeless despair. He appeared to have aged a dozen years in mere moments. 'The men who have accompanied me here today are all that remain of the armies I commanded in the north.'

Odus' mouth fell open. 'You mean one hundred soldiers – ?'

'Just that.' Fhir Oube turned away. He rested his hands against the stone wall. 'There are other survivors, no doubt. In some small number. They will make their way to me if they can.'

There was silence, then, 'And what of the south?'

'The Second Army is still positioned – at least, as far as is presently known. My cousin, Count Vess, is in command. He guards the border in anticipation of an assault from the northern Ashakite plains. In the event, Khimmur had no need of such a tactic.'

68

'Is Count Vess aware of events?' enquired Dade. 'A pincer attack now, with Khimmurian troops pouring south through Chol itself, would be disastrous.'

'I have dispatched a carrier-pigeon, and riders to apprise him in greater detail. His orders are to abandon his position immediately and join me.'

Odus digested this. 'Then what are your plans, sire?'

The Prince Regent turned back to face him. 'For the moment merely to wait until I am able to properly assess the situation and the resources still available to me. I can do little else until I have news of my cousin. We will be relatively safe here, at least in the short term.'

'Then will you make Drurn March your base and headquarters?'

Fhir Oube answered with a nod.

Odus pondered this with some ambivalence. There was little doubt that sooner or later Khimmur would learn of Fhir Oube's whereabouts. The Beast would want him eliminated, for as long as the Prince Regent lived he was the figurehead around which Chol resistance would focus. Dashed now, then, were Odus's hopes that the war would pass Drurn March by. Khimmur would come here, in force, there could be no doubt.

Ordinarily Drurn March could hold out almost indefinitely under siege. But a siege was thinkable only if there was some prospect of relief. Now there was none. Miragoff, Chol's most enduring ally, had long since fallen. No other nation possessed the strength or will to come to Chol's aid. And this was winter's end; the storehouses were less than half full. Under present conditions, with its population greatly increased, Drurn March could hope to hold out for perhaps half a year or so.

And soon there would be even more mouths to feed.

Other strongholds were dotted around the March, though none were as solid or well-situated as Drurn March. Count Vess's army, four or five thousand strong, might hold up temporarily in the nearest of these, but many of his troops would be obliged to bivouac. And some would inevitably be detailed to Drurn March.

So to what end, resisting here? When Khimmur came, it would be in overwhelming strength. Fhir Oube had lost his country, and with his current strength he could not hope to regain it.

Odus was no stranger to battle. Nor did he shrink from the prospect of combat. But he preferred odds which provided at least some glimmer of possible victory. Here a last ditch stand could result only in further defeat, and death. He was a realist, not predisposed to suicide.

Fhir Oube had evidently read, or at least deduced something of his thoughts. 'Of course, it will be a temporary arrangement. The Beast won't hesitate to send a strong army against me once he realises where I am. We could not hold out.'

'Then what?' asked Odus, in some bewilderment. The March was the veritable backside of Chol. With routes north, west, and soon south cut off there remained only a retreat eastwards. Into Qotolr. The notion fairly stunned him. 'Would you enter Enchantery?'

Fhir Oube half-closed his eyes for a moment. His hand went to the wound below his shoulder and gingerly kneaded the torn muscle and ligaments. 'Commander Odus, a blackness rises before me and denies me choice. I lack a cohesive plan. I will await my cousin. In the meantime we will convene here each day, in your hall, to discuss the most viable options presented to us.'

*I fear they are few and far between*, thought Odus, but said nothing.

Dade spoke. 'Does the Beast intend to move now against Qotolr? No one in history has dared offend the Enchanters.'

A senior officer of the Prince Regent's company, Sir Maille-Orchus, replied. 'Who knows what ambitions clamour within the mind of a creature such as he? The Beast of Rull has allies, remember, which no other leader has possessed. He may represent a threat even to Enchanters. But more likely he will do as others have done before him, and ignore Qotolr and turn south.'

Odus glanced across at Fhir Oube who merely listened with a bleak countenance, without comment, staring fixedly at the rush-strewn floor.

In Odus' mind a notion of sorts had begun to crystallise, prompted by talk of Qotolr. He addressed the Prince Regent.

'Sir, at this moment I hold within the March gaol a person you might wish to interview. I half-suspect him to be of Qotolr. Perhaps even an Enchanter. Certainly he has talents superior to those of normal men. Only yesterday he demonstrated his ability to conceal himself in our very midst.'

'Who is he?' enquired Fhir Oube, without great interest.

'He refuses to talk about himself. His purpose in this region is a mystery to me, but now, with the news you have brought, I wonder ever more at his turning up here at such a time. Perhaps to a personage of exalted status he might be willing to say more. If not, well, the means are here. He could be made to talk with little trouble.'

Fhir Oube gave a grimace of distaste. In a weary voice he said, 'Well, bring him in if you insist.'

71

The prisoner was brought to the hall, which was growing dim with the smoke from the fire and cooking. He stood in the centre, flanked by a pair of guards: a tall, dishevelled figure, dark and unspeaking, his head slightly bowed, unearthly eyes downcast. He showed no interest, one way or the other, in the occupants of the hall.

All eyes fell upon the strange young man. Odus noted, with a quiver of resentment, that the beauty from Fhir Oube's party showed an overt fascination with the prisoner. She made no move, nor did she speak, but her eyes shone and did not wander from the object of their gaze.

Fhir Oube meanwhile had gone outside to relieve himself. When at length he returned he glanced cursorily at the captive and made his way back to the head table and re-seated himself.

'Sire, this is the prisoner,' declared Odus.

'With what is he charged?' enquired the Prince Regent.

Odus hesitated. 'He– he has caused great nuisance. He evaded all attempts to apprehend him, and wounded five of my men. I suspect him at the very least of spying.'

'For whom? And, indeed, upon whom?'

'That has yet to be ascertained, sir.'

The Prince Regent turned resignedly towards the prisoner. 'What have you to say? My commander informs me you are reticent in the matter of disclosing your identity?'

The prisoner seemed at first disinclined to answer at all. He lifted his head slightly and gazed at the Prince Regent, then slowly a curious smile formed upon his lips.

'I would caution you,' said Fhir Oube impatiently. 'Your silence endangers you. These are troubled times.

The penalties are extreme for those found guilty of working against the interests of Chol.'

The young man's smile broadened, then vanished. He seemed suddenly to become interested in his situation. 'It is you,' he said in a quiet voice.

The Prince Regent frowned.

The prisoner's shoulders and back had straightened. The smile returned. 'Ah yes, good evening, Prince Fhir Oube. I had not realised by whom I was being interrogated.'

Fhir Oube appeared bemused. 'You have the advantage of me. I do not believe we have met.'

'You are mistaken. Look again.'

Fhir Oube peered curiously towards the young man. In the gloom, with wavering shadows and flickering shallow light cast by the flames of the fire and the torches set about the walls, he was able to make out little of the prisoner's dark features. He observed the tangled hair and thin beard, the skin almost equally brown, the long limbs and thick furs. He shook his head. 'You may well know me. Many do. But I believe it is you who are mistaken. I do not know you.'

The prisoner shrugged and resumed his former stance. 'Ah well, it is all one to me.'

The Prince Regent looked puzzled, taken perhaps by the cultured voice, quite unexpected, which tugged at a cord somewhere deep within the chambers of his memory. He stood, motioning to the prisoner. 'Come forward.'

The young man took two paces to position himself at the end of the table. His guards moved with him. Fhir Oube half rose, peering closely. He drew back, emitting a gasp.

The room was quite suddenly tense and soundless. Fhir Oube quickly stepped around the table and placed himself directly before the captive. He stared into his face. With his hands he reached for the man's long hair and held it aside to examine the features more fully. *'Great Demons!'*

He released the hair, stepping back. With an incredulous expression he glanced towards Odus, then back again to the prisoner.

'It is!' he breathed, as if still unable to wholly credit what he beheld. 'By the gods, yes, *it is*!'

Fhir Oube turned away, his hand agitatedly at his jaw. 'Commander Odus, plainly you have no idea who you have here.'

Returning to his seat, but remaining erect, he addressed the curious faces of the assembled company. 'He is no Qotol Enchanter, I can vouch safely for that. Nor is he the follower of any of that ilk. A spy?' He turned back to the gaunt figure. 'I believe not.'

'Then you do know him, sire?' cried Odus, dismayed.

'Indeed, I do. As do you, Commander. As does every one of us here. You know him by name, deed and reputation, if not in person. Aye, and here is an enigma. This man who stands before you is known throughout Rull. He has acquired many names in the course of his life. The Stranger; the Exile; the Nomad – these are but a few. More recently he has gained infamy and many other titles. Most notably, perhaps, he has become known as the Assassin of the Holy Wonasina-In-Preparation, Princess Seruhli of Kemahamek–'

Voices rose suddenly in astonishment and protest. Fhir Oube lifted his hands to quell the hubbub.

'Yes,' he shouted, forced to raise his voice. 'This man is called coward and traitor by his own countrymen. He is known by countless others throughout much of Rull as the Brother of the Beast, for he is the sibling of the monster that rules Khimmur and who has now trampled over our nation. Yes, I knew him, though I perceive he is scarcely the same man with whom I believed myself acquainted. Whether he is enemy or friend I cannot say. But this is he. This is Shadd, the bastard son of King Gastlan Fireheart, and former Duke of Mystoph in Khimmur.'

All had surged in excitement to their feet. Chaos threatened as they yelled and jostled, thrusting forward for a closer look at the tall man standing in their midst. A few had even drawn weapons.

Fhir Oube signalled to the guards posted at the door and around the walls. He leapt up onto the table, crying out: 'It is he! And be calm! He is not to be harmed! *I remind you all that he is under my protection!*'

# 3

## I

. . . returning. I am . . .
 . . . returning . . . I must . . . *be* again . . .

Unwilling. Unwilled. Out of bliss. Not-being. Into dream of being. Remembering. Harsh. Harsh. I do not want to . . .
 . . . but I recall.
 . . . I am . . . I . . .
 . . . Dinbig.

I must return!

I am drawn back. Sleep. Forgetfulness. Perfect disconnection. Non-being.
 But I recall . . .
 I sense . . . cannot . . . avoid.
 I recall . . .
 . . . but ah, mercy. The forgetting.

Return to life.
 No!
 Return to dream!

I died.

*But it did not end!*

No longer avoid.
 No refuge in non-existence . . . the bliss of forgetting.
I crave, and am denied. Again. Again.

I am that which I am.
Dinbig. Ronbas Dinbig.

Gone from the world. And returned.
  Now, another form.


## II

The two men faced each other along the length of an ancient, makeshift deal table set against the wall. The cell was in shadow, lit by a single torch in a sconce beside the door, augmented by the weak, slanting grey morning light which filtered in through a narrow grille set high in the north-facing wall.

The cell was not large. Its furnishings were spare and basic: a wooden pallet laid with clean straw and a rough blanket, the table, two stools (the second having been brought in to accommodate the visitor), a wood pail containing water, a tin mug and washbowl.

Enticed by the prospect of interviewing his prisoner in depth, the Prince Regent had risen early. 'I trust you were not mistreated prior to my arrival,' he said after greeting Shadd and seating himself.

Shadd smiled, a humourless half-smile. 'Indeed not. Your garrison commander was at pains to attend to my comfort – within certain bounds, of course.'

Fhir Oube nodded towards the pallet where clothing and other items lay trussed in a bundle. 'Your possessions have been returned to you. I am assured that nothing has been removed. Your weapons, of course, remain for now in my custody.'

Shadd stared at him. 'What brings you here, Prince Fhir Oube, to this neglected outpost so far from the palaces and fleshpots of Postor? And in such a condition!'

'That is one of many questions I would ask you! But all in good time!' Fhir Oube rested his hands one upon the other and raised them to lightly support his chin, his elbows on the table. 'Are you informed of events beyond this place? Do you know of your half-brother's doings? The welfare of your friends and the men and women who have served you? The fate of Kemahamek and the other nations to which Khimmur has turned its attentions?'

Shadd shrugged, his pale eyes ghostly bright against the dark mottled skin of his face. 'In detail I know little. Facets of the broader picture impose upon my consciousness from time to time, but I endeavour not to study them.'

'Endeavour? Then perhaps I am wasting my time. I was about to put it to you that we might trade. A question for a question, an answer for an answer.'

Shadd lowered his eyes. 'You are assuming I have an interest.'

'Can you say truly that you have not?'

'I have had no contact with the world I knew since the events in Twalinieh. I made a choice: to leave and live alone.'

'Is it possible to wholly renounce the world? I believe not. Surely within you there is conflict and a desire to know. Why, your friends and family may need you now. Perhaps they have been swept into the maw of the Beast. Can you truly live an untroubled life not knowing or acting?'

'Untroubled, no. But I made a decision. I still stand by it, for I see no other useful course.'

The Prince Regent shifted his weight upon the stool. He was about to say something more, but was taken with a stab of pain from the wound on his breast. He grimaced, his hand going to the wound.

Shadd leaned across the table. 'Let me look.'

Gently he removed the bandage and lint that covered the injured flesh. 'This has been neglected. Have you no doctor?'

'My physician did what he could, but he himself was sick after drinking foul water. Now he lies gravely ill in the infirmary here at Drurn March. The orderly here has done his best, but his skills are minimal and he is pressed by many more urgent cases.'

'Send someone for herbs. Comfrey, camomile, mellisa, lavendula, willow bark, calendula. I will prepare medications. They will aid your recovery and hopefully that of your physician and the other wounded. Let me think ... I will also need ingredients to make a strong purgative and emetic, and honey if available, and – '

'Hold! Do you think that here in this fortress I will find a person fit to recognise all of these?'

'The women of the villages will likely know. It is not the season for gathering or harvesting, but surely someone here will have a store of dried herbs?'

Fhir Oube considered this. 'Is this not a contradiction? Evidently you possess rare skills which could be invaluable to us here. And you are expressing yourself willing – nay, anxious – to apply them. Is this renouncing the world?'

'My direct involvement has led to tragedy and loss,' Shadd said. 'Both on a personal level, and much greater. I have no further wish to participate in the grand, intricate and ultimately futile affairs of men. But when I see others endangered, weak and helpless, the victims of unfair circumstance, I cannot find it within my heart to turn away when I might give aid.'

*Are we so pathetic to his eyes?* wondered the Prince Regent.

'A noble sentiment,' he said. 'But it poses a profound philosophical question. What if those who you

79

help become, when recovered, those who would inflict harm on others, even if inadvertently?'

'I have considered that. The question is valid, but if followed to its logical extreme would propose a condition of inertia and stagnation at all levels, with none committing themselves to activity of any kind. This in itself would result in suffering and death. Ergo we must act, hopefully for the good.'

'The good of whom? We do not all share the same goals.'

'It is the definition of good that is uncertain. Ultimately I believe we may all follow a common goal, even though we are not conscious of it. If we can by some means discover what that is, then our aims would become one.'

Intrigued, Fhir Oube pressed further, 'Then what of inertia and stagnation? Are you not, by withdrawing from the company of others to live in the wilds, knowingly surrendering yourself to a moribund state?'

'Here, I learn,' said Shadd, his voice low and impassioned. 'More than I have ever learned. I act and interact. It is only the corruptions of mankind that I have chosen to shun. One day I hope to understand something.'

Fhir Oube studied him thoughtfully for some moments, then said, 'Ah well, edifying as this debate promises to be, it is one I cannot profitably pursue just now. Your offer is accepted with gratitude. I will send out for your herbs, and if you wish you may go out this morning, under guard but without chains, to search for any other ingredients you may need. Your word, please, that you will attempt no escape.'

'It's yours.' The lips quivered for a moment. 'But can you trust me?'

'Commander Odus tells me you gave yourself voluntarily into his custody, so I assume you do not

80

intend to leave. I confess, I do not know what to make of you, but I cannot believe you have no curiosity. Well, I have been a witness to everything that has happened during these past two years. I have spoken with persons once close to you, and know of individual fates. I can tell you much. Think upon it; I think you will want to know. We will speak again presently.'

In the meadows and woodland around Drurn March Shadd, accompanied by a nervous escort of six soldiers, searched for stems, leaves, flowers and roots. Those he found he plucked tenderly from the earth or from the plants upon which they grew, conducting before he did so a brief meditation and ritual of respect and gratitude for the life he was suspending. He handled each one as though it were precious, and spoke soft benedictions to it in an unknown tongue.

With the season unfavourable he was obliged to make do with less than he would have hoped, but it was discovered that a herbalist of sorts resided in a cottage on the edge of the forest nearby. A rider was dispatched and before noon returned with several of the requisite ingredients, dried and prepared for use.

In the Drurn March infirmary Shadd made various infusions, salves and medicines to be administered to the wounded. Upon the Prince Regent's suggestion he gave these over to the orderly, with detailed instructions for their application.

'The men are fearful and mistrustful of you,' Fhir Oube explained. 'If they see who it is that tends them they will likely not accept.'

Shadd had merely nodded, then passed a linen pad steeped in a warm greenish balm to the Prince Regent. 'And you, Prince Fhir Oube. Do you trust me?'

Fhir Oube gave a weary grin and in full view of the orderly and others present pulled aside his shirt so that the compress might be applied to his wound.

'There is still a great deal I need to know about you,' he said afterwards. 'Many people believe you to be in league with your half-brother. I am not of that opinion. I know something of what transpired in Twalinieh, and I know that you opposed him.'

'Few people know of the real events in Twalinieh. How can you be among their number?'

'I was told by a friend of yours.'

'Who?'

'I will tell you in due course. But first, what of the trade I mentioned earlier? As I have said, I can tell you much that I believe you must want to know.'

With a still expression Shadd said, 'There is little to tell.'

'Nevertheless I would hear it from your own lips.'

Shadd issued a sigh, and shrugged. 'If that is what you wish.'

'Good. Then let us retire in private to Commander Odus' quarters, which he has so graciously given up for my use. Luncheon is being taken there. We will eat, drink and talk, free from distractions and the oppressive ambience of a cell.'


III


'Are you her murderer?'

Shadd, caught off-guard by the abruptness of the question, looked up sharply.

'Do you believe that I am?'

'Belief is worthless, though its consequences may be bitter. It is a characteristic of idle minds. I, like you, prefer the challenge of the pursuit of knowledge. But to answer your question: you and I met on a handful of occasions, briefly, before her death. From what little I knew of you I would not have held you capable of such an act. But love can wreak strange havoc with men's minds – and women's, come to that.'

'Love?' enquired Shadd.

'You were enamoured of her, were you not?'

'Was it so obvious?'

The Prince Regent's expression softened and he smiled. 'Aye, it was.'

Shadd assumed an intense inward look. He slumped back in his seat. 'I loved her, aye. Inasmuch as it is possible to love a woman you have seen only half-a-dozen times, and with whom you have exchanged but a few brief sentences under formal and constrained conditions. The question has beset me ever since: could I truly have loved the woman, or was it something other? A fantasy, perhaps? An attempt to fulfil a wish within my own mind? A creation of my own which bore no relation to the reality?' He shrugged disconsolately. 'Whatever . . . I knew Seruhli to be a difficult prospect, but I was not aware that she was wholly unattainable.'

'And you have discovered no satisfactory answer.'

He shook his head. 'What I felt then I feel now. The pain has not diminished. My sole desire was to know her. I did not, yet I loved her. The sight of her, the knowledge of her existence, filled me with both utter delight and almost unbearable anguish. Had I the opportunity of truly knowing her, I believe I would have loved her even more.'

'Then, I say again, are you her killer?'

Slowly Shadd nodded, avoiding his inquisitor's gaze. 'I am.'

Fhir Oube's features were transformed into a shocked and troubled expression. This was not the answer he had expected.

'You do not understand,' Shadd said. 'I am not her assassin, as is commonly believed. Seruhli died not directly by my hands – that was a calumny promulgated by the Blessed Intimates to stir the populace against Khimmur. It was a cruel ruse, for it caused the death of countless innocent Kemahamek citizens. But she died because of me: my negligence, my inaction. My criminal stupidity!'

He stood suddenly, trembling with emotion.

'I still do not understand,' said Fhir Oube, pouring fresh spring water into a mug – which was all that the prisoner, whom he was coming more and more to look upon as his guest, would drink. 'But please, be seated again. Quieten yourself a moment.'

'In my presence the Holy Wonasina committed ritual suicide,' Shadd explained. 'The Rite of Relinquishment, as the Kemahamek term it. She did so because she believed she had failed her people. The unthinkable had occurred. Homek was dead, Twalinieh was under attack, its walls breached and – as Seruhli perceived it – enemy forces and deadly spies both within and without the Holy City. Thousands of her soldiers and citizens had already lost their lives, and many more were yet to perish. Effectively Kemahamek was destroyed – almost overnight, by an enemy brilliant, cunning and utterly ruthless. It was truly a situation that none would have believed possible, and she held herself responsible. Seruhli had put her trust in Khimmur; in particular she had trusted me. Now she believed, wrongly, that I had deceived her. The awful totality of these things was too much for her to contemplate. Her final act was both an admission of defeat and a gesture of bitter defiance against Khimmur, and myself as its hateful representative.'

'Many consider it a cowardly act.'

'They do not know the Kemahamek mind, nor the traditions and customs that have been the nation's foundation for centuries. I have thought about it ceaselessly, and I know that she had no alternative. The fight was lost. For her to become the prisoner and hostage of Khimmur was unthinkable, and could have resulted in the total enslavement of the populace. The situation, as perceived by herself and the Simbissikim, demanded it. I believe she died in the hope of saving her people.'

Fhir Oube said nothing. Evidently Shadd was unaware of the sad state of Kemahamek now. No matter the Wonasina's alleged sacrifice, enslavement and forced labour had become the lot of the vast majority of the population.

'She reasoned,' went on Shadd, 'that her death would free the people of the will or the absolute necessity to fight on, and thus prevent further bloodshed. That is my interpretation of it. But I was immediately named assassin, which had the opposite effect. The citizens were roused to mindless violence. I cannot believe she had any part in that.'

'But then where does your professed negligence and criminality come in?'

'I could have prevented it all!' cried Shadd with emotion. He had reseated himself, but now thrust himself to standing once more in an impotent passion, his fists bunched at his sides. 'I foresaw it but refused to acknowledge it. I *allowed* myself to be misled. But I knew, somehow within myself *I knew* what was true, but I did not want to see it.'

Fhir Oube reflected upon these words for some moments before saying, 'A preferable course, then, once you escaped Twalinieh, would surely have been to attempt to make redress for what you perceived as the products of your negligence, rather than abandoning human society altogether?'

Shadd made a harsh scoffing sound. 'Redress? Redress Seruhli's death; the crimes of the monster that was my brother; the slaughter that still continued all around me? Very well, Fhir Oube, sage Regent Prince of Chol, tell me now how one makes redress for immensities such as these, and I will do so upon the instant.'

'I meant only that your choice is an irrational one. You are gifted with unique talents, and have commanded the love and loyalty of many. Would it not have served a greater and more worthwhile purpose to have rallied those forces still loyal to you in order to pit yourself against the storm your brother had unleashed?'

Shadd said acidly, 'One does not pit oneself against a storm such as this, Fhir Oube, unless one wishes to be crushed beneath an uprooted tree or drowned by a raging torrent.'

'You are deliberately misconstruing my words.'

Suddenly wretched, as if his spirit had abandoned him, Shadd said, 'There are dimensions to this business which you do not, and cannot perceive.'

'Then enlighten me.'

'You do not understand what has occurred, nor do you know the pattern of my life. I am cursed. I was born the by-blow of Gastlan Fireheart. Of my heritage on my mother's side I know nothing, for she was an orphan with no memory of her parents. I am said to have Savor blood, but what does that mean? The talents I have, which seem to be denied other men, are worthless. More, they are a burden, for I don't know how to command them, and it seems that they, or the mere fact of my existence, place a bane upon others – most especially upon those I love.'

'Often we interpret confusing circumstances by their appearance when their actuality, perhaps less

86

conspicuous, may bear little real resemblance. From what you have told me I see no evidence of any curse.'

'My father wished me dead,' said Shadd. 'He forced me and my mother into exile. When eventually I was able to return it was to become the unwitting tool of a power greater than any known to us. The Vulpasmage used me, as it used my brother before destroying him. Seruhli died, Dinbig discovered the truth, but he died, Khimmur's sacred mother, Hisdra, was taken. But for me they might yet be alive. How many others?' He raised his hands to his face and shook his head. 'Is all this not evidence enough? You talk of rallying loyal forces. That is risible. I am a traitor to the Khimmurian people, and the Kemahamek howl for my blood. And has anyone yet successfully fought the storm? Do any nations who have defied the Vulpasmage still survive? Does Chol?'

'None have successfully withstood it,' muttered Fhir Oube, 'including Chol. But neither have we abandoned hope. There are pockets of resistance all over Rull. If they could be united . . .'

'They would yet be crushed. You fail to realise the power of the Vulpasmage. It has been awaiting its time for centuries. It saw its opportunity when Oshalan challenged it. He believed, as did we all, that he had bound it – the first ever to do so – but in truth it was he who was bound. Now he is gone, and in his place is a monster gluttonous for power. It denies us the Realms, and now it claims our own Firstworld.'

'We must fight or become slaves, or worse.'

'I will not fight. I cannot, for fear of destroying more of those whom I love. Indeed, it has occurred to me that I too, without knowing it, may be a servant of the Vulpasmage. If that is so, then my only fight can be one of passivity, that it may manipulate me no further.'

Fhir Oube lifted his wine to sip in thoughtful silence, his eyes upon his lean-limbed companion. Shadd offered no further words; he sat with his legs up, folded, his arms wrapped around his shins and forehead resting upon his knees.

Presently Fhir Oube said, 'I will tell you something of what has come to pass throughout Rull since your flight from Twalinieh. When I have done, I will challenge you again to tell me you will do nothing.'


## IV


'I gained the details of your escape from the Holy Capital from Shimeril, Master of your Mystophian Paladins,' Fhir Oube began. 'I learned then of the terrible cost.'

'A mere fifteen paladins survived, out of one hundred that were trapped within the city,' said Shadd in a leaden voice. 'Yes, and to survive we were forced to fight our way through Kemahamek troops, we had to cut down ordinary citizens and then fight our own Khimmurians. In the end it was Fate that freed us. We would have been cut down, but Gneth came and in the ensuing carnage those of us still alive were able to retreat into the darkness of the streets. Yes, we escaped, with countless bodies piled in our wake.'

'But you fought. You believed then that something might be achieved if you could win free.'

'A madness had me. I was shocked and my thoughts were unclear. I did think then that there were possibilities. It was only later that I saw through my delusion.'

'Lord Shimeril told me of the death of your Foreign Minister.'

'Dinbig was another who lost his life through my

inaction. He believed he might have a way out of the city. We had arranged to meet, but Orl Kilroth met him instead and slew him on Holdikor's Bridge. Two of my men witnessed it from a distance, but the battle raged around us and we were unable to intervene.'

Shadd raised his head and turned to the Prince Regent, taking in suddenly the essence of what he had just revealed. 'You have seen Shimeril? When? Is he still alive?'

'He came more than a year ago to Postor on a mission of urgent diplomacy. He was endeavouring to communicate the truth of what had happened, to establish a league of nations and forces willing to stand against Khimmur. Before that neither I nor anyone else outside of Khimmur knew of the existence of the Vulpasmage. I truly believed that it was King Oshalan's doing. And he I considered at the time to be a friend and ally.

'You know that initially I had declared Chol's whole-hearted support for Khimmur when it took action against Ashakite. Chol has long been plagued by those bellicose nomads. We were pleased, if surprised, that Khimmur had taken such a resolute stand. When Lord Shimeril came he explained the deceit in fullest detail. Far too late, of course, for the course of events was irrevocably laid.'

Shadd had closed his eyes, his features compressed into an expression of anguish. 'I could have prevented it. Ah, if I had only let myself see!'

'We were all led the way the Beast wanted us led,' said Fhir Oube.

'No! This is what you do not understand! The deceit was suggested to me early on, but I failed to acknowledge it. I loved my brother; I rejected the knowledge that implicated him.'

Fhir Oube paused, troubled, but Shadd did not elucidate, so he went on: 'You will recall that I was also in Twalinieh for the Secondary Investiture, which was when Khimmur made its first move against Kemahamek. It happened that I departed only hours before the troops assaulted the capital. Thus I was ignorant of events until much later, by which time Twalinieh had fallen. When the news reached me I expressed my profound concern and condemnation in a letter to King Oshalan. I let it be known that I could no longer support him in any way unless he withdrew his forces and made appropriate reparations. My words were ignored. In the meantime it appears that some kind of arrangement had been negotiated in Twalinieh. Incredibly, the "unassailable" city had been conquered after only a couple of days fighting – testament to the military and psychological brilliance of Khimmur's king. Now the Simbissikim, who governed following the deaths of the Twin Wonas, surrendered the Sacred Citadel. But in doing so they retained some significant degree of control. It is extraordinary: knowing Kemahamek's proud history and tradition, all would have expected it to fight on to its death. Its sacred heritage was destroyed; it had nothing left to live for. But it seems that the priests found some advantage in capitulation. The terms are unknown to me, but ostensibly advantage was considered applicable to both sides. Perhaps it was simply to save the lives of Kemahamek civilians, though few can be happy with the existence they now endure. But, ever more incredibly, Kemahamek troops now make up the garrisons of many of Khimmur's subsequent conquests.'

'Kemahamek surrendered . . .' breathed Shadd. 'Yes, again I was confused. That was what I detected, but did not expect.'

'With this initial conquest Khimmur gained massive wealth and resources. Strategically its position could not be better. The whole of Lake Hiaita – apart from that northeastern strip held by Taenakipi, was under its dominion. And to the north were mountainmen of the Hulminilli, pledged to Khimmur. I have received intelligence that the mountains are rich in ores and minerals.'

Shadd nodded. 'Homek was set to exploit the wealth discovered by Gûlro miners. Oshalan—the Vulpasmage . . . beat him to it. But what of Shimeril? You have not told me if he lives.'

Fhir Oube felt a sensation of inner satisfaction. As he had hoped, the stimulus of this news of events which Shadd had until now deliberately avoided hearing was rousing him from his apathy. 'The last I heard he was still very much alive. He has gained a reputation as the Vulpasmage's bane, for he has been unceasing in his efforts to combat the evil propagated by his nation. Though his followers are comparatively few in number he has utilised them to good effect. He wages a guerilla war against the enemy, disrupting supplies and communications, harassing and ambushing ill-defended positions and vulnerable troop companies. He is elusive, popping up in one place to strike quickly, then vanishing to reappear again elsewhere, far away. He has become known as "The Windmill" by enemy and friend alike, due to a hand-weapon he wields to lethal effect.'

Shadd's eyes glittered briefly and a smile touched his lips. 'The rancet. It was a gift from Aphesuk. In the hands of a master there is scarcely a weapon to compare.'

'He has paid a high price for his actions,' Fhir Oube went on, cautiously, for fear of undoing what he had worked so carefully to achieve.

Shadd's smile faded. 'How so?'

'When the Vulpasmage learned the identity of its antagonist it sent troops to the homes of Lord Shimeril's family, the descendants of the Mi' Vhuda bloodline, in Mystoph. Shimeril and his allies had had the foresight to remove their relatives to safety, but a few remained – distant, ageing family members, too advanced in years to be uprooted; three children, the offspring of second or third cousins who were somehow overlooked. These the Vulpasmage found. They were taken to Mlanje, along with certain of Lord Shimeril's former retainers who had remained behind. They were imprisoned and demands published for Lord Shimeril's surrender. He attempted a rescue but was thwarted and was fortunate to escape with his life. Fortunately there were still Mystophian citizens willing to aid him, and he was smuggled out.'

'And the hostages?'

'Were taken to a public square, mutilated and killed. The Vulpasmage considers Mystoph to be a wellspring of underground resistance, and rightly so, I believe. It would have gone further, slaughtered whole villages to gain Shimeril's surrender, but thank the gods, it knew it could not risk turning the entire populace – and consequently the soldiery – of its own country against it.'

'Shimeril should have given himself up,' muttered Shadd, his eyes closed. 'Innocents must not be made to suffer.'

The Prince Regent shook his head. 'I do not doubt that he knew anguish. But he knew too that ultimately the cost would be far greater were he to relinquish his struggle. Surely you see that?'

'I see nothing!' Shadd snapped.

'Then it is because that is your choice.'

Shadd looked away. 'Do all Khimmurians then follow the Vulpasmage? Is there no dissent, no rebellion, no desertions from the army?'

'Only a handful follow the Vulpasmage, those at the very top. No, Khimmur follows its king. The troops, the people, they know no different. To them Oshalan is a valorous warlord who leads his nation to glory. And were they informed as to the true identity of their leader it would make little difference. The troops enjoy wealth and plunder, they experience victory upon victory. And the citizens have learned quickly that benefit is to be gained from supporting their king, but that dissent brings a visit from the militia, and imprisonment or worse. The Beast of Rull deals ruthlessly with those who resist, and many are too terrified to whisper so much as a word against their king. Others see where advantage lies and quickly seize it, while many more are untouched by events and simply do not care who rules.'

'And the dhoma-lords . . . are they of like mind?'

'Yzwul, dhoma-lord of Tiancz, fights with Shimeril, and is likewise forced to live in hiding. Of the others, I believe they have few complaints. But Chol is far removed from Khimmur. My information is limited and perhaps not always wholly reliable.'

'What is the extent of the Vulpasmage's empire?'

'Vast. Khimmur moved swiftly, and with great effect. Most countries were unprepared, and those that had warning simply could not afford the expense of a war. Khimmur, contrarily, had gained Kemahamek's bounties, which it was able to pour solely into expansion, regardless of the cost to Kemahamek itself. It moved simultaneously against Taenakipi and Putc'pii, meeting little resistance and thus securing every last inch of Lake Hiaita's shores and much of the White River. Hecra, as you surely know, was already Khimmur's.

Thus the proximal lands both north and south of the White River were now under its dominion.

'The ranks of its armies swelled. Mercenaries, attracted by the prospects of good pay and certain victory, came from far and wide. Vyshroma was invaded. I understand the Vyshromaii fought valiantly until the Vulpasmage deployed Gneth, after which the nomads were quickly overcome.'

'How many Gneth?'

'I don't know. My information is that their numbers slowly diminish. It is thought that the Vulpasmage lacks the means to replenish them: thus they are withheld for the most difficult tasks. But it is enough simply that they are known to be near. Entire regiments have broken and run at the mere knowledge that they are to confront Gneth.'

'Go on,' said Shadd grimly.

'Winter came, so the Beast sent armies south, via Sommaria.'

'Ah, King Perminias! Our most stalwart ally! Oshalan always knew how to manipulate him, even better than our father, Gastlan, before him. Perminias is vain and tunnel-visioned. He does not perceive the strings that move him. So, is he still Khimmur's friend?'

'More so than ever. He too has gained greatly. Together Khimmur and Sommaria have extended the Vulpasmage's dominion south across Rull as far as the Yphasian Ocean. The Boltar, the once great empire of Hanvat, Komamnaga, Picia and Barulia have all been overrun. Ghence resists, but the reports I have suggest it cannot hold out much longer. Here in the north Pansur and Virland were taken last spring. Long before then I had dispatched an army to Miragoff to aid King Led there. It was of no use. Led was killed, Miragoff conquered, my own troops decimated. Winter allowed us a brief respite, but now Chol itself is no more.'

'Then it is as I have said. Resistance is without point,' responded Shadd coldly.

'I hear you, Duke Shadd, but I do not recognize your voice,' said the Prince Regent with anger. 'These are the words of your oppression, which it seems you have allowed to become greater than you. You claim a curse, but I believe the only curse is the attitude you have yielded to. It is a construct of your own mind.'

Shadd's eyes were downcast. The Prince Regent waited a moment to calm his emotions. He had taken a gamble: that his revelations of events – and particularly of the measures taken in Mystoph – would arouse ever greater indignation in Shadd, stirring him to a commitment to action of some kind against their mutual foe. But he had known too that the opposite might be the result, that Mystoph's former Duke might simply withdraw even further into his depressive cocoon. To Fhir Oube's vexation it appeared that the latter was to be the case.

'Resistance *is* a possibility,' said Fhir Oube. 'And I know that you, were you to return, would have many followers.'

'I? A coward, a traitor, a base and vile murderer? You mock me, Fhir Oube.'

'Believe me, I do not. And it is not only of Mystoph and the rest of Khimmur that I speak. What of the Endless Desert?'

'The Aphesuk?' Shadd became evasive. 'They are few in number.'

'Perhaps so, but they are specialists, are they not?'

'What do you know, Fhir Oube, of the Aphesuk?'

'Only rumour, I confess. But they – '

'The people of the desert want no contact with the world beyond. It has been that way for centuries, and will remain so.'

95

'Can you be so sure? Will not the Vulpasmage at some stage turn its eyes in that direction?'

'Others have tried. To the inexperienced the desert is an enemy far more deadly than anything the Vulpasmage may command.'

'Can you continue to be so certain?'

Shadd shrugged but said nothing.

'And what of the Savor?' Fhir Oube went on. 'They are said to have intervened in the affairs of men before – '

'I know nothing of the Savor!' Shadd yelled suddenly, his huge eyes blazing white, the tracery of blue vessels prominent upon their globes. 'If the Savor exist they care nothing for me! They have forsaken me and given me up to torment!'

Fhir Oube pushed himself back in his chair. 'Think, Duke Shadd,' he said softly. 'Look within yourself. Ask yourself if this is truly what you want. Think of what is, and what will inevitably be if it is not brought to an end. Think of what might be.'

Shadd drew his knees up again. He let his head tip forward upon them. For long moments he did not speak. Eventually, without raising his head, he said, 'No longer do I think about what is, nor what can or will be. I think only of what might have been.'

'That is self-centred in the extreme.'

'Then so be it. I have had hopes, dreams, promises, aspirations. They have all been wrenched away and shattered before my eyes. Now I look back, that is all, to treasure what little remains to me, which as long as I am alive cannot be taken away.'

'Are the memories so sweet?'

'They are not. But they are precious nevertheless.'

The Prince Regent made numerous attempts to encourage his prisoner to further conversation, but Shadd, with galling obstinacy, declined to speak another word. At length Fhir Oube gave up. He considered that he had failed in his aim, and was angry both with himself and Shadd. He had no stomach at present for dealing further with this pathetic shell of a young man whom once he had liked and admired. He summoned his guards.

'You will be escorted back to your cell. I regret that for the present at least you must remain under lock and key. This is partly for your own protection. We will speak again before long.'

Shadd stood, bowed his head, and without irony said, 'I thank you.'

'One more thing,' said Fhir Oube as the prisoner turned to go. 'Your skin – when I knew you it was remarkable for its paleness. Indeed, another name by which you are known in Kemahamek and abroad is "The Pale Duke". Now . . .'

'A simple disguise effected with preparations of cam-phire, walnut and charcoal. For reasons that are self-evident I did not wish to be recognised. The stain has already begun to fade. Without re-application it will be gone within days.'

He left, accompanied by the guards.

In their wake, unnoticed by anyone, slipped a shadow – one hardly distinguishable in itself from the many within that chamber, but for the fact that it was perhaps of a more darksome quality than most. But it was a shadow cast by no perceivable object, and it darted quickly and deliberately from the room as if imbued with a life and purpose of its own.


V


Fhir Oube sat for some time gazing at the closed por-tal through which the former Duke of Mystoph had passed. He was deeply troubled. Upon first realising who this mysterious prisoner was his heart had leapt. A dozen hopes and possibilities had suggested themselves to his mind. From the beginning, speaking with Shadd, Fhir Oube had found that he did not doubt his story – somewhat to his own surprise.

Perhaps he wanted to believe it, in order simply to keep his hope alive. But upon reflection he knew himself to be less shallow. Knowing what little he had of Shadd, before the events in Twalinieh, Fhir Oube had always felt an instinctive reluctance since to credit the tales surrounding Shadd's disappearance: that he was a coward, a traitor, the murderer of the Wonasina-in-Preparation; or alternatively, that he was in league with the Vulpasmage.

Shimeril's account had subsequently persuaded him further that his instincts had not betrayed him.

And now Shadd was in his keeping.

The Prince Regent was forced to admit that his initial hopes had been unrealistic. Even had Shadd demonstrated a willingness to stand and oppose the Vulpasmage, the harsh fact had to be faced that his contribution could hardly alter the ineluctable surge of history's new tide. Rull was being swamped, swiftly and inexorably, in the mud of barbarousness and oppression. And too much ground had already been lost for there to be any hope of diverting the waves.

But Fhir Oube had not expected the oppression of spirit which Shadd evinced. Those brief moments when his apathy had been pierced and a glimmer of interest shown through had been so transient, his inquisitiveness so quickly smothered. Fhir Oube doubted now that he had the power to alter Shadd's mood.

'He is young and has experienced much,' murmured the Prince Regent to himself. 'And if the tales of his heritage are true, he is perhaps too greatly burdened.'

So what was he to do, for his people, for Chol? Certain possible courses suggested themselves. Most were unworkable, some unthinkable, and all were spawned from the womb of desperation.

He felt he occupied a dark and implacable cosmos, where the hopes and sufferings of mortals were of no consequence, where compassion and morality were bizarre aberrations, doomed to be extinguished like rushlights in Fate's wind.

He sat alone, and outside the sun settled slowly towards the hilltops. From the gloom somewhere a moth appeared and fluttered around the candleflame upon his table. As if drunk, it came too close, was burned, and fell away to land flightless upon its back. Its legs waved, its singed wings fluttered and caused it to rotate helplessly. Fhir Oube lifted his goblet of wine, hesitated, then pressed it down carefully upon the table, ending the creature's agony.

VI

Evening settled upon Drurn March. The hills and crags were enveloped in a deepening mantle of lilac-blue. Their outlines became indistinct as they began to merge with the sky. Mists, tentative at first, gathered in the hollows. The trees withdrew into the bosom of the landscape.

Within the fortress and upon its walls lanterns were lit. The sentries, leaning on their pikes alongside glowing braziers, gazed out towards the lonely hills, thought of the grog which would ease the chill and boredom of their vigil and looked forward to the termination of their watch. A moon showed briefly between passing clouds. Bats flitted about the battlements. The immense silence of the land was pierced by the screech of an owl or yap of a fox, the scream of a leveret being torn to pieces.

In his cell the prisoner sat cross-legged upon the pallet, his eyes closed, hands laid loosely in his lap, deep in concentration. Attuned to the subtle resonances of the world which enclosed his form, he reached inwards, searching, so that he might explore without. Thus he came to an awareness some moments before the door opened that a visitor approached.

He waited, unmoving. The person projected an aura unfamiliar to him and an intent obscure, but he perceived no immediate danger. The key grated and turned in the lock. The heavy wooden door swung inwards with a groan of metal on metal. Shadd's eyes opened.

Quickly a figure darted into the cell and pressed its back to the door, pushing it to. In the darkness Shadd made out nothing more than a slight form, swathed in a cloak.

'Duke Shadd!'

The figure had moved to crouch beside him. He caught a strong and sensuous perfume, of rose and musk and something else, unidentifiable. He was gazing into the face of a woman, beautiful and striking. Her hair was long and lustrous, though its colour was lost in the darkness of the cell. It was gathered at the nape of her neck. Her cloak was of a rich purple fabric, its hood thrown back between her shoulderblades.

He recognised her. She had been in the hall the previous evening when he had first been brought before Fhir Oube.

'I am Shadd. What do you want?'

She studied him with bright, intent eyes, seemingly taken by his features, then said, 'You are in danger. My brother plans treachery.'

'Your brother?'

'I am Elore, the sister of Fhir Oube. He is not to be trusted. He intends to give you to Khimmur.'

'I do not believe it!'

'Believe it! He is desperate. He thinks he can make a trade. You for Chol.'

'Then he is a fool – which is not something I had taken him for.'

'He wants only to save the people of Chol. He believes – or persuades himself – that you are the means. He will do anything, even if it means becoming the puppet of his enemy. The events of recent weeks have taken a heavy toll. I think he is becoming unhinged.'

The woman reached for the bundle that lay beside Shadd on the pallet. She thrust it into his hands. 'Come. I can help you.'

Shadd considered a moment. 'If that is what Fhir Oube wishes, if it will help, I will not resist. Perhaps this is the means by which I may at last do something of good.'

'Then it is you who are the greater fool!' She tossed back her head in scorn. 'The Vulpasmage will not bargain. My brother will be deceived. The Vulpasmage will take you, then turn upon Fhir Oube and kill him. It will never permit him power in Chol.'

Shadd weighed this, observing her in the gloom. She went on, her voice softening but imploring him: 'Please listen to me. I love my brother, and my country, but this is not the way. I have tried to dissuade him but he cannot see reason. He has announced his decision to me just now. At dawn a messenger will be dispatched to the Vulpasmage with the details of Fhir Oube's plan. You must go.'

Shadd remained immobile.

'What is wrong?'

'I will not run anymore. I will not hide or pretend. I have had enough.'

Elore rose to her full height, her hands on her hips, staring down at him. 'They told me your spirit had been crushed. I had not realised how. Did she truly mean so much?'

Shadd glanced up sharply.

Elore nodded with a sure gaze. 'I see it is so. Then let me tell you something, for there is much that you do not know. Listen, Duke of Mystoph, and listen well: *she is alive!*'

He fixed her with a rigid stare, unable to respond for some moments, then essayed a casual enquiry, though his voice shuddered with emotion. 'Of whom do you speak?'

She wheeled with a swish of fabric and a heady waft of perfume, and stepped towards the door. 'You are pathetic! Stay, then, if that is your wish! Pretend! It matters not to me.'

Shadd raised his voice. 'You are misinformed. I myself witnessed her death.'

Elore turned back. 'Did you, truly? Tell me, what did you see?'

'Seruhli administered a concoction passed to her by her Blessed Intimates. Within moments it ended her life.'

'You *are* a fool! A lumpkin! A credulous ingenue! What you witnessed was mere charade, enacted for your benefit. Her poison was a harmless mixture of coloured water.'

'Her breathing ceased.'

'Are you not trained to suspend your breathing for minutes at a time? Come now, it is an elementary exercise for any who have made serious study of the esoteric arts.'

Shadd shook his head in perplexity, overcome with a welter of emotion. 'Then to what end?'

'That she might be smuggled safely from Twalinieh. And you, whom she had been convinced were in league with your half-brother, were the perfect witness. Gullible, besotted, and – as she and the Blessed Intimates perceived it – ideally placed to spread the news of her death so that Khimmur would not doubt it.'

'No. It cannot be so.'

'It is. I can prove it.'

'How?'

The woman returned to crouch before him, and placed her hands upon his arms. 'I can guide you to her. But you must not hesitate. The Vulpasmage also is aware that Seruhli lives. She is in hiding, but it searches ceaselessly, high and low. The Beast knows her potential. Kemahamek would rise against it if she returns. Every day it comes a little closer to discovering her whereabouts.'

Shadd once more was suspicious. 'Why did not Fhir Oube tell me of this?'

'He does not know. Few do.'

'And you number yourself among the few?'

She sighed. 'I know my brother's weaknesses. I have cultivated contacts and links unbeknown to him. Now come! I can waste no more time.'

Shadd's eyes closed. His heart beat fast within his chest. He reeled under the sudden assault of this new hope and torment. Could it be true? Was there no end?

'Duke Shadd, don't you see? She is the hope of Rull! She has the power to combat the Beast, but she cannot do it without help.'

In a daze he rose to his feet, clutching the bundle which contained his few possessions. 'The guards . . .'

'Don't worry. They know me and do not suspect. I can get you out while most of the fortress is at its dinner. Nevertheless we must be careful. Once beyond this cell they will be suspicious of you. If we meet anyone I will talk to them. Now, come!'

They crossed to the door and out into the passage beyond. A short distance along Shadd's eyes fell upon a sentry, slumped spread-legged upon the floor. His shoulders and head were propped against the wall, eyes closed, mouth loosely agape.

'This one I had to drug,' Elore explained. 'He insisted upon the Prince Regent's permission before he would give me the key to your cell. He is not hurt. He will sleep till morning – and wake with a memorable headache.'

They moved on in silence. Outside night had descended. In the compound the tents housing the soldiers of Fhir Oube's company bulked before them. Voices came from barracks and hall, and shadowy forms could be seen around a fire between the tents. But no one looked their way and they quickly melted into the darkness beside the barracks.

Around the rear of the barracks they ran in almost total blackness, to the base of the fortress wall. Elore pulled him into cover beneath a wooden stairway which led up to the parapet. For a moment she was gone, then he felt her at his side again, pushing into his hands a long package wrapped in loose cloth. 'I managed to secure these from the guardroom.'

Unwrapping the cloth Shadd discovered his own weapons which had been taken from his cave by Odus's men: a pair of shortswords in scabbards upon a belt, a knife, a bow and quiver of arrows, and a length of strong rope. He quickly buckled the swords around his waist and slung the bow and quiver across his back, the rope over one shoulder.

'Here is coin,' said Elore, pressing a small leather

pouch into his hands. 'You may have need of it to pay your way.'

At his companion's bidding they waited in silence for some moments. At length the slow, even rhythm of a heavy footfall was heard above them. A sentry passed along the battlements, unseen. His footsteps faded. They waited a moment longer, until a cloud moved across the pale moon.

'Now,' she hissed. 'Up the steps!'

They crept crouching to the battlements and huddled against the wall. Elore shivered in the cold night air. 'Go over the wall here, and quickly. The sentry will be back within three minutes. Secure the rope to this post. When you are down I will untie it. Take it with you.'

'You are not coming?'

'How can I? Now listen, the climb to the roadway is difficult. Descend with care. The moonlight will aid you, but will equally serve to make you more conspicuous. At the wayside half a mile below a horse is tethered. Take it and ride east, following the path into Qotolr.'

'Qotolr? I am to enter Enchantery?'

'That is where you will find the proof, and the means to reach Seruhli. I will join you later. Ride as far as the village of Delnemere. There bear right. Continue through the forest until you come to a crossroads marked by three skulls upon three posts. Take the road along which no death's-head stares, and descend into the valley to a place called Bale, beside the Lake of Clouds. There seek out Mesmia. She is one of us. She will tell you how to find Seruhli.'

She laid a hand on the bare skin of his arm. 'Not even cold,' she said.

He smiled sardonically, invisible in the dark. 'It is elementary, like learning not to breathe.'

There was a slight increase in the weight upon

his arm, then the soft pressure of her lips upon his cheek. 'Go carefully, and once clear of this place travel as much as possible by day. It is a dangerous road through Enchantery. At night especially there are things abroad you would rather not meet. But at all times remember, she is alive! Now go. And good luck!'

He rose and stepped up onto the wall, tested the rope, then swung himself out and was gone.


## VII


The Prince Regent, Sir Maille-Orchus, Odus and various of Fhir Oube's officers and advisors assembled in Drurn March hall. They had dined well on spitted chickens with rice, corn and tomatoes in herbs, preceded by a broth of fish and vegetables and complemented with preserved fruit, bread and goats' cheese. Wine and ale had been available in abundance, but Fhir Oube had drunk sparingly, preferring a clear head to deal with the matters that beset him. With appreciation he observed that the others had followed his example, excepting Odus, who had drunk well but seemed unaffected nonetheless.

Fhir Oube had weighed the notion of inviting Shadd to join them at the table, but had dismissed it. Better perhaps to let him brood awhile. His mood had been such as to indicate that little if anything would be gained by his company this evening. Food and fresh water had been sent to his cell. Tomorrow, the Prince Regent told himself, I will speak with him again and see if I cannot by some means or other penetrate his armour and rouse his spirit.

Meanwhile the evening had brought with it some consolation and cause for celebration. A messenger

had arrived less than an hour earlier with the news
that remnants of Chol's defeated First Army had been
located some seventy miles or so to the northwest
of Drurn March. Under the command of one of Fhir
Oube's most able generals, one Sir Vicore, they had
secured control of a section of the vital link-road
between Coul and the north and were impeding the
Khimmurian advance south.

Knowing they could only eventually be beaten Sir
Vicore had been on the point of withdrawing. But
the news that the Prince Regent lived had given the
men new heart. Sir Vicore pledged to continue his
harassment of the enemy until he received new orders
from his liege. He reported his position as being strong
enough to hold for some days at least – providing
Khimmur did not deploy Gneth.

This was an encouraging development. More time
had been gained, vital hours and days which would
permit the withdrawal of Count Vess's Second Army
in the south. Moreover, Sir Vicore's position was well
forward of Drurn March. As long as he was undefeated
he could provide intelligence on Khimmurian movements, and hinder the advance of any enemy force in
this direction.

Fhir Oube and his council pondered the options now
before them. Sir Vicore's force was less than three
hundred strong. Almost certainly it would be made
to relinquish its position within a week at the very
most. A decision was made to relay orders to the
effect that Sir Vicore should attempt to hold out for
four more days, then depart in secret, at night, withdrawing a few miles further towards Drurn March. If
the possibility presented itself, they should engage the
enemy further as Khimmur renewed its march south
– but only if the enemy was disadvantaged. Seek openings; hit baggage and supplies; make lightning strikes

against its flanks, but melt away swiftly and silently before effective retaliation could be employed. This way, it was hoped, the majority of Chol troops would survive, eventually to rejoin their Prince Regent.

This resolved, Fhir Oube faced questions concerning the prisoner, Duke Shadd. He declared with sincerity his belief that Shadd was no enemy of Chol. 'But neither at present can he be said to be a true friend. He is unmanned, rendered pathetic by a deep melancholia. I am concerned that he may have lost much of his wits; certainly his nerve and will.'

'Then what is his stance?' enquired Sir Maille-Orchus.

'Effectively, abstention. But if the right impetus were found, I believe he could become a useful ally. I think there are significant numbers who would willingly serve under him still. But he is indifferent. I do not know how to rouse him.'

A Chol officer ventured the notion that Duke Shadd was perhaps under the influence of some baleful rapture, at which Fhir Oube gave a wry grimace.

'In a sense that is so. But it is one that no magical antidote can remedy – at least, none that we might employ.'

The evening wore on and all business seemed concluded. Fhir Oube, desirous of some distraction from grave and critical matters, leaned towards Odus. Aside he said, 'I notice with disappointment that a certain person has not joined us this evening.'

'Who is that, my lord?'

'The exceedingly attractive woman who graced yonder table last night.'

Odus gave him a peculiar look. 'She with the russet locks, garbed in red?'

'Exactly so,' smiled the Prince Regent. 'I had hoped to make her acquaintance. Indeed, had my attentions not been claimed by so many urgencies I would have requested an introduction last night. Tell me, who is she? The daughter of a local noble, perhaps?'

Odus' mouth hung open, his reddened eyes wide. 'My lord, do you mock me?'

'Why no!' replied the Prince Regent with some surprise. 'Forgive me, Commander, if my words have discomfited you. You are a sensitive one indeed! I am merely making polite enquiry. Is she then your daughter? Or indeed, your woman? I had assumed not, as you showed her no attention. I would not have broached the subject had I thought it would offend you.'

'No. No offence, my lord, be assured. But I am confused. The woman of whom you speak, I thought her to be of your company.'

'My company? I have not laid eyes on her before setting foot within these walls.'

'But she arrived with you.'

'You are mistaken, Commander. She did not.'

'Then I am further confused, for I too have never set eyes on her before last night. Like you, I found her fascinating, and wondered mightily as to her identity.'

By now the conversation had been picked up by others at the table. Fhir Oube threw the question open. All, it seemed, had been taken by the sight of the woman. One or two had actually spoken to her, but the conversations had been brief and – on the surface at least – frivolous. None had discovered her identity.

Fhir Oube spoke gravely. 'Where is she now?'

No one could say. The last sighting of her by any present had been some time after midday.

'Find her immediately and bring her to me!'

Guards were dispatched to search the compound, infirmary, barracks. They returned empty-handed. Fhir

Oube ordered more to the task, with every inch of the fortress being searched, from stables to stores to officers' quarters. No trace of the woman was found. During the search it was discovered that the prisoner, Shadd, erstwhile Duke of Mystoph, had escaped his cell and also departed Drurn March fortress.

# 4

## I

. . . It was a plummeting. From non-being into blissful lightness, into acknowledgement of being, then fear – and the assault.

Down, down, impelled to take form. Not knowing what, just leaping, then plummeting, joyful awareness suddenly dissolves, plunging into poisonous shadows, clotted, swollen, viscous substance. Dreadful dismay, unutterable panic. No choice. A form – sucking me down. Something flies away, shooting soundlessly past. I slide into the form, then darkness. The suffocating miasmas of the corporeal . . . The unbearable prison of flesh . . .

'He lives!'

Too much light. A weight bearing down upon me, a searing pain lancing my brain, eliciting a scream, though no sound comes. My eyes close tight. The pain diminishes but the heaviness, if anything, increases.

*I could not breathe!*

'Lie still!'

Something touched me.

*Touched! Me!*

Yes, I had feeling. I had form.

A dream? I thought, but knew somehow otherwise. I was overcome with panic, then undulating waves of nausea, then vast absorbing blackness.

'We thought you had gone.'

The pain was less intense. I was able to see, to look around, though my vision was blurred. And still the feeling of suffocation, and terrible despondency, huge weight, trammels upon me. I am no longer free.

'We almost gave up. Your heart stopped.'

Something stood alongside what was my self, over me. Its voice spoke to me, guttural, yapping, but not without tenderness. Another, close by: 'Welcome back, Huwoorsk.'

I could make out little. The forms were darkish, possibly hirsute. Protruding features: snout, jaw descending, nuzzling, warm pink tongue licked me.

'I am Dinbig!'

'What does he say?'

'I don't know. Sleep, Huwoorsk. The sisterhood protects you. We will not move on until you are well.'

The forms receded. I tried to follow. Intolerable pain! I could not move. I lay, a clamour of unspoken thoughts, mutely screaming.


II

*I was vhazz!*

This I learned, to my inexpressible dismay, soon after my initial return to consciousness.

I watched them as they moved about, though still I was immobile. My vision gradually cleared and I was able to recognise their individual forms. They were several in number – members of a pack. And when once, as they tended me, one lifted one of my forelimbs to examine an injury there, I saw to my horror that I was like them. *Vhazz!*

This realisation I could not accept. My perceptions forced it upon me, relentlessly. I felt I would go mad.

After the liberation of discarnate existence, reincarnation into the corporeal world had not been a welcome prospect. To find now that I was no longer human was a hideous shock. But to discover that I was vhazz, a dog-creature, loathsome, reviled, hunted to the death by men ... this was trauma beyond telling.

Why? Why?

And *how*?

I lay upon a litter of twigs and moss within a rock cave or tunnel. For days on end I remained motionless, incapable of stirring a limb, and so this was a period for observing and absorbing. I learned that I was a member of a family group. The females of the group tended me to the best of their abilities. Two in particular were responsible for my care, but I saw and began to recognise numerous others passing to and fro within the range of my vision.

My name was Huwoorsk. I was male, formerly vigorous and keen. I had received grievous injuries in a confrontation with humans. The pack had rescued me and brought me here, but had given me up for dead when I apparently ceased to breathe. All signs of life departed my body. I was considered lost from the world. And then, inexplicably, my lungs had begun to function again, the vital fluids in my body to flow.

I had ample time to mull over this. A vestige of a memory remained of my descent from the noncorporeal. I recalled the fleeting impression, as I was drawn towards flesh, of something silently departing, flying past me. A bizarre notion struck – was it possible? Was I the victim of some strange perversion of Fate? Had the vhazz, Huwoorsk, died, and I, destined to be reborn elsewhere, somehow been diverted, sucked into his lifeless body even as he left it? By what mysterious volition had the body been revived?

I had no answers. Neither, I accepted, were any likely to be forthcoming.

The two vhazz who tended me were named Muurh and Yaoww, both female. From them I gained much information. I had no memory of any former existence as a vhazz; I knew myself only to be Ronbas Dinbig, Grand Merchant of Khimmur. Yet I was able, as no human was, to understand vhazz speech. Quite rapidly I found myself speaking their language without difficulty. My distress did not abate. Again and again I put it to myself that this was a dream and that I must soon wake. But the dream persisted; it was real, or I was thoroughly mad.

The vhazz were on the move, my two nurses told me. The pack had repeatedly fallen foul of humans and many of its number had been killed. As a consequence the sisterhood had recently made the decision to search elsewhere for a safer homeland.

No more than a few miles had been covered when the attack had occurred in which I – Huwoorsk – was injured. The vhazz had fought off and then evaded their attackers and taken refuge in a system of natural caves situated deep in forest-clad foothills away from human habitation. Further flight had been postponed until I recovered enough to continue.

In my mind I went over what I knew of the vhazz. They were widely held to be descended from the dispossessed First Era enchanter Quirde, who millennia earlier had been bound to a body part-man part-dog. Quirde, it was said, driven to dementia by his predicament, abducted a human peasant girl, holding her prisoner for many weeks and subjecting her to unnatural acts and enforced sexual congress.

The girl at length escaped while Quirde slept. In due course she gave birth to three monstrous infants, but died – perhaps mercifully – without setting eyes upon her issue. Her parents who attended her immediately set about killing the abominable offspring, but the three newborns displayed extraordinary vigour. They struggled devilishly, nipped and scratched at the hands that endeavoured to restrain them, fought free and were away into the forest before they could be caught. These three were the first true vhazz, and from their subsequent copulations the species expanded.

Vhazz society now was fairly well-ordered and based upon large family groups or packs, but it lacked the higher administrative, organisational and manufacturing abilities characteristic of humans. Vhazz were primitively intelligent, but of foul nature and habit. Their total population had never been great – the family group of which I found myself a member currently numbered only eighty or so, of which twenty-five were not yet adults – and their groups tended to live in isolation from one another. Thus, while under favourable conditions a vhazz fighter might be the equal or better of a human in many respects, in major confrontations the vhazz had little defence against the more prolific, better-organised and armed companies of men.

The vhazz hunted both individually and in packs. Their nature was savage, but tending to cowardly, and they would attack most types of creatures if they knew their own strength to be superior.

Capable of bipedal and quadrupedal movement, vhazz possessed prehensile opposable digits on their forepaws, which enabled them to manipulate basic tools and wield weapons to good effect. In combat, however, they preferred to rely for the most part upon their powerful jaws and teeth. Individuals on occasion donned rudimentary forms of clothing and armour, but in general such adornments were rejected as trammels, the vhazz being naturally fleet and agile beasts. Sensitive to strong light, vhazz became active mainly after dusk, their night-vision bestowing upon them an advantage over many creatures, including humans. Their preferred habitat was forested terrain, where they made complex dens in labyrinthine subterranean warrens.

So much I knew. Now, without enthusiasm or choice, I was to learn more.

Of my two nurses Yaoww was the more communicative – Muurh being younger, and of a nervous and somewhat untrusting disposition. Yaoww it was who told me – reminded me, as she considered it – of the pack and its desperate need to find a safer dwelling place.

'Where then are we currently situated?' I enquired.

'We are in forest beneath Red Mountains.'

'And what is this region called?'

'We are still in our homeland, the Shadow Forest.'

I nodded, earnestly seeking some clue that would identify my whereabouts. 'And we are leaving, you say, because our enemies have grown too strong?'

'Poor Huwoorsk,' whined Yaoww, and laid her muzzle briefly upon my upper flank. 'You remember nothing, do you? For years now the men have been pushing further and further into Shadow Forest. Encounters have become more frequent. Recently they have shown greater aggression than ever before. Their leader sends them against us in training for his army. We have never encountered so many soldiers, so intent upon our extermination.'

'They train for an army? Are they then at war?'

'Men are always at war. But they seem consumed now, more than ever.'

'Their leader: do you know what he is called?'

'He is a great lord, but very old. His scions are set to succeed him. Do you not remember? His name is Gegg.'

*Gegg! The Red Mountains!*

My heart leapt. I was in Khimmur!

I struggled to contain my feelings. My concern now was that we were leaving.

'Where do we go, Yaoww?'

Yaoww suddenly twisted her neck to bite viciously at the short, dry grey-brown hair of her coat, a little below one shoulder, where a flea or some other parasite burrowed. With snuffling sounds and the aid of sharp teeth she wrenched out great tufts of coarse hair. Then, apparently satisfied, she gave a violent shake of her head. She put her nose to the floor, searching, found what she sought and hammered upon it with a pebble. She turned back to me. 'We go towards the place where the day begins. Beyond its beginning exists a region of endless night. That is where we will make our new home.'

My interpretation of this was that we were moving east, towards the rising sun.

I was growing very aware of Yaoww's proximity to me. Upon first setting eyes upon her after waking in the cave my reaction had been one of horror and revulsion. She was scrawny and thin-haired; in places her hair had come out, leaving rough pink patches; ringworm formed crusted growths upon her skin, which was generally scurfy and dry; her ears were tattered and unsightly with the marks of numerous conflicts, and her snout was likewise disfigured by scarred and swollen tissue. But my response had been born from the consciousness of a former man. Now

117

I looked upon her in another light. I was aroused by the sight and nearness of her. Her smell was powerful and intoxicating. Had I been capable I would have climbed upon her rear and rendered her there and then with pup.

My physical desire was supplanted by a sensation of alarm. Was this evidence that with the passing of the days I was becoming less human and more vhazz?

Yaoww was not indifferent to my gaze, or unaware of my arousal. She smiled – in the way that vhazz can be said to smile – with a curling of the upper lip and baring of fangs, and said, 'Huwoorsk, you are recovering! Soon we will be ready to move on again.'

She withdrew, dropping to all fours and showing me her rump as she did so. My blood surged.

A night later I was able to leave my litter. With the aid of my two nurses I took my first unsteady steps around the cave. The effort exhausted me, and I fell quickly back into sleep. But the sisterhood was pleased – and in a disquieting way so was I.

The following night, for the first time, I discovered an appetite. To date I had been fed on liquids: water, milk, broth, and small amounts of a gruel-like concoction. Now a pair of fat geckos were brought in and dropped before me, not quite dead, still twisting in their final throes. I devoured them with gusto. Next came a young rabbit, then a plump coot. Later I vomited, but when a similar procedure was followed the next evening I ate more and kept it down.

The meat gave me strength. Soon I was walking, on all fours, totteringly but unaided. A day later I awoke to find a newborn human baby lying dead beside my litter. I stared in horror for an incalculable time, then turned away, all appetite gone. When I next opened my eyes the infant had been removed.

My wounds were plentiful, but they healed rapidly. The major internal damage had been caused by a spear penetrating my left flank. Mercifully it had missed my vital organs, as my rate of recovery showed. An arrow wound in my right shoulder was painful but of lesser concern; various other lesions and contusions, though grave enough to warrant attention, were comparatively minor.

Two more nights passed and I rose upon my hind legs and walked about the cave, to yaps and whines of encouragement and appreciation from the sisterhood. On the following evening I was allowed outside.

We were situated on a rocky, forested slope at the base of a steep cliff pockmarked with cave openings. With Yaoww and Muurh at my side I gingerly entered beneath the trees, inhaling the intoxicating, invigorating aromas of oak and cedar, rhododendron, moss and grass, the reek of dark earth and droppings, the vibrant, manifold scents of creatures that had passed this way. I investigated everything with my nose, my sharp ears revelling in the variety of familiar sounds that were the spirit of the forest at night. Life poured into me as my senses rediscovered the richness and abundance of the world. With a mingling of vhazz joy and human revulsion I left my own scent upon nearby trees and rocks.

Soon after this a pack moot was convened at which it was decided that the time was at hand to leave the caves and move on again. Human soldiers – the men of Gegg's Cowm – had been observed within the forest less than five miles away. It was a virtual certainty that sooner or later our presence would be noted and the den discovered. I had almost fully recuperated, and no further purpose could be served by remaining where we were.

Before we could depart the performance of a ritual was required, a celebration of my – Huwoorsk's – return to life, and recognition of the completeness of the family group. I was about to learn facts about vhazz social structure and hierarchy that to my knowledge no human had ever been aware of.

On the night before the ritual I requested permission of my custodians to venture out alone for a short period, that I might test my limbs and faculties and familiarise myself with the landscape. The request was greeted with unanimous approval, even as if it were something the sisterhood had been anticipating or hoping for. Later I understood why a desire for solitude or a display of independence or self-sufficiency was so well-received from a pack member of my status.

I left the cave and struck out between the trees, ascending along a rabbit-track towards the high ground. The forest was vibrant with the sounds of the night. Small creatures hunted food, larger ones hunted them. Water tumbled in a mellifluous song, rushing pell-mell for the valley floor. Ice, which had formed where the daytime sun had failed to penetrate, splintered and creaked under its own weight.

I gave but cursory attention to these things, intent upon my purpose. A little way above the tree-line I paused below a jutting shoulder of rock. A panorama spread before me, the wild grandeur of the landscape invested with the mellow illumination of a waxing half-moon. Patches of snow lay in the deepest shadows. The sky was cloudless, endless and black, speckled with countless brilliant points of light. I scrambled up onto the rock, and there sat upon my haunches and gazed northwards over the hills and forests of Khimmur.

Somewhere, not so many miles beyond the limit of my sight, Lake Hiaita reflected the same moon beneath which I rested. Between here and the lake was my birthplace, and Castle Drome, seat of the Orl Kilroth, my childhood friend who had become my mortal enemy. A little to the northwest was Khimmur's capital, Hon-Hiaita, where I had made my fortune and my base.

I felt the weight of inconsolable longing. So close, my friends, my family. If they lived . . .

Rohse! With a pounding of emotion I recalled the woman who carried my child. What of her? How did she fare? And our baby? A vision of the slaughtered infant that had lain beside my litter rose before my eyes; I blinked and violently shook my head, ridding myself of the spectre.

The news that old Gegg still lived reassured me that no great time had passed since Orl Kilroth had taken my life in Twalinieh. By Yaoww's account, supplemented by the words of others I had questioned of the sisterhood, war raged, and the indication was that the Vulpasmage still ruled Khimmur. But even so, years might have gone by; I had no means of knowing. What had befallen all those I had known and loved? Had my child even been born? Was he or she perhaps now grown towards adolescence?

I sat for a long time alone upon that mountainside, thinking deep and unhappy thoughts. It was not lost upon me that a vhazz, nimble and surefooted, might easily reach Hon-Hiaita in a single night. But once there, what was to be gained? Were I to succeed in entering the town I could communicate with no one. If I was discovered I would be attacked and killed on sight. To preserve my skin I would be obliged to skulk in alleyways in the deepest hours of darkness, when

121

none but sentries of the night-watch were awake. Thus I stood a negligible chance of even glimpsing anyone I had known.

So close, so close . . . and so infinitely far away.

It was cold here, high beneath the peaks of the Red Mountains. A frost had begun to form upon the rock on which I sat. I rested a little longer, brooding, wretched. At length, without thought but prompted by some primordial instinct, I turned my snout to the great blackness overhead. Venting my feelings of loss and despair, I let loose a long and mournful howl.

The vhazz voice is distinctive. It resembles in many respects that of a wolf, but with an additional eerie quality of human-ness. It is partially this which arouses such hatred and fear among humans: many believe that the former enchanter, Quirde, hovers between realms awaiting human souls departing unexpectedly from life. These he binds by supernatural means to be born again as vhazz, and sets to torment the living. Cruel and terrible irony! Was I proof of the veracity of the belief?

Within moments of my howling I perceived the approach of numerous forms moving swift and silent up the mountainside. I slipped down from the rock. Dark shapes materialised some way off, then vanished, slinking between bushes and boulders. The scent of Yaoww entered my nostrils, then of Muurh and two others of the sisterhood. I called to them.

'Huwoorsk, what is the matter? Are you hurt?' cried Yaoww, bounding to me. 'Your voice registered such distress!'

'Ah, no. I am not hurt,' said I.

Her yellow eyes fixed solicitously upon me. 'You are different, Huwoorsk, since you were wounded. Others have noticed it. You are not like before.'

I nodded, but offered no comment. We made our way back down to the cave.

## III

The ritual of my returning took place in the early dusk, outside the cave in which I had spent my convalescence.

After waking in the afternoon I had been left alone, with instructions to remain within the cave until called. As the shadows at the cave entrance revealed that the sun had passed behind the rugged highlands of Crasmag in the west I was summoned by a single voice from without, followed by a chorus of yaps and whines.

A leather breastplate and spiked spinal guard had been left beside my litter. With them were weapons: the short, lightweight, curved and serrated sword favoured by the vhazz, a dagger, throwing-darts, and the leather scabbard, sheaths and straps appropriate. These I donned, looping the straps across my back and securing them below the breast. This done I stood erect and approached the cave entrance.

Outside numerous small fires had been ignited beneath the trees around the cave, not to provide light but, as I was to learn, as representations of those pack members who lived their lives around, but apart from, the sisterhood. The pack was assembled before me, almost eighty in number. The seniors and those who had personally tended me stood at the fore, subordinates and immature members behind. As I stood and gazed, blinking, at their faces, I noted that several males were present. Obviously this ceremony held a greater significance than I was able to appreciate.

I had also received instruction in regard to the first part of the ritual. I dutifully squatted and left my mark before the cave mouth, thus symbolically rendering it my domain. Two of the sisterhood moved up beside me and did likewise, extending my gesture to include the entire family-group.

The two withdrew. I came forward to place myself before the assembly. From this point on the ceremony was unknown to me.

The vhazz closed in, forming a circle with myself at its hub. Seven members of the sisterhood, Yaoww and Muurh among them, advanced and made an inner ring close around me. They sat upon their haunches, their eyes upon me.

One of the elders, Dopik by name, addressed me. 'We welcome you back among us, Huwoorsk. Now the time has come for you to once more take your proper place. Be low, so that you may receive the honour of the pack.'

I took this to mean I should prostrate myself. This I did, lowering my body to the earth, my head resting between my extended forelimbs. The seven came closer so that they were almost touching me. They inclined their heads and began sniffing me, their noses travelling over every portion of my body. This went on for some seconds, then they raised their heads once more.

'It is good,' said Dopik.

Now something extraordinary came to pass. As one the seven turned their rumps to me. They squatted and elevated their tails, and urinated upon me.

I lay motionless, half-stricken, not knowing how to respond as the seven warm jets of vhazz-piss streamed down on my head, my hide, my limbs, soaking me all over, through and through. When at last they ceased I blinked, shook my head, and raised my eyes, wondering what was expected of me.

And then the aroma! My nostrils quivered. I sucked in the potent, intimate musk of seven females, and was instantaneously aroused to a frenzy of lust.

I scrambled to all fours. The seven still had their rumps to me. Their heads were turned to observe me, a septuplet of female genitalia provocatively displayed while their scents imbued my entire person and wreaked havoc with my senses.

Excited beyond reason or restraint I leapt upon the back of the nearest female. But she darted from beneath me. Uncontrolled I leapt again. Once more she was gone. Now she span around, snarling, and with ferocity and speed lunged and sank sharp teeth into my foreleg. I pulled back in pain and surprise. The female faced me, ears flattened and teeth bared, emitting a low growl.

But such was my arousal that I was far from being my own master. I immediately sought elsewhere for gratification, pouncing upon another of the seven, heedless of her identity. She too darted away. I turned to a third – and was attacked without warning from all sides.

In a fury of snapping jaws the vhazz closed upon me. Razor teeth nipped at my legs and buttocks. I twisted to ward off one vhazz – four others attacked from another angle. Wheeling to deal with these, I was again set upon on flank and rear.

With snarls and growls they fought me. Their bites were sharp, but they seemed intended to disconcert and deter rather than inflict serious injury – and there was no question that had it been their wish the seven could have torn me to pieces in seconds. As it was the mêlée continued for perhaps a minute. I was forced to the defensive, unable to flee, and made to perform a wild dance of high leaps, twists and lunges in my efforts to avoid their teeth.

Suddenly it was over. The seven backed away; all were silent. I stood, panting, my legs trembling, my lower limbs a mass of small scratches and bites. The odours of the seven were still upon me – indeed, their steam rose in a cloud from my skin. My lust, dissipated in the fray, returned, commingled with confusion and fear.

'Good,' announced Dopik. 'You have received us. You are once more of the family. Now, be gone!'

The seven parted so that a passage opened between them, and between the seventy or so others gathered there to witness the ceremony of my returning. I stared nonplussed along the rows of curious vhazz faces. Beyond glowed the small lights of the fires, and there the forest loomed high. I looked back to Dopik, then Yaoww.

'Do not hesitate!' commanded Dopik sharply. 'It is done. Go!'

Yaoww, her head tilted to one side, said in a low voice, 'You must go, Huwoorsk. You know that.'

'Go where?' I said.

She looked surprised.

'Wherever you choose.'

Deep within me a memory stirred. Racial, quasi-cultural, primordial. That part of me that was truly vhazz and nothing other knew the meaning of this bizarre ritual. My confusion evaporated in a moment of clear recall. Quite suddenly I understood.

Vhazz society is ruled by females, not in a strict hierarchical or matriarchal sense, but as a body, more or less egalitarian in nature. The males exist as virtual outcasts, excluded from the day-to-day life of the pack. Their role is to perform certain vital functions, ensuring the continuance of the species, providing protection when called for, and on occasions of hardship they are expected to bring food for the weaker members.

The urination was a rite of familial and sexual bonding. All vhazz males undergo a similar initiation upon attaining adulthood, and the ritual is repeated whensoever they return to the pack for any length of time. In receiving the intimate essences of the seven I was being reminded of my attachments and duties to them and to the family-group.

The life of the vhazz male, then, is solitary. He plays no part in the running of the family-group or the upbringing and educating of the young. He lives in the wild, keeping close enough to the pack to be able to respond should trouble strike, but mingling with it only when summoned by the females, and then to a strictly limited degree. When a female is ready to bear young she summons a male, they mate, and when the function is complete part, she to return to the pack, he to the wild. The males mate solely with females of their own family; to conjoin with an outsider would incur total ostracism, thus forfeiting the protection and support of the pack. The females are as fierce in combat as the males, and the pack will act as one to protect any of its members. Thus had I – Huwoorsk – been rescued from men who would otherwise have taken my life.

There is one circumstance under which the male can be considered to benefit from the complete abandonment of his family-group. This is when it is decided within the group that a particular female should leave in order to start a new group. A suitable male is chosen to accompany her and father the first litter. Even then, however, the hapless sire serves only to oversee the raising of the initial batch of whelps. As they reach maturity he is banished once more, as are any sons he may have produced.

So I was hurt, then healed, only to receive the 'honour' of the pack and be subsequently cast out once more.

What if I refused to leave? I could not doubt that I was being offered no choice. I lifted my head, endeavouring to show some measure of dignity, and held my tail high, though inwardly I felt it to be well between my legs. In a confusion of arousal, disconcertment, dejection and wounded pride, I trotted along the passage the vhazz had formed, my wet hide steaming, and without looking back entered the dark forest beyond.


IV


It was not the kind of life I would have chosen for myself. I had been a gregarious fellow when human, inclined towards good living and the delights and benefits of wealth and high repute. Now I found myself alone in the wild, possessed of a body and personality that was half giant dog, living from night to night, hunting rabbits, deer, or any other living thing that could appease my appetite.

My wounds were at first a slight handicap, being somewhat stiff and tender, but this I quickly overcame and they were forgotten within hours. I discovered myself to be an adept hunter, finding no difficulty in locating, stalking and killing food. I was adapting rapidly to my new form – but the knowledge brought me scant comfort.

The pack resumed its journey east. Vhazz possess an unusual sense whereby they maintain a rudimentary form of mental or emotional contact when separated. They cannot communicate in any depth by this means but they do remain aware of one another over distances, and can discern something of each other's emotional condition. Hence, though I remained some way to the rear of the pack, I was aware at all times of its general movements. Had I fallen into difficulty, the pack would have known and responded. Equally, had I been required to join the pack for any reason, I had little doubt that a summons of sorts would have registered itself upon my consciousness.

On the second night the pack commenced its ascent into the western foothills of the Byar-hagkh mountains. Once on the other side we would descend into Mystoph, and thence beyond, on what was to my certainty a pointless quest. Dinbig of Khimmur had travelled great distances during his life, in all directions, to many farflung nations; he knew there existed no land of perpetual night beyond the rising sun, unless it lay in some inconceivably remote place, over the Great Eastern Ocean, which none had ever crossed and most believed had no far shores.

How I was torn! Sleeping little, I stood for hours at a time, my nose pointed towards Hon-Hiaita. There my heart lay, and with every lope, trot or bound I was taking myself further from it.

But the vhazz male is bound by a powerful, instinctual sense of loyalty and duty to its family-group. Additionally, the mere idea of not belonging to a pack provokes moral conflict and morbid terror, for to be vhazz and solitary is one thing, but to be vhazz and alone without a pack is another. A lack of contact or support equates with vulnerability and helplessness, and the fear of that condition runs constantly within vhazz veins. Though I detested being vhazz, I quailed at the idea of losing contact with my family-group.

As yet my recollection of my former, human, existence remained clear and unaffected. But with each passing day, as I grew accustomed to my vhazz form, more accepting of its nature and gradually acquainted with its quirks and idiosyncrasies, I knew that I was becoming more and more vhazz.

Late on that second night, long before the dark had begun to yield to the advancing light of dawn, I decided to test my former magical powers. I had been an advanced adept of the Zan-Chassin way in my former life, knowledgeable of magic to a formidable degree and a seasoned voyager in the Realms of Non-Corporeality, having broad experience of entities resident there. It was perhaps strange that I had not thought to test myself earlier, but shock and preoccupation with my newfound state had in truth driven all such considerations from my mind. Now I found myself prompted to action with some urgency.

Had I still the capacity to summon my allies? Gaskh, my stalwart Guardian? And Yo – perfidious Yo who had purloined my living flesh and thus brought about my end in Twalinieh?

A deeply felt sorrow passed through me as I recalled the third of my allies: my Guide, Flitzel. Brave, selfless Flitzel; playful, mercurial, enigmatic wisp of an entity, who had sacrificed her existence to the Vulpasmage in order that I might survive.

And what of the raptures I had known? Could I now employ them, or were they, and all my powers, dependent upon my being, physically, the man I had been?

The mind of a vhazz is restless and undisciplined. A multitude of distractions play upon it. The vhazz are creatures uncomfortable with themselves: parasites infest their skin and innards, boring ceaselessly, bringing out irritating boils, haemorrhages and sores or inducing varying digestive disorders. The vertebral column and its associative muscles are a further source of almost continuous discomfort, as are the internal organs. It seems they have not adapted well to supporting a creature of such bulk which is able to utilise both bipedal and quadrupedal movement.

These factors alone are sufficient to induce snappy tempers and morose moods, but there is more. Vhazz senses are readily stimulated by numerous types of sounds or odours which can galvanise the creature into primitive behavioural patterns over which it may have little conscious control. Under certain, unspecifiable stimuli the vhazz may resort to unreasoning savagery somewhat against its own better will. I was beginning to understand something of the vhazz temperament, and was discovering a growing empathy which as a human, lacking the direct experience of what it entailed to be vhazz, I could never have entertained.

Huwoorsk was no exception to these afflictions and existential burdens. His mind knew continual disquiet and did not give itself easily to the stillness required to invoke Zan-Chassin powers. And in order that Dinbig of Khimmur might apply himself fully to the task, the part of my consciousness that was vhazz had first to be somehow wholly suppressed.

I meditated for a period of some hours and gained no favourable result. Barely able to forget the creatures that crawled upon my skin, I failed to detach myself from the world, and so was unable to summon my spiritual allies or attempt to make contact with the minds of my former human associates. The most elementary raptures were beyond my ability to perform.

Dawn crept forth, subtle, sleek and silver grey, to find me exhausted and dispirited.

As evening approached the pack, awakening from its daytime slumber, prepared to move on. I had been trailing four or five miles to the rear. We were high in the Byar-hagkh now and progress had become slow due to harsh terrain and drifts of deep snow and layers of ice. I had found a sheltered place to sleep through the morning, and now gave myself to further meditation,

131

striving to drive from my thoughts all consciousness of myself as vhazz.

With immense concentration I entered at last a region of quietude. Fleetingly there was a sensation of being no longer anchored. I knew I had achieved the essential requirement which had eluded me the previous night. Thus, without thought, I dissolved the world. Slowly, leadenly, with a feeling of dragging myself through a mire, I rose above my vhazz body.

The effort was almost more than I could give. I floated free for perhaps a second or two, then was sucked back into the vhazz. I was weak and shaken – but I understood what I had accomplished. It was a small step, far from what I had hoped, but it was something! After my initial total failure it gave me new heart.

I slept for another hour, and woke with the decision made to desert the pack and return to Hon-Hiaita.

Descending out of the Byar-hagkh beneath the cover of dark trees, back down into the dhoma of Gegg's Cowm in the province of Selaor, my course took me within two miles of old Gegg's castle on a long scarp well south of the main Selaor Road. From time to time I grew aware of the proximity of men, but the night had descended to give me invisibility, and I could see while they could not.

I skirted villages, travelling west, and entered the forest of Rishal. With every step now it seemed my soul was being wrenched as I recognised familiar landmarks and locations, places I had been countless times. I kept close to the Selaor Road, then, a few miles east of Hoost's Corner, swung up to follow at some distance the northward course of the River Huss. By early morning I was positioned upon a low, wooded hilltop, looking north across the mist-blanketed Sharmanian Meadows. There, beyond the Meadows, were the stone walls and tiled and timbered roofs of Hon-Hiaita town, and the magnificent soaring battlements, towers and turrets of the Royal Palace perched high upon Hon-Hiaita rock.

## V

Soon after sunrise the town began to come alive. Smoke curled from roofs, the vibrant, varied smells of cooking, tanning, of men and animals, of the dank mist rising from the meadows, the river, Lake Hiaita beyond, wafted my way and roused me to ever-greater longing. But mingling with these smells was another, one of putrefaction, of corpses rotting on gibbets and frames.

As I observed the great Sharmanian Gate was opened. People came and went about their business: carts and wagons trundled in and out, travellers of one sort or another, on horseback or on foot, and soldiers. Many soldiers. Companies of troops rode or marched forth from time to time out of the city, or cantered in from the countryside. Most bore standards I recognised of the various dhomas of Khimmur, but twice I observed companies upholding banners I could not identify.

The Gate was well-manned, as were the walls – much more so than had been the case in my time. And every person, wagon and mount was being stopped and checked by the guards as they made to enter or leave the town. I eyed the great palace, and wondered whether the king – the Vulpasmage – was within.

The morning drew on and my vhazz eyes grew strained with the business of vigilance in the bright light of day. I withdrew to the shelter of a deep cavity beneath the roots of a toppled oak. There I slept till just before dusk.

In the dwindling light, as the sun was dipping towards the western horizon, I crept from my vantage point upon the hilltop and descended to the edge of Sharmanian Meadows. Keeping low, utilising the cover of reeds and undergrowth along the bank of the Huss, I moved up alongside Water Street towards the Sharmanian Gate. The river swung away to enter Hon-Hiaita somewhat to the west, its course there guarded by watch-towers and a heavy metal grille sunk deep into its bed. I glanced along Water Street; the way was clear. The land fell away slightly beneath the rise of the road. Here clumps of grass grew a foot or so high, and numerous small shrubs and the occasional willow provided some further cover. On my belly I crawled on beside the road, praying that no sharp-eyed sentry would spot my movement from the walls. Twenty yards from the gatehouse itself a small tangle of bramble grew. Here I halted and lay flat, concealed, I hoped, from all eyes.

In my time it had been the custom to close the Gate at sunset, after which no person would be allowed in or out of Hon-Hiaita without a special permit. I assumed this procedure to still be in force. During my morning vigil I had noted the efficiency of the guards. Everything had been checked, all passes scrutinised. Now I waited.

A couple of labourers pushing handcarts stacked with charcoal came up the road. They halted, were subjected to brusque interrogation, their carts examined, and allowed to continue on. I looked up; the sun had almost gone and the light was fading rapidly. Water Street remained free of traffic for as far as I could see.

The docan* of the guard appeared within the gatehouse entrance. He conferred with his sergeant. My

* Docan: a Khimmurian army officer in charge of a unit of ten soldiers.

heart sank as I heard him give the order to lower the portcullis. The sergeant strode to the gate to relay the command to his men. A voice called from the tower above. I pressed myself against the ground, fearing I had been spotted, awaiting the hiss and thud of arrows.

Silence. I raised my head. The docan had retired within the gatehouse. The sergeant stood, two soldiers at his side, his hands upon his hips, staring along Water Street.

The distant rumble and creak of wheels upon the road. The sound grew louder, and some moments later a wagon came into view, drawn by six sturdy bullocks. A single driver sat upon the boardseat, reins in hand. Three armed men wearing padded leather surcoats and metal helmets rode escort on horses alongside. This was perhaps what I had been waiting for. Certainly, it was my only hope if I was to enter Hon-Hiaita tonight.

The wagon drew up to the gate where the sergeant stood with one hand raised. Its nearside rear wheel rested just yards from where I lay, but my path to it was blocked by one of the armed escort who waited upon his horse on the road almost directly above my head. I held my breath. If the horse, more sensitive than men, detected my presence I would be finished.

The sergeant approached the driver. 'What is your business?'

'Good eve, sergeant,' spoke the driver. 'You know my business. It is I, Thermon from Hissik. I have come to purchase what goods I can and return with them to Mystoph and perhaps beyond, hopefully to realise a good profit.'

'Your permit,' demanded the sergeant in a gruff voice.

I assumed some form of official document or marker changed hands, though I could see nothing, for the exchange took place on the offside of the wagon. Such measures had rarely been in force when I had resided here. Other than in times of dire emergency people had come and gone within the town more or less as they pleased.

The two Hon-Hiaitan guards came around to the rear of the wagon and pulled aside the awning to inspect the contents. One of them muttered a curse, and the second marched off to fetch a lantern.

'You are lucky,' I heard the sergeant say to the merchant upon the wagon. 'Another five minutes and you would have been spending the night out here in the open. Now, let me see your face.'

The second guard returned. He held up the lantern and the two peered inside again. They poked and rummaged briefly, seemed satisfied, and left to rejoin their sergeant. A few words were spoken in an undertone and the sergeant once more addressed the merchant upon the wagon.

'You are carrying only a few bales of cloth.'

'That is so. I brought wool from Miragoff, but was offered a good price in Mlanje. With the money gained there I purchased cloth, but have managed to sell much of it along the way.'

'How long do you intend staying?'

'As soon as I have sold this, and bought other goods here, I will move on. By the way, have you heard the news? Chol has fallen.'

'Aye. I've heard.'

'They say King Oshalan fought at the head of the army like an avenging devil. I have it first-hand that he killed more than fifty of the enemy single-handed.'

'I have heard that too,' muttered the sergeant, without great interest.

'Fhir Oube is on the run. His army collapsed under the weight of Khimmur's hammerblow.'

'Yes, yes, it is good news.'

I watched the back of the wagon, so tantalisingly close if I could but get past the horseman blocking my way. Any second now the merchant would be permitted on into the town. My heart thumped as I felt my moment slip away.

The sergeant had stepped back from the wagon. There was a brief silence. Beneath the wagon I observed his booted feet as he stepped up towards the two horsemen on the other side. A further silence, then he moved back to the wagon. 'Your pass indicates an escort of three.' He raised his voice. 'Ho! You there, skulking on the other side. Come forward that I might see your face. Or do you have a reason for concealing it from me?'

The horseman above me clicked his tongue and urged his mount to the fore of the wagon. My way was as clear as it would ever be. I took the moment, came silently from my hiding place and like a shadow slipped up to the wagon and crept lightly inside beneath the awning.

Outside a horse snorted and stirred. Its rider spoke calming words. The bullocks shifted uneasily upon the road. The wagon rolled a few inches forward as they jerked on their harness. I lay in the dark, unmoving, unbreathing. The merchant, Thermon of Hissik, cussed his beasts to be still, then started up with further reports from abroad. The sergeant spoke again. 'Go your way, merchant.'

The wagon, with myself inside, rumbled on.


VI


Chol had fallen to Khimmur? The news left me somewhat mystified. Prior to the battle of Twalinieh Chol had declared herself my nation's ally. I had to assume that her Prince Regent had protested at Khimmur's hostilities, and had paid the price when the Vulpasmage turned its attentions beyond Kemahamek.

But at least now I knew for certain that I existed within my own time. King Oshalan still ruled – which is to say the Vulpasmage held power in Khimmur. My friends and loved ones, then, were they alive? Were they free? Were they within Hon-Hiaita?

The wagon made its way along Mags Urc't, Hon-Hiaita's central avenue which led to the harbourside. Once clear of the Sharmanian Gate I knew I would have to take my leave of Thermon and his escort. The harbour was a populous area, day and night, a marketplace ringed with shops and booths, warehouses, taverns, brothels and other places of entertainment. For my purposes I required a place to lie low until the night grew older and fewer people were abroad.

I moved with care to the rear of the wagon and peered out between the flaps of the awning. Two of the armed guards, it seemed, were riding up front. The third had taken up a position directly to the rear, about five paces behind.

We had passed beyond sight of the Sharmanian Gate. In a moment we would come abreast of a narrow sidestreet which led up towards the Far Prospects quarter of town, where I – the Grand Merchant, Ronbas Dinbig – had lived. There were a few people on Mags Urc't, but with the setting of the sun the evening gloom had deepened considerably.

I observed the rider behind the wagon. His attention was upon the street to either side, eyeing taverns and stalls that we passed, and especially the women passing by. It was evident that he was not about to change his position, and I had to act before the risk became too great.

Just then the rider twisted his head somewhat rear-wards, his eyes following the passage of a particularly buxom young maiden. Without hesitation I drew aside the awning and sprang into the street.

The guard's horse leapt in sudden terror, screamed and reared high. I darted to the side and bounded for the cover of an alley. No one blocked my way; I was gone from Mags Urc't before any could be the wiser, and my guess was that the rider himself had had no chance to see what it was that had so startled his mount.

Some way along the alley I paused to listen. No sound of pursuit reached my ears. I could hear the rider, who had been thrown from his saddle, swearing and emitting groans of pain. The merchant Thermon called out loudly. Other voices made vague replies. No one spoke of vhazz.

I ascended a little higher, cautiously, keeping to the darkest regions, until I came to the back of a single-storey house which had belonged to a former factor of mine. Here, tucked away behind a high timber fence, was a small lean-to used for storing logs. I carefully lifted the latch of the gate in the fence and put my head around. There was no one about. I slipped inside and crept beneath the lean-to. There I remained, hidden, until long past midnight.

In Hon-Hiaita eyes watched every street – not only the eyes of the military and those in the King's employ, but the eyes of thieves and scoundrels alert for opportunity. Strangers might pass unmolested in the town – though with the heightened tension and extra guards at this time everyone would be under suspicion – but any of non-human appearance would be quickly spotted. Dogs, cats and other animals would also quickly detect and draw attention to the presence of a vhazz.

And hatred of vhazz was such that I would be allowed no quarter, no chance to attempt to explain.

The sky grew cloudy. The moon, which had appeared high in the sky late in the afternoon, was obscured, which aided me considerably in my purpose. With the night well-advanced and the sounds of revelry from the taverns and entertainment houses of the town diminished, I came from concealment and continued on towards Far Prospects.

My former home was a stately manse set back from the street. At its front was a spacious walled-and-whitewashed courtyard bordered with laburnum, magnolia, hibiscus, bougainvillaea and acer. A venerable old Umbrella Pine occupied the centre of the court, its base ringed by pots and urns containing other plants. To this I crept in order to observe the house.

The windows were shuttered; no sounds emanated from within. I sensed that my home was occupied, but by whom? Gradually I was overcome with a feeling of futility. Why had I come here? What had I hoped to achieve? I could not gain entrance to the house. And what was there to discover if I did? I already knew that I no longer lived here, and could confidently assume that as Ronbas Dinbig had been declared a traitor to the King, my former possessions would all have been seized. Whoever occupied my home now would certainly not be a friend of mine.

I had hoped to find evidence of the fate of Rohse and my child, it is true. My awesome-tempered wife, Auvrey, too. But the only hope I had of observing anyone and perhaps finding out more would be in daylight hours. And this I could not possibly do.

I slunk away with a heavy heart.

At no great distance from my old home was the residence of the Chariness, the high-officiator of the

Zan-Chassin. To this I now made my way, drawn by the same empty sense of yearning that had brought me to Hon-Hiaita in the first place. The Chariness, like myself, had been declared an enemy of the state, so I knew I would not find her in Hon-Hiaita. But I had to see, and I had to hope. Somehow, if she and other members of the Zan-Chassin lived, there had to be a means of making contact.

I hid beneath the tall trees that ringed the Chariness's elegant home. I sensed its emptiness; unlike my manse, no one had assumed occupancy when the Chariness had been forced to flee. No doubt magical defences had been left in her wake, sufficient to discourage any who might otherwise have seized her most desirable home. Indeed, a disquieting aura of magic hung over the place, and filled me with unease.

I made to leave. A voice spoke suddenly soft but commanding in my ear: 'Halt! Who intrudes?'

I spun around, but discerned no presence.

'Speak!' commanded the voice sharply. 'Or be harmed.'

Now I saw it, a tiny bright monitor eye, set some feet overhead, concealed in moss in the crook of a branch. I attempted to reply but could summon only a harsh vhazz sound, half-growl, half-cough.

'What tongue is this?' demanded the monitor.

I tried again, but met with similar result.

'Wait!' ordered the monitor. 'Do not move. I will seek instruction.'

Seconds passed, then I sensed the manifestation of an incorporeal presence. Another voice spoke, but this time it was not borne on air, nor was it received by my aural faculties. Instead it manifested directly within my mind.

*'Who are you? And what is your purpose here?'*

141

I formed the reply with my own thought. *'I seek the Chariness, or another high-member of the Zan-Chassin.'*

*'For what purpose?'*

*'For aid.'*

*'I ask again, who are you?'*

I took a deep breath. *'I am Dinbig. Ronbas Dinbig.'*

There was a pause, then: *'Dinbig! You endanger yourself with such falsehoods. He passed beyond.'*

*'I passed beyond, Revered Sister,'* I replied, for by now I had recognised the characteristic emanations of the presence beside me, and knew myself to be communicating with none other than the Chariness herself. *'But somehow I have returned. I am Dinbig, and I am not. For I occupy another body – and to some extent am possessed of another mind.'*

I experienced a brief, gently susurrant tingling within the core of my being, barely detectable, like a psychic breath passing through my soul. I was being probed. The Chariness spoke again.

*'I sense a confusion, a divergence of personality, a mis-mingling of essence. Within I recognise something that was of Dinbig.'*

*'I can offer you indisputable proof with a single word,'* said I.

*'Do not! Others invigilate upon this place. To utter a true and secret name could endanger its owner, if you are truly he.'*

*'Revered Sister, I need help. I am trapped. I am vhazz.'*

*'Vhazz?'*

*'I do not know how to free myself.'*

*'And I do not know if we can help you. We are not strong.'*

*'But the Zan-Chassin still exist?'*

*'Yes, far from here.'*

'Then there is hope.'

'I must go,' said the Chariness with a new urgency. 'My presence is detected; entities have been summoned. I will investigate. If you are Dinbig we will find a means of contacting you again, though I do not yet know how. Now leave! Enemies approach!'

The presence beside me withdrew.

'Revered Sister, one more thing! My family. Where are they?'

The voice within my mind was faint.

'Your spouse returned to her father.'

'But Rohse? Have I a child?'

'Dinbig has a child. Rohse also returned to her family.' The voice was barely distinguishable. 'Dinbig, I perceive that it is truly you. I cannot remain, but have heart, and for now, have strength.'

These last words I barely caught, so far away did they seem, like air whispering through distant trees. The Chariness was gone. But in my mind was a new clarity, a warmth, a feeling of vigour and capacity, a vital renewal of self. She had imbued me with her strength, an aid in suppressing the bestial nature of the vhazz, Huwoorsk.

There was a vague disturbance of the atmosphere. My eardrums popped, my hackles rose. I felt a deep, sickening disorientation. The air suddenly contained a tension as something evil strove to manifest.

I sensed a conflict just beyond the fabric between this realm and the next. Entities – minions of the Vulpasmage – struggled to break through into the corporeal and were held back by the Chariness's forces.

The struggle would not last: the Vulpasmage was most powerful here. I fled from the trees and away from the Chariness's former home. The tension eased. I ran on down the nearest street, into the darkness of Hon-Hiaita.

A bleak wash of yellowish grey, low and reticent in the eastern sky, filtered through the dark cloud mass to inform the wakeful of the coming of day. At the Sharmanian Gate the sentries of the night watch were relieved by the new guard. They formed up at the head of Mags Urc't, their docan at the fore, and marched smartly away in the direction of the Royal Palace. The new docan barked out orders and the morning watch set about its duties.

With poor grace the light began to improve. One or two citizens emerged from their homes, yawning, sleepy-headed, preparing to go about the day's business. A wagon and a couple of carts rolled up Mags Urc't towards the gate, which had yet to be opened.

The sergeant came from the gatehouse, followed by two soldiers, to begin the day's inspection of traffic. A creaking, groaning sound split the morning air as the windlass within the gatehouse took the weight of the colossal iron portcullis. The portcullis ascended and two soldiers ducked beneath, to heave high the counterweighted retaining bar inside the gate. They pushed. The Sharmanian Gate swung slowly open.

From the cover of a stack of barrels beneath the eaves of a tavern some twenty yards from the gate came a large, swift, grey-brown form. Certain of its object, and as yet unseen, it sped beneath the stationary wagon before the gate, and on, between the horses' hooves, utilising them for cover. Ears flat, form elongated for speed, it raced on towards the partially-opened gate.

A shout! Horses nickered, then screamed and stamped in sudden fear. The creature shot forward, passing so close to the first soldier as to all but knock him from his feet. It gained the portcullis, then the gate, and did not pause in its flight, bounding on, out into the damp meadow beyond.

More shouts. The creature sped straight across the meadow towards the woods beyond. An arrow thudded into the ground close by, then a second. To the beast's eyes the woods seemed a mile away.

No mist offered obscurity to the creature's fleeing form. It veered, swerved, darted as more shafts flew from the battlements. Then abruptly the missiles were falling short; the vhazz had passed beyond bowshot. I bounded on, unpursued, and plunged at last into the sanctuary of the woods.

# 5

I

Virland, recently incorporated into the growing Khimmurian Empire, was a land of deep and unrelenting forest: the Forest of Magoth. Its peoples were not great in number, and consisted of a scattering of forest clans who centred themselves loosely around small settlements, some on cleared land, some within and actually upon the trees themselves.

Lacking a central government Virland had put up little concerted resistance when Khimmurian troops marched in along the rough trackways that snaked through the forest. In places remote villages had been ransacked and slaves taken, stirring up bitter resentment among the foresters there and giving rise to the formation of ragtag guerilla bands. More commonly the Khimmurians had merely marched through, causing little stir. Some of Virland's young men, eager for novelty and adventure, had volunteered for service in the ranks of the Khimmurian Army. Others had continued with their lives little changed. Some had derived profit from the influx of hungry and thirsty soldiers eager for diversion and entertainment. But many of the Vir had simply upped and withdrawn deeper into the Magoth, secure in the knowledge that they could never be found. And indeed, so rugged, dense and trackless was much of Virland's heart that it had not been penetrated by the invaders, and never would be. Its deepest denizens – not all human – lived relatively untroubled lives, wholly unaware of the rapid and far-reaching changes taking place in the lands all around them.

The village of Dalwood, set some thirty miles or so from Virland's hazy western border, was a haphazard grouping of modest wood dwellings built around a small clearing at the fork of a forest trackway. Prior to the coming of the Khimmurians Dalwood had been a tranquil place, a small universe, hidden and barely touched by the events of elsewhere. More recently it had begun to bustle and hum as soldiers moved in, bringing labourers and craftsmen, with traders close in their wake. Khimmur had hacked a trail into Virland from its frontier, linking with the forest trail that ran through Dalwood. It was set upon extending the way further to create a single road which cut right through Virland to form a direct link between Khimmur and Chol. This to avoid the hazardous route along the northern plains of the Ashakite Lands.

To this end a large wooden stockade had been constructed at no great distance from the village, one of several dotted throughout Virland. It was garrisoned with some sixty or so soldiers, with various auxiliaries. Slavegangs had been brought in from Vyshroma and Putc'pii to expedite the work. Each morning at sunrise the slaves would be marched under guard and in chains from the stockade, issued with tools and set to work till dusk. (Prudence dictated that native slaves be transported out of their former homelands to reduce the risk of insurrection from the populace. Hence, slaves taken from Virland, arguably the best men for performing the task of cutting the road through the thick forest, were necessarily assigned to works far away.)

Each day the forest around Dalwood reverberated with the sounds of chopping, sawing, digging, the crashing of mighty trees. Thick palls of smoke hung above the treetops as colossal bonfires consumed the masses of useless wood. Many considered the building of the road an impossible project: though the way would swing south to avoid Virland's impenetrable heart, the forest was still dense and unmapped, the land subject to sudden chasms or soaring, rocky heights. But the Beast of Rull had gained a reputation for thriving on the impossible, bending and forging it to comply with his own designs, undermining it so that it crumbled before him, or simply storming over it as if it were unworthy of consideration. The building of the Selaor Bridge was a prime example of achievement where none had been thought possible, as were the fall of Twalinieh and Kemahamek, the mining of the Hulminilli, and two years of unremitting conquest. Slaves were expendable and in ready supply, making the expense the road incurred in its foundation negligible in the face of eventual advantages.

Village life in Dalwood centred around a single hostelry, the Dappled Woodpecker, which also served as the local smithy. The landlord of the Dappled Woodpecker was a thickset man named Pandly, of rotund frame and direct but courteous and good-humoured manner. He bore the solid, big-boned features, chalky skin and strong dark hair and beard common to the Vir.

Pandly had lived in Dalwood all his life, as had the other villagers. He had inherited both inn and smithy from his father, who had been left it by his father before him. He was knowledgeable in the ways of the forest, and this region of the Magoth was as familiar to him as his own small vegetable plot in which he cultivated crops to garnish the meals he served to his clientele.

Far from indifferent to the presence of the Khimmurians, Pandly was nevertheless a man able to recognise and adapt to the inconstancies of circumstance. The troops had caused no direct harm to Dalwood or its modest population. Their harsh treatment of the foreign slaves was deplored, but the foresters were by and large a peaceful folk, slow to anger, and without a stalwart leader or single figurehead. In any event they lacked the manpower to make a stand against the garrison.

Pandly reckoned himself a pragmatist. He knew opportunity when he saw it, and with the coming of the soldiers had promptly trebled his prices at the inn. He maintained a precise record of every transaction; his regular customers were reimbursed in secret at monthly intervals, and the Khimmurians, knowing no different, paid over their coin with the carps and cavils reserved for landlords everywhere.* Khimmur's presence thus furnished Pandly with a handsome profit, and he in turn ensured that a portion of the dividend was directed to the exclusive benefit of the community.

One evening it happened that a traveller entered the common room of the Dappled Woodpecker. He was a man of middle-age, average in height, with thin grey hair, somewhat straggling. He wore a grey cloak over a woollen jerkin, thick brown hose and leather boots. His eyes were deep-set and grey above a long, somewhat bowed nose, and he sported a short beard. He carried a staff of seasoned ash, and at his belt hung a longsword in its scabbard.

He approached Pandly, who looked up from behind

---

* Dalwood was fortunate in this respect. Elsewhere in the burgeoning empire innkeepers who had shown themselves remiss in dispensing free drink and sustenance to the invading troops were left hanging by their necks from the eaves of their own taverns, in ghoulish imitation of the pub-signs that swung alongside them.

the counter where he was carving a haunch of venison and appraised the visitor with a mild brown gaze. Of late a small trickle of travelling folk had begun to find their way into the forest, but strangers travelling alone were still an uncommon sight.

'Good evening, sir. And how might I help you?'

'To begin with, a tankard of your best bitter,' declared the man. 'And a platter of that succulent venison, if I may.'

'Certainly,' said Pandly. The man seemed of genial disposition, but his accent Pandly could not place. 'I can offer it to you with potatoes and roots, and the speciality of the house: a gravy made with sultry red wine and a secret recipe of herbs and spices.'

'My mouth waters already, good landlord,' replied the stranger. 'That will be my choice.'

'And to follow, sir? I can recommend our baked almond pudding with hot acorn and treacle syrup. Or if you prefer something lighter, perhaps a fruit compote with thick goat's cream.'

'The almond pudding, I think. I have travelled a long way and my belly rumbles mightily in anticipation of a change from hard tack and berries.'

Pandly drew a tankard of ale. The stranger took a deep draught and smacked his lips.

'And, indeed, I would like a pallet for the night if you have one. And is there anyone in this village who can sell me a horse? I have travelled on foot, dragging a most obstreperous donkey through the forest, but I understand the way west grows somewhat easier from this point. A reliable mount would ease my journey no end. Ah yes, and stabling for the ill-tempered beast too, if you can manage that.'

'The bed and the stable I can offer you, sir. In fact they may be one and the same, as the cubicles are situated at the back, in the loft over the animals, where it's warmest,' said Pandly. 'Of course, I do have more comfortable chambers within the house itself, and can provide hot water and clean linen if you wish to incur the extra charge.'

The man shook his head. 'No, a pallet laid with clean straw will be adequate, thank you.'

'As for the horse,' Pandly went on, still seeking to place the man's accent, 'that is less easily found. Here in the forest we have little use for any but draught-animals. You might find yourself better-served at the garrison down the way, though you'll pay for the privilege.'

Pandly's customers at this time consisted of three foresters seated in muted conference close to a glowing log-fire, and a quartet of Khimmurian soldiers gambling with dice at a separate table in one corner. All seven had looked up at the stranger's entrance, and the conversation with Pandly had been conducted in tones sufficiently loud for all to hear. The stranger now turned to address the Khimmurians.

'Is this the case, to your knowledge, gentlemen?'

'It's possible,' grunted one, his eyes glued to the table. 'You'd need to see the farrier.'

'And where might he be found?'

'At the stockade, a mile or so down the road.'

'And will you good men be returning there this evening?'

'We will. Our duty commences in two hours.'

'Then perhaps I might accompany you?'

The soldier nodded. A second soldier then argued that the farrier lacked the authority to sell a horse to a civilian. The quartermaster would be the man to see, or even the Corsan, the garrison commander.

'No matter, we shall find out who soon enough!' said the traveller. 'Perhaps a deal might even be struck whereby I part company with my valuable donkey, in part payment for the horse. I was of course jesting when I referred just now to its obstreperous nature.'

The soldier and his companions chuckled and returned to their game. The traveller turned back to Pandly.

'Now, landlord, I would prefer to settle my account here and now as I shall be leaving early in the morning. Perhaps you could also furnish me with some victuals to sustain me on my journey?'

Pandly took up a blackboard and chalk, believing he had the problem of the stranger's mysterious accent solved. It was not a natural accent – the man was attempting to disguise his origins with the assumption of an accent reminiscent of eastern Vir, the inauthenticity of which was easily discerned by any keen-eared Virlander.

'And where might you be travelling to, if you don't mind my asking, sir?' enquired Pandly with renewed interest.

'Into Khimmur, and thence north to Taenakipi. I am on a pilgrimage to the shrine of the tree-god, Cara-fon-bhik, in the township of Kipitu. I hope to arrive for the celebrations of the vernal equinox. The ceremonies are particularly inspiring. I am on the right road, am I not?'

'You are. And it has been improved in recent months. There was a time when none but wild beasts, sprites and the occasional vagabond made use of it. Now it has been cleared to facilitate travel, and it is rare to go for more than two or three hours without seeing another face.'

'Good. That must at least make it safer.'

Pandly sucked in air between his teeth. 'Perhaps, and perhaps not. Increased traffic attracts an increase of robbers and cutthroats. It is best to travel carefully, and preferably in company.'

'Alas, the latter I fear I cannot do. At least, not to begin with. I have much time to make up. Still, solitary has always been my preferred mode of travel, and it has served me well.'

'Very good, sir. Well, this way will bear you eventually into Mystoph in Khimmur. Once there keep straight in a line with the Barrier Fell until you meet the north-south road called the Murth. Be sure to turn north – south is a haunted route which folk never use.'

'So I've heard tell.'

Pandly revealed his figures upon the blackboard. 'Now then, sir, here is your tally, if it pleases you.'

The stranger eyed the sum at the bottom, nodded, and withdrew a leather purse from his belt. Emptying its contents onto the counter he proceeded to count out coins. 'There, the exact amount.'

Pandly, who had been observing his movements carefully, scooped the coins into a big hand, then picked one out and eyed it with particular scrutiny.

'Sir, this silver piece – I have not seen its like before.'

The stranger leaned across. 'Ah, forgive me, landlord. That is a Dyarchim coin. There, that is the head of the current sovereign, in profile. And on the obverse is the Dyarchim symbol, the jaguar salient. I am sorry, I did not realise I still possessed any such coins. Is it not accepted tender here? I will gladly replace it.'

'No, no, sir!' Pandly tested the metal between his teeth. 'Silver is silver as far as I'm concerned. I was merely curious. We see many foreign objects these days that have never so much as entered the forest before. But this one is new to me.'

'Quite so, I'm sure. Nevertheless, if it will put you at your ease I will happily substitute a more familiar coin.'

'Not at all, sir. Now, if you would like to make yourself comfortable I will see to your food.'

The traveller took a place alone at a table near the window. His food was brought and he set to in silence, with some relish, ordering more ale.

A few minutes later one of the three foresters seated before the fire rose and crossed to the counter to engage Pandly in conversation. Their tones were hushed, the conversation brief, but from the shift of Pandly's eyes it was evident that at least one of the topics they discussed was the stranger seated by the window. The stranger was able to observe that Pandly went so far as to show a particular silver coin to the forester.

The forester rejoined his companions. Presently, as the traveller was scraping the last morsels of pudding from his bowl, a second forester, a man of advancing years, left the little group and approached him. 'My pardon, sir. I heard you say earlier that you hoped to purchase a horse.'

'Yes, that is so,' replied the stranger, dabbing his lips with a napkin.

'My brother was due to ride west tomorrow,' said the forester, 'to return a horse he borrowed some weeks ago from his son. It happens that his wife is sick with pond-fever and he cannot undertake the journey. Their son lives near the edge of the Magoth, in the village of Sawpool, close to the Khimmurian border. He requires the horse quite urgently, along with a few tools my brother had promised to deliver. My brother thought he might pay one of the villagers to deliver them in his stead, but no one here is able to leave, at least not for several days. So it occurred to me that, as you are travelling that way and he cannot, we might perhaps be able to figure some arrangement whereby both your needs and his are well-served.'

'Excellent!' declared the stranger. 'It seems my arrival here is most timely.'

'She is not the youngest or swiftest of mares, but she will get you there,' added the forester. 'And in Sawpool you will have no difficulty in purchasing another – and at a more agreeable price than you would pay at the stockade here.'

'Even better. Take me to your brother, then, and let us fix a fair price to cover my hire of his son's horse, and the delivery of his tools.'

'I can negotiate here and now on my brother's behalf,' said the forester. 'If we arrive at terms we both consider fair I will go and tell him, and bring the horse.'

The two fell to negotiation, which was quickly settled to their mutual satisfaction. The old forester left the inn to inform his brother. The traveller ordered more ale, and at length the forester returned.

'My brother is happy with the arrangement. I've brought the horse and baggage. She is stabled at the back for the night, alongside your donkey.'

'Perfect. Then I shall not be delayed in my departure tomorrow.' The traveller turned to the four Khimmurian soldiers and informed them of the changed circumstances. 'So I will not, after all, be accompanying you good fellows to the stockade this evening.'

The old forester, his task done, rejoined his two companions in front of the fire. The traveller sat on alone, neither invited nor showing any inclination to engage in further conversation with either group.

In due course the soldiers ended their game and left the inn. The landlord, Pandly, delivered to the stranger's table a cloth-bound parcel containing provisions he had prepared to fortify the fellow on his journey. The traveller drained his tankard, stood, wished everyone good-evening, and took his leave of the common room in order to retire for the night.

## II

Early the following morning, in darkness, the stranger emerged from the Dappled Woodpecker. From the stable behind the inn he led the grey mare that had been left overnight. She was a draught horse, long in the tooth and a touch sway-backed, but she seemed of even temperament and sturdy enough to sustain the journey ahead, and more. He saddled her, having earlier ascertained from the forester that she was well-used to bearing a rider, then searched the pack of tools that had been left beside her in the stable, which he was to deliver to the village of Sawpool. Being a wary fellow, canny of the situation hereabouts, and indeed throughout so much of Rull, he did not intend being the unwitting bearer of contraband or supplies to rebel bands in the region.

The tools were innocent enough – a riving froe and wedges, a set of thatcher's needles, whimbel and shearing hook, some chisels, a bow-saw, adzes, bill-hooks and various other woodsman's accessories. He strapped them onto his donkey, along with his own possessions, briefly inspected the provisions Pandly had sold him, then mounted the grey mare. With the donkey tethered behind he rode from Dalwood.

At the edge of the village was a guard-post. A pair of bleary-eyed sentries lounged within, their feet upon a bench close before a glowing brazier. At the traveller's approach they bestirred themselves with reluctance and stomped outside.

The traveller halted while his baggage was searched. He was questioned with surly directness as to his identity and purpose. He explained where he was bound and produced a tatter of parchment from a wooden tube, which revealed his name as being one Dhase Loster, a Tomian scholar. Neither sentry could read, but both were able to recognise the official seal of the council of Pher, one of Tomia's major cities, which was impressed upon the parchment. Tomia was as yet a free nation, unchanged by Khimmurian ambition, and its citizens were not bound by the restrictions placed upon others of nearby lands.

With a sardonic grin the traveller pointed out the worthlessness of the parchment to the two sentries. After all, said he, he might have stolen it from its original owner with none being the wiser. The guards found nothing to amuse them in his observation. At their demand the traveller produced markers evidencing the fact that he had passed through a succession of Khimmurian guard-posts without hindrance or delay.

The two guards were nearing the end of their duty. They were tired and ill-tempered and due to be relieved within the half-hour. The cold out here was biting and they wished for nothing more than to return to their hut to warm themselves before the embers and sit out the remaining long minutes of their watch in relative comfort. And as the traveller so gallingly insisted on reminding them, these formalities served little real purpose. It was impossible to reliably ascertain the identity of every person upon the roads of the new empire. Eighteen months earlier, soon after its conquest, a census had been attempted in Kemahamek, and quickly abandoned as futile.

This was Dalwood, an insignificant fly-blot of a place. There was nowhere this traveller could go except on into Khimmur. There, the sentries reasoned, better equipped guard-stations might see fit to deal with him at greater length. Here there was nothing more to be done.

So having rummaged through his baggage and found nothing to arouse suspicion, they issued the traveller with a new marker and sent him on his way.

\* \* \*

The darkness began to give way to dismal grey morning. Mist hung thickly along the track, enveloping the trees and limiting visibility to a few yards. The forest loomed black and featureless to either side, hanging over the trail; moisture slowly dripped from branches and new leaf. The earth was still frozen, the land silent but for the occasional rustle of a small creature in the undergrowth, or the plaintive call of a bird.

The traveller, wrapped in a waxed and waterproof cape over thick clothing to keep out the creeping cold, whistled a folk-tune to keep himself company as his horse bore him stolidly on.

The trail twisted and turned, avoiding buttresses of rock, gulleys and hummocks, and the known lairs or patrolling grounds of dire beasts. It forded a couple of shallow streams and for a stretch following the course of a deep and fast flowing river. In the main this area of the forest was without steep gradients, though soon enough the way would start to climb as the rugged hills that heralded the approach to Khimmur's border grew near. After three hours of travel the first glimmering of a sun became visible between the high branches. Slowly the mist began to burn off. Visibility improved and the temperature gradually climbed.

A cart approached, drawn by a pair of oxen, heading into Virland. Its driver, a ruddy-cheeked Vir with thick black hair and beard, hailed the traveller as he passed but did not stop to exchange further words. No other voyagers along this track did the traveller meet.

A short distance on the traveller halted beside a pond to allow his animals to drink and crop grass. He seated himself upon a tree-stump and drank from a leather flask containing Vir brandy, and ate from the provisions Pandly had packed. He gazed along the trail, which had now begun to rise. The terrain had grown more rugged, and from time to time, through the trees,

158

he had glimpsed the heights that lay before him. He rested for a few more minutes, then remounted and set off again.

Some minutes later he rounded a bend to see two men seated upon a fallen tree-trunk beside the trail. They wore leathers and forest greens, and as the traveller approached one rose unhurriedly and ambled into his path. He stood with feet casually apart, one hand resting upon the pommel of his sword, a tall, youthful man with dark beard and long hair. His companion, somewhat older and wearing upon his head a green, billed felt cap set with a panache of pheasant's plumage, remained lounging upon the tree-trunk, chewing a stalk of grass and observing the traveller with a lazy eye.

'Hold a moment, stranger,' called the man upon the trail.

The traveller brought his beasts to a halt. 'Good day, gentlemen. Can I be of service to you?'

'Perhaps. Or perhaps we to you. Where are you borne?'

'Into Khimmur, and thence north. I am on a pilgrimage. I hope to pay homage at the time of the vernal equinox, at the shrine of the tree-god Cara-fon-bhik in the township of Kipitu in Taenakipi.'

'Cara-fon-bhik?' mused the first man, with a glance to his companion. 'I know of no god by that name.'

The second man, expressionless, kept silence.

'Perhaps not,' replied the traveller, aware that other eyes watched from among the trees. 'He is not widely worshipped beyond the Taenakipi domain. But I am a scholar who has devoted much of his life to a study of the customs of that region. I have a particular sympathy for the ways of Cara-fon-bhik.'

'A scholar, you say? A poor scholar indeed, if that is truly what you are. For Cara-fon-bhik, be he god or something other, has no following in Taenakipi.'

The traveller said nothing. The second man slipped from the tree-trunk to join his companion upon the trail. Three more stepped from the trees. All wore forest greens, and each bore a bow, arrow notched and pointed casually towards the traveller.

'Speak truthfully now, stranger,' commanded the second man. 'Your life hangs upon your next words.'

'Yes, it seems I am mistaken,' said the traveller. 'For the phrase "*cara-fon-bhik*" is of course of Pansurian origin. It derives from an ancient maxim of that land: "*Bru michus hort cara, dasa het cara fon bhik*". An approximate translation runs: "Eat well of what is yours, but of another's eat only what is freely given." As I say, its message accords well with my own beliefs.'

With brisk formality the elder of the two spoke again. 'I would ask you to accompany us. Dismount, if you will. The horse will be returned to its rightful owner. We will hold your possessions, and weapons.'

The traveller complied. He slipped down to the trail and handed over his sword.

'I regret we must also take the precaution of temporarily blindfolding you.'

'It is no great inconvenience,' replied the traveller with a shrug. 'I confess, my eyes are weary with gazing upon trees and fog, fog and trees.'

A length of folded cloth was bound around his head and he was led away into the forest. Two men supported his arms, guiding him lest he stumble, and clearing branches and brambles that might snap upon his face or snag upon his clothes. The party made its way in silence, save for the occasional murmur of the two guides as they warned the traveller of a particular hazard or obstacle. For perhaps forty minutes they continued, climbing steeply, zig-zagging back and forth, and the traveller was able to gain no indication of the direction in which they moved, or their relation to the trail they had left.

In due course they came to a halt. The traveller was left standing, his blindfold still in place. Around him he could hear little, save the occasional footstep close by, and the breathing of his two guards, who remained at his side.

He heard someone approach to stand before him. The blindfold was removed. He stood blinking in the sudden glare of light.

He was within a small glade, surrounded by tall firs. It was occupied by men and women to a number of perhaps twenty, clad in similar manner to those who had accosted him at the wayside. One or two makeshift shelters had been constructed beneath the trees.

Facing the traveller was a strikingly featured man of young middle age, with long, thick, wavy, prematurely-greyed hair bound with a silver circlet. His body was loose and well-muscled, his eyes sharp, clear and steely blue. His skin bore the tan of one used to living outdoors, and flowing silver-grey sidewhiskers and a long drooping moustache adorned his lower face, framing the mouth and jaw.

He wore a quilted green jupon over a short sleeveless lamellar hauberk, and loose brown trousers of a coarse material, tucked into padded boots. Lamellar steel vambraces were strapped upon his strong forearms, which were otherwise bare. His expression was stern, but the face was one of a man neither coarse nor unduly hard. Beside him was the leader of the group that had brought the traveller from the trail.

The grey-haired warrior spoke. 'You share acquaintance with the false-god Cara-fon-bhik, I am told. Thus I will ask you bluntly, and expect easy answers: Who are you, and why have you come here?'

'I am Maille-Orchus, a knight of Chol,' replied the traveller. 'I have a message from my Prince Regent, Fhir Oube, for Lord Shimeril Mi' Vhuda, Master of the Nine Hundred Mystophian Paladins.'

'Shimeril is elsewhere,' said the warrior.

'There is one other to whom I will speak, but my instructions are that he will name himself and declare his identity with a mark. These were the conditions for secret conference agreed between Lord Shimeril and the Prince Regent in Postor.'

The warrior appraised him coolly for a moment, then tilted his head to one side and drew back his long whiskers with a hand. Running beneath the jaw and terminating in a deep puncture mark was a long scar, the tissue vivid mauve and white.

'This I gained when I fought my own countrymen who believed me to be a traitor to my king. The wound was inflicted by my uncle, whom I loved and respected, but who would have killed me. With great reluctance I was forced to take his life. I am Yzwul, dhoma-lord of Tiancz in Mystoph in Khimmur. Are your conditions now met?'

Sir Maille-Orchus nodded. 'My journey is over. Let us talk.'


III


Lord Yzwul showed Sir Maille-Orchus to a small shelter made of branches covered with hide, outside of which a chubby boy turned a spitted hog over a small campfire. The two entered the shelter and seated themselves upon goatskins laid upon the ground. Food and wine were brought, and they were left alone.

Sir Maille-Orchus said, 'My message is in two parts. First: Chol has fallen, but Fhir Oube lives and fights on. Upon my departure more than two weeks ago, Khimmur had yet to take the south. But it cannot but be taken, for our army is gravely reduced.'

'I know of the successful invasion of your country,' said Lord Yzwul sombrely. 'My sympathies go out to you and your people. But it is something that the Prince Regent lives. Has he plans for retaliation?'

'He is trapped with his back to Enchantery. As yet Khimmur does not know his whereabouts. Our Second Army has withdrawn from the south to rally to him. Other troops in some small number harass the enemy to delay their progress south. But they are but a nuisance, nothing more. Chol is lost unless a large force can be brought to attack the enemy in the rear or flank whilst we engage its front line.'

Yzwul gave a humourless smile. 'What force? We here are not strong, and there are no others.'

'That we know. I simply place the facts before you, as we know them. Our surviving army is a little over four thousand strong. The Vulpasmage, it seems, having taken Postor and the north, saw fit to withdraw many of its troops, perhaps for a campaign elsewhere. Nonetheless, those that remain are more than sufficient to take the south in time. We had half expected them to be reinforced by an army attacking out of Ashakite, but that has not materialised – at least, it had not when I left, though who knows, my words may already be redundant. Any manner of events may have come to pass in my absence.'

'It is a fact that an army was despatched from Cish in southern Mystoph some time ago,' said Lord Yzwul. 'It proceeded along northern Ashakite, intending, as far as we could determine, to strike up into Chol, to force your armies to rush south and ease the task of the troops waiting to invade from Miragoff. But three days out from Khimmur the army's advance guard was attacked by Ashakite tribesmen. It became cut off from the main force, and took heavy casualties before relief arrived. Even then a fierce battle was fought. Both sides sustained losses, though the Ashakites' were the greater. The nomads were eventually repelled, but the Khimmurian force was badly mauled, sufficient to dissuade it from advancing further. It withdrew to Cish. Hence the fact that the attack you foresaw as probable failed to materialise. And this is one reason for the road Khimmur endeavours to hack through Virland. The Vulpasmage is not yet ready to take on the Ashakite nation.'

'Ah, this would be useful information if I could but grow wings and fly swiftly back to Chol,' said Sir Maille-Orchus. 'Fhir Oube might at least be reassured that he need no longer fear attack from the south.'

'Would it alter anything?'

'It might provide more scope for manoeuvre, or at the worst, a route of escape.'

'We have pigeons, given to Shimeril by Fhir Oube.'

'And trained to fly to Postor, which the enemy now holds.'

'A pair are from one of your southern castles, Dorn, the seat of Count Vess.'

Sir Maille-Orchus put a hand to his brow in a moment of feverish thought. 'Yes, then dispatch them, or one, at least. And let us hope that the south is yet free and that someone at Castle Dorn has the means to reach Count Vess.'

Lord Yzwul arose and stepped to the entrance of the shelter, pulled aside the flap and spoke in undertones to someone outside. Returning, he said, 'The message will be sent, along with the news of your safe arrival here. Now, to your knowledge, how many troops has the Beast committed to Chol?'

'I cannot say with accuracy. Some twenty thousand were employed in the initial northern assault and the taking of Postor, plus several slave battalions used as front-line assault groups to both draw our fire and disconcert us. There was also a detachment of monsters which attacked in darkness, when our troops were least able to combat them. Now at least nine thousand remain, and probably more. They are Khimmurian nationals in the main, supplemented by Kemahamek and other foreign auxiliaries and mercenaries.'

'Kemahamek complicity in the aftermath of its defeat is mystifying,' said Yzwul. 'There is something afoot that we have yet to discover. The monsters — they are Gneth?'

'That was our assumption.'

'How many were used? And have they now been withdrawn?'

'It was difficult to assess their number — perhaps two hundred. Sufficient to create widespread panic among my troops. They may still be within Chol, but they have not been deployed in the southern advance.'

Yzwul nodded. 'I will convey your news to Lord Shimeril. And I hope you will not think me presumptuous if I offer advice. In these circumstances your Prince Regent's response must be one of prudence. Strength should be conserved; if possible, the enemy assessed and knowledge gained of his weak points. Above all, as things stand I would judge unwise any attempt to regain the capital, or confront the enemy directly. You would meet with certain defeat.'

'This we know,' said Sir Maille-Orchus stiffly. 'Fhir Oube lies low for the present. From positions of relative safety he launches swift and effective strikes, but he is an experienced soldier and leader, and avoids reckless engagement.'

Yzwul nodded. 'Now, you spoke of a second part to your message.'

Sir Maille-Orchus took a deep breath. 'It concerns the Duke Shadd.'

'You have news of him?' said Yzwul, his blue eyes widening.

'Better. He has been our guest.'

'Great Moban! This is welcome news! Where is he? How does he fare?'

Maille-Orchus shifted his weight a shade uncomfortably. 'Alas, I cannot answer those questions. We located him, yes. He was held in the gaol of one of our border forts, close to Enchantery.'

'Gaol?' Yzwul drew back in outraged astonishment. 'On what charge?'

Sir Maille-Orchus raised his hands in a gesture of appeasement. 'It was through no fault of our own, I assure you. Duke Shadd had adopted a convincing disguise, and the fortress commander, not knowing him for who he was, had him arrested on the vaguest charge of perpetrating nuisance –'

Again Lord Yzwul was moved to loud exclamation. 'This is a gross insult – !'

'Hear me out, sir, please! I am instructed by my Prince Regent to offer full and unreserved apology, and to explain the situation in all detail. It was not of our doing, and in truth it appears that Duke Shadd more or less gave himself voluntarily into the custody of the fortress commander, who acted, as he believed, in the interests of his liege. Duke Shadd passed but a single night in gaol. By the most ironic happenstance of "fortune" the Prince Regent's company, myself among its number, arrived at the fortress the following day. Fhir Oube instantly recognised the Duke and accorded him the status of honoured guest.'

'Then where is he now? Is he well? What is he doing?'

'Physically he is well,' replied Sir Maille-Orchus guardedly. 'But Fhir Oube spent some considerable time in his company and was disturbed by what he found. It seems Duke Shadd is in the thrall of a profound and immutable melancholy, perhaps of magical origin. He showed no interest in news of events in Rull, or of the fortunes of his former friends, or bitter enemies. As for what he is doing, or indeed, his whereabouts now, I deeply regret that it is beyond my capacity to tell. Having given his word that he would attempt no escape, Duke Shadd tricked his guards and slipped from the fortress and vanished. The evidence suggests that he was aided in his escape and accompanied by a woman whose identity is unknown to us.'

Lord Yzwul fixed his gaze upon Sir Maille-Orchus's face, a forbidding frown creasing his brow. 'I listen to your words but perceive a dubious quality to certain of the terms and phrases you employ. You claim Shadd was your honoured guest, yet still the descriptions you use are more often reserved for persons of prisoner status.'

'Duke Shadd was shown every respect,' replied the Chol knight. 'However, he *was* kept under guard – a precaution which he understood and to which he did not object. You must consider our position. Chol has just suffered a major, nay, a shattering defeat. Our troops are demoralised, suspicious and easily roused to anger or violence against any they hold to be unsympathetic to Chol. I do not need to tell you of Duke Shadd's reputation throughout Rull at this time. Many believe him to be an ally of the Beast of Rull. Others of our company, uninformed as to his true identity, suspected him of being in league with Enchanters. Fhir Oube, who supported neither view, nevertheless understood that in the current climate he could not permit the Duke to walk free amongst the Chol, out of fear for his safety.'

Lord Yzwul considered this and at length spoke again. 'An unidentified female, you say? Where, then, has he gone in her company?'

'The indications are that he rode east, into the domain of the Enchanters.'

'Qotolr?' Yzwul's surprise was evident. 'For what reason?'

Sir Maille-Orchus wearily shook his head. 'I regret I am unable to answer that.'

The two men spoke for a few minutes more, then Lord Yzwul rose, saying, 'I must leave you now. Please eat and drink. You will be brought hot water, linen and soap. Refresh yourself and rest overnight. In the morning my men will guide you back as far as the border with Chol. Convey my thanks, on behalf of Lord Shimeril, to the Prince Regent for his message. Tell him this: If we can be of any reasonable assistance we will. Our fight continues, even though we are few against many. We have hindered to our best abilities Khimmur's road-building efforts through Virland, but innocent slaves were made to pay with their lives for our acts of sabotage, thus we have curtailed direct operations in that respect. Nonetheless, the road will take many weeks to complete, if it is possible at all. I am sorry I can say no more at this time.'

He reached into a pouch at his belt and pulled out a silver coin which he handed to Sir Maille-Orchus. 'Yours, I believe. A Dyarchim coin, not common in these parts. You would do well to dispose of it; we will not use the same methods of contact again. A new code has been established. You will be told it when my men take their leave of you at the border.'

Sir Maille-Orchus stood. 'My thanks, and I hope we may meet again, in more fortunate circumstances.'

'That is my wish also.'


IV


The day following his meeting with the Chol knight, Lord Yzwul stood alongside Shimeril, the Commander of the Nine Hundred Mystophian Paladins, high upon a windy plateau overlooking a broad, flat valley in the heart of Mystoph in Khimmur. At their feet the valley floor, stretching away to the southwest, was occupied by an army made up of many thousands of soldiers. A stiff wind, cutting down in sudden cold gusts from the southwestern heights, stirred the various banners erected within the camps and set the tents rippling and billowing.

Shimeril, tall and erect, was garbed in quilted leather, a blue cloak hanging from his shoulders. He was armed with sword and hunting knife, and across his back was slung, sheathed, the double-bladed Aphesuk polearm, the rancet, his expert use of which had brought him renown. He gazed upon the scene below with a sober countenance, slowly clenching and unclenching the fingers of one gauntleted fist.

'I have not been able to discover where they are bound. My guess is south, to deliver what the Vulpasmage intends to be the final blow against stubborn Ghence. But perhaps a new campaign is to be born, of which we know nothing. The

Vulpasmage is elusive. Who can predict its next move? Perhaps it even intends to subdue Ashakite.'

'Then that would be its downfall,' said Yzwul.

'Are you so sure? Remember, already it has used the nomads to its own ends, and only others such as we have suffered the consequences.'

'At that time we did not know who our enemy was. The same ploy could not work again, either with us or the nomads. And the Vulpasmage was not so unwise that it attacked a major tribe. Its target was a disaffected group, weak and without support; one upon which it knew it might deliver a trouncing with minimal risk. Contrarily, it misjudged itself in its advance upon Southern Chol, and chose to pull back rather than confront a major Ashakite force.'

'I am no longer so certain,' muttered Shimeril. 'After Miragoff there was never any doubt that Chol would fall. The Vulpasmage would surely have realised that a second army was unnecessary. I ask myself whether it pulled back not so much out of fear of Ashakite, but in order to make better use of its troops elsewhere. Perhaps the whole operation was even a deliberate ploy to test the nomads.'

'Even were that so, to march now into the heart of Ashakite would be foolhardy with so much of its strength committed elsewhere.'

'It has powerful magic; allies from the Realms of which we know nothing. And one wonders how the nomads would react with Gneth set amok in their midst?'

'The Ashakites command magic of their own.'

'As do we,' Shimeril returned with undisguised sarcasm. 'But what good has it done us?' He glanced aside at the younger man. 'Have you received any communication recently?'

'None,' Yzwul admitted. 'But the Zan-Chassin are not defeated. With us, they watch and wait.'[*]

Shimeril ground his grizzled jaw in bitter abstraction. 'At all times I fear manipulation, a repeat of the events which led to Twalinieh. I question every move I make, asking myself if I – if we all – might yet be being led by the nose, the dupe and instrument of a foe infinitely more cunning than any of us.'

Yzwul kept silence, shifting his gaze out across the valley until it came to rest upon the army camps on the farther side. He narrowed his eyes. 'I see the standards of Selaor, and of Pri'in. But there are black-garbed troops in some number whose banners I do not recognise. And that furthest encampment, to the west, surely those are Cexhaut troops?'

'Cexhaut, aye. And those in black are of Anxau. The Beast of Rull has agreed a pact with those two nations. It leaves them in peace, in return for which they provide substantial troop support to reinforce Khimmur in its expansion elsewhere. It's a grim alliance, and does not bode well for free nations anywhere.'

Yzwul pensively smoothed the long whiskers of his moustache. Presently Shimeril said, 'Before you leave we must consider a new strategy in Virland.'

'We are in danger of losing the Vir fighters,' replied Yzwul. 'They are displeased that we have ceased our raids upon the forest road.'

---

[*] Lord Yzwul was not himself of the Zan-Chassin, but his spouse, the Lady Chrysdhothe, was a Second Realm Initiate. From her he had learned the techniques of mental receptivity, and was thus able to receive subtle messages projected with deliberation upon his consciousness, and, of equal importance, distinguish them from the general clutter of ideations, impulses, apprehensions and the like which are the lot and bane of human mentation.

'Would they prefer that more slaves be tortured and murdered for every action we take?'

'It is their country that is occupied, and their homes that have been destroyed, their relatives taken into slavery elsewhere. They feel kinship and sympathy for the foreign slaves, but their hatred of the Khimmurians outweighs those feelings.'

'It is a pity a few more of their kin do not share their emotions, then we might have a force we could fight with. But again Khimmur was deft in its occupation of Virland. Relatively few Vir slaves were taken, and they were from widely scattered locales, leaving no unified force of rebellion to deal with. What of your own men? Are they of similar mind?'

'They are impatient. They too have paid dearly for their loyalty. They question our reasons for ceasing actions in Virland now.'

'I cannot permit the slaughter of more innocents.'

Yzwul nodded slowly. He was aware of the subtle change that had come over his old commander in recent months. The deaths in Mlanje had deeply affected Shimeril, though he strove not to show it. Previously he had launched raid upon raid against Khimmur and her allies, causing disruption and havoc at every opportunity. Now he had grown more contemplative. His daring had been tempered by a new wariness of a particular quality. It was wholly understandable, and Yzwul shared his dilemma, for Shimeril's attitude was born out of humanity and consideration for his fellow men. But in the hands of the Beast of Rull it became an effective weapon against them. Ultimately, and paradoxically, it could be their undoing.

'We will gain little support if it becomes known that for every raid we make one hundred innocents are put to death,' Shimeril added, correctly interpreting Lord Yzwul's silence. 'We will be as one with our enemy; a limb of the very monster we oppose. And I perceive that we were wrong to try to hinder the clearing of the forest way. The Magoth itself will prove a more effective and undeterrable obstruction than we.'

'Slaves will still die as they are pitted against it.'

'As I said, a new strategy is required.'

Little more for the present was said, and Lord Yzwul made ready to depart.

'What of Duke Shadd?' he enquired before leaving. 'Will you try to find him?'

Shimeril solemnly shook his head. 'That is not for me to decide. He has to find his own way. His choice was to leave us. He has something to do. Were he to return unwillingly, or before he is ready, he would be but a burden to us, as he well knows.'

Yzwul walked away. Some distance down the forest path a guard of three men waited. They fell in now behind him. Shimeril remained as he was, staring out over the valley in deep contemplation.

Minutes passed. A figure, slender and lithe, dropped silently from the bough of an oak some yards away. It approached without a sound, to stand behind the Mystophian commander, at his left shoulder.

Shimeril turned and mutely appraised the newcomer.

'Shadd is dear to me,' he said.

'As he is to me,' replied the other, who was a female of perhaps twenty years of age. She wore loose garments of forest colours and carried a small sword, numerous knives of varying sizes and forms, and a light bow and quiver of arrows. She was slight of build, with clear, if weathered, complexion and skin of dusky olive. Her eyes were wide and faintly slanted, with an alert and vigorous expression. Her straight hair, cut short beside her ears, was a deep ebony, almost jet. She faced him with features set in sombre inscrutability.

'Will you go after him?' asked Shimeril.

'You know that I must.'

'What of the others?

'Rin will accompany me. Getshi and Abdar remain here with you, as always.'

'Witnesses to my conduct?' said Shimeril, with irony.

The girl shrugged. 'You know the Law.'

'And your other companion, Fashil?'

'Fashil will return to the Desert. He serves no purpose here, and must carry the news that Shadd has been located.'

'But he has vanished again. His trail is weeks old. He could be anywhere now. Do you really believe you can find him?'

The girl stared at him expressionlessly. 'You lived as one of us, so you know that no Aphesuk would ask such a question. In our formal language the means to phrase such a question do not even exist.'

Shimeril accepted the rebuke. 'It is simply that – '

'You doubt,' she said. 'But it is yourself that you have really come to doubt. In turn you project that doubt out upon others.'

'That is not the whole of it.'

'I know. A part of you prays that we will not find him, for fear that he has failed.'

'You will kill him then, will you not?'

'If he has transgressed, or shows indications that he will.'

'He may kill you, Kekhi. You must consider that.'

She smiled. 'The Tribe taught him many things, but some secrets are only for the Tribe. So yes, I will find him. He could have been found at any time, but it would have served no purpose. Now he has surfaced. It indicates a change, also a possible danger. Now it is imperative that he is found.'

Shimeril reached out and placed his hands upon her slim arms, stared briefly into her eyes. He spoke the traditional Aphesuk word of parting and greeting: 'Jhoso!'*

'Jhoso!' the young woman replied. She bowed, and withdrew.

He watched her, marvelling at how quickly she was gone – only yards from him, yet invisible, seeming to blend and merge with her surroundings. He turned back to the valley and the army marshalled in its cradle.

---

* 'Jhoso!' (Aphesuk). Lit: 'Blend well!'. In this single word is perhaps embodied the essence of Aphesuk mystique. Tales concerning Aphesuk abilities were myriad throughout Rull. Their fighters and agents had gained a reputation larger than life, for they were a mysterious and secretive people who shunned the world beyond the Endless Desert. Other than in the rarest instances the Aphesuk had defied all attempts to make contact with them. Hence little was actually known of them or their culture; their reputation was sinister in most aspects, their mystery amplified by hearsay and rumour.

Aphesuk warriors excelled in the arts of tracking, spying and assassination. It was commonly believed that they had mastered the secret of invisibility. It was said that an Aphesuk might dwell for a year in one's home, mingling with one's family and sharing one's food without any being the wiser. Truly, their ability to merge or blend with their surroundings lay at the core of both their renown and their martial craft. In training major emphasis was placed from infancy on the development of blending skills, for without the perfection of these all other talents were deprived of efficacy.

History records but a handful of examples of Aphesuk involvement in worldly affairs, and the authenticity of these is debatable. On those occasions when a foreign power has made use of their talents (at what cost is not known), the Aphesuk have plied their lethal trade with sure and certain effect.

# 6

Upon escaping Drurn March Shadd had not adhered precisely to Elore's directions. Descending without great difficulty the steep rocky bluff which upheld the fortress he emerged eventually onto the road. This he followed, careful in the darkness, and pausing every few yards and listening, sensing. Soon he found the horse that had been tethered at the wayside.

Leading the mount he picked his way carefully down into the pass. A three-quarter moon shone, but its light was weak and intermittent between the clouds. Beneath the trees or in the shadows of the towering cliffs it cast no illumination at all. Riding was thus inadvisable. The track was broken and scarred by crevices and potholes. All too easily the horse might stumble and break a limb, or in the darkness step right off the path to be sent crashing and flailing to the rocks below. But Shadd took some comfort in the certainty that, were his absence from the fortress to be detected, search parties would equally not venture far in pursuit of him before the first light of dawn.

The horse's hooves had been bound with linen to muffle the sounds of its passage. But bindings notwithstanding, noises travelled easily in the rarefied air to the fortress above. Shadd remained alert for indications of alarm or pursuit, but perceived none. He wondered briefly, not unimpressed, at the identity of Elore's accomplice; for almost certainly a second party would have been involved in the provisioning of the horse.

He was on the east of the fortress, facing into the no-man's-land that lay between Chol and Qotolr. Unseen somewhere before him the great mountains of mysterious Qotolr loomed.

To return to Chol a determined man might find a way back across the heights of Drurn March without recourse to the fortress road. Shadd, during his months in the wilds hereabouts, had thoroughly reconnoitred the region. He knew such a route to be possible, though it was a long and arduous climb, in places treacherous, and certainly unfeasible with a horse. Days would be required in its undertaking; and in any event he had no reason to return. His destiny did not lie within Chol.

High overhead clouds hurried across the moon. The grass and undergrowth whispered, branches sighed and creaked under the play of a light breeze. With his eyes now adjusting to the night Shadd led his horse east-wards for a couple of miles more. The road rose along a shallow incline, then more or less petered out as it gave onto a high treeless plain strewn with shattered rock. Here Shadd turned north towards a dark line of wooded hills.

He ascended into the trees, still leading his horse. The way steepened; in the moonlight he coaxed the beast up over ledges of crumbling rock and earth, across patches of loose scree. Several times the horse lost its footing. It began to show a reluctance to ascend further. Shadd paused to stroke its muzzle, whispering calming words as it regained its breath and confidence. They moved on cautiously, entering a canyon which cut up towards darkened heights. The way became choked with furze and scrub. Shadd veered right, feeling his way close beneath the canyon wall. A small spring bubbled up from beneath the rock at his feet and ran off ahead of him towards the lower ground.

A little way further a great overhang of rock projected above him, blocking out the night sky. In its shadow it provided a small area protected from wind and rain and well concealed from above. Shadd removed the saddle and bridle from his mount. With a long tether he tied the horse beside the little stream. Next he gathered leaves, grass and shrubbery to make a bed. He lay down, covering himself with his cloak and furs. He had travelled perhaps four miles, but the strain of the journey under such exacting conditions had exhausted him. Closing his eyes he fell instantly into sleep, and did not stir till morning.

With the first light Shadd arose. He washed quickly in the cold stream, then made his way further along the canyon to a point where he might ascend its steep wall. He scrambled up, to emerge at the head of a wooded rise. He climbed into a nearby tree and settled himself into the crook of a bough, gazing south towards the rocky waste from which he had ascended in the night.

Within minutes he spied what he had expected to see: a troop of horsemen rode up onto the plain out of the west. They paused a moment, seeming to confer, then spread out and proceeded east in a line across the wasteland at no great pace, plainly searching for something. At length, approaching the furthest limit of Shadd's view, the horsemen regrouped and cantered on eastwards, towards far trees, quickly disappearing from sight.

Shadd waited. An hour passed. The soldiers returned out of the east. They made their way back across the plain and descended again towards the road to Drurn March. The road and the fortress itself, and Chol beyond, were not visible from Shadd's position, the view in that direction being obscured by a steep spur. But to the west of the fortress he envisaged similar scenes. Doubtless within Chol the search would be of greater extent, for correctly he had anticipated that searchers sent east to look for him would not venture far towards the land they knew as Enchantery.

He smiled tautly to himself, climbed down from the tree and scrambled back down into the canyon. It was unlikely that a search party would be sent into these highlands, but if any came the chances of his being discovered in this isolated and hidden place were extremely remote. He knew ways of evasion and concealment taught him long ago in the Endless Desert. Already he had avoided Commander Odus's men with little effort; he did not feel it would be any greater challenge to slip through Fhir Oube's grasp.

In this spot, then, the fugitive lay low for several days. From the trees and thickets nearby he fashioned a three-pronged fishing-spear. Lower down in the canyon were numerous small pools where he caught trout and crayfish. With his bow and arrows he hunted rabbits. There was hardtack, cheese and dried fruit in his saddle-pack, and he was able to supplement his diet with a few roots and berries, while his horse suffered no inadequacy of grass and new shoots.

To cook the fish or meat Shadd burned a fire after dusk. The canyon walls hid the glow, and with the daylight gone the smoke might drift where it would without giving him away.

What made him linger here in this lonely place? Had he ridden directly for Qotolr, as Elore had bidden him do, he would have been safe from Chol pursuers. None would venture willingly into that land. Indeed, after that first morning Shadd saw no further sign of

Fhir Oube's troops out upon the plain. Nor to his knowledge did they ascend into the hills where he was camped.

But there were aspects of his escape and predicament which caused him consternation. Beyond Qotolr's borders he might be safe from Chol, and almost certainly, at the present time, from Khimmur. But Qotolr itself was a daunting and unpredictable prospect. He could not dismiss the possibility of forces unknown having been alerted to his flight east, for whatever reasons.

The ease of his escape from Drurn March left him with a vague disquiet. He wondered at himself and at how quickly he had been persuaded by Elore's words. The possibility of the Wonasina being yet alive, the thought that he and Seruhli might meet again, had fired him with hope, it was true. Perhaps no other cause existed that could so motivate him, even though past experience left him without reason to suppose that any future meeting would be a happy one.

But he was without proof that she lived. Rationally, had any other person come to him with the same information, he would have demanded evidence before committing himself to any course. And Elore was a woman of whom he knew nothing; previously he had not even been aware that the Prince Regent had a sister. Had the beautiful Elore by some subtle means befuddled his mind to influence him so effortlessly? He had detected no magic, but did that mean that none had been cast? Was it possible that he acted now under the direction of some subliminal rapture?

Whatever the truth might be Shadd knew that while there was a chance that the Wonasina, Seruhli, still lived he would enter Qotolr and seek out Mesmia.

After that, and depending upon what transpired at their meeting, he would determine a more certain course.

Nevertheless he waited in the wilds beyond Drurn March, until he adjudged that such time had passed that any within Qotolr who might have had reason to anticipate his arrival would have grown weary of their vigil. He would have been expected on that first day, or certainly on the second. By the third his intent would undoubtedly come under question.

After a week, Shadd reasoned, any who waited for him in that forbidding land would have given up. Even so he waited on. Eleven nights passed before finally, in the earliest hours of a bleak, cold morning, he saddled his horse and led it from the canyon and down onto the shattered plain.

He had changed from the furs he had previously worn. These he kept for warmth when required, rolled into a bundle and strapped behind his saddle. But now he wore clothing which, while unostentatious in any way, might nonetheless identify him as a civilised man. Heavy linen trousers of a greyish-blue, a woollen undertunic, ankle-high boots, shirt and soft leathers, and his cloak, a precious gift from Aphesuk. His skin had grown paler over the days, and he no longer saw any reason to stain it. His hair remained brown, but its roots showed a noticeable golden-white.

He proceeded across the plain following a more or less straight course from the point where the road from Drurn March petered out. There was some way to go before he entered Qotolr proper. He came to the trees into which the Chol searchers had ridden days earlier. These quickly thinned and opened out, the plain stretching again before him. He began to notice unusual features upon the landscape. Shattered granite littered the plain as far as the eye could see, but now it had begun to take on unnatural forms. The rocks appeared distorted, almost melded or *moulded* into bizarre shapes. Massive boulders and hulks of rock, at times towering above him; monolithic slabs or menhirs thrusting out of the dark peaty earth; or stones no larger than pebbles or the hoof of a horse – all took on configurations like nothing Shadd had ever seen.

Perhaps his imagination played tricks on him, but as he advanced he half-thought he descried within the strange stone forms outlandish, eldritch features. Limb-like protrusions, misshapen wings, fingers, claws, horns, armature; elastic-looking cavities and maws holding writhing tongues, stunted or gigantic teeth, wormy tentacles. The stones reared in phantasmic postures, not without menace, and the further he advanced the more it seemed that they gathered around him, until he felt that he moved between the serried ranks of some monstrous petrified army. Unbidden came recollections of scenes he had witnessed two years earlier in Twalinieh, when the Vulpasmage had unleashed an army of Gneth onto the city streets. He could not suppress a shudder.

His horse stepped nervously between the great stones. Shadd's unease increased. From time to time, out of the corner of an eye, he thought he descried movement, as though the limb of a rock had altered position, a boulder dragged itself forward, a pebble hopped or rolled deliberately aside. But when he looked more closely all was still.

Before him trees now loomed close. And beyond, rearing suddenly, the louring blue peaks of Gro'd f'ho Ib, the Harsh Maiden, the vast mountain chain of Qotolr, which extended further than any man knew.

Breaking free of the stones Shadd turned his horse to follow the line of the trees. First north, then returning south, until he discovered a path that led in from the plain.

Along this he rode. The trees closed in, shutting out the light of the day to impose a portentous gloom as of storm-bearing dusk. Like the rocks upon the plain at his back, the trees grew in quite unnatural shapes and postures. They were gnarled and twisted, their wood dark and seemingly vitiated. Many appeared rotten, yet bore leaves of an unhealthy colour, or strange flowers or fruits, as though season had no place here.

Curtains of grey, orange or other-coloured moss hung down from the branches, bizarre fungi of extraordinary hues and forms clung fast. Exotic plants covered the ground, some with pallid, poisonous looking flowers, some with lethal spines and thorns.

An unwholesome foetor pervaded the wood. The track was dank and waterlogged; his horse's hooves sunk in with every step, making sucking, gurgling noises. Strange insects flew across the path or buzzed around the woodland plants. From time to time Shadd glimpsed small creatures between the leaves or high in the branches. Shrill shrieks and twitterings, the hoarse cries of animals and birds, broke the silence. From deep within the forest he heard a mournful agonised wail, identifiable neither as human nor animal, which raised the gooseflesh upon his skin. On occasion the distant crashings of unknown beasts caused his horse to sidle nervously, but they came no closer and Shadd rode on, wary but unmolested. Something sleek, greyish-black and many limbed scuttled across his path. The horse shied and backed. Shadd peered into the undergrowth, drawing his sword, but there was nothing to be seen and the thing did not reappear. He urged his mount on.

At length the trees began to thin. Light pushed down onto the path. Soon Shadd emerged into a harsh, hilly land. In the distance the great mountains, their heads lost in clouds, seemed no closer than when he had entered the wood. He was at the head of a stony meadow, which curved down into a narrow vale. The path had become vague, but below the meadow a small hamlet, no more than a clutter of old stone farmhouses, huddled close to the slopes of the vale. Logic indicated that the way would pass through this settlement, or that if not, someone there might point him in the right direction. So towards this he rode.

He passed slowly between the dwellings, seeing no sign of inhabitants. A dry, bitter breeze whipped up spumes of dust; twigs and straw skittered about his horse's hooves. Shadd spied a few malnourished sheep huddled in a pen to the rear of a dilapidated cottage, and as he drew closer an old woman hobbled from the cottage bearing a wooden pail. She was tall and thin, raw-boned, with a bent posture and hollow features that told of a lifetime of poverty and unrelenting toil. Her eyes fell upon Shadd and she halted, mutely staring with a sour, distrustful look.

'Good-day, madam!' Shadd called. 'I seek the village of Delnemere. I wonder, could you point me in the right direction?'

The peasant-woman took him at his word. She raised a stick-like arm and pointed a finger out beyond the village, towards the southeast.

'Thank you,' said Shadd when it became apparent that she intended no further elucidation. 'And now, I will pay good coppers for a bucket of meal with which to feed my horse, and perhaps a small sackful more to take with me.'

The woman said nothing. She set down her pail, her jaw moving agitatedly, and hobbled away to disappear back inside her home, the wooden door swinging shut behind her. Shadd stared after her, somewhat mystified. He waited, and when she did not reappear, brought his horse around and rode on.

As he left the little hamlet the door of the cottage reopened and the peasant-woman reappeared, dragging a large sack outside. She stared along the way. Shadd's retreating back was still visible, he was no more than thirty yards down the road, but the old woman did not call after him. Shaking her head with a strange, glottal clucking sound, she dragged the sack of meal back indoors then went back to the business of watering her sheep.

## II

The road beyond the hamlet was somewhat better defined. It meandered into the rising hills with no obvious destination. The way became lonely, and largely without notable feature. No other sign of habitation did Shadd see.

Early in the afternoon Shadd stopped to rest beside a stream. His horse cropped grass while he took cheese and tack from his wallet and seated himself upon a stump to eat.

Cloud covered the sky, through which a hazy sun occasionally penetrated for moments at a time. Shadd gazed into the distance, and noticed something about this land which had been causing him vague mental discomfort for some time, but which had until now eluded conscious definition. He had ridden many miles that day, yet the mountains before him seemed no nearer. As he gazed upon them now it seemed to him that his vision blurred, his eyes began to swim. He looked away, blinking, then back. His vision could not hold the mountains in clear focus.

He shifted his gaze to a nearby hill. That too, now

he stared hard, seemed indistinct, ill-defined. Nearer objects were sharp enough. His vision was undisturbed as it rested upon a tree beside the road, at the icy water flowing past his feet, at the bright flowers that dotted the wayside. He looked up again at the hillside; his eyes could not properly behold it and strove of their own accord to look away.

Standing, Shadd walked closer. The base of the hill, nearer to him, shifted into sharper focus as he approached. Its crown, further away, remained uneasy to focus upon. He faced a gnarled lime-tree some dozens of yards off. It was slightly hazy, its outline vague and faintly blurred. He approached; the tree became firm and real.

The exercise grew tiresome, and the strain of gazing upon landscapes that defied normal order induced a mild sensation of nausea. Shadd returned to his horse to finish his light repast, mulling over this strange phenomenon, then resumed his journey.

Dusk approached. The road, twisting down from a ridge, bore Shadd to a small village set back in a wooded swale close by a wide tract of marshland. There was no signpost to indicate the name of the village, nor had he passed any on the way. Entering the village he enquired of the first person he encountered – a sinewy, stocky peasant carrying a bundle of hazel faggots upon his back – if this was Delnemere. The peasant glanced up without breaking his step, appraised him with a wary glance, and nodded.

'Good,' said Shadd. 'I see no inn, nor a mill. Is there somewhere here I might purchase meal for my horse?'

The peasant halted momentarily, making chewing motions with his jaw, then walked on, back bowed beneath his load. Shadd remained behind, scratching his head in perplexity.

'Does no one in this land speak?' he called after the

retreating figure. The peasant halted again, turned, and with a beckoning motion urged Shadd to follow. Dismounting, Shadd led his horse along the street. The peasant disappeared into a dry-stone outhouse. Shadd waited outside. Delnemere, like the hamlet he had passed through earlier in the day, was unusually quiet. No babies cried, no children played or called in the street. Not a single voice was to be heard from within the houses.

After a minute or so the man emerged, minus his load of faggots, but with a bulging jute sack upon his back. This he dropped upon the ground at Shadd's feet. Two other men, younger than the first, came to the doorway. They stared at Shadd with curious but cowed expressions.

'Too much,' declared Shadd. 'I have no pack-animal and cannot carry an amount this large. Give me a quarter, if you will, for which I will pay four copper pennies.'

The man nodded. He went back indoors, and returned with metal container and a smaller, empty sack. Untying the neck of the full sack he measured out meal with the container and emptied it into the second sack.

When the man had done Shadd paid over his coppers. There was no haggling for more, which would have been the norm in most other societies he had known.

'And here: two more if you will furnish me with a loaf of bread and perhaps some vegetables.'

The peasant nodded, went indoors, and came back with the provisions. Again Shadd paid over his coins. He strapped his purchases behind the saddle and remounted.

'Good evening, gentlemen.'

The three men withdrew back indoors without a word.

A short distance further was a crossroads, again

without a sign to orientate travellers. Shadd bore right, in keeping with Elore's directions. He rode on until well clear of Delnemere then directed his horse off the trail and into a copse of hazel and poplar trees. The evening had drawn closer. Shadd gathered wood and tinder, struck a spark with a flint from his pouch, and blew a hearty flame. He took meal from the sack and mixed it with water from a stream which ran through the copse, then made small cakes. The remainder of the meal he placed, in the sack, upon the ground before his horse, which immediately dumped its muzzle to eat.

From his saddle-pouch Shadd took chunks of rabbit-meat wrapped in leaves which he had brought with him from Chol. He placed the griddle-cakes on flat rocks close to the fire where they might toast; the meat he held to the flame on the tip of his hunting knife. In due course he ate a satisfying meal, drank clear water from a skin, then lay down beside the fire and slept.


III


The day dawned slowly beneath a featureless overcast. Shadd rose, discovered an ember still aglow in the fire of the night before, and blew up a flame. He cooked a little more meat, ate the last of his griddle-cakes, packed, and returned to the road.

That morning he gained his first genuine experience of the enchanted nature of Qotolr. The terrain became marked by sudden hills, upon many of which stood castles, some ruined, some showing signs of occupation. Shadd's route took him towards a low stone bridge across a small river which curled about the base of one such hill. As he approached the bridge the portcullis of the castle on the hilltop above rose, and out thundered a knight in full armour, lance held erect, mounted on a black charger.

The knight pounded down the hillside to confront Shadd before the bridge.

'Hold, vagabond, and identify yourself! By whose permission do you enter these lands?'

'I am Shadd, Duke of Mystoph,' Shadd replied, certain that his name would be without connotation in Qotolr. 'I am no vagabond, and I have the permission of no person to enter this land, for I was unaware that such was required.'

'"A duke!" he says. "A duke"!' responded the knight with haughty mockery, his voice hollow from within his visored helm. 'Where, then, is your retinue?'

'I require none.'

'A poor duke, who chooses to travel thus. I might add that your title is unknown to me.'

Shadd shrugged. 'I am not from hereabouts.'

'Hmph! Well, duke or vagabond, the fact remains. You are trespassing upon my lands.'

'And for that I readily offer apology. As I have said, I was not aware that I trespassed, nor that permission was required.'

'Nevertheless you have enacted a slight upon my noble person. I demand reparation, and will have your life.'

'My life is not something I would readily give.'

'Then you must fight me for it, for I will accept nothing less. Prepare to defend yourself, sir!'

'Sir Knight, I would prefer not to fight you,' said Shadd. 'My crime is one of ignorance, pure and simple. I am an innocent traveller, unfamiliar with the laws of this land. I apologise again for my transgression. Surely there is some means by which we might overcome this difficulty without bloodshed?'

'And compromise my honour before my own vassals?' boomed the knight. 'Nay, traveller, you have misjudged me. Ignorant or not, you are a common criminal in my eyes. Dismount, therefore, and pay the price.'

The knight put aside his lance and drew a bright broadsword from his scabbard with a whine of steel on steel.

Shadd heaved a sigh. 'I see that I have no choice. So be it, then.' Reluctantly he drew his own sword. 'Might I ask your name, Sir Knight, so that I at least know with whom I must engage in combat?'

'My name? My name? You compound the insult, oaf! Prepare to die!'

The knight spurred his mount forward.

'Hold!' called a loud voice. Shadd looked beyond. From below the castle strode a strange creature, tall and lank-limbed, furred, with a long, bearded snout, tufted ears and a long tail. It marched with long paces down the hillside until it stood beside the knight who, at the sound of its voice, had fallen silent and still.

'What is this mischief! Whom do you molest now, you non-thing!' demanded the newcomer.

'Frofandle, I merely sought to punish a criminal intent upon wanton trespass,' replied the knight in suddenly dejected tones.

The furry creature named Frofandle shook its head. 'Bah! Will you never cease in your nuisance?' He turned to Shadd. 'Stranger, I apologise for any inconvenience my accursed non-friend has caused you. Please, ignore us and pass freely on your way.'

'That he cannot!' asserted the knight. 'He is guilty of insult as well as criminal intent. Honour must be served, and justice be seen to be done!'

'Fiddle-faddle!' scolded Frofandle impatiently. 'Cease your nonsense. Begone, this instant!'

The knight seemed to droop suddenly in his saddle.

Shadd spoke. 'Sir Knight, if it will appease your sense of outrage, I again offer unreserved apology for any crime or insult I may have committed. It was inadvertent, but I understand – '

'You waste your breath, stranger,' said Frofandle with an indulgent shake of the head. 'This is no knight. This is a non-thing. Observe.'

He reached up and with a long furry paw raised the visor on the knight's helm. Shadd peered within. There was nothing to be seen; simply air, and the shadowy rear of the helmet.

'He does not exist,' said Frofandle, as if this were sufficient explanation.

Shadd sat back upon his saddle, his brow creased in perplexity. 'How so, if he occupies a suit of fine armour, rides a magnificent charger, bears weapons and speaks?'

Frofandle gave him a disconsolate look. 'Long have I pondered those very points, and the answer continues to elude me. The simple truth is that he is a non-entity, an enchantment, which believes itself extant but is not.'

'To believe one exists is surely evidence in itself of the fact,' exclaimed Shadd. 'And more: here he sits before us, as yet further proof.'

Again Frofandle shook his head. 'Forgive me, stranger, if I seem abrupt. The explanations become wearisome, most especially when I know that no satisfactory con-clusion can be gained. I will explain what I can. Up there, within Castle Glane, where I and all others of the castle's inhabitants are aware that this non-thing is a non-thing, it has no existence. It does not manifest or attempt to assert its existence in any way. It lies unobtrusively – who knows where? – and Castle Glane is a quiet place. But given the intrusion into our lands of an unknown being of intelligence like yourself, who

191

has no means of knowing that this thing is not real, it springs up, suddenly believing itself to exist, and rides out, all bluster and outrage.'

'You mean that my ignorance gives it substance?'

'That is perhaps one way of putting it, yes.'

'And if I disbelieve?'

'Then it will simply disappear. However, it is virtually impossible, I have noticed, to disbelieve when one has the substance of one's belief before one's very eyes.'

Shadd pursed his lips and expelled a breath of air. 'I can readily accept that that is so. This is an extraordinary concept.'

'This is an extraordinary land,' said Frofandle. 'Now, sir, might I ask with all politeness that you pass quickly on your way? I can offer you nothing, for the normal standards of hospitality cannot be observed here, for self-evident reasons. In truth, the sooner you are gone the sooner I can be free of this pestilent non-thing. But as long as you remain he will have reason to believe he continues to exist, and I will have the very devil of a time trying to convince him otherwise.'

'Quite so,' said Shadd, regarding the silent knight in perplexity. 'But I would plead for a moment more of your time. This is beyond the scope of my experience, and my curiosity knows no bounds. Might I ask two questions?'

Frofandle gave a tolerant sigh. 'If you must.'

'Firstly, what if this knight that is not a knight had obliged me to combat? Would the combat have been real? Might he have harmed me? Might I have harmed or killed him?'

'Those are four questions, not two.'

'They are couched as one, for I have another yet to ask.'

'Well, you are a clever fellow who can make five questions two. Nonetheless, I will answer as far as

I may. The combat would have been real, certainly, if you had believed it to be so. Equally, he might well have caused you harm, for you had no reason to believe that he could not. As for your killing him, that is something else. Consider it, sir. How might one kill something that does not exist?'

Shadd perceived that there was no answer to be had. If the latter point was valid then by all normal modes of reasoning it negated the former. But equally, how might something that existed only by dint of another's belief yet have the power to bring injury or death upon another? The debate might extend to be wrangled and pondered without end. Shadd nodded, and said, 'Lastly, then, if I might make polite enquiry, what manner of creature are you, good Frofandle? I have come across none of your ilk before.'

Frofandle gave a doleful shrug. 'I cannot answer that, for I know not. I am Frofandle, that is all. Now, I will speak no more. I wish you success on your journey, wherever it may lead you. I would have enjoyed further conversation, for such is the nature of my existence that I can spend little time with others without constant interruptions and unwelcome intrusions. But alas, that is the way of things. Begone, please, that this knight-that-is-not-a-knight may recognise again its non-substance and return to tranquil nothingness.'

Taking the rein of the black charger Frofandle turned and with long-legged strides made his way slowly back up to Castle Glane, the knight a suit of ramshackle armour slumped dishevelled in the saddle.

Shadd crossed the stone bridge and continued on his way. A minute or so passed and he turned to look back. Frofandle strode on alone into the castle gate, leading a riderless horse.

# 7

## I

A hazy light high overhead behind the overcast indicated that noon drew near. Shadd, as he rode, pondered many things. His encounter with the phantom knight of Castle Glane, and Frofandle's subsequent words intrigued and confounded him. As he dwelt upon these things it struck him that the conundrum, the paradox, might equally apply to Qotolr itself in relation to his visual experience of it the previous day. He thought about it more and more. Might his realisation of this land be somehow engendered out of his belief, his expectations? Would that explain the haziness and ill-definition of the landscape? Was it possible that his very considerations of what ought to be were somehow contributing to, or even shaping, the landscape he beheld? Might others experience this world differently?

The notion both thrilled and disconcerted him.

Thick forest closed in about the trail. Great crags and turrets of rock reared up out of the trees on either side. The way soared and swooped, looped around and back upon itself as it negotiated the rugged land. The mountains had appeared with abruptness, seeming to materialise suddenly out of the distance to stand close before and all around him.

In an intersection of valley passes Shadd came upon a crossroads marked by three ancient posts driven into the rocky earth. Upon each was fixed a human skull, their gaping eye-sockets staring sightless in three directions. One faced the north, one the west, one the south. Shadd's route took him upon the road which led most nearly eastwards, along which no death's eye stared.

A little later he decided to stop to eat and rest his horse. Some yards from the roadside he spied a grassy glade where green willows fringed a placid pool. Leaving his horse to graze, Shadd seated himself in this pleasant spot, his back against a mossy boulder. He took hardtack and cheese from his pack, along with his skin of water, and ate and drank.

It had grown warmer. A few insects hovered about the surface of the pond. A pair of goldfinches fluttered down from the branches of a tree, then took flight again. A young fox, unaware of its human observer, padded from the bushes to quench its thirst at the water's edge. Shadd watched with a sense of growing enchantment. This was a pleasant and tranquil site. The tensions and concerns of his journey were forgotten as he relaxed in its ambience. He slipped into a light reverie, grew drowsy, felt himself being gently borne towards welcome, comforting sleep.

'An hour's rest,' he thought to himself. 'It will restore my vigour, preparatory to undertaking the remainder of my journey.'

Deep within his consciousness a small voice warned: *Do not sleep!* But he gave it no regard. His eyes closed, opened again, refused to remain open. Sleep. Sleep. It was perfect here. He was very tired.

He drifted out of consciousness into sleep's protecting womb.

*'You will never leave this place!'*

Shadd's eyes opened. He gazed around blearily. He was alone, yet he was certain he had heard a voice which was not his own. His imaginings, it had to be. Slumber plays strange tricks upon the mind. His eyes

195

rolled back in their sockets, his head lolled against the rock. Consciousness drifted from him once more.

Again the voice, loud and mordant. *'Be warned, if you succumb you will never rise again!'*

With a supreme effort Shadd forced himself to sit erect. Still he found himself alone beside the still pool.

'Who speaks?' he demanded. 'Who awakens me with such dire warnings?'

'It is I,' came the voice, so close as to cause Shadd to leap to his feet, drawing his sword.

'I see no one. Reveal yourself, please, if you are not some wispy phantom.'

'I am no phantom, and I am plainly revealed if you would but look. Here, down here, beside your feet.'

Shadd examined the ground but there was nothing to see but grass, earth, moss, a few fallen catkins and a single stone. Shadd bent closer, frowning.

'Still I see nothing.'

'It is I,' asserted the voice peevishly. 'You are staring right at me.'

With a confounded expression Shadd sank to one knee and bent his head more closely to the earth. 'I am staring at a rock, that is all. A rock half-concealed in grass and moss, of irregular rounded shape, somewhat larger than a duck's egg. There is nothing else here.'

'Quite so,' came the reply.

'You?' enquired Shadd. 'I am addressed by a rock? That cannot be so, for rocks do not speak. Ah, I understand. I have in truth fallen asleep and now I dream.'

'You do not dream,' came the voice, with irritation. 'And I am not merely a rock.'

'Then what are you?'

'A hylozote.'

'I am unfamiliar with the term.'

'I am rock imbued with life. Inanimate matter upon which conscious awareness has been bestowed. A hylozote.'

'Extraordinary,' muttered Shadd, still not wholly convinced that he was awake. He extended a hand towards the rock.

'What are you doing?'

'I would pick you up, to examine you more closely.'

'Very well. It will be refreshing to view the world from another vantage. However, it would be a common politeness to ask my permission first. You have already lain yourself down with your cloak thrown upon me.'

'Forgive me. Of course you are right. My excuse is that I was not to know.' Shadd lifted the rock from the earth and laid it carefully in the flat of his palm. It was of a whitish, marble-like substance, striated with broken bands of reddish-amber. It was hard and cold to the touch, seemingly undistinguished from any other piece of rock. Shadd shook his head in wonder. 'A hylozote. Most strange. How can you be? I know of no natural laws or principles, not even those of magic, that would permit a sentience such as yours.'

'I can only guess at how I came to be,' said the hylozote, 'for once I was not and then, quite suddenly, I was. I believe I am the result of a quirk of happenstance, created by hazard rather than design, at a time when great wars raged between creatures with the powers of gods, who commanded forces unknown today.'

'The Enchanters?' asked Shadd. 'You are a by-product of the Enchanter Wars?'

'I believe so.'

'Then you have existed for a very long time. Have you always rested here, in this glade?'

'Not quite. For many ages I lay high upon the

mountainside which rears here above you. I had a fine view over many miles of countryside. But I was dislodged one day by a passing goat. I tumbled and rolled down the mountainside, and came to rest here, where you have found me. Here I have lain ever since.'

'And how long is that?'

'Two-thousand four hundred and fifty-two years, plus four lunar cycles, eight sidereal days, thirteen hours, seven minutes and twenty-three degrees thereof.'

Shadd straightened, dumbfounded. 'That is indeed a long time.'

'It is, indeed.'

Shadd stared for some time at the hylozote. 'Forgive me for asking, but I am struck by the enigma of your existence. You possess consciousness; do you then also possess a soul?'

'Well of course!' retorted the hylozote indignantly. 'Soul is not particularised, it is everywhere, in everything: every bird, every tree, every cloud, every grain of sand. You are human, and like all humans believe yourself both exclusive and superior, as if chosen for some exalted role. But you are simply incapable of perceiving. Of course you have scarcely evolved from mud, so it would be unfair to expect more.'

Shadd nodded to himself, considering this. 'Yes, your words make sense. I have learned much from listening to the messages carried on the breeze, words whispered between trees.'

'Then in some respects you may be an exceptional man.'

'Yet, since entering this land, I find a silence. I no longer perceive such subtle messages.'

'Aha!' declared the hylozote, but did not expand.

'Tell me, why did you wake me?'

'You were about to fall asleep.'

'Is that such a bad thing?'

'Not if it is your desire to remain here forever. This is an enchanted place. Look around, the evidence is before you.'

Shadd cast his eyes about the glade. 'I see nothing to excite attention or alarm.'

'Then that is because you see only the enchantment, which is all that the others saw also.'

'Others? What others?'

'An exception in some respects you may be, but mostly you are a man. It is hopeless to explain. The only way to see is to penetrate the enchantment.'

Vestiges of drowsiness still clung to Shadd's mind. He blinked and shook his head, then closed his eyes. For some moments he remained motionless, withdrawing within himself. Concentrating deeply he strove to dispel the sleepiness, work through his mind's distractions to provide access to the perceptive powers which would enable him to see through the deceptions of this place. He reopened his eyes.

For a fleeting moment he gazed upon something quite different from that which he had beheld only moments before. The pleasant glade in which he stood still remained, but now it held a darker aspect. Scattered across the ground all about his feet were human remains. Skeletons, some clothed, some mere naked bones. Many were half overgrown by grass and other vegetation; some indeed seemed to be half buried in the earth itself, or sunk into the mud at the edge of the pond; others lay prominent at his feet. The clear perception lasted but a second before the power of the enchantment once more overcame his capacity to see beyond it.

'I see by your face that you have perceived the actuality,' said the hylozote.

'How many?' asked Shadd in a shaking voice. 'And who were they?'

'More than I can remember,' the hylozote replied. 'Like you they were drawn from the roadside by the subliminal attraction of this site. Innocent travellers in the main, who came to take a brief rest, succumbed to slumber and never woke again. You are the first I have ever saved. No others were able to free themselves of their desire to sleep. One did survive, but it was by reason of insanity rather than any intervention on my part. He seemed impervious to the worst effects of this glade, by dint of his extreme mental condition.'

'Then I am indebted to you. You have saved my life. My sincere thanks. And now I shall remove myself from this place without further delay.'

He bent to replace the hylozote upon the ground.

'Take me with you!' the rock cried, its voice suddenly imploring.

Shadd hesitated. 'Where? Where would you wish to go?'

'Anywhere! Anywhere at all.' A new note entered the hylozote's voice. 'Perhaps I might even travel with you as your companion?'

'A rock for a travelling companion? It is a novel idea.'

'I can be of service to you.'

'In what way?'

'I know actuality where you can perceive it not.'

'Perhaps,' said Shadd. 'But then, in this place you had the advantage of me by some two thousand years.'

'Ah, but I see other things,' insisted the hylozote. 'For instance, are you aware that you have been followed here? Even now you are observed.'

'By whom?'

'By something which you will never perceive. Look, beside the bole of that willow close to the water.'

Turning, Shadd squinnied his eyes. 'I see nothing. Just a tree.'

The hylozote's voice became a whisper. 'And the shadows beneath it?'

'What of them?'

'Among them lurks one that is not a shadow. I saw it come, just after you settled yourself here. Go closer and look again.'

Warily Shadd edged closer to the bole of the willow. He peered into its shade, his sword in his hand. There was a flicker of movement, almost nothing. It might have been his imagining, or a leaf shadow shifting in the breeze. Yet he believed something had slipped away.

'Did you see?' asked the hylozote.

Grimly Shadd straightened. 'Perhaps. I am not sure.'

'I believe you are. And you see that I speak the truth: I can be of service to you.'

'That may be so,' said Shadd.

'If it is yet insufficient, then I would exhort you to search your conscience,' went on the hylozote. 'Put yourself in my place. Ask yourself how it must feel to be a conscious rock, doomed to lie wherever you fall for all eternity. I crave company. All that I have ever known in this place are humans who come and sleep and die and rot, or woodland creatures who pay me even less heed, other than to bestow upon me some profound indignity. For to them a rock is merely something to rub their nether parts upon, or to spray with their dreadful spore to mark territory. I have had enough of being pissed on and ignored. I wish to see, to exp – '

'Hold!' cried Shadd. 'You have persuaded me. Come, you are no great burden.

'You will be my travelling companion, and as we ride perhaps you can tell me more of the history of this strange and unnatural land. Though you have scarcely moved in all the years of your existence, it is evident that you have assimilated much, and there is much that I would learn. Now, let us leave this glade forthwith. It gives me the shivers.'


## II


The remainder of the day passed without notable event. The hylozote Shadd placed within a pouch at his belt. Its percipience was unaffected by confinement. Lacking physical organs of sight or hearing, it assimilated impressions of its surroundings by some other, mysterious means. Obstacles, the want of light, and those other factors which would act to the detriment of human perceptions were of no consequence to the hylozote.

As they rode the hylozote enquired of Shadd, 'If I might be so bold as to enquire, what precisely is the nature of your quest here?'

Shadd did not immediately reply. When he did his manner was preoccupied, his tones subdued. 'I seek a woman.'

'A common affliction among your kind, so I have learned.'

'You misconstrue me. She is not just any woman,' replied Shadd shortly.

'They never are.'

Shadd fell silent. A while later the hylozote asked, 'If you find her, what then?'

Again he replied only after some consideration, and then simply to admit that he did not know. The hylozote did not press further, and for the time being no more was spoken on the subject.

As evening drew close Shadd stopped at a lonely wayside inn set in wooded heights. He ordered a meal of meat balls and parsnip fritters with, for a change, a small pitcher of local wine. His horse was stabled and given fodder and water. Though his preference was to sleep beneath the stars Shadd chose now to pay for a pallet at the inn rather than risk the nighttime hazards of this land.

He stated his requirements and retired to a table in the common room. He was the sole customer. The place was dreary and cold, no fire cheered the hearth. His food, when it arrived, proved to be flavourless, the meat tough, the vegetables stringy and somewhat beyond their prime. His wine had a rough, resinous quality and was barely palatable. Still, he was not over-charged, and knowing something of the conditions under which the population of Qotolr lived, he felt it inappropriate to complain.

As he ate he withdrew the hylozote from its pouch and placed it upon the table before him.

'The landlord of this place is a taciturn fellow, to say the least,' observed Shadd in an undertone, 'but he does speak, even if it is no more than a gruff syllable at a time. Elsewhere I have encountered folk whom I could not coax to utter a single word, no matter my efforts to show cordiality and respect.'

'Did you come from a westerly direction?' enquired the hylozote.

'I did.'

'Ah well, it is explained, then. You passed through the fringes of a domain ruled by a diabolic presence, one of the five who dominate this land.'

'Has he imposed a rule of silence upon the land?'

'Worse. He is known for his obsession with privacy. To that end he decreed long ago that none might speak of him, or make reference to him in any way. As insurance that his decree was not abused he sent out squads of vile henchmen to every settlement within his dominion. Their instruction was to remove the

203

tongues of each and every person. This they did, without ceremony, with the crudest methods, and I believe with some relish. And they continue to do so. Whenever a child is born Urch-Malmain is informed of the event and his henchmen dispatched immediately with orders to return with its tongue. It has been that way for as long as I have known.'

Shadd stopped eating and pushed aside his plate in anger. 'This is a devilish land!'

'Is it not the same everywhere?'

'No. In my own country – ' Shadd stopped short. A rueful expression clouded his face. ' . . . perhaps in many ways it is not so different after all.'

The hylozote lowered its voice. 'By the way, you are exciting attention.'

Shadd raised his eyes to see the landlord, a short, squat, heavy-countenanced fellow, hovering at the kitchen door behind the counter. Beside him was a wizened crone whom Shadd took to be his spouse. Finding themselves observed they set to busily, attending to suddenly urgent chores.

Shadd sat as he was. 'A strange-eyed fellow in conversation with a rock. No doubt they consider me mad.'

'Or a magician muttering invocations over his effectuary. Whichever, they are too fearful to intervene in any way, and are too far away to have overheard.'

'Nonetheless, I would rather not be the object of their scrutiny.'

Picking up the hylozote he returned it to its pouch, rose, and with a nod to the landlord and his wife, left the common room.

Next morning he arose early and prepared to continue his journey. After settling his account he enquired of the landlord the distance to the Lake of Clouds and the village of Bale.

The man was unable to look him in the eye. He answered quickly, with perspiring brow and quick nervous movements. 'Half a day.'

Shadd thanked him and rode away; as he did so the fellow made a strange sign across his breast then sat down and mopped his brow, muttering to himself with relief.

### III

The Lake of Clouds was aptly named. It was enclosed on all sides by snow-peaked mountains, and over its waters hung a dense, grey-white pall. Its far shores were obscured by this mist, and the mountain peaks rose from it as if without a solid base. As Shadd descended via steep traverses towards the shoreline it appeared that he gazed towards mountains suspended in the sky itself.

A cluster of buildings close to the lake's western shore marked the village of Bale. Shadd arrived eventually by the water's edge and turned towards the village. The mist hung close, a high wall forming some twenty yards out from the shore. From this elevation it blocked out all that lay beyond, the peaks above and the water beneath. The sun barely penetrated to earth, and the air held a penetrating damp chill.

Shadd walked his horse along the trail beside a long shingle beach, drawing his cloak close to ward off the cold. Some distance ahead he spied a lonely figure upon the strand, standing at the water's edge, wreathed in drifting tendrils of mist.

Shadd craned forward in the saddle, straining to see more clearly, a strange and urgent thumping starting in his chest. He approached as near as the road would take him to where the figure stood, then drew his horse to a halt. The figure was still some distance away but he could see that it was a woman, though he was able to make out little of her features. She stood motionless, facing towards him across the shingle. The water lapped around her ankles with a languid rattling of the pebbles.

She wore a garment of some light, thin material, of a soft whitish colour, which fell to midway down her calves. Shadd saw that she was young and slender, of perhaps medium height, with pale blonde hair which fell almost to her shoulders. Her arms and legs were slim and graceful, her feet naked.

With a nervous quickening within him Shadd climbed down from the saddle and began to approach her across the shingle.

'Take care, Duke Shadd,' came the voice of the hylozote. 'This is a strange and unnatural land.'

Shadd took no heed, so taken was he with what he beheld. He continued until he stood within a few feet of the young woman. He waited before her silently, not knowing what to say.

She returned his gaze with a half-smile, her eyes pale blue, calm and appraising. There was an aura about her of mystery and sadness, a look in her pale, freck-led features of gentle provocation; yet she remained serene and perhaps childlike. To Shadd's eyes she was most exquisitely beautiful.

'So you have come, then, Duke of Mystoph.'

He nodded slowly, as though in a dream, unable to take his eyes from her. 'I have come.'

'To find me?'

'Yes, though I did not expect that I would.'

'You believed me dead, then?'

'For long ages.'

She seemed for a moment to express regret in her look. 'It was a cruel ruse, but necessary, as I then believed.'

Shadd closed his eyes. The weight of a profound sorrow and almost unbearable longing pressed upon him.

She spoke again. 'Are you ill?'

He opened his eyes, breathing deeply. 'No. Simply . . . Is it truly you?'

Her pale golden hair, falling neatly beside her face, moved slightly with a cold breath of breeze from the lake. A small smile returned to her lips. 'It is I, Seruhli. But you should understand that though you see me, I am not here.'

Shadd frowned. 'I do not understand.'

'I am waiting for you, far from this place. There is something you must do.' As she spoke these last words the substance of her form seemed to shift and fade. Shadd stared, blinked. Seruhli was barely more than a wraith, her image dissolving before his eyes. He stepped forward and reached out to take her hand, but his own hand passed through air.

'No!' he cried. 'No! Don't go.'

'There is something you must do,' came her voice. 'Say that you will do it.'

'I will do it if it is in my power. But do not leave! Tell me what I must do.'

'Do not fail me, Duke Shadd.'

The ghost, for it was nothing more, retreated from him across the water, fading even as it was enveloped in the mist.

For long minutes Shadd stood at the shore's edge, staring into the blank greyness that hung over the Lake of Clouds, shaking his head, from time to time uttering words of anguished confoundment. Eventually he turned away and with head bowed trudged back up the shingle to the wayside.

He mounted his horse and rode on in gloomy silence, and the hylozote, wisely, kept its own counsel.

207

The village of Bale drew near. Upon the shingle two men worked upon an upturned fishing boat, beating fresh caulking into its seams. Shadd stopped and called across to them. 'I am looking for the home of the woman, Mesmia. Do you know her?'

The two ceased working and eyed him with measured glances. One rose unhurriedly to his feet, caulking mallet and iron in his hands. 'What might you be wanting with her?'

'I was advised to seek her out by someone far from here. I understand she will be expecting me.'

The fisherman eyed him with an expression not wholly removed from contempt. 'Up there.' He nodded towards the mountainous slopes at Shadd's back. 'Two hours' ride. You'll find the track on the other side of the village, behind the church.'

Shadd thanked him and tugged the horse's rein to move on.

'Be warned,' said the fisherman. 'If you're seeking something that the Drear-hag has you'll pay for it in certain kind.'

## IV

Approximately two hours later Shadd, ascending along a rough, twisting stony path, came upon a tall rounded tower of dilapidated aspect, tapering towards its top, made of dark ancient stone and timber. It occupied a bare clearing upon the side of a high cliff, at the base of which, more than one hundred feet below, a fast river flowed. Two massive curs were chained to posts at the front entrance. At Shadd's approach they set up a blood-chilling baying and strained upon their chains to reach him.

'This is not an easy place,' muttered Shadd, reining the horse to a halt.

'I can readily understand that you would feel that way,' said the hylozote. 'Still, to one who has not moved in long ages, it is a novelty.'

'Do you detect magic here? Or perceive anything that I might not?'

The hylozote hesitated, then spoke with a certain guarded manner. 'I am not sure.'

'That implies that you detect something.'

'Magic is here, in some form. But – I cannot – I do not – ' The hylozote created a sound resembling an exasperated grunt, then continued in a voice more formal and strained. 'Nothing specific is revealed to me.'

Shadd cast his eyes around him. 'This must be the place I seek. The track goes no further, and the cliff ascends sheer behind the tower.'

As if in reply the door at the base of the tower opened with a jarring rattle. A crone appeared, short and grotesquely fat, with frizzy hair the colour of ripe aubergine, which jutted out in all directions. She was dressed in a vast, shapeless garment of black and orange. Advancing with a lumbering gait with the aid of a gnarled stick towards the gateway she silenced the two great dogs with a word. She stared up at her visitor with small, dark, squinting eyes.

'The Pale Duke. I expected you sooner.'

'You are Mesmia?' Shadd enquired.

The crone nodded.

'Plain caution overcame my impulse to ride here at fullest speed,' explained Shadd. 'Still, I am here now, which may or may not be evidence of the wisdom of my strategy.'

'Enter then, please. My pets will not harm you now. You may stable your horse yonder.' Mesmia gestured towards a low stone outhouse beside the tower.

When he had attended to the horse Shadd followed the old woman into the tower. He was obliged to bend low to step through the wooden outer door, and within, straightening, found that the top of his head brushed the ceiling. He was in a small lobby, its walls caked with grime. This gave onto a larger room of circular shape, so gloomy as to be almost dark. Slim shafts of light stabbed in through chinks in three small shuttered windows, and two candles set upon a table provided the only other illumination. The gloom was intense, the heavy oak beams and rafters of the ceiling low and oppressive. Dust and cobwebs covered everything. About the walls were set rickety shelves holding ancient books, urns and pots of earthenware or glazed clay, and artefacts of one kind or another, though it was impossible to see anything clearly. To one side of the room a wooden stairway led up to the first floor. The aura of magic hung close and disconcerting in the frowsty air.

Mesmia was not to be seen, but her voice called down from the head of the stairs. 'Ascend, Duke Shadd.'

Shadd climbed, to find a door confronting him, partially closed. He pushed upon it with one hand and stepped across the threshold, to stand blinking in surprise at the sight that greeted his eyes.

The room, circular like the former, was otherwise in complete contrast. This was a grand and spacious gallery set with sumptuous furnishings and works of art. The circular wall bore dozens of paintings, large and small; mounted upon the floor, and in cabinets and upon shelves and pedestals were sculpted works, ornate figurines, life-sized statues, miniatures – formed out of a variety of woods, precious and semi-precious stones, ivory, gems, or metals. All of them were of an erotic nature depicting men, women, beasts and

210

creatures of myth or pure fantasy in attitudes and postures of erotic play.

Shadd stared around him, rendered speechless as much by the contrast as the content. This sudden, unexpected assault upon his perceptions was as disconcerting, in its own way, as the sense of magical presence had been below.

Mesmia had seated her bulk to one side behind a low table of dark green serpentine set upon golden legs. The gold had been painstakingly carved and moulded to display multiple figures in full relief curving sinuously about its form. The serpentine bore engravings of a similar nature. Mesmia herself, old, filthy, grossly formed, was an incongruous presence amidst such decadent finery.

'I see you are impressed by my little collection,' she said with a toothless grin, plainly amused at her guest's reaction. 'It has taken more than a lifetime to bring all these pieces together. Many come from lands far from here. They are the works of the greatest artists and craftsmen of many ages. And of course, they are priceless.'

'You must constantly fear theft,' said Shadd.

The old woman's watery eyes gleamed. 'Few know of this place. Those that do would never dare come near. I am feared and shunned.'

'It must be a lonely existence.'

Mesmia cackled. 'Not so! Not so at all!'

'At the lakeside I heard the term "Drear-hag" applied to you,' said Shadd.

Mesmia grinned and chuckled to herself. 'The locals believe me a witch, capable of many things. It serves a purpose and I allow them to think as they will.'

'You know why I have come,' Shadd said without further diversion. 'Perhaps I am foolish to have journeyed so far and risked so many dangers upon the word of a woman I do not even know, but nevertheless I am here. So speak frankly please, and tell me whether I have wasted my time.'

'You seek the Wonasina-In-Preparation, the Holy Princess Seruhli of Kemahamek, do you not?'

'That is so.'

'Then your time is not wasted. I can help you find her.'

'She is alive?'

Mesmia nodded.

Shadd grew agitated. 'I require proof. Already today I have encountered her ghost upon the lakeshore. I am not here to pursue phantoms.'

'I am aware of your encounter,' replied Mesmia. 'But it had its purpose.'

'Purpose? To demonstrate what I already know to be true: that nothing in this land is to be believed!'

'Have you given consideration to the hidden agency which projected this vision?'

Shadd gave a cynical shrug. 'There are persons aplenty who would prevent me from finding Seruhli if they can. I do not doubt that many of them are capable of performing such magic.'

'That is one explanation, certainly. But there are others.'

'I would hear them, then.'

'You may have conjured the vision, or ghost as you call it, yourself. The atmosphere of Enchantery is imbued with unusual properties. A person with powerful, perhaps latent, powers of imagining and visualisation may find that out of their own desires or fears a certain reality is formed.'

Shadd contemplated this, relating it to his earlier thoughts and experiences since entering Qotolr. Mesmia spoke again. 'But I proffer another alternative, which is that the projection may have originated from Seruhli herself. I believe she may now be aware of your quest to find her, and wishes to reach you. Did she pass you a message of any kind?'

'She had me promise to do something for her, but did not specify the task.'

'Then I can tell you. She wishes to be set free.'

'Is she imprisoned?'

'In a manner of speaking. Seruhli lives, as you were told. She is in hiding, or more precisely, she is hidden by those loyal to her. But when you left Chol you were not given the precise circumstances under which she now exists. This was for a reason. We had to persuade you to come, and had you known everything, in the state of mind to which you have succumbed you might have been discouraged. For this . . . expedience, I apologise.'

Fighting back bitter anger Shadd said, 'Then give me the truth now. What are these "circumstances", and what is it that has to be done?'

'Seruhli was betrayed in Twalinieh, by someone close to her, a person of exalted rank within the Blessed Intimates,' Mesmia said. 'The potion she imbibed during the ceremony of Relinquishment, at which you were a witness, was not mere coloured water as was intended. It was a magical infusion which induces a Semblance of Death, a condition outwardly similar in all respects to death. But it is in fact more accurately a profound and total withdrawal from life. Bodily functions cease, yet the body is preserved. None but the most highly-trained would know the difference. The condition endures without interruption.'

'Is there no antidote?'

'The Simbissikim possessed a formula for making the antidote. But just as only a few knew how to concoct the poison, only a few knew the formula for the antidote. These all died in the battle for Twalinieh.

Some mystery surrounds the circumstances of their deaths, and it is to be assumed that they were not merely coincidental. Seruhli was smuggled from the city via secret underground tunnels and taken to ...' the old woman smiled thinly, ' ... taken to where she is now. But those Blessed Intimates who guard Seruhli's body have no means now of reviving her.'

'Then you are saying that she is dead after all.'

'She is worse than dead, Duke Shadd. The full import of this I must impress upon you at all costs, so that you may understand the true extent of her betrayal. You see, had her enemies simply wished her dead they might have accomplished that without recourse to the complex and uncertain plot that led to her ingesting the poison. But they required much more, for once dead, Seruhli would be bound to be reborn and thus return to the Kemahamek people. But Semblance of Death is just that: a semblance. The body is not truly dead and so the soul is not released. She lives on, suspended between death and life, held to her body and so prevented both from reviving and from dying that she might live again.'

Shadd swayed as he took in the full implications of what he was being told. He turned away, his face grey, etched with deep lines of consternation and remorse. 'Was the Vulpasmage behind this?' he asked in a shaking voice.

'We have no proof, but that is our assumption. It is certain that this plot was long in its preparation. Some form of secret pact must have been made between an outside agent and certain of the priests, but we are beginning to believe that the Vulpasmage was establishing the groundwork for its coming long before it took over the mind of your half-brother. Whomsoever betrayed the Wonasina could only have been a trusted Intimate, trained since childhood to occupy high station within the Simbissikim hierarchy. The

214

corruption, then, would have begun at a very early age. We know that the Simbissikim surrendered the Holy Citadel to Khimmur's forces soon after Seruhli's "assassination" was announced. Kemahamek suffers, but certain of her priests and warriors have grown fat and wealthy under Khimmurian occupation.'

It was some time before Shadd found words. When they came they were bitter and distraught. 'Why, then, have I been sent here to you?'

'There is a task which you must fulfil. Seruhli must return. She represents a power which may be able to resist the evil that has taken over Kemahamek. Without her there is no foreseeable end to the Vulpasmage's reign there.'

'But how? You have already said – '

Mesmia silenced him with a gesture of her wrinkled hand. 'Within Qotolr there is an ancient scroll upon which is inscribed the only other transcript of the formula for the antidote to Semblance of Death known to exist. The language it is written in is one that has been dead for centuries, but I am to some degree familiar with ancient tongues. I believe I may be able to decipher it.'

She looked up at him alertly, observing the reactions upon his face. With a flaccid smile she said, 'Ah, all is not so hopeless, Duke Shadd. You see, the location of the scroll is known to me. It lies buried in an underground chamber, along with many other treasures. But I cannot gain access to it. The chamber is within the domain of the Enchanter, Yxon. He, I am certain, is unaware of its existence. But he is not sympathetic to me. Were I to venture into his land he would know of it, and would destroy me. Therefore, someone else must go.'

'And that is why I have been sent here?'

Mesmia nodded, causing her cheeks and jowls to

ripple. 'If you accept the task I can show you the route and provide you with certain aids. But be warned, the way is dangerous, the chamber trapped and guarded by I know not what.'

'Why me?' said Shadd.

She gave him a candid stare. 'Because you love Seruhli.'

'Many love her and would willingly give their lives for her.'

'We do not seek someone who will willingly give up his life! Whoever goes must have at least a slim hope of returning. Your talents are your second qualification.'

Shadd shook his head. 'You are mistaken. I am a man with pale skin and strange eyes, nothing more.'

Mesmia tapped fat stumpy fingers upon the serpentine table. 'You possess talents of which you are not yet aware, Duke Shadd. Under ideal circumstances we would wait and observe, allow them to burgeon naturally over the course of your lifetime. Of course, they may never do so; so much depends upon eventuality. But you, now, are Seruhli's only hope, and we must rely upon necessity as an instrument of growth. All depends upon you and your ability to realise and call forth what is within you.' She pulled herself laboriously to her feet and leaned heavily upon her stick. 'Even then, it may not be enough.'

Mesmia bore herself away towards the stairs. 'I will leave you to consider.'

'There is no need,' said Shadd. 'I will go, as you surely knew I would.'

## V

Shadd quickly returned to the outhouse beside the tower where his horse was stabled. He took his weapons and other possessions, and returned to the first-floor gallery. Mesmia awaited him. In her hand she held a rolled parchment which she spread upon the serpentine table.

'Here is where you must go.' She indicated a symbol upon the map, at a position beyond a long mountain range, some distance north of her tower. Alongside the symbol was a name, Ciracar's Warren. 'There are numerous entrances. The warren is inhabited by a variety of creatures. A companion will join you later. He has skills which may complement your own. He will guide you there and will know which entrances are most favourable. To some degree he may also be able to guide you when you are within. The scroll is contained in a sealed ivory tube. Its markings are distinctive.' She pointed to a series of inscriptions upon the edge of the map. 'Like these. Now follow me.'

Leaving the map Mesmia crossed the room to stand before a large marble composite, of ancient Bethic style, which depicted a trio of wood-nymphs engaged in erotic concourse with a minotaur. Her eyes on Shadd, she reached down and grasped the minotaur's heroically-sculpted phallus. She gave a small tug, looking back at Shadd with a lewd chuckle. There was a click. Mesmia pushed upon a panel in the wall behind the composite. The panel swung back with a soft grating sound.

Mesmia stepped through, Shadd following, to enter a second chamber, this one much smaller. This contained little other than a large wooden chest. The walls of the room were hewn out of solid rock, and Shadd calculated that it was not a part of the tower, but was situated within the cliff itself. The panel slid closed behind him as he entered.

A greenish-yellow light of indiscernible origin illuminated this chamber; the aura of magic was of a much greater intensity here. Mesmia produced a huge iron key, Shadd did not see from where, and bent over the chest. Unlocking it she raised the lid. From within she took a leather pouch with a draw neck. This she opened and withdrew a small glasslike ball.

'This is a Stepforth. Toss it into the air and it will float before you, bonded to you and moving as you do to provide light where there is none. When not in darkness keep it secure in this pouch where no light penetrates, or it will lose its power.'

Shadd took the pouch and the little ball and was surprised to note that when the ball rested upon his palm it seemed to be of no weight.

Next Mesmia took out a brilliant cut crystal of pale blue hue, within which was a fragment of another crystal in deepest red. A light silver chain was attached to this. She held it up; the blue seemed to shimmer with motes of darting light; the red sent out minute tongues of subtle fire.

'Wear this around your neck. Keep it upon you at all times. Both stones have been magically infused. They will work upon the subtle energies within you, and encourage the development of your powers. In times of need they could aid you in making the right decisions.'

Shadd took the twin-crystal and held it for a moment in his hand. He closed his eyes, then nodded, satisfied that the stones contained no evil property.

Mesmia had closed the chest-lid and was eyeing him closely. 'Return these articles to me when you have done. Do not lose them or pass them on to any other. Do you understand?'

He nodded.

'Now, it is time for you to leave.'

Shadd saw that Mesmia held within her hand a short metal rod. She turned her broad back and inserted the rod into a small fissure in the rock wall.

'One more thing,' she said, her hand upon the protruding end of the rod. 'Your companion will be interested in the other treasures that you will find along with the scroll. He is welcome to whatever he can take; in fact, that is his reward for accompanying you. You too, if such is your desire, may avail yourself of what you find. But beware, many of the treasures are of magical nature and could cause an unwitting bearer great harm. Others have rightful owners who will go to extreme lengths to have them back. The scroll, Duke Shadd, is your one objective.'

She pressed down upon the metal bar. A trapdoor opened in the floor of the chamber. Shadd stepped across and peered into the cavity at his feet. Stone stairs led down into blackness.

'This tunnel will take you through the Gro'd f'ho Ib. Your companion will meet you when you emerge. Go now. Take care. There are many dangers. I wish you success and a safe return.'

Shadd stood before the open trapdoor and looked back at her. 'If I fail, what then?'

Mesmia shrugged her huge shoulders. 'There is no one else we can send. Seruhli will remain forever as she is, neither alive nor dead, and Kemahamek will never rise against the Vulpasmage.'

He nodded, and descended into the dark.

# 8

## I

Following my frantic flight from Hon-Hiaita I made straightway for the village of Little Malme, which lay at the fringe of the forest only minutes from Hon-Hiaita's walls, within Khim province. I was spurred by the last words of the Chariness, made manifest in my mind as we communicated within the garden of her former home. I had the vaguest memory, recalled quite literally from a former life, of words spoken to me long years earlier. Rohse: sweet, spirited, good-natured, flame-haired Rohse, who had entered my life as chambermaid to my wife, Auvrey, and quickly become my lover, had once told me of her upbringing and home.

Her parents had a small farmstead at Little Malme where they raised a few pigs and goats, and grew crops. They made a basic living selling vegetables and fruit, and occasionally a fattened pig or kid at the town market. Rohse had lived her childhood there, with her younger brother, Farli. The children worked with their parents upon the land, until Rohse's fifteenth birthday when her father had brought her to Hon-Hiaita. Here he had hoped she might find work with a wealthy family and gain something of an education which would serve her in good stead in future years.

Rohse worked first in a tavern, then for three years was employed as a servant within the house of a wool merchant of fairly low status. The merchant's business fell into decline and he himself became ill and died. His remaining assets I absorbed into my own flourishing mercantile empire, thus providing for the family he had left behind, and at this time Rohse had been taken into my household to attend to the needs of my wife.

Without difficulty I found my way to Little Malme. The village was beginning to stir as the sun rose above the hills and burned off the cold morning mist.

Little Malme consisted of only a couple of dozen dwellings, and I recalled that Rohse had mentioned that her home lay on the edge, on the western side. This area I scouted, and quickly narrowed down to two the number of homes that fitted the descriptions I recalled. In undergrowth before the first of these I settled myself to wait.

The dwelling was a small thatched cottage built of stone. A fenced garden extended before it, where neat rows of soil were tilled in preparation for the new season's growth. At the back goats roamed in an orchard where apple, pear and cherry trees grew, their branches sleeved in blossom. Pigs snuffled in a sty nearby, a dozen or so hens were penned in a spacious run, and two small meadows spotted with wildflowers ran off behind thick hedgerows towards the woods beyond. Smoke curled from the roof of the cottage, and from within came faint sounds of movement.

At length the door of the cottage opened. An elderly man emerged, grey-haired and spare of frame, and traipsed with a somewhat arthritic gait towards the rear of the cottage. There he took up an axe and commenced splitting logs upon a stump close beside the pigsty.

Some moments later a stocky woman in smock and shawl came out of the house carrying a bucket. She too went around to the rear, humming a song to herself, and entered a shed. I knew, from the sounds which still emanated from within the cottage, that someone else remained inside. I waited, my eyes upon the doorway, growing more nervous by the minute.

A tiny movement drew my eye. A white, amorphous shape had appeared low on the edge of the cottage door. I made out a little pale hand. My breath stopped. Five small fingers drew the door inwards as I watched. Into the doorway came a doll-like figure, a child, a little girl, in a blue smock dress. She peered into the garden, a round, innocent face, all inquisitive, then advanced two paces, clambered over the stone step set at the doorway, and wandered a little uncertainly onto the garden path.

In her hands the child held a tattered rag doll. She squatted beside a cluster of bright anemones, holding the doll before her and talking to it. She waggled a forefinger at the doll, scolding it for some imagined misdemeanour. I stared transfixed.

Behind her the door opened wider. Suddenly, there stood Rohse. She was identical in all respects to the vision I retained of her in my memory. She looked out, satisfied herself that her daughter was close. 'Don't you go wandering off now, Eroniss,' she called, and withdrew inside again, leaving the door wide.

Eroniss! I felt a tug of poignant emotion within my chest. The name was the feminised version of my own, Ronbas. My daughter had been named in honour of my memory!

Welling with emotion I turned back to the child once more. From here she was the image of her mother. Clusters of bright curls, the colour of burnished copper, tumbled about her head and shoulders. Her face was small, round, possibly freckled like her mother's. Her little arms and legs were so fine, so perfectly formed.

'You've been a bad, bad girl,' I heard her tell her doll in a little, faltering voice, just succeeding in forming the words. 'Do you want me to tell Grandad?'

Nothing in my experience, human or vhazz, had prepared me for the intensity of feeling that surged within me as I lay there in the bushes, staring at this sweet, tiny girl who I had fathered, who was mine, my very own. My heart ached, almost forcing itself from my ribcage, and the tears started to my eyes, brimmed and spilled down my coarse vhazz cheeks.

I edged forward on my belly; I could not restrain myself. I had to see my daughter more closely. Unnoticed, I reached the garden gate and peered through between the bars. Eroniss played on, now cuddling the doll and rocking it in her arms.

A bright blue butterfly flew past. Eroniss watched as it fluttered away to alight upon a strawberry flower only feet from where I crouched behind the gate. Discarding her doll my daughter stood and approached, fascinated by the insect.

She was so close to me! I breathed in the frail, milky freshness of her pure child's skin, listened to the air entering and leaving her little lungs.

She reached for the butterfly. It rose and flew away, upwards, over the gate, into the sky and beyond. Eroniss's eyes – green, as mine had been – followed it.

Her mouth formed into a small, petulant droop.

At length the insect was lost to her view, or perhaps her interest waned. Her round eyes fell. They came to rest on the gate. She looked at the creature hidden beyond.

Eroniss showed no fear. She merely stared, her pretty head tilted slightly to one side.

Slowly, trembling with emotion, I rose onto my hindlegs. I wanted to see her more closely, without the barrier of the gate. My little daughter stared up at me curiously. I leaned a little way over the gate and extended a paw. I wished only to touch her; perhaps, if she would permit it, to hold her. Words formed in my mind, but when I spoke it was with a soft growl.

The little girl took a step towards me. Quite suddenly everything changed.

I gazed upon that tiny, vulnerable child and was overcome by another emotion which came not from Dinbig, but from the creature I was now. The savage, troubled vha'zz: hunter, killer, coward, tyrannised by its nature. The little girl's scent rose to my nostrils, and it was no longer I who gazed down upon her, but Huwoorsk, whose belly rumbled, who had not eaten for an entire night. The saliva filled my mouth and drooled from my jowls. I was consumed with my hunger, my savagery, my need. I reached down for her.

There was a shriek. I glanced up. Rohse was in the doorway of the cottage, her face a mask of horror. She rushed forward without fear or hesitation, along the garden path towards me, shouting, a broom in her hands.

Rohse! Rohse! How I have pondered that moment since! I have no doubt of what would have occurred had you not acted as you did. My nature was not my own; I could not help myself. But for you I would have committed the most vile and horrible crime; it would have destroyed you and haunted me for my lifetime.

Heedless of her own safety Rohse threw herself upon me, shrieking, striking out wildly with the broom again and again. I backed away a step, fielding her blows, brought somewhat to my true senses by her intrusion. She was no threat to me. I could have torn her to pieces effortlessly. But her brave actions brought me to an abrupt awareness of the horror I had been on the verge of perpetrating.

I took her blows. They were painful, and anger came. I might yet have dealt with her, but mercifully the part of me that was Dinbig of Khimmur again became uppermost.The vhazz was roused to fury, but somehow I contained it.

Now came another voice, raised in shock and anger. Rohse's father rushed out from beside the house, his woodcutter's axe grasped before him in both hands.

Still I could have killed them. And in those moments of vhazz rage and hunger I almost did. But my child was screaming, and her pain and terror rent Dinbig's soul. Huwoorsk snarled, but I backed away. Rohse came at me, blind, weeping, red-faced, furious, hitting me again and again. If I could have just spoken a word . . .

*Oh Rohse, how I loved you then!*

I turned and bounded away into the trees.


## II


I did not pause. I ran and ran, through woods, over hills, through pools of mist and clots of dappled sunlight. I ran for miles, until I could run no more. My lungs burned, my legs were lead and scarcely able to support me. I collapsed, exhausted, and lay gasping.

Minutes passed. I regained my breath and lay staring at the sky through the new green canopy overhead. The relentless image of what had almost occurred preyed upon me. I thought of Eroniss, my child.

*I was her father!*

How I wanted to see her again! And Rohse. Brave, beautiful Rohse. I longed to be able to return.

Then I wept, there in the woods of Khim province, trapped as I was in the flesh of a beast, never to be one of my family.

At length I – that is, Huwoorsk – was reminded of my hunger. I sniffed the air, scented a faint spore, and left the place where I lay. I found a trail. A short distance on I came upon a porcupine snuffling at the roots of a toppled tree.

The creature detected my presence and raised its spines. But they were no hazard to me. With my vhazz sword I flipped it onto its back and exposed its soft belly. With lust, with bestial relish, I sank my teeth deep into the warm flesh.

The porcupine squealed. I held on, closing my eyes and revelling in its suffering. Its sharp claws ripped at my snout, but I feasted upon the pain. Vital organs burst in the grip of my jaws; life juices bubbled and gushed. This was indulgence, vengeance, demonic need, pure, cruel and sweet. I was vhazz.

I sank my teeth deeper, tore away the porcupine's flesh while it still lived and kicked and squealed. When it lay still I gorged myself. Later, skulking and ashamed, I slunk away into the forest, my appetite appeased.

I made my way eastwards, with a new terror growing. I – Huwoorsk – was alone. A vague awareness of my pack remained, but they were far from me now, and moving away. My sense of them was diminishing with every passing hour. In its place I contemplated a loneliness more engulfing than any I had known, as human or vhazz, and I knew that I had to return to the pack.

I ran on, deep into the Forest of Rishal, but by midday my limbs were again growing weak from the exertion. I found a small cavern deep in the forest, and there curled up and slept until nightfall.

The night brought rain. I travelled on, pausing only to kill and eat. I made use of the Selaor Road to speed my passage into Mystoph. It was deserted at night, though the risk was ever present that guard-posts or depots unknown to me in my former life had been set up along its route. Still, I had the advantage of sight, and I steered clear when approaching known human settlements, leaving the road to skirt carefully around them.

As light dawned I was approaching One Thousand Rannon Ford, close to the village of Boundary on the Selaor-Mystoph border. My sense of the vhazz pack had grown no stronger, but my unease was increased now by a sensation of shared alarm or fear. I was picking up signals, still faint, of distress. The pack, far ahead, had run into difficulties, I was certain of it. But I could discern nothing of what the difficulties entailed, or the gravity of the situation. This provoked a heightened sense of guilt and alarm. My duty in times of trouble or need was to my pack. I would have been summoned to aid them, but I had not been there to respond. I had failed the sisterhood.

I slept fitfully, awoke early, and moved on, into the wild heart of Mystoph.

A day later I came upon an unexpected sight. To make up ground I was sleeping only for a few hours in the afternoon, then travelling through the night and on into the daylight hours. As the first light of day dawned I crested a low wooded ridge to look down upon a great army encamped in a valley before me. I say encamped, but from the measure of activity I witnessed, large sections of troops were evidently preparing to move. Since entering Mystoph I had come across several companies of soldiers. Some had been of considerable strength, though insignificant in comparison to what I now beheld, and they had in the main been heading south or eastwards. Their orders, it would now appear, had been to join this massive force.

The army was composed predominantly of Khimmurian nationals: I recognised the standards of numerous of the dhomas of my homeland. Former friends and associates of mine were down there, and enemies too. But I was mystified at the sight of Kemahamek troops camped alongside them. And, equally surprisingly, large contingents of fighting men from the nations of Cexhaut and Anxau, beyond Hecra; and auxiliary groups who bore no national colours or emblem. This was unquestionably an army of conquest; I wondered where its destination might be.

I watched as some of the camps across the valley were taken apart, equipment and appurtenances packed into a second army of wagons and carts. Many remained; it was obvious that not all were preparing to leave.

The first of the troops formed up on horseback and began to move out of the valley. Behind marched infantry, then more horsemen. They were led by a giant of a figure seated upon a great stallion. He was some distance off, but I could not mistake him. He was Orl Kilroth, my killer.

Kilroth's men marched southwestward, heading, it was my guess, for the West Road which flanked the Byar-hagkh mountains. The road would take them south to the edge of Ashakite. But whence where were they bound? The possibilities were numerous, and I could not travel with them to find out.

Half a mile on I came upon another disturbing sight. Camped at the edge of the valley, beside a rivulet shielded from the main army by a wooded knoll, was another force. This one was much smaller. It consisted of thirty or so black wagons, guarded by a small contingent of troops.

This was a chilling discovery. The black wagons were known and feared, in Khimmur and beyond. They

228

were used to transport H'padir warriors, Khimmur's beastmen who, in battle, were incomparable. Beside the wagons, on long chains, were the H'padirs' partners in combat, the great warhounds, savage armoured mastiffs which can weigh more than a man.

I bypassed this camp, but as I trotted on the question kept arising in my mind: how many H'padir? Thirty wagons could mean as much as three hundred of the wildmen, yet Khimmur had never possessed that many. These men were psychopaths, uncontrollables. They were difficult and expensive to train; only one man had any degree of command over them, their brutish leader, Kuno. In battle the H'padir were capable of wreaking immense havoc upon an enemy force many times their size. But they rarely survived, generally fighting on in an insane fury until they were eventually cut down. Thus their numbers were not easily replenished.

My thoughts travelled back to the events of Twalinieh two years earlier. There Shimeril had told me how, upon the road to Kemahamek, he had encountered Kuno riding at the head of twenty black wagons. Even then, two hundred H'padir were far more than Kuno was known to command. If the beastmen had since been deployed in Kemahamek, or elsewhere, they would surely have taken heavy losses. Yet now I witnessed with my own eyes that Kuno had more. How could this be? Or did these shrouded wagons contain something else?

Midday was drawing nigh. With the countryside rife with soldiery I deemed it safer to travel no further until nightfall. I found a secluded hollow deep within a bramble thicket, and slept.

I was woken almost by a sixth sense, a forewarning of danger. I lay still, listening, my nostrils testing the air. Men were close by. Horses, too. Their odours were carried to me on a breath of a breeze. I lay as still as a stone.

Soft footsteps: the crack of a twig, the light jingle of a harness or creak of leather. On my belly I inched towards the edge of the thicket.

It was dusk. Beneath the trees a deep gloom had gathered. I picked out the shapes of men creeping like spectres through the wood. Six or seven I saw, but sensed others close by. They advanced with swords drawn or bows at the ready, and I caught the occasional glint of a steel breastplate or helmet. Others came slowly behind, leading horses.

A footfall within feet of me! A warrior passed, and I saw with a tingle of excitement that he wore the green and black uniform of Mystoph.

At first I thought I must be the object of their search, but as I realised this was not so I became intrigued. When the last soldier had passed I left my hiding place and followed, keeping low, at a safe distance behind the last horse. They were moving in the direction from which I had come, back towards the valley in which the army was encamped. As I followed, they swung somewhat northeast, bringing them on a course with the rivulet and Kuno's black wagons.

The Mystophians halted within the trees just short of the clearing where Kuno's camp lay. I crept up closer to observe those on foot spreading out to take up positions in the wood, while those with the horses, numbering about twenty in all, waited to the rear.

For some time no further move was made. I crept onto the knoll above Kuno's position. The black wagons were formed into a laager. At their centre burned a large cooking-fire. Dusky figures sat within its glow and moved about the camp. From time to time, from the wagons where the H'padir were kept chained and subdued, came strange moans or ululations.

I moved a little higher in order to look across into the broad valley beyond the knoll. An army was still encamped, though many of the troops had departed during the day. Hundreds of small fires flickered red and orange across the valley floor.

The evening darkened. The gloom beneath the trees was broken in frail filigree patches by wan moonlight cast down between the branches. I moved from the knoll, for there I felt trapped between two, or perhaps three hostile forces.

As I arrived back at an observation point close to where the horsemen were mustered there was movement among them. A tall figure wearing a blue cloak, armoured in leather and a steel breastplate, issued curt orders. The horses were led through the trees to the north of Kuno's camp. I watched, enthralled. This man was known to me. He was Shimeril, the Commander of the Nine Hundred Mystophian Paladins, my old and loyal friend and guardian of Duke Shadd.

Shimeril led his own horse north with his men. Moments later I caught a flicker of flame, just briefly, among the trees in the direction in which they had gone.

I crept onto a bank of earth and scrub, careful to avoid the notice of the men hidden in the trees. From here I was able to look out onto Kuno's camp. I had scarcely settled myself when I heard the faint drum of hooves upon the earth and the accompanying jangle of harness and equipment. Out of the trees to the north broke Shimeril's paladins. Each man held a bow, notched with a flaming arrow. They pounded down upon the laager of wagons.

They burst into the laager unopposed, releasing their shafts as they galloped through. Startled guards leapt aside to avoid the horses. Others ran forward from the wagons, brandishing weapons, to intercept the raiders.

The burning shafts struck into the nearest wagons. Their flames caught the tarpaulin covers. From within came yells, then roars of terror and pain as chained men, unable to flee, realised they were about to be burned alive.

The paladins, their fiery arrows spent, put aside their bows and drew swords.

Figures tumbled from two of the wagons: H'padir, half-naked, drugged and confused, who had through sheer brute strength broken free of their chains. From the woods more arrows hummed as the hidden Mystophians let fly. Guards fell. The horsemen rode on, not breaking their pace, making for the southern perimeter of the camp.

The camp was a scene of chaos. Eight wagons were ablaze; on three the timbers had caught, threatening the entire structure. Men milled in panic within the circle. Shouts turned to groans and cries as arrows rained from the woods to strike into flesh. H'padir, trapped in the flames, thrashed and writhed, their screams terrible to hear. Some of the guards ran to the rivulet for water; others attempted to retaliate, but illuminated by the fires they were easy targets for Shimeril's archers, who were themselves shielded by the dark.

The wardogs bayed, the flames crackled as men shouted and died. The H'padir who had fought clear of the blazing wagons were hardly warriors now. Indeed, they made pathetic figures, stumbling around, banging into one another, calling out incoherently. Some fell, struck down by murderous arrows; others made off into the woods, away from the raiders; but none fought. Such a contrast with the bestial warriors I had witnessed when roused for battle, striking terror into their opponents, hacking down men by the dozen.

The last of Shimeril's riders were almost clear of the camp. The foremost galloped free, passing below where I lay. Shimeril himself rode by, crouched low in the saddle. I glimpsed his face, pallid and ghostly, a taut smile stretched across his teeth.

A single paladin had been caught up in fighting within the circle of wagons. Two of Kuno's guards had rushed forward to intercept him. He drew his sword and swung at the first, forcing him aside. The second drove forward with a pike, and the rider was obliged to swerve.

Diverted from his course the paladin broke free of the wagons to the west. He galloped on towards me, about thirty yards behind the last of his companions. A figure scuttled out behind him, squat, broad, of immensely powerful build. I recognized Kuno, the H'padir master.

From a strap across his torso Kuno slipped free a throwing-iron. He drew back his arm and took aim at the retreating rider. With grim concentration he hurled the weapon, emitting a guttural yell as it flew from his fingers.

The iron sang as it sped through the moonlight. Impelled by Kuno's immense strength, it struck hard between the paladin's shoulder blades. He arched his back with a terrible moan. His features, as he passed below me, were clenched hard with sudden agony. He rode on, slewing in the saddle, his horse bearing him away into the woods.

For a few more seconds the arrows rained on into Kuno's camp, then quite suddenly ceased. The raiders melted away into the night.

It would take only moments, I knew, before soldiers arrived from the main army camped in the valley. I slipped down from the bank and made off in the wake of Shimeril's troop.

## III

Eighty yards into the woods I came upon the body.

The last paladin had fallen from his mount and lay face down upon the grass. Kuno's bloody iron had dropped, or he had succeeded in wresting it, from his back. Blood flowed darkly from the wound and soaked his clothing. At first I believed him dead, but as I crept closer I noted he still breathed, though he was unconscious.

I quickly examined the wound. The iron had penetrated the paladin's mail shirt and buried itself deep into the flesh. Minute fragments of metal had been driven inwards, into the lesion. Bone was shattered, the mutilated flesh gaped wide, the blood flowed freely from severed veins. Without medical attention the man would soon die.

Shimeril could attempt no rescue, of that I was fairly certain. In minutes this area would be swarming with Khimmurian soldiers. The raiders had timed their action precisely. They had struck out of nowhere, caused sudden damage, and vanished, all within seconds. Each man would have known the risk and accepted the rules of engagement.

Thus I was faced with a dilemma. To try to aid the dying paladin, or to abandon him. If I chose the former I would be delaying my attempts to rejoin my vhazz pack – possibly relinquishing all hope of contact with them. I would be at immediate risk from Khimmurians searching the area, and further, from any other humans to whom I might endeavour to take the wounded man.

And not least, there was my vhazz nature to contend with. The vhazz are not averse to scavenging; helplessness or vulnerability in others excites their savagery. Even now I was greatly aroused by the scent and sight of the paladin's blood.

But this man was Mystophian. He had fought for all I held dear. He deserved better than to die alone in this wild wood, or at the hands of the torturers of the Beast of Rull.

From the direction of the burning camp I heard raised voices. Torches flickered some distance off among the trees. I had little time for decision.

I looked again at the dying man, and for the first time took note of his face. A wide jaw, covered by a neatly trimmed black beard, noble brow beneath his helmet, eyes closed. I realised suddenly that I knew him. He was Sar B'hut, a Mystophian noble whose estate lay close to Mlanje. In my former existence I had ridden with him, and fought with him when bandits – unbeknown to us in the employ of the Beast of Rull – had ambushed us in an attempt to take my life.

My decision was made.

My immediate priority was to get Sar B'hut into cover. I took his weight beneath the shoulders and began to drag him, away from the searchers who were now penetrating the woods. For the present the thicket where I had slept during the daylight hours would provide sufficient concealment, but as I hauled the limp body closer I heard a chilling sound from the direction of Kuno's camp. A great baying as the wardogs on their chains led the searchers into the forest.

Now I knew the full scope of our peril. Men I could have hoped to avoid. They would not have searched far in the night, and once they had given up I could have utilised the remaining hours of darkness to carry

Sar B'hut away from the area. But the hounds would quickly scent his blood, and from them there was nowhere to hide. In moments they would be upon us.

Even as I thought it the mournful baying became agitated and triumphal. The hounds had our scent.

Would they be released from their chains, or would their handlers, for fear of losing them, hold them close? I listened. From the speed of their approach I knew that at least two of the hounds had been freed.

I dragged Sar B'hut to the bole of a great oak. It was dark here, where no moonlight penetrated the canopy. I left the paladin there and bounded back along the way we had come. The first of the great hounds was almost upon us. I drew my vhazz sword and took cover behind a mossy boulder.

The animal came hurtling out of the undergrowth, its snout to the ground. As it passed me, unaware of my presence, I crouched low and swept my blade out into its path. The dog hit the earth, its forelimbs severed, and howled.

Another was behind it. I rose, sword high, and brought the blade down.

The weapon glanced off the hound's spinal guard. The creature wheeled, snarling. I struck again, slashing this time across its unprotected muzzle. The dog screamed. I leapt upon it and bowled it onto its back, stabbing deep till it lay still.

I scrambled erect. A third wardog charged into view. Like the others it wore guard and spikes over its most vulnerable parts. Seeing me it skidded to a halt in sudden surprise, perhaps disconcerted, for few dogs will willingly contend with a vhazz. I advanced, chopping with my sword. The wardog backed away, its teeth bared.

But now another joined it, and another I saw, streak past, a huge black shadow, making straight along the

236

trail towards Sar B'hut. In desperation I grabbed darts from my harness and hurled them at the two hounds facing me. One at least struck home, but I did not wait to see its effect. I spun around to race back to the stricken paladin.

The wardog was already upon him, like a great homunculus, tearing at his flesh. I sprang at it, stabbing with my blade. The hound rolled away, taken by surprise. As it twisted beneath me I sank my fangs into its throat, beside the spiked collar, twisted, ripped, tore away its gullet.

A searing pain hammered into my side, a heavy weight pounding into me. The other hounds were upon me. In numbers they had no fear. I heard shouts as men approached.

I rolled, spun, biting, stabbing, kicking. Somehow I fought momentarily free of the two hounds. One attacked again; the other held back, whimpering, blood pouring from its neck.

I dodged the attack, but soldiers were here now, rushing suddenly from between the trees. Desperately I hurled a dart. The first man, illuminated by his own torch, staggered and cried out, stared about him in surprise, clutching the dart which had pierced his hip. In the darkness he had yet to see me.

I leapt, struck with my sword into his belly. He fell dead, never knowing what had killed him. But others ran forward, and the warhound was upon me again, hampering my movement. More dogs bayed close by, as yet still chained.

I had no hope. I was outnumbered.

A soldier came at me, sword raised, another behind him. I lifted my own weapon to ward the blow, but staggered as the hound leapt again at my throat. I fell back. The Khimmurian lunged. I rolled, stabbing now at the dog.

A second hound flew, bearing me down. The Khimmurian raised his sword again, stepped in, his companion in close support.

Quite suddenly the first soldier grunted, staggered, and toppled to the ground. I glimpsed fleeting movement; the second Khimmurian fell backwards, blood blossoming suddenly on his chest.

One of the two wardogs attacking me collapsed, lifeless. A figure moved by, a blur of motion. I rolled and stabbed, fought off the second hound. Half-rising, I glanced around me. Yards away I saw Shimeril advance upon the nearest Khimmurians, weaving, side-stepping. His twin-bladed rancet spun and whirled, dealing death to any who came to meet it.

Others of Shimeril's men ran forward to engage the enemy. The night was full of shouts and clanging steel. I glanced back. Two men bent over the still form of Sar B'hut. They lifted him gently and bore him off to a waiting horse.

Shimeril. I had misjudged him. He had returned.

For a few more seconds the woods rang with the sound of battle, then abruptly it was over. The Khimmurians, few in number at this point, retreated with their dogs. In the darkness the Mystophians did not pursue. Shimeril wheeled and strode back. The horse carrying Sar B'hut was led away into the forest dark. I stood before my old friend, face to face. He held his weapon before him, guarded, not fully certain of me.

'This is an extraordinary thing,' said he. 'A vhazz intervenes in a human conflict, to save a man.'

I said nothing. I could not. Not anything that would be understood.

'Ordinarily I would kill you on sight,' said Shimeril. 'As you would I. What am I to make of this?'

He stared at me with narrowed eyes. 'Do you understand me?'

. I nodded. Shimeril raised his eyebrows in surprise. 'By Moban, I believe you do!'

Desperately I struggled to form words, but again only vhazz sounds emerged.

Shimeril shook his head in mystification. 'There is something here that I am not capable of understanding.'

Again I nodded, and tears clouded my eyes. My old friend peered at me, totally bemused. Shouts rang again from the woods. More dogs howled. Shimeril glanced around him. His men, all but two, had vanished.

'We must go. They may yet come with more troops.' He inhaled a deep breath. 'I can offer you nothing, vhazz, but my deep and sincere gratitude, and the opportunity to escape this place unhindered. Go quickly, and with our thanks, friend.'

He backed away, gave a quick bow of his head, then turned and with his two fighters at his side, ran off into the night. I waited scarcely a moment longer before likewise fleeing that place.˙


IV


The following days, as I continued east in pursuit of my pack, passed without major incident. From Mystoph I plunged into the Magoth, the great forest which ranges across the whole of Virland. Here I discovered too the evidence of Khimmurian occupation. Patrols along the forest road, guard-posts and depots, gangs of slaves labouring in the forest. I began

˙ It is now widely believed that the above incident forms the basis for the popular Rullian folk-tale: 'The Good Vhazz'. See 'Folk-tales and Fables of Rull', compiled, edited and revised by Parvis Parvislopis.

to appreciate something of the extent of the Vulpasmage's new empire.

The wounds I had sustained fighting to save Sar B'hut were fortunately not grave enough to warrant detailed attention. I bathed them in a stream, applied healing plants, and let them mend at their own pace.

The way through Virland proved hard. The forest was so dense in places as to present an impenetrable wall, even to a creature such as I for whom forest was a natural and preferred habitat. Always, as I moved on, the sense of the pack somewhere before me . . . East, moving east, in search of perpetual night. And within me was the terrible division as I sought the vhazz: the terror that I might lose them, and the anguish of leaving ever further behind me the land and peoples to whom I truly belonged, and of whom I longed to be a part once more.

Was I in any way coming to accept myself now as vhazz? With the passing weeks was I becoming the creature whose body I occupied? Repeatedly I demanded of myself whether my destiny was to live out my existence in this bestial form, gradually losing all recollection of ever having been something other. I tested my mental faculties as I ran, going back over events in my life as Dinbig of Khimmur to reassure myself that my memories remained sharp and clear. And each evening when I awoke, I spent a period in Zan-Chassin meditation and focus, concerned that what meagre powers still remained to me were not permitted to diminish.

Often I stopped in my tracks to stare back along the way I had come. The yearning to return to Khimmur was so great that I almost turned around to make my way back. But I knew there was nothing for me there; no means of becoming human again. Something kept me moving east, something other than the ever-present vhazz fear of abandonment. A whispered voice, so deep within me that it was barely heard. It prompted me, goaded me on, east, ever east. As though there might lie an answer, a resolution, some means of making my existence at least tolerable.

From Virland I passed into Chol, and at about the same time grew conscious of having made ground, having gained a little on the sisterhood. The pack was closer, more distinct in my awareness. There was still a distance between us, but I felt that we were separated by hours now, rather than days.

The Khimmurian presence in Chol was much greater than in Virland. I understood that, down here towards the south, fighting still continued. Khimmur did not yet have full control of this nation. I moved on with greater caution. Troops were concentrated in strength, ever vigilant and alert. I kept to the night, and to the wildlands away from human habitation; too easily I might have walked inadvertently into a concealed troop position, or been spotted from a lookout-post.

One evening I had skirted around a small Chol township when I picked up a faint scent, a vaguest intimation of something familiar to me, carried in a fine tendril by the wind. I stood stock still, my nostrils dilating, searching the air. It came again, stronger this time. Seconds later, out of the bushes ahead of me, bounded Yaoww.

'Huwoorsk!'

She ran forward and leapt upon me. I was overjoyed at the sight of her. We rolled together in the dust, clasped each other warmly, sucking in one another's odours. Yaoww's musk was powerful, wildly intoxicating. Before I knew it she was on all fours, her rump towards me. I climbed eagerly upon her haunches.

241

Our coupling was breathless, over in moments, as is the vhazz way, then we trotted away together, still eastwards, and I asked, 'How did you find me?'

'We were concerned,' said Yaoww. 'We could not understand what had happened to you, Huwoorsk, for we were losing contact with you, yet we detected no great distress. You seemed simply to grow more distant. A moot was held, but it was decided we could not risk turning back for you. We did not know whether you had chosen to abandon us, but if that were so there was nothing to be done. I argued that you might yet be unwell, due to your injuries, and in need of our help. But I was overruled. The greater duty was to the family-group. We had to keep moving to find our new homeland.'

'And have you found it?' I asked, with cynicism I do not think Yaoww detected.

'Every day we move closer.'

'Why have you come now to me?'

Yaoww looked at me sidelong, her yellowed teeth bared in a smile. 'The decision was made some time ago that my time for bearing young again was at hand. I designated you for my partner. When it seemed we had lost you I was urged to choose again, but I waited. Some nights ago we grew aware that you were still pursuing us. You grew closer. Yesternight I was given permission to turn back alone and find you.'

'Then how far ahead is the pack?'

'Not far. Perhaps a night at the most. The sisterhood moves at a lesser pace so that we may catch up. Battles are being fought hereabouts, so we must take great care. Twice the sisterhood has come under attack. Eleven members were killed in the first attack; we stumbled into the path of a human army. It was a terrible fight.'

Yaoww's eyes had misted as she looked back. I recalled the sense of distress I had picked up from the pack as I entered Mystoph.

'I am happy to see you, Yaoww,' I said, truthfully. The oppressive loneliness that had characterised my days for so long now was partly dispelled by her presence.

Yaoww turned her head and nuzzled me. 'And I you, Huwoorsk.'

We moved on, towards the east and a land that did not exist.

# 9

## I

What of events elsewhere at this time?

The behemoth of war pushed remorselessly on. In the south, once mighty Ghence stood staunchly in defiance of its foe. A massive wall constructed a century and a half earlier spanned the border between Ghence and her former ally, Hanvat.˙ Later augmentations extended to cover the Soland border. These, manned along their entire length by thousands of Ghentine troops, had halted the Khimmurian advance and for months kept at bay the massed armies of the Beast of Rull.

The Ghentine navy, the pride of Rull, successfully held control of the southern waters, thwarting any hopes the Beast had entertained of a seaborne invasion from Barulia or Komamnaga. But the Beast's army was not idle as it sat before the outer gates of Ghence. The defenders knew no rest; battalions of siege engines pounded without cease the great wall and its towers. Khimmur's most stalwart ally, Sommaria, whose troops had conquered Komamnaga and Picia, and whose army now supplemented the Khimmurians before the wall, sent an assault force into Soland. Horsetroops and elephant cavalry, with thousands of infantry in support, razed towns and villages, looting

---

˙ Ironically, the wall had been built by the Hanvatians to keep out the Ghentines. In a massive coup Ghence 'purloined' the wall within days of its completion by Hanvat.

244

and pillaging as they went. Soland, a wild land with little organisation, offered no concerted resistance and was swiftly overcome. The Sommarian army established itself before Ghence's northern frontier wall. Ghence's defenders were stretched to their limits.

As the siege progressed Khimmurian envoys approached the Ghentine commanders at frequent intervals with calls for capitulation. Each time they were rebuffed. The great trebuchets continued their bombardment, but now, from time to time, their payloads of rock were substituted with more ghoulish cargo. Before the eyes of the defenders rows of prisoners were lined up beside the war machines. Men, women, children, many of them civilians, taken randomly from Hanvatian or Solandian towns and villages; or Ghentine settlers who had taken up residence on the wrong side of the wall. Others were soldiers, from Ghence or elsewhere, who had been captured in battle.

These unfortunates were loaded into the machines. Some were smothered in pitch or wildfire, and put, still living, to the torch. In their hundreds they were hurled flailing and screaming across the Ghentine wall, into the ranks of the defending troops.

More calls for surrender, answered with stubborn refusal. But inevitably, Ghentine morale suffered a serious decline. Occasional sallies against apparent enemy weak points revealed only that appearances may be deceptive. Khimmur and her ally at all times maintained strong infantry support around their artillery units, and battalions of light and heavy cavalry were stationed within easy reach of every besieging position, able to ride swiftly to provide support where needed.

A counterattack was required, a blow that would cause Khimmur to stagger while re-establishing Ghence's dwindling faith in her ability to withstand the invaders. A plan was laid for a seaborne strike from the south.

One hundred warships and merchant transports landed a force near the Barulian border. There, as spy reports had indicated, the Khimmurian garrison was found to be ill defended. It was quickly overcome and the Ghentines marched on without pause to engage Sommaria's southern siege force before the wall.

Fierce battle ensued. The defenders on the wall sallied out in strength and the Sommarians, sandwiched between two forces, were beaten back, taking heavy losses before relief arrived from the north. Ghence had a beach-head; but the plan had been ill-conceived. Further northern expansion was impossible, due to the weight of enemy forces. To move west would gain Ghence nothing, merely stretching its resources and laying its lines open to exploitation and division by the enemy. A stalemate endured for several days, during which Khimmur moved a strong detachment of horse and foot southwest into Barulia. As Sommaria pressed down from the north, this force struck hard into the Ghentine left flank.

The pressure was too great, and the Ghentine army was pushed inexorably back. Slowly the Beast's troops whittled away at their defences. Then a brilliant tactical manoeuvre by one of Sommaria's generals led to a wedge being driven through the centre of the Ghentine force, isolating its western flank.

Utilising captured naval vessels Khimmur was able to blockade the Blue Gulf between Barulia and Ghence, preventing supplies and reinforcements being brought in to relieve the troops on the flank. The beleaguered Ghentine force was butchered; the survivors, along with the bodies of the dead, were returned to Ghence via the Khimmurian trebuchets.

The remaining Ghentine troops lost heart. Outnumbered and outmanoeuvred they retreated again to the comparative safety of the wall.

Meanwhile urgent missives had been dispatched by Ghence's ruling oligarchal council to the rulers of lands near and far, even to the distant island nations of the Yphasian Ocean. They were couched in the form of dire caveats and appeals for assistance, 'that a united stand be made upon the hallowed soil of Ghence, to drive back once and for all this northern scum, these insolent barbarians, to the lands whence they have issued'. Tomia, March and Dyarchim, understanding at last something of the gravity of the threat, began to build up their own border defences. Diplomats and advisors entered Ghence to learn what they could, but as yet no foreign army mustered beside Ghence's own.

Later a message was to be brought by pigeon to Ghence's Chambers of Grand Council, in the capital, Trore. Another enemy army had been sighted leaving Khimmur to thread its way south along the Sommarian Spice Road. This force was as great as that which sat before Ghence's border walls. Auxiliary troops from several northern nations supplemented its numbers. Following such a route, under such circumstances, its destination could only be Ghence.

New letters went out from Ghence, apprising her neighbours of the new development and renewing calls for military aid. The great oligarchal council convened in crisis to thrash out last minute plans for defence and possible evacuation.

The shadow of the Beast of Rull loomed ever darker in the south.

Ghence waited.


II


Bitter fighting had continued in Chol as the remnants of the First Chol Army, led by Sir Vicore, struggled to delay Khimmur's push south along the Coul Road. Two hundred and seventy determined men had launched repeated forays against an army some six thousand strong. They struck from the heights; rolled great boulders or tumbles of logs down onto the enemy train below. From the cover of woods they made swift and sudden attacks; flights of arrows raining suddenly into a chosen section of the army as it trudged past; a sudden charge by mounted lancers, who were then gone again, defying attempts to give chase. The Chol dug up the road, set barricades, destroyed bridges. The loss to Khimmur in actual manpower was minimal, but with each obstacle encountered the army was obliged to halt and set up a defended camp while workgangs laboured to repair the damage. Thus vital days were gained in which Count Vess's Second Army had been able to withdraw in secret from the southern border and rally to the Prince Regent, Fhir Oube.

Reports flew back to Postor, and thence to the Beast of Rull, the Vulpasmage incarnate, King Oshalan of Khimmur, who had left the Chol capital to return to Khimmur. He grew increasingly angered at the news. Inevitably the Khimmurian force, whose commander was the dhoma-lord Marsinenicon of Rishal, would win through by sheer weight of numbers, but the Vulpasmage had anticipated a swift defeat of Chol. With the Chol army crushed he wished to deploy the bulk of Lord Marsinenicon's troops elsewhere. It was unthinkable that his advance should be so impeded by a tiny band of Chol.

Gneth would have routed the Chol in no time. But the nether-spawn were not great in number, and as things stood at present, irreplaceable. To preserve them for maximum effect elsewhere they had been pulled out of battle after Postor fell. The Vulpasmage rode now at their head, to join the army that still waited in Mystoph and ride on for the southern lands and the greater prize of Ghence.

Orders were sent back to Postor, where the Khimmurian dhoma-lord Hhubith of Poisse, charged with overseeing the administration of Khimmur's newest conquest, held temporary residence in the Palace of the Prince Regent. Under Lord Hhubith's personal command a contingent of troops left the capital to march southeast via an unconventional overland route.

A Sommarian captain called Fland had earlier arrived in Postor. He came with a small company, and brought a gift for the Vulpasmage of rare hunting beasts extracted from the menagerie of exotic creatures that was King Perminias's pride and joy. These animals, trained in Sommaria, came with Perminias's effusive greetings and sincere hopes that they would prove a delight and distraction for his most valued and respected Khimmurian ally. The Vulpasmage had inspected the gift with interest, but with little time or inclination for anything but the swift subdual of his adversaries, had given them no further thought. Now Fland travelled south with his company towards Coul, bearing a message for Lord Marsinenicon.

At Drurn March the arrival of the Prince Regent's cousin, Count Vess, with Chol's Second Army, provided a valuable boost to morale. Count Vess and the Prince Regent, with officers and advisors, convened in Drurn March hall for urgent appraisal of their situation. Learning that Sir Vicore still commanded the road north of Coul, Count Vess pressed for reinforcements to be sent to his aid. This was agreed, and a major assault upon the Khimmurian advance planned.

Lord Marsinenicon would be expecting further ambush, but now the opportunity existed to spring a surprise. Khimmurian losses had been negligible, inflicted by a force too small to cause much more than nuisance. Now that force, properly augmented, might take advantage of Khimmurian complacency and deal a sound and punishing blow.

It was agreed that this would be the final strike of its kind. Khimmur was too strong; it could not be stopped. Its king was wily, its warlords experienced. Fhir Oube had achieved his immediate objective. With bitterness he had acknowledged the fall of southern Chol as being inevitable. It was a matter now of strategic withdrawal in order to fight another day.

Maps were studied in detail, the most auspicious site for an ambush upon the Coul Road chosen. A complex plan of engagement was drawn up. It was decided that eight hundred Chol soldiers would supplement Sir Vicore's company. More would have been cumbersome, for the terrain and circumstance did not favour massed battle; less might have diminished the effect of the blow Chol planned to deliver. A messenger was dispatched immediately to Sir Vicore, with orders that he withdraw forthwith to the allotted location, make preparations and await further word. Two days later, in the early morning, Count Vess led his eight hundred from Drurn March, determined that a battle would be fought which Khimmur would not quickly forget.

III

In accordance with instructions Sir Vicore withdrew his small force some twenty-five miles south towards Coul. There stood a wooden bridge, called Demon's Bridge, which spanned a steep-sided, narrow chasm some forty feet deep, along which the river Isk bounded north towards Lake Chol. Immediately upstream of the bridge the road climbed and was flanked by banks and slopes, wooded and rocky, which afforded cover for an ambushing force. The land behind provided a ready route of escape into surrounding highlands.

The terrain on the northern approach to the bridge was open meadowland which funnelled into a narrow, sheer-sided pass through which the Isk flowed. Sir Vicore's brief was to take up hidden positions on the south side of Demon's Bridge, leaving the bridge itself apparently intact. Khimmurian suspicions would be kindled, it was reasoned, by finding the bridge in such a state, for to date no bridge on the Coul Road had been left whole. Thus Lord Marsinenicon's army would create its own delay by halting and setting up camp in the meadows while exploratory teams came forward to investigate the bridge and its environs.

Sir Vicore's men worked swiftly. Vital struts and supports beneath Demon's Bridge where it stretched out from the south bank were weakened and undermined. The work was done in positions that could not be easily sighted without close inspection. Long ropes were attached to enable men hidden on the slopes to pull away the supports at a given signal, causing the bridge to collapse. Concealed ditches and short tunnels were excavated, providing the saboteurs with escape routes into the country beyond. A covering of brush, earth, grass and transplanted shrubs ensured that no trace of the work was visible from the road.

Count Vess arrived with his eight hundred soldiers. He and Sir Vicore held conference. The plan devised at Drurn March was declared sound: Count Vess was to swing northeast, taking a circuitous overland route to avoid the Coul Road and any risk of sighting by Khimmurian scouts. His own scouts would locate the approaching enemy army and he would take up position to its left rear flank when it encamped in the meadows beyond the pass.

Terrain precluded the entry of a large force into the pass in anything more than triple file. If the weakened timbers of the bridge were not discovered it was calculated that a sizeable company would attempt to cross and establish a bridgehead. More troops would then move up to protect the road. This being achieved, the army would attempt to renew its trek south.

At about this point Sir Vicore would launch his assault. The bridge supports would be pulled away, bringing down Demon's Bridge to leave the soldiers on the southern side cut off from the main army. Troops from the encampment would forge up in support of the beleaguered company, at which time, taking advantage of the confusion, Count Vess would attack the camp from the north, striking hard at a single point, then retreating.

It was likely, however, that the sabotage upon the bridge would be discovered before any sizeable force crossed. If that were so Sir Vicore was to pull back his men. Khimmurian engineers, with a strong guard, would undoubtedly be brought up to make repairs. These Sir Vicore would harry with missiles.

When the bridge was eventually made sound once more a similar scenario to the first could be expected. But with Sir Vicore's presence now known a much larger Khimmurian van would almost certainly cross the bridge. They too would be harried, then Sir Vicore's company would quickly vanish. The army would begin to file into the pass. Count Vess, choosing his moment, would attack from behind. Sir Vicore would reappear to provide supporting fire. Thus, again, the Khimmurian force would be split when at its most vulnerable. And again, there would be no protracted engagement. Both Chol forces, knowing the land, would strike quickly and be gone.

The Khimmurians, advancing cautiously from the north, were expected to arrive within sight of Demon's Bridge within two days. Count Vess's overland route, which required that he travel first south, then leave the road to tramp northeastwards at the back of the nearest range of hills, required perhaps a day-and-a-half. Without further delay Count Vess departed.

As predicted, late on the morning of the second day following, lookouts for Sir Vicore on the high ridges above the pass reported the approach of the Khimmurian advance guard. About one hundred soldiers, well-armed and riding sturdy mounts, had broken out of the woodlands on the Coul Road some seven miles to the north and were proceeding cautiously through the open meadows.

Sir Vicore climbed to the heights to observe. The Khimmurians halted before the head of the pass. A party of fifteen came on forward at walking pace along the road above the Isk. Scanning the cliffs on either side they moved to a point where the road, twisting, would have taken them out of sight of their companions. Here they paused. A second party rode forward to join them. The original fifteen then advanced further until they came in sight of Demon's Bridge.

Again they halted, observing the bridge from a distance of some fifty yards but making no attempt to approach closer. A single horseman galloped back along the pass to the main group waiting in the meadows. From there two riders rode north, up the road over the meadows and into the woods beyond, presumably to report their findings to Lord Marsinenicon.

The company made camp close to the head of the pass. The two parties within the pass were relieved at regular intervals, and the hours passed without incident. In the middle of the afternoon Lord Marsinenicon's army began to march out of the woodlands north of the meadows. As anticipated it broke ranks and commenced to set up camp. Swiftly and systematically a large wooden palisade was erected, within which blossomed tents, some small huts and the various impedimenta of an army on the move, all in orderly array. Bodies of infantry and archers took up defensive positions behind a wall of pavises until the palisade was complete, and flying columns of mounted troops stood by, ready to respond instantly to attack.

A small party of cavalry detached itself from this scene of industry and rode into the pass to join those already positioned before Demon's Bridge. At the head of the party rode a man resplendent in gleaming armour and a helm supporting a plume of orange and green. His shield bore the coat of arms of Rishal, and the standards carried by the riders at his rear were of Rishal and Khimmur. This was Lord Marsinenicon. He conferred briefly with his officers, gesturing from time to time towards the bridge and the ravine it spanned, then rode with his retinue back to camp.

Soon after a body of perhaps one hundred infantry and archers marched up towards the bridge. They wore heavy mail or lamellar hauberks, and carried large, slightly convex, rectangular shields. They halted on the narrow road before the bridge, in front of the waiting horsemen. Some climbed up onto the slopes and cliffs flanking the pass and took up secure positions among the rocks.

A second body of similar size marched into the pass and established a position upon the road half a mile downstream, and a third beyond that. Men were set to chopping trees, digging into the rocky earth and rolling boulders down to the roadside. As the daylight waned hastily constructed but sturdy fortifications commanded the limited space immediately north of the bridge and secured the road as far back as the camp.

From his vantage overhead Sir Vicore nodded to himself, and murmured to the guard at his side, 'They are thorough and efficient. One cannot help but admire their order.'

A platoon of thirty infantry now advanced behind a cordon of shields to within yards of the bridge. Ten horsemen rode forward. Two infantrymen, one on either side, crept gingerly onto the bridge. A pair of horsemen followed in similar fashion. They stepped forward, inspecting the timbers as they came, until they reached the midpoint, directly above the churning Isk. All four then turned and made their way quickly back to the shelter of the fortifications. Footsoldiers ran up carrying a pair of metal cressets with conical rain hats. These were erected at the head of the bridge, filled, and set to burning so that Demon's Bridge was illuminated throughout the night. No further moves were made by the Khimmurians that day.

While sufficient light still held Sir Vicore scrambled back down to rejoin his men south of the bridge.

The evening grew chill. In the Khimmurian meadow-camp, and along the road, fires burned. The smell of cooking wafted into the clear air as the army took its evening meal. The Chol fighters ate cold food and huddled for the night in blankets and furs beneath make-shift shelters, concealed among the trees. The morning dawned misty and damp. Sir Vicore moved up to observe the bridge again. Tension was high. Today, almost certainly, the Khimmurians would attempt to cross.

From the Khimmurian camp a single wagon rolled up the road. Out of it were unloaded structures of wickerwork and timber. These were assembled to make a pair of movable shelters large enough to contain a squad of soldiers.

A platoon of infantry slipped cautiously across the bridge, shields at the fore. On the southern side they took up defensive positions. More followed and moved into the trees and rocks. Sir Vicore's men, concealed well back from the bridge, made no move. They were as yet in no danger of being sighted, though the two teams of saboteurs, dug-in on both sides only fifty yards from the bridge, were now in much closer proximity to the enemy infantry.

With the bridgehead secured the Khimmurians showed no inclination to further explore the surrounding terrain. On the north shore men slipped beneath the movable shelters. Like huge crabs the shelters shuffled forward, one a little behind the other as the way was of insufficient width to permit them to proceed abreast.

Sir Vicore watched, waited, prepared at any moment to give the signal to attack. The men beneath the shelters he assumed to be engineers set to inspect the timbers before an attempt was made to bring anything of bulk across the chasm. As it stood the bridge was still capable of supporting almost any load, but at his signal, with minimal effort, the entire span could be brought down. Timing was crucial to create the greatest disruption to the Khimmurian army while providing the Chol with every possible advantage.

The shelters moved fitfully towards the southern shore; from time to time a head poked out to peer down over the railings of the bridge to the supports beneath. Now the engineers were almost over the concealed works. If any were to spot the damage it would be these men. And if they failed, would they descend for a closer examination beneath the span?

They reached the southern side. The two shelters shuffled together that their occupants might confer, then made their way quickly back again to the waiting troops. The engineers came from their cover. Further discussion followed with the Khimmurian officers. A rider galloped back down the pass to the camp.

Minutes passed. Veils of mist swirled down from the heights to the northwest. They curled across the meadows, up into the pass. Visibility was reduced to mere yards, and with the mist came a light cold drizzle.

Little could be seen around Demon's Bridge, though the silence indicated no renewed Khimmurian activity. The Chol covered their bows to protect the strings from the damp. After a short interval the drizzle ceased and the mist dispersed. Brittle golden sunlight burned down, creating dazzling mirrors of the moisture upon the road and vegetation.

A curious company was seen approaching Demon's Bridge along the pass: five box wagons drawn by teams of bullocks. Each wagon carried a seemingly identical load, large and rectangular in shape, shrouded in tarpaulin. Escorting the wagons was a troop of light cavalry in tan-and-red uniforms.

'Sommarians,' said Sir Vicore in a harsh whisper. 'I was not aware that they had been deployed in Chol.'

The officer beside him nodded. 'Nor I. And I wonder, what is it that they carry hidden on their wagons?'

The wagons halted at the bridge. Behind them a body of Khimmurian infantry had marched up from the camp and waited now upon the road.

'No doubt we will discover soon enough,' whispered Sir Vicore. 'I sense that the time for battle is nigh.'

He glanced upwards to a clifftop high above and to the west. There, unseen, two Chol waited beside a beacon, ready at a signal relayed from below to set it alight. Smoke from the beacon would inform Count Vess, should he not be aware from activities within the Khimmurian camp, that the battle for Demon's Bridge had commenced.

The first of the Sommarian wagons rumbled slowly onto the bridge, the bullocks guided by men upon the ground. Soldiers walked ahead of it, checking for signs of weakness in the timbers.

Sir Vicore watched, calculating, nervous, intrigued. He was aware of many eyes fixed upon him as his men awaited his order. Should he attack now, to bring down the bridge before the wagons had crossed, or wait in order to isolate the wagons? The cargo was significant, that was certain. Khimmur was taking a risk in allowing it over so early. It must certainly be a deliberate ploy. What if soldiers were hidden beneath those shrouds? He considered, and dismissed it. Five wagons could not contain sufficient troops to threaten his men waiting in ambush.

So, then, should he wait, and allow all five to cross? If he then sprang the ambush the wagons, with the bridge down, would be isolated. His men might gain their cargo, and if not they could certainly ensure that Lord Marsinenicon was deprived of it.

The first wagon reached the southern side and halted. A second was brought up.

'Sir,' the officer beside him urged. 'We should attack.'

Sir Vicore hesitated, brow furrowed, his lips drawn taut. Everything focused upon this moment.

'Sir, what is your order? Do we attack now?'

'No!' He clenched hard the pommel of his sword. 'We wait, and let them cross!'

It was to prove a fateful decision, compounded by events as yet unsuspected that were to befall Count Vess and his eight hundred men in the woods to the northeast.


IV


Upon departing Demon's Bridge Count Vess had marched his men south towards Coul until they reached a point where the hills fell away and the land became more even. Here they left the road to swing north again behind a row of hills to the east. Utilising woodland and valleys of fairly gentle nature, they made good headway. Twenty-four hours after leaving Demon's Bridge they were well within reach once more of the craggy Isk valley and the Coul Road along which the enemy army approached.

They marched to a position which would enable them to close quickly upon the Khimmurian rear flank once the army arrived in the meadows. Beneath the cover of woods they had made camp. Count Vess, though doubtful that Lord Marsinenicon would send scouts so deep into hostile countryside, nevertheless passed an order forbidding the lighting of campfires, the erecting of tents, and emphasising that as far as possible silence be maintained. Chol rangers were then sent forward to observe the road and report on the enemy's advance.

But unbeknown to Count Vess his own movements had been observed. A lone horseman, seated high on a northeastern ridge where no enemy was thought to be, watched with interest as the eight hundred trooped up the valley and entered the woods at its head. As the Chol made their camp the horseman turned his mount and rode away, back into the northeast.

Lord Hhubith of Poisse in Khimmur was a heavy-jowled, dour-countenanced man, born to the sword, the proud descendant of one of Khimmur's most notable families. He had smiled shrewdly to himself at the news brought in by his scout. His long overland toil was vindicated. He wondered, not for the first time, in admiration at the insight of his King who had ordered him south via this route.

Lord Hhubith's force was two thousand strong, consisting predominantly of infantry. His present position was less than ten miles from Count Vess's camp.

Without delay he had sent observers forward to spy on the Chol, and a mounted messenger back overland towards the Coul/Postor road, there to ride south in the hope of contacting Lord Marsinenicon's army.

The following day a Chol ranger had returned to camp to inform Count Vess of Lord Marsinenicon's approach. In accordance with Chol anticipations the Khimmurian army entered the wide valley north of Demon's Bridge and established camp in the meadows. Count Vess moved further north, to deploy in woods three miles from the enemy camp. From there, observing circumstance and opportunity, he would edge his men nearer in preparation for a full assault when the attack upon Demon's Bridge began.

At the bridge the fifth wagon creaked towards the southern shore. The first three, with a small escort of Sommarian soldiers, had rolled on perhaps seventy or eighty yards along the road, then halted. The fifth came to rest in front of the bridge. A Sommarian officer strode forward.

Sir Vicore raised his hand to give the signal. He hesitated yet: there was movement among the Khimmurian officers on the far bank. Would someone of rank cross, to join the men this side of the bridge? It would be an added prize.

The soldiers beside the wagons turned and began to march back towards the bridge, leaving two men beside each wagon. Sir Vicore frowned: so vulnerable! He was suddenly afraid.

Without warning there was uproar on the north side of the river. The Khimmurian troops that had formed up on the road behind the wagons were charging forward, with yells and shouts, brandishing their weapons. They surged straight towards the bridge. Others, further downstream, scrambled into the chasm itself.

Sir Vicore's hand fell, his attention distracted for a moment from the wagons. A Chol horn blew. From cover all around arrows showered down towards the soldiers by the bridge.

But simultaneous with the Khimmurian charge the Sommarian officer had barked an order. In unison the men at the wagons peeled back the tarpaulins. The mysterious cargo was revealed: huge cages made of sturdy metallic mesh. Within each tawny shapes moved. Even as the tarpaulins came off, sprung doors on the cages flew open. Out onto the road leapt great hunting lions, twenty-five in number, sleek and powerful. The Sommarian officer yelled, gesticulating. Ignoring the friendly troops by the road the lions bounded for the slopes where the Chol were hidden.

High above a torch was put to the Chol beacon.

The Khimmurians at the bridge were well-organised. As the Chol arrows fell they held their positions behind their big shields. They made no attempt to engage the Chol, other than to loose their own shafts when a target presented itself.

Sir Vicore stared in horror. Already, within the first few seconds, his strategy had gone badly awry. The bridge was to have been pulled and his men then move in upon the stranded Khimmurians. But the trained lions were already among his troops, creating panic and forcing many of the Chol to abandon their assault upon the Khimmurians in order to deal with this more lethal foe.

And the bridge had not fallen!

On the one side the supports had come away cleanly; but on the other something had jammed. The bridge listed dangerously, but it still held sufficiently to permit men to cross. The team of Chol saboteurs heaved upon the ropes, struggling to bring the structure down. But now they too were distracted. Sir Vicore, his eyes alighting on the Sommarian officer beside the road, realised that this man was somehow directing the lions. From the nearest of the wagons three of the great beasts made straight for the Chol trenches.

Sir Vicore pointed at the Sommarian. 'There! That man! Bring him down!'

But the officer, his job done, now ran to where his own men crouched. Their shields opened and he vanished into cover.

There were screams from the Chol in the trenches as the lions leapt upon them. All hope now of bringing down the bridge was dashed as they fought for their lives. Men scrambled from cover and ran, to be picked off by enemy bowmen.

Higher up the slopes Chol had already died, others struggled desperately against the huge cats. Though the lions were few in number they were evidently well-trained, each in effect counting for more than ten men. Several were already slain or severely wounded, but too many Chol were forced to deal with those that remained.

With his heart pounding Sir Vicore acknowledged the worst. Khimmurian infantry were clambering over the sagging bridge, clinging hard to the unstable timbers. Many were felled by Chol arrows, but several now were gaining the south road. Others were in the chasm, grappling with ropes, irons, poles and logs, working furiously to establish footways across the Isk. By the time the lions were dealt with, Sir Vicore knew, the enemy would have crossed the river in strength. He had lost the element of surprise. Already the Chol had taken dozens of casualties. With or without Count Vess's support, the bridge was lost.

Sir Vicore stared about him in hollow-eyed devastation. This final strike against the enemy had turned upon its head, been transformed into a humiliating débâcle. The blame was his. He had hesitated, seeking the greater victory. Now he could only watch as valiant Chol fighters, with whom he had fought many battles, were brought down before him.

His one hope was to preserve his remaining troops. He turned and bawled the order to withdraw.

North of the pass further carnage ensued.

Count Vess and his eight hundred, hidden within the woods fringing the wide meadows, observed sudden activity in the Khimmurian camp. Khimmurian soldiers in their hundreds were rushing forward, leaving the camp to make for the pass. Glancing to a high ridge beyond, Count Vess spied the first slow curls of smoke climbing into the blue. Immediately he passed the order to assault the camp. An area had been preselected on the southern perimeter. There the Khimmurians had constructed a gate, around which defences appeared relatively weak. Dozens of baggage wagons and carts were assembled just within, and if these could be hit, and as many nearby Khimmurians as possible slain, it could prove a major setback to the enemy army.

To gain this area meant leaving the trees to cross a hundred yards or so of relatively open land. Some minimal cover was available in the form of small grassy hillocks and shallow gulleys, plus a few scattered trees. But approaching from the north the Chol would be invisible to the main body of Khimmurians, which was marshalling at the other end of the camp.

The Chol poured from the woods. They had covered thirty yards before the first arrows flew from behind the palisade. They charged on undeterred. But now there came renewed activity within the Khimmurian camp. From the wagons and carts soldiers suddenly appeared, running to reinforce the guards at the palisade. Similarly from the rows of tents set further back came soldiers ready and equipped for battle.

As yet unsuspecting of what this heralded, the Chol eight hundred swarmed forward. Arrows began flying into their ranks from the rear, out of the very woods they had just left. Dozens of Chol fell in the open fields before it was realised that they were under assault not only from the camp but simultaneously from behind.

At last the presence of the second Khimmurian force under Lord Hhubith was realised. The Chol charge began to falter. Men panicked, tried to run back to the woods to regain their former positions, and were picked off by Lord Hhubith's men. And now the Khimmurians at the south of the meadow, who had been making ostensibly for Demon's Bridge, suddenly swung around. In tight battle array they bore down upon the stricken Chol.

Trapped there in the open between three hostile forces Count Vess's men had little hope. As the sun glared down from its lofty azure reach, raising thin tendrils of mist from the damp meadows, they were slaughtered. Count Vess died, a spear penetrating his mail shirt, toppling him from his horse and bursting through his chest and back to pin his body to the earth. The eight hundred were annihilated almost to the man. The green meadows north of Demon's Bridge were stained red with their blood as the smoke from an abandoned beacon curled languidly into the sky.

Sir Vicore, by dint of a speedy retreat into the countryside, saved most of his small band of warriors. Days later they arrived at Drurn March, demoralised and disgraced, to report the news to the Prince Regent that Southern Chol belonged to Khimmur.

With this Fhir Oube knew that Drurn March was no longer secure. Prisoners would certainly have been taken. Loyal though they might be to Chol, he did not doubt that the facts of his whereabouts and details of the force he commanded would be quickly elicited. He was faced with a simple decision: to remain where he was and face inevitable siege, or to leave Chol and withdraw along the only remaining road, east, into Qotolr.

V

Dalwood village in Virland had itself been the scene of unusual activity at about this time.

At the end of a long day during which the sun had not once penetrated the dense cloud which lay over the great Magoth Forest, one hundred and thirty foreign slaves formed up in the dimming light on the track they themselves had cleared. Exhausted and begrimed, they were counted by their Khimmurian guards, then began their weary trudge back to the Dalwood stockade.

From the cover of the trees flew arrows. Men dropped, first with barely a sound, then with groans and cries of alarm.

The slaves watched, stunned, as their gaolers were assailed with darting shafts. In seconds it was over. Men in leathers and greens came from the undergrowth and engaged with sword or axe those few Khimmurians still standing. They removed the slaves' fetters and urged them to take weapons from the fallen guards. Then, unrestrained, the former slaves continued on towards Dalwood in company with their rescuers.

At Dalwood they found the stockade burning. A surprise attack by a force of one hundred or so men, led by a warrior who fought like a devil with long grey hair and flowing sidewhiskers and moustache, had quickly overrun the garrison. The fighting had been sudden and fierce, and the Khimmurians, lulled by long months of routine and boredom, had been ill-prepared and slack. They had fought bravely, but were nevertheless soon overcome. The survivors were now gathered in a ragged knot in a clearing beside the track, ringed by armed warriors.

As the erstwhile slaves gathered round, as yet bemused and uncertain of their freedom or what it entailed, the grey-haired warrior climbed upon a felled tree to address them. He gazed upon the haggard faces, lit by the flickering orange of the flames that consumed the nearby stockade.

'I am Yzwul, rightful dhoma-lord of Tiancz in the province of Mystoph in Khimmur. It is my privilege and pleasure to tell you that you are again free men, at liberty to go where you choose and do as you will.'

There was a brief silence. Men cowed by brutality and deprivation sought to find expression for their emotions. Then, quite suddenly a rousing cheer went up. Those who held weapons thrust them high.

Lord Yzwul waited until he could again be heard, then continued: 'Those of you who wish may join our band.

You will be required to swear an oath, as we have done, to fight with us and for us, unceasingly, giving of your lives if necessary, in order to end the oppression that grips our homelands. You will be provided with weapons and equipment, taken just now from this stockade along with its stores and livestock. Or, if you prefer, you may leave now with my goodwill, to return to your homes and families. But if the latter is your choice, be warned: the world is not as you knew it. Khimmur is everywhere, and you may too easily find yourselves recaptured and returned to slavery.'

He jumped down from the tree-trunk in order to inspect the prisoners, who numbered perhaps twenty in all. They stood before him, some sullen, some shifting and uneasy, one or two attempting an unconvincing display of disdain or indifference.

'It gives me no pleasure to confront you thus, my own countrymen, my enemies,' said Yzwul. 'You, Egil Falmane from Su'um S'ol, and you, Dain M'kan from Sigath: I know you well. And who is this? You, corsan of this gang of sorry brigands; your name escapes me, but I have you marked as a disciplined officer and a skilled soldier. Fate has dealt an unfair hand that we should meet in these circumstances.'

The corsan whom Yzwul had addressed raised his head contemptuously. 'We are Khimmurians, loyal to our King. And you, Yzwul, whom once I admired, are a cur who has betrayed his country. I revile you, thoroughly.'

He tilted his head and spat upon the grass. Yzwul maintained an impassive mien. The soldier named Dain M'kan stepped forward, his features strained, his voice beseeching. 'Lord Yzwul, do not assume this attitude to be ours to the man. We are simply soldiers who have followed the orders of our commanders, as was our duty.

267

Give us the opportunity to prove ourselves and we will gladly join you and make our weapons yours.'

Lord Yzwul turned back to the erstwhile slaves. 'What say you? You have lived in thralldom under these men, and are better qualified than I to assess them now. They were your illegal jailers, aye, but now the tables have been turned. Was their treatment of you fair and just, or did they in any way exceed the bounds of soldierly duty?'

Cries and jeers came from the former slaves. 'Hang them! They beat and starved us! They should not be allowed to live!'

A man stepped forward, thin as a rake, his eyes hollow and moist. He pointed a shaking finger at the soldier Dain M'kan. 'Was it duty when before my very eyes you beat my brother until he died?'

'He was refusing to work!' cried the soldier.

'He was too weak to work!' snapped back his accuser. 'He collapsed upon the ground with no strength remaining in his limbs. Why, he could not even stand!' He wheeled upon another of the prisoners, tears in his eyes. 'And you, who from sheer perversity wielded your whip so freely and indiscriminately. How now do you defend yourself?'

More cries came. 'And what of those who starved to death while you gorged yourselves upon venison and roast pheasant? And those who froze in winter while just yards away you warmed your toes before your fires?'

The prisoners moved closer together, a woeful-looking bunch. Yzwul raised his hands. 'Are all these men then guilty of crimes against you? I ask you, look closely at each of the prisoners assembled here. Enemies in war they may be, but that in itself is not a crime that demands their lives in reparation. Is not one of them deserving of your mercy?'

The cries and accusations grew more vehement. Some of the former slaves were overcome with emotion, weeping openly as they recounted the injustices perpetrated against them and their wives and children by the Khimmurians. Eventually, having heard enough, Yzwul turned and strode away. He passed orders to his men, 'Bring ropes. Hang these reptiles from the trees and let us begone.'

Similar scenes were enacted elsewhere in western Virland. Four more slave camps were liberated, and in each instance words of mercy for the Khimmurian guards were not easily come by. With reluctance Lord Yzwul was obliged to continue with the business of executing his own countrymen. In all, less than thirty Khimmurian guards were held blameless, out of more than one hundred taken prisoner. These were stripped to their undertunics and sent west upon the road to Khimmur.


VI


News of these events was received by the Vulpasmage as he arrived at Mlanje in Mystoph, preparatory to riding on south to Ghence in the wake of the army led by Orl Kilroth. First came word of Shimeril's daring raid upon the H'padir wagons. Later on the same day followed the news of the liberation of the Virland slavegangs, for both actions had been timed to coincide as nearly as possible.

In flesh and blood the monster that was the Beast of Rull was still the man, King Oshalan of Khimmur. But the body, powerful and erect, held an unusual tension and seemed almost to vibrate with a terrible prepotency. The flesh of the once-handsome face had

269

grown grey and deeply seamed. The features were twisted and contorted into a near-chronic expression of agonised fury; the eyes burned with a predatory glare, red-rimmed and sunken; the mouth was set into a taut grimace. The hair, once lustrous, was left unbound and untrimmed, allowed to grow wild and uncared for. To any capable of reading the truth, it was as if mind and body were insufficient vessels to contain the energies of the creature that now possessed them.

The Vulpasmage gave ear intently as the news was recounted, rage visibly mounting. The message-bearer was a minor aide, no doubt bullied into his task by superiors too fearful to deliver such dire news themselves. When he had done the Vulpasmage wheeled upon him, taking brief perverse amusement at the sight of the poor fellow cowering back, blanch-faced.

He addressed his relative, the commander of his personal guard, Count Genelb Phan. 'Send troops into Virland, to the villages where the deeds were done. Round up every man, woman and child and hang them from the trees beside the road. Their bodies will dangle there till they drop. All who pass that way may know what it is to defy me.'

Count Phan stiffened to attention, tilted his head in a stiff bow, and departed. Khimmur's King turned back to the message-bearer. 'You, what is your name?'

The man stuttered and stammered. 'Sire, your Grace, if it pleases you, my name is Croman.'

'Whether it pleases me is of no account. Your station?'

'Sire, I am an under-secretary to the chamberlain of this house in which you now reside.'

The Vulpasmage gave a mordant laugh. 'And where just now is the chamberlain, or the head footman, one of whom would surely have been a more apposite message-bringer than an insignificant clerk like yourself?'

'Sire, I do not know. At present they are both engaged in other duties.'

'Then return to your masters. Inform them both that they are relieved of their posts, as of this moment. They may report forthwith to the courtyard outside, where an expert will await them. Under his guidance they will learn quickly the cost of their cowardice. You, Croman, I appoint chamberlain of this house. Now begone.'

Stammering and bowing, scarcely able to believe what he heard, Croman departed. Already he was forgotten. The Vulpasmage turned and strode to stare out of a window.

*Shimeril!*

Retaliation against the Master of Paladins and his band of rebels was effected less easily in Mystoph than in Virland. It served no purpose to alienate the populace here, on home territory. Though a war of propaganda had earlier been launched, damning Shimeril and Yzwul and their followers, and rewards offered for information leading to their arrest, they had brought no favourable result. All attempts to turn the people against 'The Windmill', as Shimeril had become known, to gain informers or infiltrate spies had failed. Magic had been employed, but it had revealed nothing that would lead to Shimeril's whereabouts. Bound spirit allies occupying the bodies of wild beasts and birds had roamed the countryside, but had likewise failed to unearth the rebels.

Shimeril's activities indicated that he maintained no permanent camp. He was too cunning and experienced to make serious mistakes; and his intimate knowledge of Khimmur and its ways declared him a dangerous foe. At present he was not strong, but if he gained more support . . . Somehow Shimeril had to be caught, the wind taken from the Windmill's sails.

But for now a decision as to how best to respond to his latest impudences was postponed.

The following day there arrived word from the dhoma-lords Hhubith and Marsinenicon of their victory over the Chol at Demon's Bridge. The Vulpasmage's wrath was somewhat salved. Briefly the anguished face of King Oshalan was transformed into an expression of glee-filled triumph. Straightway he made preparations to leave. Now, undistracted, the Beast of Rull could ride at the head of his armies for Ghence, to engineer and witness its final collapse.

## VI

Into Dalwood Khimmurian soldiers rode. The village was cordoned-off, that none might leave. The soldiers smashed their way into every dwelling, to haul out the foresters and their kin. But the houses they discovered to be empty. The villagers had gone.

Elsewhere in the region the story was the same. The small, scattered communities had gathered everything they could carry and vanished, deep into the protective heart of the great Magoth. Not even domestic animals remained. Western Virland had been evacuated.

Tales were later told of the soldiers who penetrated the forest in search of the Vir. One group was annihilated when it came under ambush from forest fighters led, it was claimed, by a warrior with long grey hair and flowing sidewhiskers and moustache. A second party was said to have stumbled into a swamp, where dire creatures rose to engulf them. Folk speak of their screams lingering there still, held in strange stasis above the unnatural air of the swamp. Any who venture now into that part of the Magoth may, if perfect conditions prevail, hear again the cries of the dying soldiers.

Other parties, more fortunate, returned empty-handed, and Khimmur made no further attempt to locate the missing villagers of Virland.

# 10

The passage through the mountain was long and unbroken, with frequent variations of elevation, and occasional sweeps or sudden corners. It extended for miles, a single great wormhole driven through the rock.

Shadd proceeded, guided by the Stepforth which floated before him, illuminating the way with a frail but clear, moonlike luminescence. The roof of the tunnel was high enough to enable Shadd to walk erect; the rock walls he could brush with his fingers as he walked. The dimensions were unchanging, save for those occasions when the tunnel opened into natural chambers or caverns of rock. The floor beneath his feet was harsh stone, sometimes hewn into rough steps as the way steepened, and from time to time giving way to sand or gravel beds.

Shadd marvelled at the hands that had created this way through the mountain – for it was most certainly not a natural occurrence. The way had been bored not through mere earth but through solid rock. No evidence existed of excavations for ore or mineral extraction, nor were there any branching shafts. On occasion he passed massive beams of timber shoring up the roof or walls, but for the most part the tunnel appeared secure and without hazard – a secret way, built for the sole purpose of providing access between Mesmia's tower above the Lake of Clouds, and the land on the other side of the Gro'd f'ho Ib.

*Gûlro?* Shadd wondered momentarily. He considered

the stocky mountain folk from the north, renowned for their mining and engineering skills. A company was at work even now in the Hulminilli Mountains north of Kemahamek, mining riches for Khimmur. But Shadd dismissed the thought. Throughout known history the Gûlro had not ventured this far from their homelands. That a group was as far southeast as the Hulminilli was explained by recent civil strife at home. But this passage was no recent construct. And, he believed, its accomplishment surpassed even the bounds of Gûlro abilities. Men would have taken centuries to chip and drill their way through here, even if such a feat were possible. And nowhere did he see the impressions of man-made tools scored into the rock.

No, this seemed to be the work of a greater force, something ancient and formidable. Something, hope-fully, no longer in existence, or at least beyond the reach of any man to command.

Within the mountain the air was cold and eddyless, but Shadd worked up a sweat as he walked. The light of the Stepforth extended only a few feet before him; beyond and all around was a wall of enclosing blackness, so intense as to appear solid. He wondered, with a tingle of unease, what he would do were the light of the Stepforth for some reason to fail.

He had walked for perhaps three hours. The passage dipped, Shadd felt the soft resistance of sand beneath his feet. The way grew more level and opened into a small rock chamber. The Stepforth showed walls of orange-red stone. From a crevice above Shadd's head a dribble of water ran down the wall, collected into a pool beside the path, then scurried across the path and away into the chamber.

Shadd paused to rest and take stock, seating himself on a ledge of rock and taking out food and his water sack. He ate in pensive silence, absorbed in the motion

of the little stream at his feet. Presently he took the
hylozote from its pouch and placed it upon the ledge
beside him.

'What opinion, if any, did you form of Mesmia?' he
asked.

'I am uncertain of her. My impression is that she
speaks truth, but not all of it. She is wily, deceptive,
and is keeping something back. There is something
she did not wish you to know.'

Shadd nodded. 'My sentiments, also. Do you believe
I am in danger?'

'There is little doubt that danger exists in this undertaking. But at this juncture I do not think it derives from
the Drear-hag. My feeling was that she is anxious for you
to succeed, though I cannot help but feel that her moti-
vations may not precisely correspond with your own.'

'Aye, there is a mystery here. And I am ever fearful
that no matter what course I take I will bring disaster
upon those I would hope to aid.'

'You speak like a man doomed or cursed by another.'

'That is perhaps what I am.'

'Then are you not committed on this course?'

'I am committed. But I fear that my hopes, my
dreams, my good intentions are but instruments to be
manipulated in secret by a mind that is not my own,
and corrupted into base things which cause suffering
and death.'

'Ah, that would explain it, then,' said the hylozote.

'Explain what?'

'Your glum countenance. I have not yet seen you
smile, nor do you engage in small talk or banter,
which is the stuff of common exchange between all
other persons I have observed. In truth, I have you
marked as a serious fellow indeed.'

At this Shadd could not suppress a quiver of a smile.
'Am I such a dull companion, then, hylozote? If so you

have only to say the word and I will gladly relieve you of the burden of my company forthwith!'

'Ah, not so! Not so at all, Duke Shadd. Indeed, I could not have hoped for a more interesting companion. I find you sympathetic and engaging. And I am intrigued, to say the least, by your circumstances and your apparent courtship with Fate.'

'Good. It would be vexing indeed to think that eternity passed in the gloom of this subterranean passage might be preferable to another minute spent in my company!'

'Quite so!'

Shadd chewed thoughtfully, his mood somewhat lifted by the hylozote's gentle ribbing. He drank a deep draught of water from his sack, said, 'Aye, perhaps you are right. Mayhap my curse is only that I am too deeply immersed in weighty concerns. But I would argue that they are not of my own making.'

'Sometimes the mere consideration of his concerns can be sufficient to distract a man and drag him down to a level where he is beaten before he ever confronts their substance.'

'There is some truth in that, and it echoes words spoken to me quite recently by a man whom I believed honourable. He said that often we may interpret confusing circumstances by their appearance, which in truth may scarcely resemble their actuality.'

'Then that man was no fool. Yet I detect an edge of bitterness, of cynicism in your voice.'

Shadd expelled a long breath of air into the gloom of the chamber. 'I later learned that that man planned to betray me. He pretended friendship while secretly planning to barter me with my enemies.'

The hylozote was silent for a moment, then said, 'May I ask how you learned of this betrayal, Duke Shadd?'

Briefly, Shadd recounted the events in Drurn March fortress which had led to his escape and subsequent adventures.

'Then you have no real proof of the Prince Regent's intention to betray you,' observed the hylozote when he had done.

'The evidence is circumstantial, it is true – '

'No – forgive me, Duke Shadd, but it is not. You have no evidence, only the word of another, a woman whom you do not know.'

'Fhir Oube is a desperate man, reduced by harsh circumstance. Such a course would be not unreasonable; indeed, as he viewed it, it was perhaps his only hope. I do not consider him dishonourable. He sought to save his nation and its people; and I, who am a criminal in my country's eyes, was the means by which he might do so.'

'Perhaps. But firm evidence is still lacking. Do not misconstrue me: I think you took the correct course in escaping, for I cannot see that there was anything to be gained from your remaining in the Chol fortress. But, I must repeat, you do not know what Fhir Oube planned.'

Shadd swallowed. 'Very well. I will admit, the notion of Fhir Oube as my betrayer does not sit easily or pleasantly in my mind.'

'Then let us, with caution, suspend judgement until we are better placed to judge.'

'So be it.' Shadd turned his head to gaze down upon the hylozote, and again a half-smile came to his lips. 'You are a profound fellow indeed, for a lump of stone.'

'I have had ample time for reflection. And you, Duke Shadd, though somewhat the thrall of your emotions, are nevertheless not grossly insensible – for an assemblage of meat, bone and tacky fluids.'

Shadd capped his water sack and returned his uneaten food to his pack. 'Now, what of our uninvited companion, hylozote—the shadow-that-is-not-a-shadow? I have wondered whether it still dogs my footsteps since we left the enchanted glade?'

The hylozote's voice, when it came, was stiff and hesitant, devoid of the humour of moments ago. 'I – er, I did believe it to have followed us after we left the glade. I thought also to have spied a certain unnatural motion upon the stones at the lake-shore. After that, well, I cannot say.'

'Overall you seem less than confident.'

Again the hylozote faltered. 'Duke Shadd, I have a confession.'

Shadd raised his eyebrows, noting the tremor in the hylozote's voice. 'Speak, then.'

'I realise now that, quite unintentionally, I made false representation of myself to you.'

'How so?'

'In the enchanted glade, I indicated, in good faith, that I was capable of perceiving actualities that you could not.'

'And you then demonstrated the veracity of your claim.'

'I did, but I am guilty of having failed to take into account the precise factors contributing to my enhanced sight. You see, I now realise that there was a very good reason why I was able to spot the intrusive shadow so readily. It was because of the age I had spent within that glade.'

'A period of well over two thousand years, if I remember correctly,' said Shadd.

'Yes. And in that time, unable to move, I had little to do with myself but gaze upon my surroundings. Over the centuries, then, quite naturally, an awareness evolved within me – an acute and encompassing intimacy with the landscape around me. I became aware of every leaf, every blade of grass, every pebble or grain of soil – and every shadow – that existed within that glade. With the changes of seasons, the vagaries of weather, I still knew that glade to the last minute detail. Any intrusion, no matter how small or insignificant, was an event that registered itself immediately upon my consciousness.'

Understanding dawned. Shadd nodded to himself. 'And removed from that familiar environment you find that your apprehension of the world has become somewhat more selective; the minutiae of a place or situation no longer impinge so forcefully upon your senses.'

'That is correct. Duke Shadd, I spoke and acted with sincerity, but I realise that I have misled you. You will perhaps no longer consider me a fit companion. I will harbour no grudge, therefore, if you choose now to part company with me. It would be regrettable from my point of view, but I would quite understand your decision.'

'It does rather alter the terms of our relationship,' said Shadd stiffly.

The hylozote's voice quavered. 'I would ask but one thing.'

'What is that?'

'That you do not discard me here, in this dank and gloomy tunnel, where nothing lives or moves. Rather, if you can but tolerate my company for a short while longer, could you not leave me in a place where there is at least a view, a prospect of some kind which can to some small degree engage my senses?'

'Considering the circumstances, it is a great deal to ask.'

'I understand that, but I appeal to you, trusting you to be not a cruel or callous man.'

Shadd's stern countenance broke; his frown dissolved.

280

'Fear not, hylozote. I know you did not speak dishonestly. And I value your clear-sightedness, and believe yet that you have awareness where I have not. Furthermore, I may still come to rely upon you. Should the light of this Stepforth fail, then you, who perceive without light, could become my eyes and guide me from this rock tomb. And as it happens, I enjoy your company. It would sadden me to part company with so unique a companion.'

'I am relieved that you feel that way,' said the hylozote.

Shadd slipped down from the ledge and proceeded to remove his furs and blanket from his pack. 'Now tell me, hylozote, do you sleep?'

'Sleep, Duke Shadd?'

'Yes, sleep. Do you at any time relinquish consciousness in order to gain rest?'

'What need have I of rest? I am at all times alert. Have you ever known a stone to grow tired through exerting itself?'

'As I thought.' Shadd spread the furs upon the rock ledge. 'I, who am but meat, bone and tacky fluids, need rest at regular intervals. Such a time is now. I wish to sleep, briefly. Would you then keep watch, alert me to any danger, and if none threatens awaken me when approximately three hours have passed?'

'Gladly.'

Shadd stretched upon the ledge and covered himself with his Aphesuk cloak and blanket. 'Then I bid you goodnight.'


II


He awoke in the clammy cave air, aware of the harsh chill of the place, yet kept warm by his precious cloak

281

which was of a fabric and weave which enabled it to both reflect or absorb heat. The hylozote's voice sounded in his ear.

'Three hours have passed, Duke Shadd.'

Shadd sat up, briefly centred and focused his mind in meditation taught him by elders of the Aphesuk tribe with whom, deep in the Endless Desert, he had passed so much of his youth. Quickly he shook off the blear of sleep. An additional technique set his blood to flowing and brought alertness and precision to his thoughts. He hopped down onto the sand and ran swiftly through a discipline of exercises to relieve the sluggishness of his limbs, then gathered his belongings, returned the hylozote to its pouch, and resumed his journey.

The passage bore on, as if without end, into the mountain's core. Shadd's footsteps and the sound of his breathing were all that broke the silence. The sounds were exaggerated, amplified, reverberating from the rock.

The hylozote spoke. 'Duke Shadd, while you slept I have been communicating with the Stepforth.'

Shadd ceased walking. 'Communicating? Is this Stepforth possessed of intelligence, then, like yourself?'

'That is very much the case, though she is not precisely like myself. A Stepforth is not her natural form. She is a Gwynad, a fairy-creature. Her name is Temminee. Many years ago she found herself the prisoner of a rogue imp named Twando, a wicked fellow, who sought to have his way with her. She resisted by means both subtle and direct, and despite all his efforts her captor failed to impose his will upon her. In fury Twando bound her by powerful magic into a new form, the Stepforth, and gave her away. I am the first being she has spoken with since that time.'

'I had no idea,' said Shadd. 'I will speak with her. Temminee – '

He was interrupted by the hylozote. 'Forgive me, Duke Shadd, but in her current form Temminee is dumb. It would appear that fortune has brought us into one another's company, for my consciousness and hers are in natural attunement. If you will permit me, then, I will be pleased to act as your go-between.'

'Then please tell Temminee of my concern at learning of her plight. Is there a way of unbinding the magic that holds her?'

'Indeed there is,' replied the hylozote after a pause. 'The great cruelty of Twando's spell lay in the simplicity with which it might be broken but which, due to the muteness inflicted upon Temminee, she might never reveal. She has only to be allowed to remain in light for a full day and she will return to her original form.'

'And Mesmia cautioned me to keep the Stepforth always in darkness when not in use,' murmured Shadd, resuming his pace. 'Surely then, Mesmia knows of this.'

'According to Temminee, that is so. Twando gave the Stepforth to Mesmia in return for a small favour. Mesmia had no reason to believe you could communicate with the Stepforth. As long as you obeyed her instruction none would be the wiser.'

'Tell Temminee this: The moment we step from this passage into light I will release her from service to me. As a measure of security, to ensure that none interferes with her, I will, if she wishes, carry her with me in full daylight for as long as she requires to complete her transformation. She will then be free to do as she wishes. Or if she prefers I will place her somewhere of her own choosing and leave her there.'

The hylozote relayed his message. 'She offers you

her most profound gratitude, Duke Shadd. As a token of her thanks she has asked me to inform you of something. The crystal that you wear around your neck, which was given to you by Mesmia – Temminee says it is a most valuable and powerful object.'

Unconsciously Shadd's hand went to the stone on the chain. 'I have sensed a subtle resonance. What does Temminee know of it?'

'It is called the Soul Crystal. It belonged to her people, the Gwynad. To them it is a sacred object, held in reverence. Long ago it was taken from them during a time of great strife.'

'Taken? By Mesmia?'

'It is not known who stole it, or to where it was taken. Temminee believes it unlikely that Mesmia was the original thief, for the Gwynad had scant contact with her kind. How it came into Mesmia's possession is a mystery.'

'Then what of its properties?' asked Shadd. 'Can Temminee tell me anything of these?'

'She says it is as Mesmia told you. The Soul Crystal has the power to harmonise with and enhance the subtle energies of its bearer. Its full power and the extent to which its resonances can respond are unknown, and perhaps unknowable, for all depends upon the character of the bearer. The most advanced elders of Temminee's race had a greater knowledge of its potential, but they kept it secret, and even they did not know everything. Temminee quotes a line from a sacred Gwynad text: "The Crystal of the Soul gives what is already possessed". She expresses surprise that Mesmia should allow so valuable an object into another's hands.'

'Perhaps she is ignorant of its true value,' mused Shadd.

'She is aware, Temminee says. Do not doubt it.'

'Then it is further proof of her desire for me to succeed.'

'Perhaps so. Yet my earlier reservations are not dispelled. I am wary of her motives. Temminee states that the Drear-hag reveals little of herself, but is a woman of great power.'

Shadd nodded grimly. 'That too is something of which I have little doubt. I am caught in a web of intrigue; a mummer upon another's stage. It has become a familiar role, and one I tire of. But for the present at least I have accepted my part. Ciracar's Warren lies somewhere ahead, and within it the scroll. That is where I must go.'

He fingered the Soul Crystal, observing in the soft glow from the Stepforth the subtle interplay and dispersion of light between its two gems.

'I am grateful to Temminee for her information,' he said. 'Now, behold! There is a change in the quality of the air in this place. It's no longer as stale, nor as still. I feel a draught upon my cheek. Tell Temminee I believe she will soon be rid of her present form, for almost certainly we are approaching the exit from this tunnel.'

Moments later the passage took a slightly upward turn, to reveal, quite suddenly, a ragged oval of brilliant white some twenty paces ahead. Shadd slowed his pace and approached with caution, keeping to the passage wall. So bright was the light that it hurt his eyes to gaze upon it, and he could make out no features beyond the cave mouth.

He stopped, still within the passage, and knelt for cover beside a low stone abutment. There he waited while his eyes adjusted to the light outside and he was able to make out something of the landscape. The passage appeared to open into woodland; dappled green grass and shrubs grew at the entrance. The roof of the cave barred Shadd's vision of the sky, but rays of bright sunlight beamed down between overhead branches at an acute angle, telling him that the time was early morning. The walk from Mesmia's tower had taken longer than he had realised. He listened intently, heard nothing of note, and made to move forward.

To the hylozote he said in an undertone, 'It is perhaps an idea if we maintain silence between ourselves once my guide is met. Until I am certain of this person I would prefer that he or she has no knowledge of you or Temminee. Suggest to Temminee that she try to attach herself closely to my person so that she is inconspicuous while still gaining the light she needs.'

This was done. The Stepforth floated down to a position behind Shadd's shoulder and neck, where she was part-concealed by his long hair and the pack upon his back. Shadd rose and stepped cautiously from the tunnel.

The light still blinded. He screwed up his eyes and shaded them with a hand, ran forward, half-crouching, across the grass to enter the shade of a pendulous mulberry. He knelt beside its trunk, alert, one hand upon a sword-hilt, peering out between the hanging leaves. The sky overhead he saw was clear blue, and he was aware of the warmth of the day, despite the hour and the early season.

The hylozote whispered from its pouch. 'Duke Shadd, the passage!'

Shadd glanced back. A tumble of rock rose behind him at the base of a sheer rock wall. The mouth of the passage from which he had just emerged was not visible. He stared uneasily, reluctant yet to move again. At length, satisfied that he was not observed, or at least not threatened, his curiosity overcame him

He crept from beneath the mulberry and returned to where the passage entrance should have been.

Shadd inspected the rock. It was solid, impenetrable. There was no passage into the cliff face. He clambered onto a boulder to peer behind, but again found no entrance.

From behind him came a baritone laugh, and a voice spoke. 'Don't be alarmed, my friend! The lady merely guards her back door against unwelcome intruders.'

Shadd spun around, drawing his two shortswords. A few yards away a man had stepped from the trees. He was tall, dark-haired, bearded, dressed in light, patched clothing. He stood with his hands upon his hips, grinning broadly. Two daggers hung at his belt and across his back was strapped a weighty battleaxe.

The man strode confidently towards Shadd, raising his hands, open, in a gesture of appeasement. 'Sheathe your weapons, sir, if you will. I mean you no harm. I am Thufor, your guide. It is I who will lead you to Ciracar's Warren.'

He halted, gazing up at Shadd, and the two men appraised one another. Thufor's eyes, brown, keen, artful, took in Shadd's tall, spare figure, his pale skin, now almost wholly free of its darker stain. Seeing Shadd's own eyes Thufor showed no surprise, nor even interest. To a native of Qotolr, no doubt, few things were considered strange.

For his part Shadd saw a swarthy, leather-complexioned man in his thirties, of easy posture and strong but sinewy build. He was a little shorter and somewhat broader than Shadd. His full brown beard covered much of his face. He had a long aquiline nose, craggy features, and eyes that were deep-set and lined. Though Thufor's grin was wide, his gaze had a veiled quality. Shadd was aware of the thoroughness of Thufor's inspection of his person.

Shadd sheathed his swords and leapt down to stand before the newcomer. With a motion of his head he indicated the rock face behind him. 'Is there a means of re-entering the passage?'

'If you return with your mission complete you will find the door open.'

'And if not?'

Thufor produced an indifferent shrug. 'That would depend. There is no other way through the Gro'd f'ho Ib.'

Shadd extended his gaze beyond the nearby trees. The place in which they stood was a small plateau high upon a slope. In the distance, some way below, he glimpsed the varied greens of sunlit meadows and woods. Further beyond, encircling on all sides, mountain peaks rose, purple and misted blue, capped with snow.

'Is it far to our destination?' Shadd enquired.

'With luck on our side we can be there on the morrow,' Thufor said. 'Come, I have horses tethered nearby.'

He turned without waiting for Shadd's response, and marched away through the trees. Shadd cast a final rueful gaze at the rock face behind him, then followed.


III


They made their way on horseback slowly into the valley. The morning grew hot. The rising heat-addled air distorted the landscape, and Shadd was unable to tell whether the distant land features here held the same lack of fixity or solidity that he had experienced earlier.

When they reached the valley floor Thufor led the way north along a meandering dirt track. The way climbed, and as they passed from the valley the terrain underwent an abrupt change. Now they were overshadowed by crags of tortured black rock. The ground was rubble-strewn, and rent with gaping crevices and pits. Pocked, jagged outcrops of rock splayed in irregular 'clumps' as far as the eye could see. Few plants grew, and apart from the occasional basking lizard, and eagles circling high overhead, Shadd saw no sign of life.

Thufor, slowing his mount, leaned back in his saddle, to call out, basso-voiced, 'Tread carefully, my friend. These rocks are as sharp as any blade.'

For two hours or more they picked their way across this treacherous wasteland, speaking little as they concentrated upon safe passage. In due course the rock fell away behind them and they passed onto arid heathland. A wind gusted, driving plumes of choking yellow dust across their path, stinging eyes and clogging nose and throat. Ever present were the mountains, never nearer, never further away, crouched and huddled on all sides.

At midday they paused to eat in a shallow gulley beneath the wind, where a clump of stunted scrub-oaks grew around a seeping spring. Tethering the horses beside the spring, they seated themselves upon rocks and ate lunch from their packs.

Shadd attempted conversation, but Thufor's mood had undergone a change. He had lost the cheerful openness of earlier; now he evinced tension. His replies to Shadd's questions were guarded, terse if not actually monosyllabic. On the matter of his relationship with Mesmia in particular he would not be drawn, saying only that in the past she had employed him for numerous tasks, and that he was adequately rewarded for his services.

'What of this Ciracar, whose underground domain we are to infiltrate?' asked Shadd. 'Who is he?'

Thufor gave a noncommittal shrug, chewing on a

piece of dried meat. 'Legends surround him and his origins. Some say he was an Enchanter of yore, others that he was a gigantic thing who lived underground and did battle with gods.'

'Then he is dead now?'

Again the shrug. 'So it is said.'

'You do not appear over-concerned.'

'I am a pragmatist,' said Thufor. 'None know what is true and what is not. Ciracar is dead; Ciracar only slumbers. He exists; he is gone. Perhaps his legend is greater than he. Perhaps he never was.'

'Then, apart from the legend, who or what inhabits the warren now?'

'Foul creatures in the main. Slaths in some number, I understand. It is some time since I have been there. I hope for more recent information before we enter. But expect anything and you will not be disappointed. Who knows, perhaps you will be truly lucky and find nothing.'

Shadd gazed at him, wondering whether there was deliberate ambiguity in that last statement. He said, 'And the Enchanter, Yxon, within whose lands the warren lies – what of him?'

'We will soon be entering his territories,' said Thufor. 'I am his sworn enemy. If you are caught by him in my company you will be slain. I will meet another fate.'

He rose, signalling an end to the conversation, and went to relieve himself behind a bush. When he returned he packed his belongings in silence. Shadd followed suit and they continued on their way.

They travelled along a seemingly trackless course. The countryside changed again: they passed through leafy woodland, skirted remote foothills. The wind had dropped and the heat of the day became oppressive.

Infrequently they encountered a small hamlet or village, or passed within sight of isolated cottages. Invariably the peasants of the region withdrew indoors at their approach. Shadd grew conscious of fear-filled eyes observing him from behind shuttered windows and doors, and was happier to leave such settlements behind.

Late in the afternoon, as they proceeded at walking pace along a rough woodland road, Shadd was alerted by the whispered voice of the hylozote at his belt. 'Duke Shadd, Temminee has something she wishes to communicate to you.'

'A moment,' said Shadd. He slowed his mount, allowing himself to fall some paces behind Thufor. 'Now, speak on.'

'The end of the day draws nigh,' said the hylozote. 'Temminee has absorbed the light of the sun for several hours. She grows aware of the first promptings of change within her.'

'That is good news.'

'But she has this to say: she wishes to repay you for the liberation you have granted her. In our conversations I have made her aware of something of the nature of your quest. She tells me she would like to remain with you to aid you in any way she can. But she adds that in her true form, that of a Gwynad, she cannot cast light. That is a property of the Stepforth which she will relinquish with her transformation. Thus she is prepared to forego her liberation for a further period if by doing so she can aid you in the darkness of Ciracar's Warren.'

'This is a noble sentiment indeed!' said Shadd. 'But I cannot possibly accept. What guarantee have I that I will survive this journey? Were I to die in Ciracar's Warren, Temminee would be trapped forever beneath the earth. That is a responsibility I do not wish to bear. No, tell Temminee that I am honoured and profoundly moved by her offer, but that I must decline. I will find another means of providing light, but before I enter that place I would rather see her free of the foul magic that binds her.'

A moment later the hylozote spoke again. 'Temminee replies that when her transformation is complete she will, with your permission, still accompany you into the warren, to be of whatever assistance she may.'

'The decision is hers to make. Certainly she has my permission; I would value another companion and aide. But remind her of the dangers we may face, and inform her that she is under no bond of fealty to me. She is free to return to her people, or otherwise do as she chooses.'

They rode on, and as evening approached Thufor led Shadd from the road, along a narrow woodland track to the ruins of a stone dwelling, behind which grew fruit trees.

'Here we will rest till morning,' he said.

After seeing to his horse Shadd explored the ruin. It had been a cottage of two simple rooms, but little remained now save tumbling stone walls, a few decaying timbers and bowed rafters, leaving the interior open to the sky. Outside he found plums and peaches not yet ripe, but bright, sweet red cherries hung in abundance, and with these he was able to supplement his and Thufor's evening meal.

Thufor's mood had lifted somewhat as the afternoon progressed. His smile had returned and he spoke more readily as they partook of their meal, though of general matters rather than anything of import or great relevance to their situation. Perhaps, reasoned Shadd, they had earlier passed close to some peril of which he, Shadd, was ignorant, but which had made Thufor wary.

Darkness drew in, and with the sun gone the evening turned chill. Thufor cautioned against lighting a fire

'There are strange things hereabouts which I would rather not attract,' said he, and added, 'We are fairly safe here, but if you value your skin do not stray beyond these walls before morning.'

They had gathered grass and leaves to make up beds, and presently Thufor lay down at the base of one wall. Soon Shadd found himself listening to the deep and even sound of his companion's breathing as he slumbered.

Shadd lay on, thinking, observing the moon, almost full, which hung brightly in the night sky. It reflected an unusual hue, being tinged with greenish-ochre, and from time to time he half-thought to observe something strange about its rim: a shifting, blurring motion, as though its very shape and form were subject to inconstancy. This he put down to the strange effects of the land that he had already observed, and resolved to give it no further notice. Once or twice his attention was drawn by a flittering silhouette darting across the shining par-globe. And just once the globe was blotted out entirely as something huge passed in front of it, causing Shadd to sit upright and stare. But he saw nothing more, and lay down again. Eventually he slept.

Later he was awoken, tense and alert. A glance at the night sky showed him that the moon had covered only a quarter of its journey across the firmament. Listening, he discerned what it was that had brought him from sleep: a distant voice, that of a man, or mannish thing, raised in lilting, erratic song in some strange babbling tongue. It issued from the direction of the road.

Leaving his bed Shadd crept to the wall of the ruin. The track from the gaping cottage door was visible, disappearing into a screen of black trees. He heard the voice again, closer this time. Something about it, an indefinable quality, eerily familiar yet alien, drew him to know more of its owner.

Disregarding Thufor's warning, Shadd slipped from the ruin. He stole along the track and entered the trees, halting at a point where, with the green-tinged moonlight to aid him, he commanded a view of the road close by. Even as he watched a figure appeared some way down the road. It was a man, garbed in a loose robe, who walked with an odd, drunken gait. As he walked he sang, or babbled, in a broken voice. His song was undisciplined, the words nonsensical: *'Haddle-addle, biddle-baddle, oh, oh, oh! Dimbly-dambly, pimbly-pambly, I don't know! Oh dear me, oh master me, what am I to do! Catch a coodle, whack a snoodle, mmmmmmm . . .'*

As he sang he threw up his arms, tossed back his head, giggled, twirled, performed a hop and a kick-step, stumbled and almost fell. He recovered himself, stopped in the centre of the road, and hung his head. His arms rose, went to the sides of his head. He rocked it from side to side.

*'Oh, woe is me! Woe is me!'* he cried in a suddenly plaintive voice. He turned his bearded face to the stars, still clutching his head. *'Aa-ieee! Aa-ieee! Aaiee!'*

Shadd stared, crouching low, his eyes narrowed in bemusement. Something about what he was witnessing disturbed and puzzled him, incited a response within him that he could not fathom.

The strange fellow resumed his stumbling walk, spinning around, babbling incessantly. Now, as he drew closer, Shadd observed an inequality in the man's physical form. One arm was far shorter than the other: the left limb terminated in a stump some way below the elbow.

The man was almost opposite Shadd now, just paces away. He skipped forward and twirled, and the delicate light of the moon fell full upon his face.

Shadd's eyes widened in shock. Involuntarily he

rose, stared again as the man whirled away. He was about to call out when another sound drew his attention. A snort; the thump of hooves upon the road. Riders approached!

Sensing danger, Shadd drew back. At the same time the madman upon the road, hearing the sound of the riders behind him, shrieked and leapt high. He glanced once over his shoulder, then dashed as fast as his legs would carry him, away down the road.

Shadd slipped back between the trees and lay prone. From the road came the jangle of harness. A party of mounted warriors rounded the bend at a brisk trot.

They came close. Shadd saw that the mounts were not horses, but strange half-skeletal creatures, vaguely equine in form, but with broad stunted heads which were clustered with short horns, and wide jaws which displayed rows of curving teeth. Shadd observed the riders, who wore heavy armour of a dark hue. Upon their heads were great helmets set with horns and spines. As they passed, nine or ten in number, one turned his head in Shadd's general direction. Shadd saw a face of glistening reptilian skin, a strange bone-like protuberance beneath the jaw, and eyes that glittered like obsidian in the moonlight.

These eldritch warriors rode on, unaware of his presence. When all sounds of their passage had faded he withdrew to the ruin and lay down once more upon his bed, deeply troubled.


IV


The following morning Thufor built a fire and produced bacon from his saddle-pack, which he cut into thin strips and proceeded to toast in the flames. For some time he said nothing, but Shadd grew aware of

295

sour glances being cast his way from beneath a beetled brow. As they ate Thufor said, 'You ignored my warning.'

Shadd looked up. 'Then it was true. I half thought upon waking that what I witnessed must have been a dream.'

Thufor gave a harsh laugh. 'Everything in this land is a dream, my friend. Yet it is no less than reality. You are lucky to have survived the night.'

Shadd cast his gaze to the dilapidated walls of the ruin, and beyond. An overcast marked the day, dense unmoving cloud covering the sky and obscuring the loftiest of the distant peaks. He nodded to himself, observing that the furthermost features of the land still defied the focusing of his vision. He said, 'Last night I believed I encountered someone I once knew, a friend dear to me, yet whom I know to be dead. That is why I believed I had dreamed. And in some ways I would prefer to believe still that it was a dream. Yet . . .' He frowned in consternation, and shook his head. 'I will be glad to leave this land.'

Thufor regarded him with a sombre expression. 'You are a stranger here. You know nothing. If you wish to survive, heed my words. I have been appointed your guide, and be assured, my reward depends upon your returning with that which you have come for. But if you persist in disregarding my instructions, and thus endangering yourself and me, I will not hesitate to abandon you here. Remember your quest, and do not be diverted from it.'

Later, as Shadd saddled his horse, he was addressed by the hylozote. 'Duke Shadd, may I speak?'

Shadd glanced across at Thufor, who was already leading his horse back towards the road. 'Aye, speak ahead.'

'The person you observed last night, he is known to

me. He is the addle-brain I spoke of, who survived the enchanted glade where all others slept.'

'Stranger and yet stranger again,' mused Shadd.

'He came three times to that glade in recent months,' the hylozote added. 'Not once was he affected. And I understand, from the conversations of others who paused to rest and never moved on, that he is a familiar presence, and a source of some amusement.'

'I do not know what to make of it,' Shadd said. He adjusted the girth straps beneath his saddle and began to lead his horse around to the front of the ruin.

'Before you rejoin Thufor, there is someone who would like to speak to you,' said the hylozote quickly.

Something which Shadd at first took to be a large winged insect flew before his eyes, then alighted upon the seat of his horse's saddle. Shadd saw a tiny female of human form, scarcely larger than a dragonfly. Delicate transparent wings, trembling in the morning air, spread from between her shoulders. Her form was exquisite, her figure slender, her skin pale as porcelain. Fine clusters of olive-black hair tumbled about her shoulders. She wore a garment of light-grey silky material, and in her hand held a slender metallic rod no larger than a pin.

'Temminee,' said Shadd. He gazed upon her in wonderment, smiling. 'You are most beautiful, as I knew – from the light the Stepforth cast – that you must be. I am happy to see you free.'

Temminee bowed her head. Her voice, when she spoke, was clear and musical, bringing to mind the sound of wind-chimes. 'Thank you, Duke Shadd. But for your intervention I would have passed an eternity in that form.'

'And now, is your choice to return to your people? You are free, as I have said, to do as you will.'

297

A cloud passed across the perfect, tiny features. 'It has been a long time. The Gwynad were never many; with the war, and the long years, I do not know if they exist any more. For now, if you will allow me, I would remain with you.'

'By all means. But conceal yourself. It may not be to your advantage to be seen by others. Now, I hear Thufor calling from the roadside. Let us go.'

At midday Thufor led Shadd down a shallow declivity into a hollow beside a small river, where a cluster of rude dwellings had grown up around an ancient circle of stones. Within and about the circle a fair or festival was in progress. Stalls and booths had been set up, entertainers played. People milled within and without the circle, viewing the wares of the merchants, or the shows and diversions put on for their diversion. Many wore peasants' garb, others sported gaudy and outrageous costumes; some, evidently not of the village, were dressed in finery and showed expensive tastes. To Shadd's eyes, in fact, it was apparent that folk had come from far around to be at this fair, for the simple homes of the village were not enough to house such a population as he now witnessed.

The cloud had begun to break up, the day growing warm and characterised by intermittent sunshine. With Thufor Shadd strolled awhile among the booths set up outside the perimeter of the stone circle. He was glad of the respite, his spirits uplifted by the gaiety of the occasion, for it was the first sign of levity or conviviality that he had encountered in Qotolr. He would have gone further, to inspect the goods and mingle with the crowds within the circle itself, but Thufor steered him away.

'My belly rumbles and cries out for good food and ale. Come, let's eat.'

They repaired to an inn, called The Fallen Star, set not far from the stone circle. Chairs, tables and benches had been set up outside. The two chose an unoccupied table beneath a plane tree and stated their requirements to the serving-girl.

Thufor, though in affable enough mood, chose to concentrate upon his meal rather than conversation. When he had wiped his plate clean he excused himself. 'I have a certain business to transact. Await me here. Do not leave under any circumstances. I will not be long.'

He left and entered the inn. Shadd remained where he was, observing the folk, bemused by Thufor's words, which were freighted with strange warning. Minutes passed, and Thufor returned. With him was a second person, a man of perhaps forty years, of slight, almost spare build, and shortish stature, who sported an immaculately trimmed, pointed beard.

'This is Sleen,' announced Thufor, re-seating himself. 'A fellow well known to me. He will accompany us to Ciracar's Warren.'

With some surprise Shadd registered the newcomer, who also seated himself at their table. Sleen wore a loose purple tunic of fine cloth and superior cut, trousers and boots of equal excellence, a floppy, wide-brimmed hat of crushed green velvet, and an embroidered cloak pinned at his breast with an opal cabochon. As he sat he removed the hat with a flourish, revealing long thin grey hair, which was slicked down tight upon his skull and gathered into a pigtail with a clasp of leather and silver set with garnets. A dagger and slim-bladed sword were strapped at his waist.

'Your servant, sir.'

'I was not expecting another companion,' said Shadd.

'Sleen has valuable information,' Thufor replied. 'He has been to the warren and has collected data from others who have ventured in there. He knows the most favourable portals by which we might gain entrance and egress.'

'Is this true?' Shadd asked, not easy with this turn of events.

Sleen, his hands with ring-adorned fingers clasped before him and his head thrust forward in an attitude eager and almost servile, nodded. 'Indeed, sir, it is.'

Sleen's smile was thin, his features sharp, his complexion pale. Small dark mobile eyes glittered, betraying a shrewd and clever mind. Shadd marked him down as a man to be watched. 'Then enlarge, please,' said he.

Sleen separated his hands and stretched the fingers. 'Parts of the warren I have entered several times. Of course, I have not been to the depths. No one has. But I have succeeded in drawing up a plan of parts of the interior. I believe it could prove invaluable to any intending to enter now.'

'This is heartening news,' declared Shadd. 'What price do you ask for a copy of your plan?'

'Ah no, sir, you misunderstand,' said Sleen, with a widening smile. 'Regrettably, copies are not for sale. The plan, you see, exists in only one place.' He lifted one hand and with a knob-knuckled forefinger tapped the side of his head. 'My price is that I accompany you. And I assure you, you will be glad to have me at your side.'

Shadd appraised him without expression. 'You wear a sword and dagger, but you do not strike me as being the kind of man to needlessly place himself in peril. Perils there are aplenty where we are venturing, as you surely know. What entices you to enter Ciracar's Warren?'

'Ha-ha!' laughed Sleen. 'Appearances can be deceptive! But I will confess, it is sheer cupidity that motivates me. I count myself as something of an adventurer, and a merchant of fine goods to boot. And I have grown rich from looting the lairs of beasts within that warren – I say it without shame, and I am not alone in my fortunes. Ah, but beasts have been slain, their hoards taken – and not a few men have lost their lives in the process – and now the rewards grow smaller. Most recently I have brought out little more than trinkets, yet I know that deep within that warren lie riches untold. You intend to journey deep within, and I am assured by Thufor here that our interests do not conflict.' He narrowed his eyes, tilted his head, and grinned slyly. 'I know an optimal route into the warren, which avoids the more populated areas, and which will take us directly to the hidden entrance to the vault which you must enter. No other has this information, and without it you might spend weeks searching and still not find your way to what you seek. Others have been lost in there, for the warren is large and complex. But I am willing to add my talents to yours, to provide you with the benefits of my experience, and risk the dangers in the knowledge that a better life will come of it.'

'If we return,' said Shadd.

'Ah, quite so. But life without risk is a stagnant thing, sir. And I am not one to sit and watch my buttocks spread and my belly grow over my belt.'

Shadd nodded slowly, recognising that he had little choice but to accept. The feeling grew more strongly that he was caught up in a grander plan, the true dimensions of which were being kept carefully hidden from him.

'Very well, then,' he said. 'You will join us.'

'Good.' Sleen sat back and rubbed his hands. 'Then let us drink a toast to success!'

Sleen called for ale. When it had been brought to their table, and the three had raised their mugs and downed a draught, Shadd turned to Thufor. 'Yesterday

301

you indicated that we could expect to arrive at the warren today. Do we have far to go?'

'If we leave immediately we can be there before nightfall,' came the reply. 'However, there is a problem. Sleen tells me that Fahn raiders have been foraging close to the warren. They have a sizeable camp there, and it would be wise to avoid them.'

'Fahn?'

'Brutish warriors, remnants of unnatural legions of an Enchanter of yore, Vaclad the Grim. They have become nomadic in habit, appearing from time to time, laying waste indiscriminately, stealing, murdering. Fortunately they are not great in number now. Nonetheless, I would not willingly meet with them.'

'Would the warriors I saw last night be of the Fahn?' Shadd enquired, and described the eldritch party he had spied upon the trail.

Thufor nodded. 'Those are they. I would suggest we wait. They will not remain long in one place. For one thing, this is Yxon's domain. His troops will move quickly against the Fahn once he learns of their presence. We will have access to the warren soon enough.'

'If that is how it must be,' said Shadd. He gazed around him. 'At least we have a pleasant place to tarry. I would happily enjoy further the distractions of this festival while we wait.'

Sleen and Thufor exchanged arch glances. Sleen said, 'It is not all that it seems, sir.'

'How is that?'

'This is the Festival of the Lost. When night falls all this will disappear, as will the people you see before you. There will remain only the standing stones, and the few hovels scattered beyond them.'

'I don't understand. How can this be?'

'This place is Skirdon, known in ancient times as Lale,' Thufor explained. 'History relates that in the time of the Wars it was a thriving and prosperous township. But a conflict was fought in the skies over Lale, between the gods – the Enchanters. One day, while a festival of Spring was in progress, a bolt of magical origin fell, destroying all that lay here. These stones which form the circle are fragments of that bolt.

'Lale and its people, then, are no more. But once a year, on the anniversary of that day, their ghosts return to mingle again and enjoy the festival that was brought to so abrupt and tragic an end. The inhabitants of Skirdon now are superstitious peasants who dwell in the hovels here. They worship the stones, believing them to be objects of power. On this day, though, the peasants remain indoors. They know that, come the evening, the ghosts will be called back to that uncertain place which is their domain now, and that any who have mingled with them inside the circle will be called there too, and will be powerless to resist. And that is another reason why we should not tarry.'

'But that cannot be so!' declared Shadd. He stared around him. 'These people are not all ghosts. I have observed them: they drink, and eat solid food as we have. Their coin is real; the landlord is happy to accept it. And some have brushed against me; I have felt the bulk of their flesh.'

'The landlord is a canny fellow, right enough,' said Thufor. 'He advertises this event far and wide, and people come simply to observe the strange spectacle. It is they who you see eating, drinking and exchanging their coin. He makes a good profit. But within that circle there are only ghosts. You may enter and mingle with them, you may even speak with them, but once there you are theirs. You can no longer count yourself among the living. I say again, Shadd, heed my words if you would survive Enchantery.'

303

Thufor placed his palms upon the table and heaved himself to standing. 'Now, our business is complete. Strange things can happen in Skirdon, even to those who merely observe. Let us begone while our wits and resolve are still sound.'

# 11

## I

Three nights and two days they were obliged to wait before the Fahn warriors broke camp and rode from the vicinity of Ciracar's Warren.

Shadd and his companions, two and a half hours' ride from Skirdon, waited upon a hill overlooking the lowland where Ciracar's Warren lay. Externally, the warren was a huge, elongated mound of irregular shape, splayed across the flat. Its slopes ranged from gentle gradients to steep, rocky inclines, in places broken up by sheer high cliff faces. Its surface was long grown over with trees and vegetation. In all it was unremarkable, at least from their vantage some two miles distant, and might well have been nothing more than a natural feature of the land.

The Fahn were encamped on the low ground, beside a stream running close to the base of the warren. Shadd estimated between fifty and sixty, but companies of ten or so rode out at frequent intervals, while others rode in with booty, making it impossible to precisely determine their complement.

Thufor, at first, was confident that the Fahn would be gone within hours. But the day wore on and the hours accumulated, stretched into a night, then another day, and he began to express surprise and impatience. He had anticipated swift intervention from Yxon's troops. The Fahn and Yxon's Laughing Blue Knights, as they were known, were mortal enemies. The Blue Knights' love of fighting was renowned. They

305

were ruthless, fierce and skilful, maintained harsh but efficient justice in the region, and far outnumbered the Fahn. Typically they descended without hesitation or enquiry upon any encroaching force and drove it from Yxon's lands.

By noon of the second day Thufor was becoming irritable. His nervousness was compounded by the knowledge that the longer they remained where they were the more likely they were to be discovered by the Fahn, who regularly reconnoitred the area.

Thufor decided to set out himself to scout north-westwards in the direction of Madgard Keep, Yxon's stronghold, for signs of the Enchanter's forces. If something was preventing Yxon from responding to the Fahn presence a choice would have to be made. They – Shadd and his companions – could take the considerable risk of attempting to enter Ciracar's Warren with the Fahn still in place. That risk might be diminished somewhat by circling around to one of the northern entrances, furthest from the Fahn camp. However, by choosing to enter from the north they would lose the advantage of Sleen's memorised plan of the interior, which depended upon ingress by one of three entrances on the southern side of the warren.

Alternatively they could abandon all present intentions and repair to some nearby village or town, there to twiddle their thumbs until news came of the departure of the marauding Fahn.

Thufor's mission was itself not without risk, for both the Fahn and Yxon's knights were hostile to him. But he was an experienced scout, familiar with the terrain of the region, and was confident that, alone, he could keep himself free of trouble. Shadd watched him leave with renewed disquiet, apprehensive lest this development be something contrived, another element in the grander design which lay beyond the scope of his perception.

Thufor was gone four hours, returning in the early evening to report the presence of Yxon's guard, the Laughing Blue Knights, less than twelve miles away. The three slept again through a freezing night on the hillside beneath the stars, and when next morning they awoke it was to find that the Fahn had departed. At Thufor's behest they waited a while longer on the hill. Within the hour a force of some two hundred mounted knights appeared riding out of the northwest. As they drew closer Shadd observed that they wore armour of brilliant metallic-blue mail, their chargers clothed in elaborate barding of identical hue. Standards and shields carried a blazon of dark blue upon a metallic-blue field, but its details Shadd could not make out. The Blue Knights halted briefly to inspect the abandoned Fahn camp, then rode on around Ciracar's Warren to disappear into woodland to the south.

Thufor led his companions from the hilltop, saying, 'They will be back. We should not tarry.'

Close to the base of the warren the ground broke up into a series of high grassy hummocks. Sleen, who upon leaving Skirdon had exchanged his foppish outfit for one of light leathers and strong cloth more suited to the task ahead, guided them between these, to where the slope reared suddenly before them. He indicated with his hand a narrow trail cutting around the hummocks. 'That way leads to one of the entrances. It is a direct route in, but well known. Further around is an ancient doorway. It is fortified and well-guarded. I would enter by that means only if I were a slath. But up there – ' he pointed up the slope, ' – lies a concealed entrance which is little used. I discovered it myself more or less by accident. It is an uncomfortable way in and will take us by a somewhat circuitous route, but it will deliver us to the warren's heart with little risk of serious encounter.'

'Do you possess accurate information in regard to the denizens of this place?' enquired Shadd. He observed Sleen warily, then shifted his gaze to Thufor who stood a few paces away, keening the blade of his axe with an oiled cloth and gazing up the slope of the warren.

Shadd's mind reached back, to recollections of long years of training and discipline – as a child at Hon-Hiaita, schooled by the Zan-Chassin; later, deep in the Endless Desert, where extremes of Aphesuk tutelage had on several occasions come close to depriving him of his sanity or his life; and underscoring these, constantly, throughout his youth, even more esoteric disciplines which were taught to him by his mother, Mercy. *'These are for you alone,'* she had said, emphasising the fact again and again, *'in order that, Fate willing, you may one day realise your true heritage. Guard them well; reveal them to no one. In time, perhaps, you may come to know their value.'*

Those exercises had meant little to him. Long, long hours he had passed in apparently meaningless performances: in meditations, maintaining strange and uncomfortable postures, reciting incantations, litanies, invocations, listening to tales without sense, histories without relation to anything he knew or understood. All without discernible effect. The Zan-Chassin meditations he had quickly comprehended; even more so those taught him by the Aphesuk. They had revealed their purpose in time to practical application, the development and honing of varying faculties and talents. But his mother's disciplines had remained a mystery.

Now all his senses alerted him to the danger he was about to face. And from within, as though he glimpsed a movement, an opening in the flux of the future, Shadd became aware of something else. He faced immense danger, yes. Perilous uncertainties within the warren; the likelihood of treachery from one or both of his companions, Thufor and Sleen. But beyond this was a greater peril, one far less distinct yet more engulfing, of much greater consequence.

With a shock of intuitive understanding Shadd recognised a deeper truth: the greater danger lay not in his failing in this task, and thereby losing his life. No, the greater danger lay in his succeeding, his living on.

*There is movement here*, he thought, *and I am component in it. But I do not control it. There is a purpose, but I do not know what it is. I am not my own master. What is my role? And for whom or what do I play it?*

The vision was gone. A glimmer of understanding had come and passed away, revealing nothing of the details, nothing to identify the character of the darker design that he was convinced manipulated the events in which he now participated. He returned, shaken, blinking, to the present. Sleen was speaking.

'A tribe of slaths. They are organised, and can be deadly in battle. But I am acquainted with many of their patrol routes. With luck we may avoid most of them. A family of ogres have a den towards the northern side. There may be other creatures, it is impossible to say. And of course, there is the Sentinel.'

'The Sentinel?' said Shadd. 'What is this?'

'A strange, many-limbed thing with flaming eyes which seems able to appear from nowhere. And further down, where we must go – that will be a place of dire magic and grim encounters.'

His eyes on Shadd, Thufor said, 'Are we agreed then, that we will enter here, as Sleen recommends?'

Slowly, still shaken by his premonition, Shadd nodded.

They led their horses into a thicket of elder close beside the stream, and there left them on long tethers. From their saddle-packs the three took provisions and equipment: rope, a strong net, climbing irons, a pair of oil-lamps. Sleen led the way up the steep slope of the warren, pursuing a nebulous track towards the skyline. Dense vegetation hindered their passage, and they wound and looped back and forth. At length, after some ten minutes, Sleen halted, panting, beside a clutch of boulders fifty feet below the crest of the warren.

'We are here.'

He leaned upon one of the boulders, hanging his head to catch his breath. Shadd gazed thoughtfully around. Thufor, standing upon a rock, said, 'The Blue Men return.'

They stared in the direction he indicated. Far away across the flat a faint cloud of dust rose, and before it came a faint shimmering of blue, sparks of sunlight glinting off metal.

'The horses are well hidden. They will not discover them,' said Sleen.

'Unless they are expecting to,' Thufor muttered.

'I see no opening, Sleen,' said Shadd with impatience. 'Yet you claim this is our destination.'

Sleen grinned and winked. He patted the boulder upon which he leaned. 'Come, I am weakened by the climb. Perhaps you would oblige?'

Shadd stepped across.

'Merely lift and push, that way,' said Sleen.

Shadd crouched, slipped his fingers into a niche at the boulder's base, and lifted. The rock rolled aside with surprisingly little effort. Beneath was a dense tangle of roots which Sleen dragged aside. A dark hole gaped in the earth, large enough for a man to enter.

Sleen grinned again. 'Who will go first?'

## II

They crawled in single file in total darkness, on hands and knees, their packs dragging behind them, attached by cords around their waists. At times, so narrow was the tunnel, they were forced to crawl upon their bellies.

Perhaps to allay fears, Thufor had volunteered to go first, followed by Shadd, with Sleen bringing up the rear. They used no lamp, for there was no space to bear it properly.

'It will deprive its holder of air, and will tend to dazzle rather than reveal,' Sleen had said. 'The tunnel extends for about one hundred yards, then opens into an area where the lamp will be of better use. Until then there is only earth, clay and rock. Feel your way forward with care and you will not go wrong.'

The air in the tunnel was stale, rank with the smell of earth and roots, and stifling. Elbows and knees grew sore as they crawled; the muscles of thighs, back, neck and arms ached with the effort. The passage wound down into the hillside at a gentle gradient, and the warmth and claustrophobic blackness became oppressive.

The three maintained silence as best they could, for this would be a terrible place to be caught by an enemy. Sleen had repeated his assurances as they'd entered that this was by far the least hazardous route into the warren. Ogres and slaths were too bulky to enter the tunnel, and he was convinced, furthermore, that they had no knowledge of its existence. Shadd drew some comfort from the company of Temminee and the hylozote, both of whom, with sight undiminished by the lack of light, maintained a vigil on his behalf.

Sixty yards into the tunnel they encountered trouble. Ahead of Shadd Thufor emitted a sudden barking grunt, followed by a curse, then a groan of pain.

'What ails you?' Shadd rasped in a low voice.

'I have been struck, I know not by what.'

'Are you badly hurt?'

'I think not. A sharp blow upon the cheek. It has drawn blood, but that is all. But I d – '

He was cut short by a voice from the blackness ahead. 'Halt, intruders! Advance no further unless you have a yen for further pain. Who are you, and what do you wish here in my burrow?'

The three at first maintained stunned silence. The voice called again, pitched high, thin and muffled in the heavy air, carrying a peevish tone. 'Answer, or you will suffer! Lo!'

Thufor gave another cry. '*Aiee!!*' He swore again, then called out: 'Sir, whoever you are, hold, please! We are travellers, nothing more. Our destination is the domain below. We intend you no harm.'

'But are you aware that you pass through my burrow?'

'We did not know this tunnel was occupied. We simply wish to pass.'

From behind him Shadd called, 'Might I enquire, sir, whom do we address?'

The reply, when it came, issued from another direction, to their right, and somewhat below them. 'Whom? Why, I, the Burrower, of course. And do not think you can sneak past, or push through. You are three, but were you three thousand you would not pass without my consent. I command the burrow. Witness!'

Close beside Shadd there was a scuffling noise. Something sharp prodded him rudely between the ribs, then again in the abdomen. He grunted and squirmed. A second later, ahead of him, Thufor groaned once more and Shadd heard him writhe helplessly.

'You see!' cried the Burrower. 'With my sling and prongs I can hold off an army. And my aim, should I wish it, is precise and deadly.'

The voice of Temminee whispered softly in Shadd's ear. 'There is a honeycomb of smaller interlinking passages and holes running off this large one. It is from these that this Burrower assaults you.'

Shadd ran his hands over the sides of the tunnel. He felt numerous openings of varying size angling off the main passage. He called out, 'Sir Burrower, I reiterate my companion's words. We come without ill intent. We simply wish to pass.'

In a harsh whisper he addressed Sleen behind him. 'This is your simple route? You made no mention of this Burrower!'

'The tunnel was empty when I passed this way before,' hissed Sleen, then gave a yelp of pain.

'Cease your sly whisperings!' cried the Burrower. 'Do not think even for an instant that you can outwit me. Now, you desire passage, you say?'

'That is so,' Shadd replied. To Temminee he whispered, 'Can you see this creature?'

'Not yet. But wait, I will look.'

She slipped from Shadd's shoulder, and was gone.

The Burrower called again, this time from his original position ahead of them. 'A toll then, if you please.'

'A toll?' barked Thufor. 'What manner – '

There was a *ping!* as something hard and fast-moving rebounded off metal. Thufor gasped.

'Next time it will be your fingers, not merely the dagger hilt they closed around!' cried the Burrower. 'Or better, the next stone may shatter your skull and take up permanent lodging in your brain. Now, it is your choice: pay my toll and you may proceed or return the way you came. Or if you prefer, pay nothing and remain where you are. In truth, that would be pleasing to me, for when you have succumbed to thirst or starvation I will inherit everything you carry.'

'How much is your toll?' Shadd called.

'Three gold pieces.'

Behind him Shadd heard Sleen mutter imprecations.

'Each!' added the Burrower.

'And if we pay, we will be allowed to continue unmolested?'

'That is so.'

'Then we will pay your toll. Here – here are my coins.'

The Burrower spoke close beside his head, above and to the left. 'Place them upon the tunnel floor, then move on.'

Shadd felt a light tug at his hair as Temminee re-alighted upon his shoulder. 'The Burrower is a fur-covered two-legged manling. He stands less than a foot tall. His burrow appears vast and complex. And he speaks the truth: an army could not pass without his say so.'

Shadd spoke to Thufor and Sleen. 'We are left no choice but to pay the toll, which is after all fair recompense, for we are lumbering creatures who have rudely invaded this Burrower's home.'

'Well said!' came the voice of the Burrower, from another direction again. 'You at least are a perceptive and principled man.'

'We will continue on our way, then.'

The Burrower gave a sigh, audible even in the close air of his burrow. 'Yes, that is the exchange. A pity, though; I would have enjoyed further sport. Ah well, begone!'

They crawled on. Temminee whispered, 'Duke Shadd, did you see?'

'I can see nothing in this darkness,' growled Shadd.

'Perhaps you did not know,' said Temminee. 'I will go back.'

'Why? Of what do you speak?'

'You carry the Soul Crystal, Duke Shadd. Test yourself now. Attune yourself. My eyes may be yours.'

She was gone. Mystified, Shadd lifted a hand to clasp the crystal upon the chain at his breast. He crawled on, puzzling over Temminee's meaning.

Into his mind came an image: he seemed to glide along a narrow, earthen passage – a passage within a complex of passages, twisting and angling, of differing diameters. As he focused in bemused fascination upon this image, he observed a figure ahead of him, squat and sleekly furred. It stood at an intersection of passages, leaning out to peer around a corner into the larger of the tunnels, its back to Shadd. In one hand, which was wide and furry with powerful splayed claws, the strange creature held a sling. Around its rotund waist was a belt which secured several short javelins or darts. As Shadd observed the little creature stepped out into the larger passage. It fitted a round pebble into the sling, spun the sling with a strong, stubby arm, and let fly.

There came a loud yelp from the darkness to the rear of where Shadd crawled. He stopped and called back, 'Sleen! Are you hurt?'

'I have been struck most painfully,' came the aggrieved reply. 'Upon my right buttock!'

From the passageway some distance to their rear came the sound of high-pitched laughter.

Within Shadd's mind the image persisted. The small furry man-thing clutched its ample belly and rocked upon its heels, momentarily helpless with mirth. Then it quickly gathered itself and scampered forward, down the larger passage. In his mind's eye Shadd followed. He saw the Burrower halt and stoop to gather up something from the earth floor. He moved closer, found himself peering over the Burrower's shoulder. In his hand the Burrower held three gold pieces; six others lay upon the floor nearby, in two little piles. These the Burrower also collected.

Shadd's vision retreated. He was flying back, veering into a smaller passage. Seconds later Temminee was at his shoulder again.

'Now,' said she, 'I will ask you again. Did you see?'

'I saw. But I do not understand.'

'Good! It is as I hoped! You are in harmony with the Crystal. It has aided you in bringing forth a faculty latent within you. You can see through others' eyes. I think it is the beginning; time will show.'

'Then there is more?'

'The Crystal can only respond to qualities already inherent in the bearer. For now you may use the sight of others – providing they are willing to allow you. With time I believe you may learn to hear, speak, even feel through others. Truly the totality is for you to discover, but I will tell you one thing: the Crystal will respond most effectively when your need is such that thought plays no part. Now, shall I go back and cause some dismay to this malapert Burrower? I can at least return the coins he has exacted from you.'

'Are we clear now of his maze?'

'Yes.'

'Then leave him. We entered his home uninvited and have paid the price. And we may have need to return this way. His character is mischievous but without true malice, I think. If we meet again I would prefer that he remembers us without ire or desire for revenge.'

III

'A high price to pay,' grumbled Thufor, his hand at his cheek from which flowed a trickle of blood, engendered by the Burrower's first stone.

'The alternative would have been far higher,' said Shadd. To himself he thought, *we were helpless and at the mercy of one no larger than a rabbit.*

They had emerged from the Burrower's cramped passage into a wider chamber in which they could stand. Sleen had lighted an oil-lamp, to illuminate a small cavern perhaps five yards in diameter. Now they eased and stretched their limbs, and rubbed at grazed elbows and knees. Sleen, his eyes on the blackness of the hole from which they had crawled, commented ruefully, 'I'll warrant he hoards a small fortune within that maze.'

'Likely,' Thufor agreed. 'But it is one you will never see.'

Shadd cast his eyes around the chamber. The ceiling was high, lost in blackness which the light from the lamp could not penetrate. Upon the rock walls trails of wetness glistened. Black shadows trembled; juts and hollows of rock seeming to quiver and writhe under the influence of the little flame. He could see no other entrance or exit.

He looked questioningly at Sleen, who grinned and

stepped across the rock floor to where a scar of dense black shadow streaked up the wall. Sleen disappeared. They heard his voice, hollow. 'Here, sir, to answer your unspoken question, is the way out.'

He reappeared, smiling. 'A narrow passage leads to steps hewn into the rock, which descend to the main part of the warren. It is steep and slippery. We should descend with care.'

Temminee whispered to Shadd, 'Use your new gift. I will scout ahead; you may observe through my eyes. Your two companions will wonder at your "clairvoyance", and will surely think again if treachery is their intention.'

She departed, skimming unseen across the floor of the cavern and darting into the gap in the rock.

Thufor, taking the lamp, made to step from the cavern.

'A moment!' said Shadd. The two men paused; they observed him curiously. He concentrated upon Temminee, the union with her consciousness. The wavering light of the lamp was a distraction. The image within his mind did not form as readily as it had in the total darkness of the Burrower's tunnel, nor was it as distinct. Still, he was able to see enough. Temminee flew down, down, above narrow steps that were sickeningly steep, arriving at length at their foot, where an ancient arched portal of grime-covered timber bound with iron straps stood in a recess cut into the natural rock. Three great bolts of iron held the portal closed.

'There is a door at the base of these steps,' said Shadd. 'To where does it lead?'

Sleen's jaw went slack. 'You have been here?'

'Never.'

Sleen exchanged an apprehensive glance with Thufor beside him. 'Beyond the door is the domain of the slaths. The door is bolted, and may only be opened from this side.'

Shadd nodded. 'It is as you say.' He relinquished the image to focus fully upon his companions once more. 'Thufor, do you prefer that I take the lead this time?'

Thufor shrugged. 'It is all one. I will lead, if you wish.'

'I would advise that you take one of the lamps. I or Sleen can hold the other. The stairs are precipitous, and a black void gapes to one side which I would not care to explore.'

Again Sleen gaped at Shadd. 'Your description is accurate. You *have* been here before.'

Shadd pursed his lips into a sombre smile and shook his head.

'Then how do you know this?'

'Perhaps I read your mind.'

Sleen seemed to writhe slightly, discomfited by this notion, though in the limited light it was impossible to read the expression on his face. Shadd shifted his gaze to Thufor. 'Remember, there are many reasons why I was chosen for this task.'

Thufor studied him with interest, then laughed. 'Come. We waste time.'

He stepped forward and disappeared through the slit in the rock. Shadd followed, and Sleen again came last, carrying the second lamp. The passage extended a mere yard or two before opening onto the chasm. The steps followed the form of the rock face, down, plunging into darkness. From the chasm came occasional updraughts of warm, foetid air, and as they descended they heard from time to time faint disturbances from far below, a wet, thrashing sound, as though something of great bulk flailed in a watery domain.

At length they arrived before the portal at the bottom.

Temminee had pressed herself back out of sight into a fissure in the rock above the arch of the door. Thufor put the heel of his hand to the bolts, drawing them back one by one with a dry rasping of metal on metal. He pulled upon a large iron handle shaped as a grimacing leonine head. The door swung slowly inwards. Unnoticed, Temminee darted out into the corridor beyond.

Thufor made to step through the portal, but Shadd stayed him with a hand upon his arm. Turning from the glare of the lamps Shadd focused his mind once more.

Through Temminee's eyes he saw that the portal gave onto an alcove which opened onto a passageway stretching to left and right.

'Which way?' Shadd asked Sleen.

'Right.'

Immediately Temminee veered right and, keeping close to the rock ceiling, glided along the passage. After fifty yards the passage split into three. Temminee peered along the two new ways, revealing them to be deserted, but she advanced no further.

'Which way at the intersection?' asked Shadd.

'Left,' replied Sleen with a pettish tone. 'But the way may be guarded.'

'Come.' Drawing his two shortswords Shadd slipped through the door.

They crept to the intersection where Temminee waited. She, unbidden, flew on to explore further. A little way down the corridor curved towards the right, and her sight revealed a long passage partially illuminated by torches set in brackets upon the walls. Along this passage could be seen doors and alcoves.

'Extinguish the lamps,' said Shadd. 'We will not need them here.'

With weapons drawn the three moved on in Temminee's wake. At a point just beyond the reach of the wavering light of the first torch they halted. Temminee waited ten paces ahead, above the first door. Some way beyond they could see another intersection of corridors.

'We are entering the main living quarters of the slaths,' whispered Sleen. 'These are guardrooms, sleeping areas, cells. The second passage on the left will lead us to a central chamber, from where we may descend into the vault.'

Temminee drew back, rising into the shadows of the rocky ceiling. Shadd, his shared vision disturbed by the light from the torches in the corridor, had only a fleeting image of what had alarmed her.

'Hold still!' he warned. 'Something approaches.'

They crouched back in the darkness. From down the corridor came the sound of heavy marching steps: *thap-thap-thap-thap.* It was accompanied by a dull, dragging, slithering sound. Slaths, their long fleshy tails trailing behind them upon the floor.

There was no time to withdraw. Shadd pressed himself into the rock. The dark provided scant cover, for slath sight was well-adapted to poor light. If the slaths turned their way they would be seen.

*Thap-thap-thap.*

Out of the first passage marched a party of four slaths: lizard creatures, six feet tall and twice the bulk of any man. They strode erect on squat, muscle-packed hindlegs, clawed, splaying feet smacking the ground. Each clasped a spear between the digits of its smaller forelimbs. Immense barbed tails, up to four feet in length and armoured in tough, tooth-edged scales, swept the floor behind them. The slaths turned, and marched on into the shadowy light, away down the main passage.

Temminee descended and moved along the corridor. She watched until the slaths had disappeared into a further passage.

For the moment the way seemed clear. Shadd crept soundlessly forward, Thufor at his shoulder, Sleen just behind. Shadd paused outside the first door. Erratic sounds issued from within: thumps, scrapes, muffled grunts and harsh gibbers. Shadd stole past, Thufor likewise. But as Sleen made to follow the door resounded to a heavy thud and flew violently open.

A slath stood there, blinking in momentary surprise.

Like lightning Sleen attacked. He darted into the slath, lunging hard with dagger and slim sword. He slashed, stabbed, ripped, slitting open the brute's soft pale underbelly before it had time to gather its wits. The slath vented a strangled roar as its guts spilled out onto the dirt. Sleen's sword drove up under its jaw, penetrating deep into its brain. It jerked and shuddered, and was dead before it knew what had happened.

But others came behind. As the first slath folded in the doorway another sprang out, using tail and hindlegs to clear its dead companion. It slammed into Sleen, bowling him over. He fell violently to the floor, where he lay stunned. The slath was upon him, slivers of teeth bared, jaws widening to tear him apart.

Thufor, axe swinging, hurled himself forward. His blade sank into the scaly hide of the slath's neck. Reddish ichor spurted from the wound. The slath screamed, hissed, spun around, its barbed tail raised high. Thufor ducked, then charged forward again. The axe bit deep into the slath's chest. It staggered back and fell, trapping Sleen beneath its dead weight.

A third slath had come from the chamber, lunging with its spear at Thufor. Shadd advanced, slashing with bright shortswords. The creature screamed as a foreclaw, still clutching the haft of the spear, dropped to the dirt. It swung in a frenzy of pain. Shadd darted in, crouching, stabbed swiftly with shortswords. The lethal tail flew around. Shadd leapt back, cleared its offensive arc, leapt in again.

The creature went onto its belly and shot forward with astonishing speed, massive head swinging from side to side, jaws snapping. Shadd dived, hit the ground, rolled and came erect. He drove his sword hard into the brute's flank, but so tough were the scales that the blade barely penetrated. The slath wheeled around again. Shadd stepped back, slipped on the ichor-splattered floor, and lost his footing. The slath flew at him. Something flashed across his vision. The blade of Thufor's battleaxe fell in a deadly arc to sink deep into the slath's skull. The lizard twitched and lay still, its brains and fluids dribbling about its face, its eyes still glaring.

From behind Thufor came another slath, and yet another was leaping from the doorway.

The first sprang, claws, spear and mighty jaws aimed at Thufor's back. Shadd lunged, rolling beneath it and thrusting with both swords up into its exposed abdomen. Thufor, sensing the danger, hurled himself away, relinquishing his axe which was still embedded in the dead slath's skull.

The springing slath let out a seething roar as Shadd's swords pierced its flesh. It twisted mid-leap, its legs kicking out wildly, forelimbs clutching at the two blades. It fell heavily onto its side, and Shadd was up, stabbing savagely into eye and throat.

Thufor had scrambled forward to wrench his axe free as the last of the creatures came at him. This one, unnerved now at the sight of its dead companions, hesitated. Shadd was in with darting blades. The slath backed away. Thufor's axe descended, but the slath reeled and dodged the blow. It lunged at Thufor with its spear. Shadd saw an opening, took it. His blade sank into the slath's neck. The creature gurgled, clawing wildly. Thufor ended its life with a final blow of his axe.

Shadd glanced around him. Five slaths lay dead in the corridor. Cautiously, with Thufor beside him, he stepped into the chamber. It was empty: a guardroom containing nothing of interest. They moved back into the corridor, and Thufor crossed to where Sleen lay trapped beneath the corpse.

From the pouch at Shadd's waist the hylozote quietly spoke. 'Are you hurt, Duke Shadd?'

'No.'

He felt the lightest touch upon his shoulder as Temminee settled there once more. Joining Thufor he hauled aside the dead slath to free Sleen. They stood for a moment, regaining their breath.

'We should drag these bodies into the chamber,' said Thufor.

This they did, not without difficulty, for the slaths were of great weight. It required the strength of the three of them to shift each corpse. Temminee, meanwhile, departed again to keep watch down the corridor.

A warning from the hylozote caused Shadd to bid the others cease and take cover. Temminee, in silent communication to the hylozote, had reported the approach of another slath patrol. The three waited at the door of the chamber, poised for further combat, but the patrol turned off before entering their corridor.

They completed their labour without further interruption, closed the chamber door and made off down the passage. Darting forward, pausing, moving again, they followed Sleen's directions, passed several more doors, entered new passages.

A door creaked open at their backs. They took cover in a natural alcove behind a jut of hard blue granite. Out of the door came a stream of the great lizards. Twelve in all, they stomped away up the passage in the opposite direction.

Shadd took the moment to fuse his vision once more with Temminee's.

'This passage ends at an arched double-door. Two sentries are stationed there,' he said to Sleen.

Sleen, regarding him with an extraordinary expression, nodded. 'That is the central hall. In there lies the entrance to the vault beneath. It is likely that there will be slaths within, but with luck we will find them sleeping, for this is not their active period. I would have chosen this time deliberately, had not our encounter with the Fahn imposed it upon us. At other times we could have expected to encounter far more of the beasts.'

A faint, sickening smell hung in the air, growing stronger as they moved towards the central hall. They came to a curve in the corridor, beyond which, some thirty yards away, was the double-door and its two guards. Shadd received a whispered message from the hylozote: 'Temminee has returned. She slipped beneath the door of the central chamber. It is more or less as Sleen reported, though there are other sights in there that are not pleasant.'

Drawing back, Shadd consulted his two companions. 'We cannot approach without being seen.' He touched his bow, which was slung across his shoulder. 'Even with arrows I do not think we could kill the guards instantly. They would have time to cry out and alert others.' He looked back along the passageway. 'We are very vulnerable here.'

'These slaths are deadly but slow-witted,' said Sleen. 'And therein lies our own strength.'

Moments later, with Shadd and Thufor crouched out of sight, Sleen stepped into the centre of the passage. With a staggering gait he moved towards the door of the hall in full view of the slath guards, who stiffened in surprise. Sleen stumbled a few paces more, clutched his chest with both hands, tottered and fell, first to his knees, then onto his back upon the dirt floor.

With their short spears held before them the two guards approached, testing the air with darting tongues. They halted before the fallen Sleen, made to prod him with their spears. Thufor and Shadd came from hiding, loosed an arrow apiece. Both arrows struck home. The slaths gave out sudden gibbers of pain. Sleen came alive, stabbing up with his dagger, into the gut of the closest slath. He ripped, wrenched, rolled away, clear of the thrashing tail as Shadd and Thufor leapt into the fray.

The combat was brief, the two lizards quickly dispatched. The three men ran to the double-door and waited tensely, alert for indications that the sounds of their scuffle had roused others.

When he was satisfied that this was not the case Thufor raised the heavy iron latch on the door. He pressed his shoulder to the timber. The door moved inwards. Shadd slid forward and put his head inside the chamber.

He gagged upon the stench within this place; an overpowering foetor of rotting flesh, faecal matter and other foul and unidentifiable odours. The hall was a gloomy rock cavern of indiscernible proportions. It was rudely furnished with rough-hewn tables, benches and stools. A central cooking-fire sited in a depression in the earth floor was its sole illumination, and smoke from this, finding scant avenues of escape, had filled the chamber with an acrid, choking fog.

The bodies of slaths could be seen within the smoke, slumped at tables or upon the floor. The noise of their uneven, stertorous breathing filled the air. Huge discarded flagons and mugs were strewn amidst puddles of some kind of beer or crude wine, evidencing the reasons for the slaths' brutish slumber.

Wiping his eyes, which burned and watered with the smoke, Shadd saw half-gnawed lumps of meat and uncountable bones scattered everywhere.

He slipped inside. Sleen, at his side, whispered, 'Over there. The entrance to the vault is beneath the ceremonial seat.'

Beyond the fire Shadd made out the shape of a massive block of stone worked roughly into the form of a long, couch-like throne, set upon a low dais. An obese slath, larger than any he had seen, was sprawled unconscious upon it. Glancing around him he calculated that there were perhaps ten or a dozen slaths within his range of vision. Others may have lain in the shadows in the further reaches of the hall. He picked his way carefully forward. From the discarded meat, some raw, some partially cooked, clouds of flies arose in agitation at his passing.

As he passed close to the fire Shadd's eyes were drawn back towards the low flames. The putrefying haunch of a deer lay nearby; he saw the remains of a hog, even parts of the cadaver of a bear. Then his eyes fell upon something which caused him to stop and stare in mute horror.

At his feet lay a man's arm, torn off below the shoulder, the humerus stripped bare. Ribbons of rank, shrivelled flesh hung off the forearm and wrist.

He tore his eyes away, his stomach heaving. Now he recognised other human remains scattered about the chamber amidst the general carnage.

Sleen materialised at his side. He stared down at the arm, then stooped and lifted the decaying hand. 'Ah, Rebic,' he rasped. 'So this is where you ended your days.'

He glanced up at Shadd, reading his ashen face, and pointed. 'The ring.'

Upon the second finger of the rotting hand was an engraved silver band set with a large ruby.

'Then you knew this man?' said Shadd, choking in the foul atmosphere.

'I knew the man who wore this, and assume he still wears it. He was Rebic, a companion who entered here with me some time ago. We entered by another route which was much more heavily guarded. Our party became divided. I was isolated and forced to seek a way out alone. Evidently Rebic and the others were less fortunate than I.'

Sleen pulled the ring from the finger, rose and dropped it into a pocket. He moved off. To Shadd's disgust he saw that Sleen was scanning the floor, stooping among the remains from time to time to remove some item of value from dead flesh. Shadd glanced across to Thufor, who was proceeding in a similar manner. He fought down his revulsion. This was not the moment to dispute the moral conduct of his two companions.

His attention was diverted by a low mewling sound from the gloom beyond the fire. Sleen, who was closest to its source, darted across the floor. Shadd saw him, half lost in the smoky gloom, drop to one knee before some large, low object.

Shadd made his way around the fire. As he approached he saw that Sleen was bent over a body, his own body shielding its upper half from sight. Shadd lowered himself to a crouch beside Sleen, who made a quick, surreptitious movement with one hand close to his belt.

The dead man was horribly mutilated. His skin had been gored and pierced and allowed to fester. Pieces of flesh had been torn or hacked away from his bones, and within the wounds maggots feasted.

'He died even as I reached him,' muttered Sleen.

Shadd put his hand to the base of the dead man's skull. A trickle of warm blood flowed from a small incision there. He looked at Sleen. 'It would appear he was helped on his way.'

He half-expected a challenge, but Sleen merely said, 'Had he been able to speak he would have begged for release. Look. He could not live.'

That this was so was undeniable, yet Shadd could not suppress a quiver of outrage. He rose to his feet, saying, 'And was this man also a friend of yours?'

Sleen busied himself for a moment about the corpse, then rose to face him, his narrow eyes wet and glittering. 'I knew him, sir, aye.'

He turned away and made off towards the low dais of rock on which the ceremonial seat rested.


IV


Thufor, upon the dais, hefted his axe and with one mighty blow sank it deep into the neck of the sleeping brute upon the seat. So massive was the slath's neck that the head did not sever, though the blade sliced through arteries, windpipe and spinal cord. The slath's body lurched violently into semi-awareness as its life fluids spewed. It gurgled and spat, then the axe-blade split its skull, dividing it almost in two, and the monster shuddered and died.

The three men scanned the chamber. No other slath stirred. Together, Thufor and Sleen took the dead slath's forelimbs and hauled it from the seat. The body rolled heavily onto the floor, spilling dark blood over the lip of the dais, to soak into the fouled earth beneath.

Sleen lowered himself onto his buttocks upon the dais and extended an arm beneath the seat. 'Somewhere here, if I have not been misled ... Ah! I have it.'

They heard a dull click as he pulled upon something hidden. He stood. 'Now, get behind the seat, yes, and push!'

Under their combined effort the massive rock seat slid back upon the dais with a heavy grating noise. Fitted into the rock beneath it was a single flat flagstone, a little over two feet square.

Sleen delved in his pack and brought out a pair of sturdy iron rods, wedged and flattened at one end. He handed one to Thufor, and with the other began to scrape and prise around one edge of the flag. Thufor did likewise. Close beside the dais a sleeping slath stirred, opened a bleary eye, snorted. Thufor abandoned his work, grabbed his axe, stepped down and splintered the creature's skull.

Speaking to Shadd, Sleen indicated the second tool. 'Aid me, sir, if you will.'

Together they drove the wedges beneath the flag and levered it up. Sleen got his fingers beneath it, and Thufor returned to help. The stone lifted and was eased back to settle upon the dais. Where it had lain was a narrow stairway twisting down into darkness.

Sleen straightened, breathing heavily, a film of sweat glistening upon his skin. He placed his hands upon his hips. 'Gentlemen, we are at the threshold to the vault. To my knowledge no one has come this far in centuries. From this point on my knowledge of this place is no greater than yours.'

'Do the slaths not know of this stairway, or what is said to lie beneath?' enquired Shadd.

'I believe not. They are neither clever nor acquisitive. When they made this warren their home it would not have occurred to them to investigate further. Nor would they have had any interest in the previous inhabitants.'

Thufor had descended the first two steps. Shadd was about to follow when a flickering motion caught his eye. He stayed Thufor with a hand upon his shoulder, and pointed.

Across the chamber, through the murky haze, could be seen a figure. Its form was not easy to make out. It seemed shapeless and indistinct, about eight feet in height and floating almost motionless in the air, some inches above the ground. Numerous limbs or tentacles of varying lengths and dimensions extended from its body. It had no head as such, but three eyes, glowing bright orange-red, shimmered in its upper part as if composed of fire.

'The Sentinel!' breathed Sleen. 'In every report I have gained from adventurers who have entered this place, it has appeared. I have seen it myself each time I have been here. Never yet has it interfered with men.'

They stood where they were, facing the thing with uncertainty. The Sentinel made no move other than the restless writhing, quivering motion which seemed native to its being. After a moment it began to withdraw, soundlessly, merging into the shadow on the far side of the hall until only the fiery glow of its eyes remained. Then that too was gone.

Sleen wiped his brow upon his arm. He turned, contriving an arch smile. 'From previous experience, I believe it will not return.'

They descended. The air beneath the hall of the slaths was cooler, dank but free of the vile odours of above. Thufor insisted upon a lamp, and Sleen supported him, though Shadd, for the present, advised against it. Temminee had flown on ahead, and using her vision Shadd had glimpsed something of what lay before them. A dozen rough-hewn steps wound down to an enclosed passage. Nothing moved there, and he would have preferred entering without the light which would give away their presence.

He was overruled. The other two would not descend in darkness.

A damp covering of lichen or mould lay upon the steps, and cobwebs hung across the passage, making it appear that no one had recently walked this way. Temminee returned, alighted on Shadd's shoulder to whisper in his ear, 'The passage ends after a few yards. I can find no other exit.'

The passage ended in a blunt face of rock. It was as though it had been begun and then abandoned, leading nowhere. Shadd stepped forward, gazing at the rock for some moments. He extended a hand and touched it with his fingertips.

'I sense powerful magic here.'

Thufor pressed against the rock. 'I sense nothing but cold, unbudging stone. Yet my instincts, or perhaps my wishes, tell me that there is a way through.'

Shadd turned to look back along the passage. With the movement of his head he noticed in the corner of his vision a slight shimmering at the angle formed between one side of the passage and the rock face. It was gone as he turned back to focus his eyes upon it. Perhaps it had been no more than a play of light and shadow cast by Thufor's lamp. Nevertheless he stepped forward and peered closer. Within the crook of the passage was a small area that, upon close inspection, seemed of uncertain texture.

Sleen pushed up to investigate. 'Have you found something?'

'Something, but I know not what.'

Temminee whispered, 'Caution, Duke Shadd!'

Sleen, seeing the area Shadd indicated, leaned forward, reaching to touch the rock.

'No!' hissed Shadd. He knocked Sleen's arm aside. He cast his eyes swiftly over the rock, then up to the ceiling overhead. He stepped back, grabbing Sleen and yanking him with him.

'What is this?' protested Sleen, bristling.

'I believe it would have been your end,' said Shadd. 'Wait here, both of you, and as you value your lives do not move from where you stand.'

He ran silently back along the passage and up the stairs to the hall of the slaths. There he grabbed a pair of spears and returned. Thufor and Sleen stood as he had left them, their eyes upon the angle of rock. Sleen was muttering something in a low voice.

'Now, let us put this to the test,' said Shadd. Holding the spear out and extending his arm to its fullest length, he touched the spearhead to the area of rock that had drawn his attention. He pushed.

Nothing.

He pushed again, more vigorously this time. The suspect rock gave with an abrasive sound. At the same time there was a harsh grating noise overhead. A massive pillar of rock dropped suddenly from the ceiling and crashed to the floor of the passage at the angle of wall and rock face where, just moments before, both Sleen and Shadd had been standing. The thunder of its fall reverberated deafeningly through the enclosed passage. A thick pall of powdery dust was thrown up, obscuring everything.

Shadd, who had darted back as the rock fell, said nothing. His eyes stayed on the pillar as the dust settled. Sleen had paled, aware that had he pressed upon the suspect rock as he'd intended, he would now be lying crushed beneath it.

Shadd stepped up to the pillar. It stood seven feet high, reaching almost to the ceiling. Taking the lantern he peered up into the gap it had left overhead. 'There are small niches which will serve as footholds,' he said, running a hand over the face of the pillar. He handed the lantern back to Thufor. 'It appears that this is our way through.'

Temminee had already darted up into the black. With her eyes Shadd saw a short narrow shaft leading through into a cavern chamber, which was illuminated, though he could not see by what. He reached up to grab the lip of the pillar, placed a foot in the first niche, and began to climb. Once up on the top of the pillar he eased his way into the shaft. It struck him that the fact that the rock pillar had been in place when they arrived was almost certain proof that no one had passed this way before them – unless there existed some mechanism for returning the pillar to its recess. If this was the case, then there must also reside within the vault some kind of intelligence which could operate the mechanism.

He reached the end of the shaft and lowered himself gingerly into the new chamber. Thufor, then Sleen, came behind him. The cavern held a soft, delicate luminescence, of a pale mauvish colour, which seemed to emanate from the harsh rock walls themselves. It was of no great size, and curved away in a leftward sweep, tapering abruptly into a tunnel whose end was obscured behind the angle of its wall. Rough, uneven rock formed the floor, and from somewhere could be heard the echoing music of running water.

Temminee flitted away around the curve, returned, whispered to Shadd that a wooden door stood there. Shadd advanced cautiously, Thufor beside him, Sleen a little to their rear.

They entered the tunnel to see the door twenty paces away. They moved up, scanning walls, floor, roof, but found nothing to arouse concern. Shadd observed the door for some seconds, then prodded it with the remaining slath spear. 'It seems sound. I detect no magic, other than what is intrinsic to this place.'

Thufor stepped forward and grasped the iron door-handle. With extreme care, as though he were holding a newborn babe, he began to ease it around. All three tuned their senses for signs of another trap.

The handle turned, the latch slowly lifted. Thufor pushed upon the door, which swung silently open to reveal another short corridor. This too was bathed in mauvish light, though its walls were smooth and flat. At its end it opened into what gave every appearance of being an empty chamber.

They moved forward into this new passage, the door swinging to behind them, and Shadd felt his skin begin to tingle and his inner awareness rise under the increase of subtle magic here. The chamber was rectangular, no more than eight paces in length and six wide. Its walls were dull grey and of perfectly smooth stone. At its far side was a recess housing another timbered door.

They crossed the chamber and with similar precautions opened this door. They passed into another corridor leading to another chamber identical in all respects, except that its luminescence was of a greenish shade. And on, into a third chamber, this one filled with ice-blue light; and a fourth, amber; and fifth, roseate. As they passed through this last, Temminee alighted again on Shadd's shoulder and whispered in his ear. He halted, glanced behind him, frowning, then said, 'Thufor, Sleen, stand as you are.'

The two stopped near the centre of the chamber. Shadd walked by them to the door. 'Wait a moment, and observe. I wish to test something.'

Shadd opened the door and stepped through. As with the previous doors it closed behind him. Thufor and Sleen waited uneasily. A voice spoke from behind them: 'Indeed, this is a diabolically clever device.'

They both spun around, weapons before them, to see Shadd standing at the entrance to the chamber through which they had just walked.

'How is this?' cried Thufor, looking back in bafflement at the door, then to Shadd once more.

'How, I do not know,' said Shadd. 'But the fact of it is that this is a nexus of magical contrivance. We have been proceeding endlessly through the same chamber, going nowhere, and might conceivably have continued to do so for as long as the strength remained in our limbs to carry us forward.'

'Then we should return and seek another route,' said Sleen.

'There was no other route,' Thufor remarked.

'Then we must break the pattern.'

Shadd turned to stare back with a contemplative expression into the corridor. He noticed now a distortion within its atmosphere which had not been apparent when entering from the other direction. A limpid, liquid film appeared to ripple in the rose-hued air.

With the slath spear Shadd probed the space of the corridor. To no effect. He stood back, then tossed the spear so that it fell to the corridor floor with a *clack* and a *clang*.

Immediately there was a loud rumbling sound. The walls of the corridor suddenly trembled and slipped back. Scurries of dust and rubble tumbled towards the floor, and the roof of the corridor, a gigantic block of solid stone, dropped. It slammed into the floor, sending shock waves hammering into the chamber where they stood. The ground shook with the impact and the chamber clouded quickly with dust.

The dust settled and the three men saw that the way back had been tightly sealed by the great stone. Not even Temminee could have passed that way now.

Thufor gave a warning cry. Shadd wheeled, to see rising from the floor of the chamber, out of the very stone upon which they stood, wispy tendrils, like smoke or mist. The wisps became vaporous columns which seemed to wreathe into solidity, becoming indistinct yet specific forms. As the three stared the forms became recognisable: wraithlike warriors in glimmering grey armour, bearing swords and axes. They rose up, twelve or more, from every corner of the chamber, and silently, menacingly, advanced upon the humans in their midst.

# 12

## I

The voice of Khimmur called silently across nations, tearing me, calling me home. Already we had passed beyond Chol, had entered the Enchanted Land. My heart grew heavier with every step; so frequently did I turn to look back along my tracks! East we went, ever east, further and further from everything I had ever known and loved. Where would this path take me? To what end?

Rohse, I thought of you ceaselessly then. I ached to be with you, to hold you as I had held you before. I wanted to be your protector, your husband, your lover; the doting father of Eroniss, nothing more.

*How I longed to be human again!*

On several occasions Yaoww trotted back to where I had stopped in my tracks and turned my face to the west, and enquired with a concerned expression as to what was troubling me. I could tell her nothing. How could I hope to explain?

'I am troubled by this journey,' I began, thinking I might attempt to convey to her something of the futility of the quest the vhazz had undertaken. But that, too, was a doomed undertaking.

'I too,' replied Yaoww. 'But it is our one hope.'

A forlorn hope, but she would never see it. We differed fundamentally in our conceptions of the world and events, in our aspirations and our fears. I looked back, afraid of what the future might hold, longing for what lay behind me. Yaoww's eyes saw ahead, into illusion born of groundless myth and desperate belief. For her the past was to be abandoned, rejected, feared, while for me it had somehow to be regained. The vhazz mind drew sustenance from its reliance upon a future that could never be.

'A part of me resides back there,' was all I could say as reluctantly I let her lead me on into the east.

Yaoww seemed to be acquainted with a tortuous route over the harsh mountainous terrain of eastern Chol, and beyond, ascending into the night-clasped mountains of Qotolr – mountains sometimes called by humans 'The Ghosting Peaks', for it is true, when gazed upon from a distance these mountains seem to mist, to blur, to defy the eye and irk the brain, almost as though they too are illusory.

To my knowledge no human, not even the Chol, knew a way across these mountains. And as far as I was aware Yaoww had never passed this way before. Yet she advanced with confidence, apparently following an unmarked path, and never once seeming to doubt her route.

I questioned her about this, and she regarded me curiously.

'I have never used this route before, Huwoorsk. But vhazz packs in the past have, and their memories have been passed on to us. Surely you are aware of this?'

I wasn't. I was blind. Without Yaoww I would have perished in this forbidding land. I could not have stayed on the trail she followed. We soared and dived, scrambled up rearing cliffs, through harsh vegetation, traversed ice-walls and glaciers, snow-fields and chasms. We chased pell-mell into lush moon-silvered vales, then climbed again into barren wintry rock and ice.

Advancing into the future, seeking a myth, following a memory.

As best I could I committed every detail of the

journey to memory, holding the hope that perhaps one day I might have need to retrace my steps.

Each day, as evening drew nigh, I would awake from sleep an hour or so before Yaoww to immerse myself in Zan-Chassin meditations. As before, contact was denied me, either with former ally-entities from the Realms of Non-Corporeality, or with my human associates. And no raptures could I cast still, not even the most trifling. The restless, disquieted nature of the vhazz, its existential torment compounding my own many times over, its flesh aching and itching, denied me vital dissociation. It was all I could do each time to drag myself free of the vhazz body.

Into this single exercise, then, I continued to concentrate all my effort, striving to prolong the precious moments of incorporeality. Gradually the seconds had become half a minute. Now that stretched into a minute, the minute strove to become two. Then the dreadful pull of Huwoorsk's corporeal self overcame my capacity to resist. Everything became the effort instead of the deed, and I fell back into dire flesh.

But it was something. In truth it was everything – for as long as I retained the capacity to at least rise out of that body I could reassure myself, without self-duplicity, that I was still something other than vhazz.

We descended one night towards a wide valley bathed in frail moonlight, which opened into less rugged terrain than that we had so far encountered. A river, almost phosphorescent, wound across the valley floor. We found cover and prepared to rest, for the night was all but over and we had travelled hard and were greatly fatigued.

I was awakened in full daylight, seized suddenly with a violent sense of alarm. Yaoww was already on her feet, frozen in an attitude of questing anxiety, staring across the valley. As I moved up beside her I saw that her whole body trembled. Her eyes had filled with tears.

'They are dying, Huwoorsk!' she whispered hoarsely, in a voice so tremulous and despairing that I shuddered. 'Can you feel them? *Oh!*' She winced, gave a whimper of pain. 'They are dying! All of them!'

And I sensed something of what she felt. Somewhere ahead, perhaps just hours away, something terrible was happening. The pack, our sisterhood, was in distress, dreadful distress. Their summons was an assault upon me like nothing I had felt before; their mutual call for aid so tragic that I was all but paralysed by the sense of their fear and agony. I could scarcely imagine what Yaoww felt, knowing that she experienced it with an intensity far greater than I.

With a scream Yaoww bounded away, with no heed for the daylight. 'To them! Quickly!'

I raced behind her. We followed the course of the river, then swerved away through woods, over freshly tilled meadows and orchards, hardly bothering to keep to cover. We passed close to an isolated farmstead on the outskirts of a village of stone huts. Bounding over a dry stone wall we surprised a small herd of scrawny cattle driven along a track by a peasant lad. The cattle scattered in panic, scrambling madly up over the wall, or galloping back along the track. The drover was too shocked to respond immediately, and we were gone before he could gather his wits.

For an hour we ran at breakneck speed. Eventually my pace slackened. My lungs were scorched, my legs unable to summon the strength to continue. The way steepened as we ascended onto a rocky hill, and to my relief I saw that Yaoww, too, was beginning to falter.

At the hill crest she stopped and sagged to the earth.

I dragged myself up beside her, my lungs heaving, and collapsed, an agonising pain racking my innards. When at last I could breathe again I raised my head. The hill commanded a prospect of a broad, wild plain. In the far distance could be seen the mountains rising once more, shimmering and uncertain.

Yaoww turned her head to me. Her tormented expression reinforced the new sense of desolation that had overcome me. The terror I had sensed earlier had diminished, but in its place was a different fear, something even deeper and more disturbing which I could not yet fully grasp. It was a feeling of emptiness, of utter, inexpressible loss.

'They are gone,' whispered Yaoww.

It came to me then, in full and awful recognition. The pack's agony had ceased, but not because of vhazz triumph or successful escape. The unimaginable had occurred, and my entire being went rigid as I faced the ineffable, terrifying gulf that opened within me. The sisterhood was no more.

Yaoww stared away across the landscape, tears streaking the hair of her cheeks. 'How can this be?'

And I too, though I knew it, still could not grasp it. All dead? Almost seventy proud and fierce vhazz, skilled warriors in the main. Even the youngest was capable of spirited resistance against any normal foe.

Ah, but this is Enchantery, I reminded myself, for no other explanation could reasonably suffice. In Enchantery it is possible that there exists no such thing as a normal foe.

'Some must have survived,' declared Yaoww feebly. 'They must have. It is impossible that they have all died. The survivors may be scattered, weakened. We cannot sense them.'

She rose to all fours and pushed herself forward, down the hillside.

It was twenty minutes later that we scented blood. Faint at first, no more than a delicate trace dispersed upon a south-westerly breeze. Yaoww whined; we veered towards the scent. It became stronger, brought to us in thick, drenching wafts. It was vhazz blood. The blood of others mingled with it, too, but predominantly, overpoweringly, it was vhazz.

We quickened our pace, heading for a line of dark trees which marked the fringe of a forest. As we entered those trees we came upon the first bodies.

Two vhazz lay sprawled in the shade, their corpses torn and bloody. The first, whose name, I recalled, was Morad, was splayed upon her back, a gaping hole driven right through her chest. Her companion, whom I did not know, had been hacked to death with a sword. Yaoww moved to them tearfully, lowering her muzzle to lick bright blood from their matted hair. She whispered their names softly. Around her the breeze took up her whisper and passed it among the trees.

I scoured the immediate area and found the marks of horses' hooves impressed deep into the soil. There was no indication of who had ridden the horses.

There was little we could do. We moved on.

More bodies, all vhazz. In all we came across fifteen, but the stench of death grew ever stronger, drawing us further into the wood.

In the deepest part of the forest vast oaks and chestnut trees spread a dense canopy over a gulley choked with bracken and scrub. Shoulders of limestone clothed in green moss and lichen, butted up from the earth. In this place we came upon the most dreadful sight of all.

Here, and all around, the bodies of vhazz were strewn. In places they lay on top of one another, so close-quartered had been the fighting. We moved

343

among them, searching for life and finding none. We counted forty-four corpses, male and female, young and old. All bore the evidence of brutal fighting, and nowhere was there any sign of their assailants, other than hoofprints in the earth and arrows protruding from the hides of the dead vhazz.

I took passing note of one of the arrows. Its shaft was of white ash, its flights of feathers coloured a deep metallic-blue. The arrowhead I could not see, for it was buried in vhazz flesh.

I came across Muurh, who with Yaoww had been responsible for nursing me back to health when – how long ago? – I first came to occupy the body of Huwoorsk. She lay upon her side, her body contorted into a wholly unnatural posture. She still grasped a bloody vhazz sword, a shield strapped upon one forelimb. Her muzzle and face had been smashed beyond recognition by a mace or some other blunt, heavy weapon. Her spine was broken; a blue-fletched arrow stuck out from her chest. I knew her only by her scent.

Yaoww stood a few feet away, surrounded by the corpses of her family, shocked into silence. I moved across to her and pressed my muzzle to her cheek in a hopeless gesture of consolation.

'They were caught sleeping,' Yaoww said, her voice choked and quavering. 'It is the only explanation. They were trapped here, surprised by an enemy many times stronger. Whoever or whatever did this terrible thing, they must have followed the sisterhood here and waited until all but the sentries were asleep.'

She said more, repeating herself over and over in an attempt to derive sense out of what confronted us. But there was no solace to be had in words, no meaning to be found. We faced slaughter, stark and terrible. Yaoww, as she spoke, pressed herself against me, returning my own gesture. Before I was aware of what was happening she had twisted her body around and was beneath me, and I had entered her. We coupled, fervidly, almost irrationally, moved by a primordial impulse greater than we: the need, not simply to distract ourselves in this dreadful moment, but to continue, to ensure survival, for our species, of which we might conceivably be the last.

And when we had done and lay together, faced once more with death and horror, Yaoww wept. I lay in silence, bewildered and desolate, grieving even as I wondered what I had become.

## II

'Some still live!' declared Yaoww abruptly. She had risen onto her haunches, her nostrils tasting the air. 'Do you feel it, Huwoorsk? It is faint, but the life-pulse is there still. It is not a total void.'

I directed my mind inwards, searching that emptiness, that bleak abyss that was both within me and I within it. And, yes! Something! Feeble, barely living . . . but there. Some – perhaps even only one – had survived.

Already Yaoww had gone, racing in the direction of the pulse. I followed, passing more bodies, all vhazz – those who had tried to flee. The enemy had been remorseless, allowing them no quarter or escape. And still there was no sign of enemy casualties.

We weaved between the trees, seeking the source of that pulse. Beside a dense tangle of briar we came upon a male member of the pack. He rested at the base of an oak, a red stain of blood matting the hair of his shoulder and chest. At the sound of our approach he had sprung erect, weapons bared, but at the sight of us he slumped to the ground once more.

'Vis!' cried Yaoww. She ran to him, examined his wound. It was a sword-slash, deep but not fatal. She licked it clean. Vis lay back, his head upon the earth.

He stared dully at the two of us, too exhausted or despondent for emotion.

'Are there others?' cried Yaoww. 'What happened?'

'There may be others,' replied Vis in a voice flat and slurred. 'The slaughter was great. At the last several of us tried to escape. We were pursued to the end. Perhaps half-a-dozen got away, probably less. You were the lucky one, Yaoww. You who went back to find Huwoorsk.'

There was no mistaking the acrimony in his voice. His eyes settled briefly upon me. Yaoww chose not to respond. She gave a moan of disbelief, shaking her head in grief. Wearily Vis told his tale.

The pack had come upon the gulley some time before dawn, and had chosen to rest there through the day, it being well-concealed and – as they'd thought – easily defensible. Vis had been trailing a mile or so behind, in the manner of the vhazz male. He had not been aware of any threat, though he had spotted warriors during the night.

'They were dark, strange-skinned creatures who rode warmounts unlike any I had seen. They were ten in number, following a course roughly parallel to our own. They were unaware of us, and not close enough to represent danger. When we stopped to rest they rode on. I followed them for a time, until they were well clear of our area. They were not the ones who attacked us. Indeed, my feeling was that they themselves were pursued and anxious to be far from this place.'

The attack had come an hour or so later, while the pack, and Vis, slept. Vis had been woken by the summons of the sisterhood and the noise of battle filtering to him through the trees. He had raced down to the gulley, to confront a terrible sight.

'The gulley was surrounded, and our vhazz were trapped within. Warriors fell upon them, two hundred strong or more, it was difficult to tell. They were formidable fighters: blue men – their armour blue, their weapons, even their faces. Many were mounted, though the terrain was unsuitable for horses. Yet the horses suffered no disadvantage. They were surefooted, swift and as agile as panthers! Others were on foot, hidden in the trees and rocks. Our vhazz were dying, unable to escape the gulley. And how those blue men fought! They were not ordinary men. I threw myself upon the back of the nearest and buried my sword deep. He whirled, dying, but even as his life left him he laughed. His mouth stretched wide and he laughed out loud!

'Then two others attacked me, but I was aided now by Ozors, of our pack.'

Vis shook his head. There really was so little he could say. The evidence lay in the woods behind us.

'You say you killed one,' I said, 'yet we have searched. We found no sign of these blue men.'

'Do you doubt me, Huwoorsk?'

'I do not doubt you. I merely wonder at what we have witnessed.'

Vis looked away into the trees. 'I killed more than one, and each time they died with shouts of laughter. And other blue men lay dead on the forest floor. What happened to their dead I cannot say, but for every one that we brought down it seemed that three or four of our own were slain. We were defeated and I and those that still could, when it was apparent that all was lost, tried to escape, for there was no quarter. The blue men were not satisfied with simple victory. They demanded the deaths of us all.'

347

With water from a nearby stream we bathed Vis's wound. Yaoww applied balm and a compress of leaves and moss. She bound the wound with a strip of cloth.

'We will move on now,' she said. 'We must search for other survivors.'

Though we were greatly fatigued, and it was still full daylight, neither I nor Vis saw fit to argue. Yaoww was the female of our little band, and the elders of the sisterhood were now gone. Naturally she had assumed leadership.

Within the hour we came upon three more survivors, females of the pack. All had been wounded in the massacre or during their subsequent escape. One, Shavis by name, was in a grave condition. A hindleg had been smashed with a heavy blow and a swordblade had penetrated deep between her ribs. She was weak, semi-delirious, and could barely walk. We dressed her wounds and bound her leg with hazel splints, but it was evident that Shavis had severe internal bleeding.

The other two told of their relentless pursuit by the blue men. They had eventually escaped by going to ground, and had been fortunate, for the blue men were intent on hunting them down to the last. Even now they had not given up the hunt, and continued to scour the land.

It was Yaoww's decision now that we find a hiding-place and rest until nightfall. We climbed into higher ground, came across an abandoned lair upon a ridge of broken sandstone, and rested there.

We saw no sign of our enemy for the remainder of that day. When night came Shavis was too weak to be moved so we stayed into the following day. Late in the afternoon Shavis's soul quietly slipped free of her mauled and shattered flesh. With the evening we placed her corporeal form in the open, to become sustenance for others. We departed our hiding-place and moved on eastwards, and though no one spoke their thoughts I believe that none of us now were confident of our destination.

## III

Twice we spied scouting parties of the blue men, each about half a dozen strong. Mindful of Vis's description I gave particular attention to their horses. They were indeed exceptionally swift and light-footed, their movements graceful yet quick and darting, though the mounts themselves were chargers, heavily-caparisoned for battle. Certainly these were enchanted beasts, and their riders rode with a certainty unreduced by the night. We faced formidable foes indeed.

Late in the night we startled a buck from its resting-place, a handsome three-year-old with newly budding antlers. We gave chase as it made a wild dash down through the woods into a river gorge, then up the rocky hillside beyond. The buck was fleet, but so were we, though injured Vis could not keep pace and fell back to follow our trail at his own pace.

For an hour we chased the buck. He was vigorous and determined, and more than once we came close to losing him. But we were three, and were able to drive him along our own course. In the end we cornered him at the foot of a granite buttress, and there brought him down. Ravenous, we feasted upon his rich flesh, leaving ample for Vis who limped in to join us twenty minutes later.

As Vis ate his fill Yaoww touched upon the subject of the future. As we were two males and three females the sisterhood's dream did not have to perish. We would move on, still making for the place where day begins, and beyond its beginning, the land of endless night. And from the offspring which we would bear a new and strong pack would grow. We would survive, to prosper in a new homeland where we might live without the constant fear of slaughter at the hands of men.

It was rousing talk, set to kindle hope and renewed purpose. It was the stuff of desperation, bonding us anew and directing our thoughts from the horrors just past.

But as Yaoww drew towards the end of her speech she was interrupted by a sudden crashing in the woods at her back, then a heavy pounding and a wild, blood-curdling cry. I spun, to see a mounted knight in blue armour break from the trees just yards away. He charged down upon us, a savage grin upon his face, his eyes glaring white. His battle-cry sundering the stillness of the night, his long lance couched, tip low.

I flung myself aside, as did the others. But Vis, who was still devouring the buck's carcass, was slower. He, turning to identify the source of the disturbance, rose onto his hindlegs. He glimpsed his assailant, then the knight was upon him. The lance drove clean through Vis's chest and out through his back. He was lifted bodily from the ground and carried along with the horse's charge, skewered upon the lance.

The blue knight vented a great ululation of glee. He tilted his lance high, Vis's limp body still impaled upon it, and I marvelled, even as I gaped aghast, at the strength of the arm that could raise a load like that, almost as heavy as a man.

The knight's charge had carried him beyond us by some twenty yards. The horse wheeled quickly around. The knight drew the beast to a halt to gather himself.

'Stand together!' hissed Yaoww. 'He is but one. We can take him if he charges again.'

With a scornful laugh the knight tossed aside his encumbered lance. He drew his sword, while with his other hand he tipped a horn to his lips, threw back his head and blew a single bright note into the night. Then he crouched again in his saddle, sword high, and spurred his mount forward.

We readied ourselves as he thundered down upon us. He leaned from his saddle, aiming a swordblow at Yaoww. I was forced to leap aside, as were the other two females, to avoid being struck by the great warhorse. The horse was between Yaoww and I; I did not see the outcome of the blow.

I slashed with my sword at the mount's foreleg as it passed. It stumbled, went down. The blue knight pitched headlong from his saddle.

With relief I glimpsed Yaoww, crouching. As the knight smashed into the earth she bounded forward and leapt upon him. He rolled, fending off her swordblow with the edge of his own blade. One hand got beneath her chest and he thrust her away, almost without effort. He clambered to one knee, laughing insanely.

Now I and the other two were upon him. I stabbed while one of the females took the knight by the throat with her jaws. The other lunged with her sword, and its blade sank deep into his abdomen. The blue knight's eyes widened. His mouth stretched and he laughed as the life went from his body. He toppled backwards and lay grinning in death upon the bloodied earth.

From the woods came the pounding of hooves, the crash of foliage, the yells of men.

'*Run!*' cried Yaoww.

We fled that place. Somewhere behind us came the

blue men upon their horses, whooping with the joy of the chase.

We ran a wild and erratic course, weaving and hurtling through the trees. We broke out into the open, up across a patch of meadow, down into a marshy pit, then up again into trees and uneven ground. Here we should have had the advantage, for the earth was strewn with outcrops of rock. We could dart between the boulders, unhindered by the tortuous passage they forced. But I glanced back to see the blue horses riding the terrain almost as easily as we. Nimble and undeterred, they came like supernatural things over land that would have stalled any normal mount.

Inexorably they were gaining on us. We came out of the rocks into a wide field of long grass. Here we were invisible, though we left trails like markers in our wake. The din of the hunt came closer, filling the night.

We were faced abruptly with a sheer rocky cliff. Panic rose like a great wave in my brain. We veered to the right. Over my shoulder I glimpsed a mounted form bearing down, almost upon me. I threw myself flat, pressed to the earth. The warhorse bounded over me. Something whizzed by my head, all but scraping the top of my skull. I was up again on all fours, and running.

The cliff began to break up. Ahead of us four blue knights suddenly galloped across our path. They spotted us, wheeled their mounts around for the charge. We swerved to the left, into a narrow, furze-choked opening in the rock.

Up over broken earth, loose stone, slabs of rotten grey rock. Still the blue horses came on. An arrow whined by my ear, bounced off a rock just ahead of me. Yaoww and the other two were before me, disappearing now as the ground suddenly gave way onto a steep, stony slope.

I hurled myself forward, regardless of what lay beyond, and pitched headlong down the slope. Ahead of me I glimpsed the others, sliding, careening down over loose rock and earth.

We reached the bottom, the thunder of our pursuers like an avalanche in our wake. Here was a small stream and dense woods. We bounded across the water. A horseman drove down suddenly upon one of the females, Escre by name. I screamed a warning. Escre leapt to the side, dodged the arcing sword, and raced on.

Suddenly a shout from Yaoww: 'Here! A cave!'

I saw it – a black fissure among thick brush at the base of a tumble of rocks rearing up beside the stream. With the others I charged towards it. It was too small for a horse – but was it a refuge or a trap?

There was no time to consider. Outside we were lost. As one we plunged into the opening.

The cave drove back into the hillside, its ceiling low, coming eventually to meet the ground fifteen yards in. Here, gasping for breath, we pressed ourselves against the uneven rock walls, hugging what cover there was lest our pursuers loose arrows in our wake.

Looking back I saw the opening framed against the night beyond. Voices called from outside, cursing, demanding. A figure appeared in silhouette, bent on one knee to peer into the cave. Quick as a flash Escre flicked a dart. The blue knight reeled back with a cry, clutching his face.

Yaoww was exploring the interior of the cave. 'It seems we may be fortunate. The rock here is split; the roof does not quite meet the ground and a way seems to extend further back.'

She flattened herself to wriggle through the gap she had found. Her voice came back to us, hollow and muffled. 'There is a passage. I cannot see how far it leads.'

Even as she spoke an arrow zinged in from outside, glancing off the cave wall. Another followed, and another, forcing us to duck and scramble for cover. We were without a choice. To remain where we were was to die eventually at the hands of the blue knights. One by one we squeezed ourselves through the rock and followed Yaoww.

# 13

The first of the wraith-warriors aimed a scything blow
with its axe at Shadd's middle. He dodged aside, and
returned the attack with flashing shortswords. The
edge of his first blade bit deeply into the wraith-
warrior's neck; the second slipped between its scaled
armour to cleanly penetrate the flesh of its breast. The
warrior displayed no reaction. It came on, thrusting
hard with the sharpened metal beak mounted upon
the axe-helve. Shadd parried the blow and danced back,
dismayed.

To his side Thufor swung his mighty axe. It
slammed into a shield, buckling the metal. The
warrior staggered under the impact. Thufor's second
blow sliced into its flank, but again, the warrior shed
no blood, nor was it stayed or deterred by its injury.
With a great yell Thufor struck again, this time
bringing his blade around the attack of another of the
wraiths. His axe severed the warrior's arm above the
elbow, revealing bloodless 'flesh' of the consistency
and colour of greyish clay. Before Thufor's astonished
eyes the truncated arm immediately began to grow
again. And from the limb that had fallen to the
flagstones spouted a vaporous column which took
on the form of a new warrior.

Thufor cried out in alarm, 'Hold! They do not die!
And more are born from their parts!'

The wraith-warriors pressed hard, forcing the three
of them back.

Sleen had already retreated to the doorway. 'We must run!'

There was little choice, though they could not know now what lay beyond that door. Would they enter to find themselves back once again in this same chamber, as before? Perhaps worse, would they somehow be projected into the block of stone that had fallen into the passageway, there to be embedded forever? Or was the pattern of the magical nexus now broken? Had the way through been breached with the falling of the stone?

Sleen no longer hesitated. He pushed upon the door and ran through. Shadd and Thufor followed, warding blows but discouraged from renewing the attack. The wraith-warriors crowded after them with mute and emotionless menace.

The nexus *had* been broken! They ran into a softly-illuminated rock cavern of cathedral proportions. Columns of ancient rock struck up from the floor or grew out of the ceiling high overhead, in formations beautiful, wondrous and bizarre. An underground river flowed through the middle of the cavern and out beneath the rock, its water swirling, black and even as silk, its precise point of egress undiscernible. Spanning this was a footbridge made of heavy, age-worn timber, which appeared to be suspended on chains secured to the rock ceiling. Over the bridge a natural portal opened in the rock.

Without time for thought or precaution Sleen bounded onto the bridge and over, the others close at his heels. The bridge quivered and rattled as they crossed, but it proved sturdy, its timbers unvitiated by time. They ran through the portal and entered the passage on the other side.

For twenty paces they ran on. The passage twisted away deep into the rock. Suddenly they were confronted

356

with an iron grille set into ceiling, walls and floor, which barred the way into a large chamber beyond.

With a shout of alarm Sleen threw aside his sword and flung himself at the grille, endeavouring to raise it with his bare hands. Thufor joined him, to no effect. The grille would not budge. They wheeled, taking up their weapons once more, to face the oncoming wraiths.

But the passageway behind was empty. They waited. The wraiths did not appear. With caution they edged back along the passage, expecting at any moment to find the weird-warriors bearing down upon them. They reached the entrance of the passage. Over the bridge, on the far shore of the underground river, the wraiths were gathered, milling in agitation.

'It seems they are unwilling to cross,' said Thufor, breathing hard, his face flushed from the exertion.

'As well for us that they are,' Shadd muttered.

They stood awhile, observing the wraiths, which still made no attempt to set foot upon the bridge. Presently Shadd turned to make his way back along the passage. The others followed.

At the grille they examined the walls and floor for signs of a trigger or mechanism that might raise the barrier. They found nothing. In the chamber beyond they could see, at the far end, an altar-like table carved out of stone, its facing side engraved with arcane cyphers and mysterious designs. Upon it stood a fabulous golden chalice set with gems. Two small wooden chests bound with straps of iron rested upon the floor, one each side of the altar. Upon the walls were ornate tapestries, richly embroidered drapes and other decorative hangings.

Temminee flitted between the bars of the grille into the chamber. She returned after moments. 'I see nothing to indicate a means of entering.'

Together the three men strove with sheer brute strength to raise the grille. It remained fast. They pushed, first to one side, then to the other, in the hope that it might slide back into the rock. Still they failed to move it. Thufor stepped back, his hands upon his hips. 'We can go neither forward nor back.'

Shadd stood beside him, immersed in thought, his eyes wandering over the ceiling and walls. 'So far the pattern has been consistent. There has always been a way forward. Surely that will prove to be the case here, too.'

Sleen, who had wandered away along the passage to check on the wraiths, returned. 'They are still there. We cannot go back.'

He sat down upon the floor, his back to the rock. Presently Thufor joined him. Shadd stood a while longer, contemplating the grille. 'It rests within a housing, in floor, ceiling and walls,' he murmured, half to himself. 'It is not set directly into the rock.'

He walked back down the passage to the bridge. On the other side the wraith-warriors had fallen still. At his approach they stirred and began to press forward. None, however, stepped upon the bridge.

Shadd stared across, his hand raised pensively to his jaw. His eyes swept the vast interior of the cavern. He observed the obsidian water, the rock walls, the bridge. He stepped onto the bridge, noting its slight sway and vibration beneath his weight. He turned, the fingers of one hand touching the Soul Crystal at his breast, and stared back into the tunnel where Thufor and Sleen waited.

Shadd's eyes fell upon the chains which held the bridge. His gaze travelled upwards, to the rock ceiling. He saw now that the chains were not actually secured into the rock as he had previously supposed. They rose, two at each end of the bridge, to link with a single more massive chain overhead. This followed a perpendicular course to disappear into the high vault of the ceiling itself.

He stared for some moments, puzzled without knowing quite why. He looked down to his feet, at the planks of ancient larch beneath, laid across massive oak beams and struts. He bent his knees and jumped upon the spot, observant of the slight motion of the bridge. Crossing back to the shore he knelt and examined the base of the bridge, where it met the shore at each side, then its entire span.

Quite suddenly he had it. He stared again, a half-smile lightening his sombre face. He rose to his feet and called back into the passage, 'We are fools! Look, here is the way through!'

Thufor and Sleen came smartly.

'The grille cannot be raised,' said Shadd, 'and neither is it meant to be. Look, this bridge is suspended. It is a counterweight. It is this that holds the grille in place. Free the bridge from its chains and the grille, I am certain, will drop.'

Thufor, his brow furrowed, studied the bridge, then shook his head. 'The bridge appears to be suspended, aye. But there is a narrow lip of rock directly beneath its ends here. Free it of its chains and its weight will merely come to rest upon this lip.'

'Look more closely!' insisted Shadd. 'The chains must be freed in a specific order. In fact, only those upon the other side should be released. There is no rock directly beneath the bridge there. That end will fall straight into the river beneath.'

'And this end will then rise and swing into the centre. The weight will be as before; nothing will have been achieved, except that it will then be impossible to reach the bridge to free the remaining chains.'

'No. Again you have not looked closely enough.

This entire structure is an ingenious and meticulously crafted device. Observe the centre of the bridge. What do you see?'

Thufor studied the bridge. 'The timbers are not whole. It is sectioned in the middle.'

'Quite so. The two sections are held fast by mortice and tenon joints. Nothing else that I can see holds them together. Thus were the bridge up-ended it would divide into its two sections. One would fall away into the river, so halving its weight.'

'And destroying its effectiveness as a counterweight to the grille! By the gods, you are right!'

Sleen, who had followed Shadd's reasoning with a moot expression, now made a sceptical grimace and said, 'But can we be certain that that is indeed the bridge's function? If you are wrong, if we destroy this bridge only to find that the grille has still not budged, we will still be unable to advance and will additionally have cut off our only way back across this river.'

Shadd made a dismissive gesture. 'There is no way back. We cannot fight those creatures mustered on the other shore. But I am convinced that this is the way. Why else such a subtle but painstaking design? It would have been no simple task to construct it thus and set it in place.'

Sleen seemed to concur, though it was evident he was not entirely happy at the prospect of destroying the bridge.

As Shadd had pointed out, the chains had to be released on the far side, so that that end of the bridge would drop and the section fall away. The easiest means of achieving this was to cut through the solid oak beams into which the chains were secured. The man whose task it was to sunder the wood would be obliged to stand upon the bridge. As the bridge up-ended he, inevitably, would be pitched into the dark waters beneath.

Thufor, being the axe-bearer, made no attempt to deny his suitability for the task. Nor did he shrink from it. He stripped to his loincloth, then lowered himself onto the rock to dip a foot into the water. He drew it back with a gasp.

'A man will last but seconds in that water!' He stared at the two of them. 'The current is strong; I will be unable to swim to the shore, and may well be sucked under – moreso as I would prefer not to lose my axe.'

Shadd held out a rope. 'We will haul you back.'

'And do it quickly. I have little choice but to trust you.'

'Your trust will not be misplaced.'

Thufor wound the rope about his girth, knotted it, and strode out onto the bridge.

For the next few minutes Thufor worked, his feet well apart, striking again and again with his axe at the wood. The wraiths on the other shore pushed forward excitedly, thrusting and jabbing with their weapons. But Thufor had positioned himself beyond their reach, and they would not commit themselves to the bridge where they might properly engage him.

He worked upon the two beams alternately, reducing each so that, when the first was released, destabilising the footway on which he stood, he would have no great amount of work to do to free the second. The muscles of his broad back, arms and thighs rippled as he worked, and he was quickly drenched in a gleaming film of sweat. But he did not pause to rest. Eventually he called back, 'The first beam is almost through.'

Shadd and Sleen took up the slack of the rope, bracing themselves. Thufor swung another three times. There was the sound of splitting wood. The first chain, freed, sprang back into the air, the butt of the oak beam swinging at its end. The bridge lurched precipitously. Thufor lunged and grabbed the rail, struggling to stay on his feet.

He looked back at the others with a broad grin. Hooking one arm about the rail he hefted the axe with the other and brought it down upon the remaining beam.

Again. And again. The wood creaked, sagged under the strain of the sudden extra weight, and gave.

The end of the bridge dropped suddenly, while that nearest to Shadd and Sleen was yanked abruptly away and roofwards. The bridge parted. Behind them, in the passage, there was a hollow rumbling sound, and a thunderous metallic crash. At the same time Thufor was skidding across the planks, thrown onto his back. He rolled violently with the motion of the sundered bridge and was propelled backwards and down, into the water. He disappeared beneath the surface.

Immediately Shadd and Sleen hauled upon the rope. The current was more powerful than they had supposed. Thufor did not resurface and his body dragged hard, seeming to possess the weight of two or three men. They pulled again. A murky white shape appeared beneath the surface of the water.

They heaved. A pale arm broke the surface, groped for the rock. Then Thufor's head of dark hair, his mouth open and gasping. His other arm came up, thrusting his axe out onto dry land. He clung to the rock, his limbs so shocked by the cold that he could not pull himself up. The two took his weight and brought him to safety.

Thufor half lay for some seconds, seemingly in shock, regaining his breath. Before them the section of bridge dangled on its chain high above the water, swinging and rotating slowly. The other section had drifted away downstream and was lodged against the rock where the river appeared to flow out beneath the cavern. Shadd strode quickly back along the passage to inspect the grille. As he had deduced, it had dropped into the floor. Nothing was to be seen of it now, other than its uppermost rim sunk into its housing an inch or so beneath the ground. The way was clear to enter the chamber beyond.

## II

Thufor dried and dressed himself and seemed none the worse for his watery ordeal. They stood together at the threshold of the chamber. Before entering Shadd slipped his pack from his shoulders. He removed all essential items, then loaded the pack with stones from the floor of the tunnel. He swung it and let it fly from his grasp so that it fell upon the smooth flagstones deep inside the chamber.

When nothing happened he said, 'I believe we may enter. But with extreme caution all the same. This vault will surely be designed to bring grief to the unwary.'

They stepped over the fallen grille and entered the chamber, to stand some paces before the altar.

Sleen eyed the golden chalice. 'Were we in any other place but this, my instinct would be to take that cup and stuff it in my bag.'

'Aye, and those chests are a temptation to any adventurer,' agreed Thufor.

Sleen explored his inner cheek with his tongue. 'However . . .'

Shadd had recovered his pack, emptying the stones onto the floor. Sleen now took one of these and carefully tossed it so that it struck the golden chalice and caused it to topple back upon the altar. The flagstones immediately before the altar, where a person attempting to take the chalice would ordinarily have stood, dropped away. A dark and musty pit was revealed, filled with long and vicious metal spikes.

Sleen advanced to the edge of the pit, stroking his beard. He turned to them with a puckish grin. 'Well, sirs, it appears I have saved myself an amount of discomfort. Now, let us examine the other furnishings of this inhospitable chamber.'

He crossed to the first of the tapestries hanging upon the wall. On this were woven complex images and words or symbols in an unfamiliar language. Sleen stood before it for some moments as if studying it. Then he moved to its side, his back against the wall, and motioned for the other two to join him. 'I believe there are other traps. Were we to touch either of the two chests, or the altar itself, I believe we would die.'

Shadd, his heart beating fast, said, 'Do you read these symbols?'

His eyes were on the altar. Engraved upon the stone were figures similar to those upon the tapestry. A language unfamiliar, yes, but not unrecognised. In Mesmia's tower he had seen something similar. Describing the scroll she was sending him to retrieve she had indicated figures like these, inscribed upon the edge of her map. He scarcely doubted now that he was in the chamber where the scroll was to be found.

Sleen was shaking his head. 'Simply a hunch.'

With his rope he had fashioned a wide noose. This he cast at the closer of the two chests. The noose fell across the top of the chest, failing to encircle it as had been his intention. However, its mere weight upon the lid was enough. Small cavities flipped open low in the wall behind the chest. Metal bolts flew from these, shooting across the chamber, faster than eyes could follow. They smashed into the wall, chipping it deeply and sending brief clouds of powdered stone into the air, then fell with a clatter to the flags.

Thufor arched a brow, but made no comment. Sleen grinned and said, 'As well I was not positioned before that chest.'

Retrieving his rope he cast it once more. This time it looped cleanly over the chest. He motioned the others to lie flat, then did so himself. Carefully taking up the slack, and with Thufor's aid, he dragged the chest across the floor towards them.

Only now, with the chest standing before them, did they notice that the lock which secured its lid had been forced.

'Someone has been here before us!' Sleen hissed.

'Impossible!' snapped Shadd, his eyes flashing.

Still suspecting further traps, Sleen slipped the tip of his sword beneath the lid and tipped it open. It lifted back with a soft creak. The chest was empty.

'The other is the same,' growled Thufor squinting at the lock and hasp of the second chest.

They crossed the chamber. Sleen lassooed the second chest, springing another trap, this one a double ring of sharpened metal spikes thrusting up out of the floor, sufficient to have disembowelled any persons standing within a two pace radius of the chest. They approached the spikes. Sleen stretched through with his sword and opened the chest lid. Again there was nothing within.

'Have we come all this way for nothing?' demanded Thufor angrily.

Sleen turned a rueful gaze to the passage outside the vault. 'And destroyed our sole means of retreat in the process.'

Shadd stared vexedly at the empty chest. 'Something is not right. The traps had not been sprung.

The bridge was intact.' He shook his head. 'No one can have preceded us and looted these chests.'

'Then where is the treasure they contained?'

Shadd held silence for a moment, before exclaiming, 'There was none! It is another trick! These chests have always been empty, their locks broken by whomsoever first placed them here. They are decoys; the chamber is set up to mislead. The treasure, and the scroll, lie elsewhere.'

He stared around the vault. 'There is perhaps yet another chamber beyond this one.'

His eyes came to rest once again upon the stone altar, and in a flash understanding dawned. 'No! There! There is our goal!'

Temminee, as if sharing his thought, flew to the altar. Unnoticed by the others, she glided once around it and returned, saying, 'It is possible. The top of the altar may well lift free.'

Shadd spoke to the other two. 'We must remove the altar top. Perhaps it can be lifted off, or there may be a lever or trigger which will release it.'

They approached the altar from the side. After careful inspection Thufor put his shoulder beneath the lip of the stone slab which composed the table surface. He eased upwards; the stone gave a fraction.

'Aye, it will come free.'

Together they got beneath the stone and lifted. Slowly they were able to ease it to one side, until at last a gap was made, allowing them to peer into the interior of the altar. Sleen chuckled; Thufor gave a booming bark of laughter: the altar was a storehouse of priceless articles: gems, jewellery, ornaments, artefacts and other precious objects. Sleen reached in and with two hands scooped up a mass of fine glittering stones: emeralds, rubies, diamonds, amethysts and citrines, opals, pearls, worked agate and jasper . . . riches diverse and dazzling, far beyond counting. With a wild laugh he let them fall between his fingers, back into the interior of the altar, then reached for an empty sack within his pack.

They pushed the stone slab further back. Thufor reached in and withdrew a golden-hilted dagger studded with jewels. His eyes widened in wonder. Like Sleen he now produced an empty sack and proceeded to load it with treasure from the altar.

Shadd, meanwhile, had seen but one item. It was half-buried among the treasures: a time-stained ivory tube, carved with distinctive and complex symbols. Half in a trance he reached in and withdrew it.

He held it for a moment, balancing its weight in both hands, staring, his heart hammering.

'You have found what you came for, my friend?' enquired Thufor, pausing for a moment.

Hardly hearing him, Shadd twisted the ivory plug which sealed one end of the tube. It came away without great effort. He tipped up the tube and extracted a thick roll of ancient yellowed parchment of a fine but unfamiliar texture. This he unrolled and held it up for examination.

The scroll turned out to be several separate leaves of parchment. Ancient figures, meaningless to his eyes, covered one face of each. He stared at the leaves one by one. The language of the inscriptions was as on the tapestries upon the walls of the vault, as on the engravings on the altar; the same as that which Mesmia had shown him upon her map.

'I have found it,' he murmured, while his heart pounded and his mind reeled under the surge of a myriad conflicting emotions. With shuddering breath, almost in awe, he carefully rolled the leaves of parchment back, slid them into the tube and resealed it. *Seruhli, I have found it! But is it what Mesmia has*

*promised? Will it truly free you of the terrible force
that binds you?*

He pushed the ivory tube into his waistband and
stepped back from the altar. *What next?* he thought.
*Where does this now lead me?*

He stared around the chamber. How were they to
escape this place?

## III

The answer was to come from an unexpected source.

Thufor and Sleen had done with their looting. Their
sacks now bulged. A few items were left behind –
namely those deemed to be of questionable origin, or to
which clung curses or fateful resonances of one kind or
another. The two men seemed amply acquainted with
many of the items they found. These were objects
steeped in lore and legend, recognisable to any who
had devoted themselves to sufficient research.

'Morteroy's Circlet!' declared Sleen, holding up a
slender hoop of dark gold bounded by mysterious
veined stone and tiny, many-coloured gems. 'It will
induce violent madness in any upon whose head it
is set.'

He tossed it aside, reached in and brought up a small
dark green figurine sculpted of nephrite. 'The Dryad of
the Long Pool. Crafted by a servant of Grool of the
Creeping Veil. Even now I sense the quiver of its evil
upon my fingertips.'

He shuddered, and let the object fall. Thufor held
up a red metallic object, like an irregularly shaped
ball set with knobs of varying size. 'Manomin's Fist.
A mighty weapon for any who know how to wield it,
but it will destroy a bearer ignorant of controlling its
powers.'

Other objects they brought out and named, along with many more lacking historic distinction though of similar or even greater value. Most went into their sacks. Some they debated over then left aside, sensing or suspecting bewitchments or other harmful properties. Others they passed to Shadd for further examination, unable to make up their own minds. He inspected each carefully, seeking within himself for dissonances or disharmony cast upon his deeper mind. He passed back only those he sensed to be wholly free of enchantment or bane. Even so the possibility existed that more subtle curses had escaped detection, and that even now Thufor and Sleen were the holders of valuables that worked to bring them to their doom. But they seemed willing to accept that risk. When they had done, as an afterthought, Sleen stepped behind the altar and collected the golden, gem-encrusted chalice that had stood atop it when they'd entered the vault.

Now all three turned their minds to escape. They inspected the vault – the walls, the floor, the ceiling. They removed the tapestries from the walls in the hope of discovering behind them a secret door or a hidden mechanism for opening or revealing a way of egress. None did they find. Still unperceived by the other two, Temminee searched the nooks and crannies where human fingers could not reach, or the shadows which human eyes could not penetrate. She too found nothing.

They returned to the hanging bridge. Across the river the wraiths attended in silence, gathered close upon the floor of the rock hall. Ghoul-eyed and expressionless they shifted like plants played by a breeze as the three reappeared.

'The river flows out,' said Shadd, his eyes upon the water-borne section of the bridge which was still trapped against the rock at the end of the cavern.

'Conceivably that is our route of escape, though it means exploring beneath the rock, beneath the water itself.'

Thufor shook his head. 'The water holds a chill like none I have ever known. It is colder than the coldest mountain stream – unnaturally so. Likewise its currents and vortices. I am a strong swimmer, but I was pulled under as though dragged by invisible hands. I would not willingly enter that river again.'

They reviewed other possibilities, arrived at no result, and returned once more to the vault. There they seated themselves against a wall, took rations from their packs, and ate. A deepening gloom, as yet unspoken, was descending upon each. It was Thufor who finally gave voice to thoughts they all shared.

'This is profound irony, to be entombed here when we have each found what we came for! Ye devils, Sleen and I have become perhaps the richest men in all Enchantery, yet our wealth benefits us not at all. And you, my friend, whose mission was of a selfless and more noble character, having completed your quest are as helpless and impotent as we.'

'My quest is not complete,' corrected Shadd, beads of sweat standing out in the soft light upon his pale skin, for the air within the vault had become uncomfortably close. 'It is true, I appear to have what I came for. But if it cannot be applied to the end for which it was designed, then the achievement is without meaning.'

'It is a sad end to contemplate.'

'I am not given to such contemplation. It is my intention to escape this place and return with the scroll.'

'Resolutely said! And yet the evidence is that you sit here with us, with no notion of how to effect your escape. And should you succeed, what then? The scroll is delivered. Is that the end?'

'It is not, as I suspect you know. It will mark the opening of another phase, whose precise nature or end I cannot predict.'

'I have heard death described in like terms.'

'Perhaps, but it is not death I speak of.'

After a short pause, Thufor resumed. 'Do you fear death, my friend?'

Shadd frowned. 'Fear? Not in itself. But I have no desire yet to experience death's embrace. Nor do I wish presently to pursue the topic further.'

Thufor shrugged. 'I was merely considering all eventualities. It intrigues me that we take such extreme measures to avoid that consequence, which is after all inevitable.'

Shadd re-wrapped his remaining provisions in their cloth and returned them to his pack. Once more he swept his eyes around the vault, searching for some clue to a way out.

Thufor spoke ruminatively to himself. 'Aye, you are perhaps right. It is not the end.'

Shadd glanced around, taken by the sudden weight of his tone. He was struck by the inward focus of Thufor's gaze, the leaden, almost mournful expression upon his face. Then Sleen touched Shadd's arm, drawing his attention, and said, 'Perhaps there is our answer.'

At the entrance to the vault a shape was materialising, seemingly out of the air. A vague mass of dark hues, maroon to purplish to black; a shifting, amorphous blotch about eight feet in height, which hovered above the flagstones. In its upper part three glowing orange-red orbs like eyes of flame appeared.

As one the three scrambled to their feet, hands flying instinctively to their weapons.

The creature, which Sleen had earlier named the Sentinel, slowly moved towards them over the stones. It halted before them. As they stood, fearful and uncertain of how to respond, a puff of its substance extended suddenly from its middle and reached out towards Shadd. Shadd stepped backwards, dodging, ducking, but the Sentinel's limb was faster. Unerringly it followed his movement, caught him, enfolded itself around his skull.

Shadd felt nothing. The Sentinel's touch was like vapour, or air. There was no pain, no physical sense of being held or restrained, and yet, quite suddenly, he was unable to move. His brain sent out signals of alarm but his limbs would not answer its summons to respond. He was numbed and paralysed.

Out of the corner of his eye he could see Sleen and Thufor. They stood in attitudes of shocked surprise. Both held their weapons ready but neither attempted to move against the Sentinel, perhaps because they sensed the futility of such effort.

The limb which held Shadd began to dilate, its substance extending to travel over him until it swathed his entire body like an ethereal cocoon. His eyes were drawn to the three candescent orbs, whose brightness seemed to increase as he stared. He was mesmerised by their glow; their fiery light seemed to bore into him, painlessly but with an irresistible force. Abruptly a terrible shrieking tore through him, a cacophony which threatened to shatter both his mind and his eardrums. His body went rigid. His lips drew back in an involuntary grimace of agony. He screamed, though he was not certain that he made any sound.

The cacophony ceased. Shadd's limbs sagged and grew suddenly heavy. The agony was gone, but he felt as though his spirit had been sucked out of him, leaving him feeble and almost lifeless. With relief he sensed himself sinking into oblivion. Then a voice.

*'So you have come!'*

It was like no voice he had ever heard. He could not have described its tones or timbre, he was not even certain that it had a sound. Rather, it seemed as though it spoke within him and was not a voice as much as a strand of something alien intruding upon his own thought. His eyes, which had fallen closed, opened, stared into the Sentinel's flaring orbs. He found his own voice, which again was a response within his consciousness, a question he did not have to speak, a simple declaration of his confusion.

*'I do not understand.'*

*'You have come. My vigil is over.'*

*'Vigil? For what have you maintained a vigil?'*

*'For the one who would come with specific purpose, bearing certain signs. No other has entered here. My task was to wait, to be certain.'*

*'Certain of what?'*

*'That it was not a false one who came. You solved the puzzles which thwart lesser minds; you have seen the treasures but taken only that which was predicted, and which would be of no value to ordinary mortals. And, as final proof, you survived the Savor pulse, which, regrettably, would have killed any other.'*

Shadd's blood quickened. *'Are you Savor?'*.

Within him he sensed something that might have been resonant laughter. *'Oh, perhaps, in a manner of speaking. But no, also. But the pulse was your final test, and it has brought to a close my ages of waiting.'*

*'Who, then, or what are you?'*

*'This is a queer thing. You enter my home, then ask who I am?'*

*'Ciracar? You are Ciracar?'*

'It is one name by which I am known. But what is a name? I am the one who has waited; you are the one who has come. That is all that is important. A cycle is complete. I may go, at last. As may you.'

'Is there a way out?'

'That is my last task, to reveal it. But do not think it is without peril. Destiny is mutable. Though your span is interwoven into its pattern, Destiny may change even as it evolves. Chance events, the workings of those who do not know what they do . . . anything may alter the weft or warp of its unfolding. That you are chosen does not mean that you will succeed. Nothing is certain.'

'Chosen for what? Succeed in what?'

The answer was less than direct. 'Go now, do as you will. You may take what you wish from this place – and we have joined, so it is possible that you may take something of myself. Remember, Savor, your purpose is before you.'

Shadd found he was lying upon the floor. Sensation had returned to his limbs. The blood flowed in his veins. Above him still hovered the form of Ciracar, but it no longer held him. Ciracar was withdrawing, his form dissolving.

'Wait!' cried out Shadd, though his voice emerged as a dry croak. 'I must know more!'

Ciracar, now distant within his mind, spoke once more. 'My task is done. I go, and yours now is the burden. Act wisely.'


IV


His mind reeling, Shadd climbed to his feet. Close by stood Thufor and Sleen, staring as if awestruck. Ciracar was gone. Shadd faced them, haggard, his limbs shaking.

'Are you injured, Duke Shadd?' It was Temminee's voice, but almost simultaneously Thufor asked the same question.

Shadd shook his head. 'I believe not.'

'We thought you were dying,' said Sleen, 'and believed a similar fate awaited us. We could not intercede. We could not move.'

'And what did you hear?'

'Hear? There was nothing to hear. We saw only your body lifted from the ground by the Sentinel, held there, writhing in mute agony, then lowered and let be.'

Thufor, picking up on Shadd's enquiry, said, 'The Sentinel spoke to you?'

Shadd gave a wary nod. Evidently it was as he had surmised: the communication between himself and Ciracar had been inaudible to the others. And he thought: *Savor. He called me Savor.*

Thufor's curiosity was heightened. 'Then what passed between you?'

'It told me that there is a way out of this place.'

The two regarded him darkly, doubtless suspecting that there was more.

Sleen spoke. 'It is true, a way has opened.'

Shadd turned to where he indicated. He saw that the floor of the spike-filled pit before the altar had dropped away. A narrow shaft led beneath the altar.

Immediately Temminee was gone. Still half-stupefied from the encounter with Ciracar, Shadd made no union with her vision, but she returned to tell that the shaft led into an underground cave system. No immediate danger had been apparent.

'Come,' said Shadd when he had sufficiently recovered.

They lowered themselves into the pit and entered the shaft. A short crawl brought them into a modestly proportioned cavern. Light from Sleen's rekindled lamp revealed numerous passages leading off. Temminee explored a couple at random; Shadd, now better able to utilise her eyes, chose the second. 'It appears to lead upwards, and that is the direction we must go.'

The roof of the passage was low and they were obliged for some time to proceed with bent backs, Thufor and Sleen further hampered by their bulging sacks of booty. Shadd had taken the lead, with Temminee, as ever, revealing the way ahead. From behind Shadd there came suddenly a wrenching, cracking sound, followed by a muffled outcry. He spun around, to see the top of Thufor's head and the sack he bore upon his back disappearing into the ground, where a hole gaped suddenly beneath his feet. From within the hole came a scraping, sliding sound, then silence but for the gentle patter of tumbling particles of earth and stone.

Shadd immediately dropped to his knees to peer into the hole, as did Sleen on the other side. The lamp revealed nothing but gaping blackness beyond the first couple of feet. Shadd cupped his hands to his mouth to hail Thufor. There was no reply.

Standing, Shadd took rope from his back. 'The extra weight of his sack must have caused the trap to give way after I had passed safely over. I will climb down and try to locate him.'

Temminee had already darted into the hole. Back at Shadd's ear she whispered what she had discovered.

'Will you remain up and take my weight?' said Shadd to Sleen.

Sleen looked not altogether happy at the prospect. 'Thufor may already be dead.'

'He is alive but unconscious at the bottom of a chute. It is vital I get to him quickly; his position is precarious. The chute empties into a den where a pair of ogres sleep. It is fortunate that the noise of his fall has not awoken them, but should he wake now and inadvertently cry out or in some other way disturb them, it will be his end.'

Sleen was plainly in two minds.

'There is another exit from the den,' pressed Shadd. 'Evidently it is used by the ogres, and must surely therefore lead out of the warren. It may prove to be our best and quickest route of escape.'

Sleen appeared to accept the logic of this. He nodded. 'You have not so far told me untrue, though I wonder more and more how you know these things.'

Shadd had secured the rope around his chest. He tossed the end across the hole to Sleen. 'When Thufor is safe I will signal with two sharp tugs upon the rope. Slide down the chute. I will be at the bottom to break your descent. Do not move before the signal, nor let go of the rope. If things go awry we may have to retreat urgently back up the chute.'

So saying he sat upon the edge of the hole and carefully lowered himself in.

The chute, though steep with sides of smoothed earth and stone, proved narrow enough to permit a man to check his rate of descent by use of feet, hands, knees and elbows upon its walls. By this means, and with the aid of Sleen bearing much of his weight from above, Shadd had little difficulty in making his way down. Furthermore, it was evident that with care Sleen would himself be able to descend without hazard.

Feet first, Shadd slipped into the lair where the ogres slept. Temminee's eyes revealed Thufor, sprawled on the floor, his sack of booty beside him. Likely it was this that had struck his head and knocked him senseless, for Shadd could not see that the slide down the chute, rapid as it may have been, would of itself have rendered him unconscious.

The den contained a foul and frowsty stink. The

air was fuggy, and from disturbingly close by came the uneven sound of stertorous breathing. Temminee flitted over to the ogres, permitting Shadd to view them. Both lay on a litter of mouldering leaves and branches. A mother, huge and grotesque, with vast shuddering belly and sagging, wrinkled, warty paps like the flayed hides of monstrous toads; and curled beside her, beneath the protection of her mightily muscled arm, her offspring, an ogre of perhaps two years, itself almost eight feet tall, repulsive in all aspects and strong enough to tear a man's head from his shoulders with its giant's hands.

There issued a groan from Thufor. Shadd quickly slid a hand across his mouth. Half-conscious, Thufor stiffened, made to struggle.

'It is I, Shadd!' Shadd hissed into his ear. 'Hold still, and make no sound.'

Thufor relaxed; Shadd removed his hand. In a whisper he described their situation. Thufor sat up, rubbing his crown. He felt in the dark, first for the helve of his axe, then his sack. He made to rise. 'Curse this blackness! I can see nothing. Show me where these monsters lie and I will split their brains with my axe.'

Shadd took Thufor's arm. 'No. There has been enough killing. There is a doorway here. I will summon Sleen and we will make our escape while the ogres still sleep.'

He sensed Thufor's eyes upon him. 'These are murderous, flesh-eating monsters! They do not deserve mercy.'

'So might be their view of us, and who can argue the difference? As we stand, they offer no immediate threat. I am sickened by this slaughter. Let us at least attempt to make free without further blood-letting.'

Temminee still hovered above the sleeping ogres,

providing Shadd assurance that he and Thufor remained unmenaced. At his behest Thufor felt his
way grudgingly along the rock wall of the den to
the door, a dilapidated affair of rotting, worm-riddled
timbers. This he lifted aside. A pallid shade of unstill,
uneven light slid in from outside. Thufor put his head
out, returned.

'A passage, lit by torches.'

'Good.' Shadd tugged twice upon the rope. A moment later came a slithering and scraping from high up
in the chute, followed by muttered curses and laboured
breathing. Sleen slid down, his heavy sack pressing
heavily upon him as it followed in his wake.

'I am here, sir,' said he in the darkness, dusting himself off. 'Is Thufor with us? Are the monsters disposed
of?'

Shadd cautioned him to silence. Together they stole
from the ogres' den.

The passage outside led to right and left. Temminee
went left. Shadd, distracted by the torches set in brackets some distance apart along the walls, lost her vision.
She returned suddenly. 'A third ogre! Flee!'

Even as she spoke a shadow loomed around a bend in
the passage twenty paces away. There was nowhere to
run without being seen. The three pressed themselves
into shadows.

Into view came a monster, a male ogre standing
more than twelve feet tall, striding upon massively
thewed, bowed legs. Its loins were bound with tattered
hide, its torso and arms bulged with wads and ridges of
raw muscle. Over one shoulder it carried the carcass of
a bullock.

As it rounded the curve the ogre slowed in its stride,
then lurched to a halt. It lowered its weight, flaring
nostrils searching the air, and peered forward into the
half-light. It stared directly into the shadows where the

three hid. Something caught its attention. Its great head thrust forward, blinking in surprise. Then with a sudden bellow it cast aside the bullock, reared to its fullest height and charged.

'It believes we menace its family! Run!' yelled Shadd.

His words were scarcely necessary. Thufor and Sleen had already bolted, fleeing along the corridor as fast as their burdens would permit.

The ogre's charge proved to be a feint, intended perhaps to instil terror and test the mettle of its opponents. With the entrance to its den clear it halted, glaring at the three fleeing figures. It flung its arms high, then down, beating massive fists upon the floor, venting furious roars. It strode to the door. From within came answering bellows and grunts. The door flew back and the female rushed out, fangs bared, her hideous weanling at her heels.

The respite had given the three humans space to put desperate yards between themselves and the monsters. Now all three ogres resumed the chase, the passage reverberating with their clamour.

The way split into three. Sleen, who had somehow taken the lead, hared into the narrower in the hope that its close walls would hinder the ogres' pursuit. The others came close behind. Temminee raced ahead, seeking a way out.

The ogres entered the new passage, obliged to pursue in single file. The male was at the fore, massive feet thudding, bellowing its wrath. With long strides it gained upon the three, being now no more than fifteen paces behind them.

Temminee raced back to Shadd. 'There is an opening, a cleft, too small for the ogres. I've no time to see where it leads.'

Shadd glanced back over his shoulder. Thufor was

two paces behind him, and beyond was looming black-ness, filled with the ogres' roars.

'We will take it! We have no choice!'

Temminee guided him around a sharp bend in the passage, to the cleft. Sleen, in his haste, had rushed straight past. Shadd called him back, and dived between the rocks. Thufor came next, but his sack caught in the cleft, trapping Sleen in the passage outside. Sleen shrieked, pushing frantically at the bulging sack as the others pulled. The sack came free. Sleen tumbled through, his own sack held before him, and fell sprawling upon the floor.

There was a blood-curdling roar from outside, and the rock around the cleft shuddered as the ogre's massive bulk slammed into it. As Sleen scrambled to his knees a long arm reached through. The hand groped, found Sleen's ankle as he strove to pull away. The gigantic fingers closed around his leg and dragged him back.

Shadd leapt and struck with his swords at the ogre's hand. There came a howl of distress from outside. Releasing Sleen, the hand snatched back through the gap.

Sleen shot across the floor, to put himself well beyond reach.

The three took stock of their situation. They had entered into another, wider passage. High above was a ragged ribbon of bright grey-gold sky, impossible to reach. Light stabbed down to partially illuminate the area they had entered. Before them was a small cavern, narrowing at one side into another black tunnel. For the moment they were safe.

All three sagged in exhaustion onto the earth floor which was covered in the droppings of bats and birds. Beyond the cleft, just feet away, the three ogres stamped and hammered. The weanling might have squeezed through the gap, but plainly it was not about to do so.

'What price squeamishness, or mercy to sleeping monsters?' demanded Thufor with contempt when he had found his breath. Shadd, his eyes closed, made no reply. Sleen sat with his lamp between his feet, his eyes travelling from cleft to tunnel to sky, and back to cleft again.

Outside, the tone of the ogres' hammering suddenly altered. Dull, heavy thumps upon the rock wall and floor became louder, sharper, more precise. Shadd opened his eyes. With a chill he realised that the ogres had taken up heavy stones and were hammering at the edges of the cleft. Cracks appeared in the rock at one side, and it began slowly to crumble. Six huge hands appeared, one pouring blood. The fingers closed around the rock and wrenched it free. A portion of the cleft was suddenly a hand's span wider.

The three men leapt erect. Thufor and Sleen hefted their sacks. Shadd lunged towards the cleft with his swords. From outside a monstrous face peered through, then shifted aside. A second later a stone as large as a man's head was hurled with force through the opening, narrowly missing Shadd, who threw himself to the side. The stone smashed into the far wall.

'They will win through eventually!' Shadd cried.

The other two were already at the entrance to the tunnel. Without further pause they ran in, Thufor first, then Sleen. Shadd quickly crossed the cavern behind them.

The tunnel was high-roofed and wide enough for the ogres to penetrate once they had forced a way through the rock cleft. Thufor had taken the lamp, which illuminated the path immediately before him. With Temminee's eyes Shadd was able to see a way twisting seemingly without purpose through the rock, rising slightly. Intermittently a vague semblance of light from the outside world filtered in through natural flues overhead. They caught glimpses of sky far above, though no negotiable outlet presented itself.

The path continued to climb. In the depths behind them the hammering and crashing, the rumble of rock being torn away, accompanied by muffled roars, indicated that the ogres were not abandoning their task.

Surely now it could not be far to the outside world? The patches of sky were a reassuring sign, but as yet they had no sure indication that this tunnel would provide an exit.

From far behind them came a renewed bellow, dampened by the layers of rock, but charged with triumph and dreadful menace. The crashing had ceased. The ogres were through the cleft and once more in pursuit.

*How much further?* thought Shadd, stumbling over a mound of rubble. His lungs were on fire. Before him, in the glow of the lantern, the dim shapes of Sleen and Thufor pushed on. Suddenly, a glimpse of motion further ahead. A shadow – several shadows, darting. Shadd blinked, uncertain of what he had seen, realised it was Temminee's view. He had no chance to see more; Temminee was retreating, returning to him.

Thufor stumbled out into a wider section of the passage. Some paces off another corridor branched away. Temminee was back at Shadd's shoulder, but before she could speak he saw motion with his own eyes. Something bounded from above directly into Thufor's path. Another followed. Other things hovered on a ledge above their path.

Thufor showed no hesitation. They could not go back. It was fight or be destroyed. In instant response he thrust his heavy sack at the first creature, reached for his axe.

'*Vhazz!*' he yelled, and charged forward to the attack.

# 14

I

We had wandered for some time, following a directionless path through a network of chambers and gaping tunnel mouths which offered themselves at random junctures to our eyes. It became plain that we had entered a labyrinth of tremendous complexity and extent. An occasional eddy of cool air funnelled in from behind us, bringing the scent of the Laughing Blue Knights. Whether they had entered the cave and pursued us now, or whether they still waited outside we could not tell. Their scent gradually grew fainter, so we knew they came no closer. At least for the moment we could disregard the danger they presented.

There was minimal communication between us. All were preoccupied. Yaoww led, her muzzle testing ground and air, seeking traces of other inhabitants of the labyrinth, or of fresh currents of air which would indicate a way out. From somewhere ahead, deep within the warren, came a series of sounds, or rather, a continuous sound, a distant thunderous echo broken up into muffled, reverberant crashings and rumblings, smothered by the dense firmament of rock. A rockfall somewhere in the depths, perhaps – yet there seemed an erratic rhythm of sorts to it, and it persisted, surely too long for any single fall of rock, unless a very large part of the labyrinth was under collapse.

I was considering that perhaps it came from a subterranean waterfall when abruptly the sound altered timbre, then ceased. We paused, listening. Nothing more was heard and we resumed our path.

A minute later came other sounds. Echoing footsteps; muffled and distorted, bounced off rock walls and columns, borne through numberless passages, shafts and flues, so that their precise direction was indeterminable. The air, carried still from behind us, brought no scent.

Yaoww cast a glance over her shoulder, anxious and desperately weary, as were we all. She moved on. The path came to a sudden end upon a ledge of rock overlooking another passage some feet below. Yaoww peered over the brink, assessed the distance, and leapt down. Escre followed. Beinea, the last female, paused a moment before joining them. As she leapt there came a sudden cry, a wild human voice, deep and resonant, filled with warning.

*'Vhazz!'*

Yaoww spun, startled, snarling. Something of bulk slammed into her, knocking her momentarily off balance, then fell to the floor with a clank and jingle of metal. Suddenly into the midst of the three vhazz leapt a fearsome figure, a human fighter, yelling a battle cry and swinging a great axe.

Yaoww was closest to this man. She neatly dodged his initial blow, but he lunged on forward without a pause, his axe curving again. Beinea leapt back, but Escre was not so quick. The axe bit savagely into her neck, almost severing head from shoulders. Her legs buckled, blood gushed in great rivulets from her neck, and she dropped dead to the earth without a sound.

Now behind the axeman came a second figure brandishing a slim sword. I leapt down to engage him, but Yaoww was quicker. A third fighter jumped forward around the angle of rock. I drew my vhazz sword, readying myself.

The third man stepped fully into my vision. I froze.

Seeing me, the fellow drove forward. He gave a harsh shout, stabbing and thrusting with a pair of shortswords. Somehow I found enough sense to leap back, but I could not engage him. I gaped in utter astonishment as he pressed on, pale and grim-visaged, mouth set in concentration.

Duke Shadd! It could not be – I had believed he'd perished in Twalinieh. Yet it was. Duke Shadd.

Retreating, I somehow fended off his first blows. But he came at me like a demon – and I well knew what he was capable of in battle. Still in shock at the sight of him, I dodged, and retreated further. I blundered into the back of the axeman, who had Beinea cornered in an angle of the passage. Fortuitously my error caused him to stumble. Beinea took the moment, slipping beneath his upraised blade and out. Now she faced Shadd, while the axeman, wheeling, came face-to-face with me.

I heard a whine, and out of the corner of my vision glimpsed Yaoww stagger back, blood seeping from her chest as the first swordsman's flickering blade penetrated her defence. I had no time to see more. With a bellow the axeman was upon me.

Still I could barely respond, so great was my bewilderment at finding myself face-to-face with Shadd. I twisted away from the blow as the axe-head swept through the air where I had stood. I drew a dart and flicked it; it sank into the axeman's chest. He grunted, stared down at the missile. Had I been alert I could have attacked in that moment. I didn't. The axeman lunged again.

I backed away. Behind the axeman Shadd advanced with flurrying swordplay, pressing Beinea back. I saw Yaoww sag to the floor, the first swordsman's blade plunged deep into her breast.

Suddenly, in confusion, in dreadful turmoil, I was without stomach for the fight. I glanced again at Shadd. *If only I had words!* Ah, but we may as well have been separated by miles for all the good our close proximity did. The axeman was upon me again. I whirled, crouched, rolled away, and ran, blindly.

A rocky buttress thrust out into my path. I swerved around it, to find two ways confronting me. I took the second, which curved sharply around a high shoulder of rock. Too late, I skidded around the rock and saw that the passage led nowhere. I was faced with a blank rock wall. I turned with sword drawn, the rock at my back, with no choice but to face my pursuer.

The axeman charged into the entrance, saw me and halted. Ten paces separated us. He firmed his stance and steadied his grip upon the helve of his weapon. His eyes blazed with the savage fire of combat; his broad chest rose and fell. Beneath the thick bush of his beard his lips spread into a fierce smile. Blood soaked his coarse linen shirt where my dart had struck him. The dart had gone, and he seemed scarcely troubled by the wound. He eased forward.

That part of me that was Huwoorsk, that was pure vhazz, drew back its lips into a snarl and prepared to fight and, almost certainly, to die. Two of our number were already slain or incapacitated. Should the axeman fail to take me alone, I had little doubt that at least one of his companions would be here in moments to render him aid.

And Dinbig of Khimmur cried out in heavy-hearted sorrow. Was my life truly to be ended here, ended by the companions – or perhaps the very sword – of the one man I loved above all others? Such cruel irony – after all that had gone before, to stand mute before Shadd and be perceived as his mortal foe.

The axeman moved, and was suddenly upon me. My

greater agility saved me. I slipped aside, stabbed with my sword, but he fended my blow with his blade, and was ready once more for the attack.

My manoeuvre had taken me out from the rock wall. I backed away again. My adversary stepped across to block my path, assuming, wrongly, that I planned to run back for the main passage. From behind him came the sound of footsteps. A shadow loomed; Shadd came at speed around the angle of rock.

At the sight of him my will to fight on fled me once more. I stared beyond the axe-wielder for an instant into the huge pale mysterious eyes of my old friend and ward. He breathed hard; the grim mask of battle set his features. I could not reach him. I saw him, but he saw only a vhazz. There would be no mercy.

What possessed me to do what I did next I cannot say. I acted almost without thought. Scarcely even was there a conscious notion of attempted submission. Hope. Yes, perhaps that was there, though my action was so quick and spontaneous, that I was not even aware that I hoped. As likely it was despair that prompted me, resignation, the total absence of hope. I don't know, other than that, out of a sudden inner impulse, I acted.

As the two men stood poised and wary before me I dropped my sword. I sank onto all fours, then onto my belly upon the stale earth beneath me. Then I rolled over onto my back, allowing my limbs to loll, exposing my unprotected abdomen and underparts to my attackers.

The axeman jerked back his head, momentarily taken aback. Vhazz do not surrender! Then with a guffaw of contempt he hefted his weapon, stepped forward and struck.

Shadd leapt. 'Hold!'

His arm stayed the axeman's blow.

'I have said, enough of needless slaying!'

A flicker of anger crossed the axeman's face. He turned. For a moment the two faced each other, and I was aware of the third man approaching behind them: my vhazz (*my vhazz!*) then, were surely dead. The axeman seemed to relax. He lowered his weapon with a shrug of a shoulder.

'So be it.'

I breathed again. The three men formed an arc about me, staring. Shadd spoke first, shaking his head with a baffled frown. 'This is an extraordinary thing.'

Slowly, so as to cause them no startlement, I rolled again onto my belly. Now, I perceived, I had one opportunity. I might yet be left to live, but if I could not act now it would be to live the lifeless, terrified existence of a vhazz alone, without pack or companions. I summoned from the depths of myself the strength of consciousness that was all that could save me. Somehow I pushed conscious awareness aside, withdrew from the world, dissolved all. I rose out of the vhazz body and projected a single thought.

*'Duke Shadd, old friend, it is I, Dinbig.'*

Had I the focus or the strength to enter his mind? Would he even be receptive?

I saw his frown deepen as he stared, but no other reaction was evident. I spoke again, freighting my message with probing urgency.

*'Shadd, do you perceive my voice? Do not doubt. Old friend, it is truly I.'*

Shadd's face grew ever more baffled. Then came a light of surprise to his eyes, which melded into an expression suddenly grave. His look became inward. I sensed – hoped – that he attempted to communicate with me, but no voice penetrated my consciousness.

*'Shadd, I do not hear you. If you hear me, speak now. I lack the strength to communicate further.'*

389

Shadd spoke aloud, and his two companions turned to stare at him in surprise. 'Dinbig? How can this be? Dinbig died at Twalinieh.'

A sense of unbounded relief swept through me. Desperately I strove to remain aloof of my body, that I might say something more. *'As, I believed, did you. I was slain by Orl Kilroth, yet I returned in this form. Do not ask me more, my strength is waning. The vhazz body exerts terrible pressure upon me. Just believe, old friend. I beg of you, believe.'*

I added a word, my true and secret name, known only to adepts of the Zan-Chassin way. Though Shadd had never received formal Zan-Chassin initiation, he was trained in many of our techniques and privileged by right of rank and direct connection to share many of our secrets. He took the word, his eyes narrowing, then he nodded as I, unable to resist, was dragged back into the body of Huwoorsk.

Shadd addressed his companions. 'This vhazz, whom we have almost slain, is not what he appears. It seems that fortune has brought us together here, for this is an old and valued friend, who by some foul means has been transformed. Mark, then: from this moment on he has my protection, and will travel now at my side.'

He reached down to help me to my feet. We faced each other.

'I find I am lost for appropriate words,' said Shadd. 'Forgive me, Dinbig, if I look at you and, seeing a vhazz, find my tongue falters as it tries to pronounce your name. The sight of you thus gives me little comfort; but I do not doubt your word. And I rejoice at having found you, whom I believed gone from this world forever.'

So saying he clasped my shoulders and drew me to him. We embraced, warmly, as the tears made free and liberal passage down my cheeks.

'Now,' said Shadd, releasing me. 'We have no time to lose. These are my companions, Thufor and Sleen, on what is turning out to be an ever more extraordinary adventure. We have faced great danger here, and it is not yet past. We must be gone from this place.'

## II

We stepped back out into the passage. Beinea lay close by, the gashes of brutal sword cuts crimson upon her chest and neck. Escre's mutilated corpse was a little way beyond. Further down, stretched upon her side, was Yaoww.

I halted and stared, a sudden lurching sensation robbing me of all awareness of Shadd or the other two, or the surroundings in which I stood. I crossed to where Yaoww lay and lowered myself beside her. Her eyes were open, glassy and staring. Her purple-pink tongue hung limply between her jaws, onto the dank ground. Blood drained from her wounds into the earth. Her snout was horribly lacerated.

A movement! A flicker of the eyelid! She lived! With immense effort Yaoww turned her eye to focus upon me.

'Huwoorsk . . .'

It was the last word she spoke. Her final breath escaped her in a tired sigh and the life passed from her body. Yaoww, who had nursed me, brought me back to health, travelled with me, loved me. She had taught me much.

I considered her death. The odds in this battle had surely been in favour of the vhazz. We were four to the humans' three. We possessed superior sight, in the main the greater agility and, arguably, ferocity. Although the flow of air within the tunnels had been against us, we should nevertheless have detected something of the pungent human scent before we actually came upon the three men. And we had approached from overhead; we could have dropped down upon the humans before they had become aware of our presence.

Yet we had blundered into them, and then Yaoww, Beinea and Escre had died so quickly, so easily. Why? It was almost as if they had not wanted to save themselves. Could that be true? With the massacre of the pack, had their spirit left them? Had this last encounter been one too many to bear? We were all exhausted, but had they simply given up?

An unbearable weight throbbed within my chest. I pressed my muzzle to Yaoww's cheek, then gently closed her sightless eyes. And the thought came that at last she had found her land of perpetual night.

Shadd stood beside me, placing a hand upon my shoulder as I rose. 'She was dear to you?'

I nodded weakly. A few paces off, Thufor and Sleen wiped vhazz blood from their blades.

'I am sorry, old friend.' I sensed Shadd's gaze, remorseful, intent and quizzical upon me, and he said softly, 'There is much to be told, that much is evident.'

We removed ourselves swiftly from that place, continuing along the passage the humans had been following. After a short distance a way branched off to the left. I sensed fresher air coming from it, and was about to indicate as much, but already Shadd had chosen that route. A little further on he bade us halt.

'There is an opening ahead,' he announced. I wondered how he knew. 'Take care. Dangers may lurk outside.'

'They will hardly be greater than those within,' commented Thufor with a wary glance over his shoulder.

We approached the exit from the labyrinth: a tall, contorted column of light. I, whose faculties were perhaps the best developed for exploring the immediate vicinity, would have crept ahead, but Shadd stayed me. It seemed he had some means of knowing what lay beyond, for he waited for a period of some seconds, then said, 'It appears to be clear.'

One by one we slipped outside into a wooded land. It was mid-afternoon. Overhead a lowering sky was laden with iron-grey clouds pushed laboriously by a cool breeze blowing out of the mountains to the north-west. Thufor quickly climbed a nearby tree to survey the landscape. He returned, saying, 'We are about half a mile from our point of entry.'

We began a cautious march through the trees along the base of the warren in the direction he had indicated. Lacking the strength to leave my body again I endeavoured, with yapping sounds, to alert Shadd to my concern. He brought the others to a halt, and stared at me for some moments. The fingers of one hand rested upon a crystal he wore upon a silver chain around his neck. Quite suddenly I was aware of his voice within my mind.

*'Shadd, I hear you!'*

Shadd smiled. *'Thank Moban! Now we may tell each other all that has come to pass.'*

Briefly I related to him the danger I believed us to be in. I told him of the Laughing Blue Knights, of the massacre of the vhazz and my subsequent flight with Yaoww and the other two. *'It was but an hour or two ago. The knights may still be close by. These are devils, Shadd. They are not normal fighters.'*

*'I know something of them. They are the troops of an Enchanter named Yxon, whose domain this is.'*

'Come,' said Sleen impatiently. 'Let's away now to the horses. The quicker we are gone from here the better.'

He turned and strode on. Something whined out of the undergrowth nearby. Sleen grunted, staggered and sat down abruptly, a blue-fletched arrow sticking from high upon his breast.

From the bushes came loud whoops and screeches. Seven mounted blue knights thundered out of the trees. They galloped forward and formed a circle around us as we drew weapons and faced them.

'And what have we here?' cried one, a tall, bearded man, much of his face obscured by his gleaming blue helm. He leaned forward upon his charger and grinned widely. 'A motley company. What's this, humans, or near-humans, in company with this mangy dog-thing? I have never before seen such a raggle-taggle party.'

He sat back in his saddle, laughing, then his eyes came to rest upon Thufor. 'Aye, Thufor, we believed it was you. You were unwise to return to this land. Now you will be ours again.'

'Not while I live,' growled the axeman with a defiant grimace.

The knight gave a mocking laugh. 'Why, alive or dead, it is one to us. You know that. You are ours, and that is all there is to be said. Your companions, of course, must die.'

He unsheathed his broadsword with a shrill whinge and spurred his mount forward, barking, 'Take them!'

From somewhere above me and to my rear came an ear-splitting roar. A shadow passed fleetingly across my vision. A rock the size of a hogshead smashed hard into the blue knight's chest, propelling him backwards out of his saddle. He tumbled to the earth with a dull clatter, his sword flying from his hand, and lay still.

A second rock hammered into one of the blue

chargers, and a third thudded into the ground only inches from where Shadd stood.

Spinning around, I saw perched upon the slope behind us three ogres. With roars and bellows they plucked massive stones from the slope and rained them down. Another knight was bowled headlong from his horse; the remaining mounts wheeled in frightened disarray, stamping, neighing, snorting.

The biggest of the three ogres, a monster more than twelve feet tall, wrenched a sturdy sapling from the earth and hurled it down, then charged towards us in its wake.

Thufor leapt, his axe biting into the armoured flank of a knight whose sword had been raised to strike him. Shadd gave a yell, 'Quickly! Help Sleen!'

Taking advantage of the confusion, Shadd and Thufor raised Sleen to his feet. He was sorely wounded, ashen-faced, but with their support was able to stumble away. Fending off blows, dodging flying rocks and ramping, rearing horses, we fought our way free, the Blue Knights now forced to concentrate all their effort upon the enraged ogres.

We ran through thick undergrowth, beneath the boughs of great elms and oaks, Sleen gasping, half-carried by his two companions, though his arms clutched hard around the large sack he carried. The ground was uneven and gave way to grassy hummocks. Between these we raced, the sounds of furious battle never far enough behind. In a covert of elder trees three horses were tethered. The men climbed upon these. Sleen, half-slumped in his saddle, then Thufor, were away without pause. Shadd calmed his horse, which had grown skittish at the sight of me. He stretched an arm down to help me. I jumped up behind him and we made off behind the others.

# III

Darkness found us in an abandoned woodcutter's hut situated upon a sheltered hillside. In the vale below a cluster of rude dwellings had been built around a ring of standing stones. By Thufor's account the village was named Skirdon. It boasted an inn which could have furnished us with more comfortable accommodation, but he advised against it, for the Blue Knights would almost certainly be searching for us.

We risked a fire to boil water to bathe Sleen's wound. By its light Shadd carefully cut Sleen's flesh where the arrow had pierced it, and eased free the blue arrowhead. He bathed, tended and dressed the wound. Sleen had lost much blood. He quickly became feverish, but the wound, though deep, did not threaten his life; with time it would heal, leaving him none the worse but for a livid scar.

As Sleen, with the aid of Shadd's ministration, slipped into sleep, Shadd questioned Thufor. 'I am curious as to the exchange of words between you and the Blue Knight. Evidently you are known to them. Indeed, the implication was that they hold some form of power over you. They seemed almost to consider you their property.'

Thufor, squatting upon his haunches, ruminatively carved cheese and bacon from his pack, and for long moments did not reply. Nor would he meet Shadd's eyes. At length, the bacon cut into strips and toasting beside the flames, he sat back upon his buttocks and leaned against the hut wall, his knife dangling loosely between fingers and thumb. 'I was one of them,' he said.

Shadd's face revealed nothing. 'And now you are not?'

'You may recall that in answer to your enquiry

some days ago, I told you that were we to be captured by Yxon you would be slain, while I would meet another fate. That is it. Yxon would unwork the magic that keeps me free of him. I would become his again.'

Shadd stared at him for some time, then said, 'They seem proud, if somewhat belligerent knights. Is the prospect of being one of them so wholly without appeal?'

'The Laughing Blue Knights are crazed things,' said Thufor. 'Fanatical enchanted warriors without minds of their own. They are guided and controlled by Yxon. He has instilled within them the conviction that they are invincible and immortal, that they can never be brought to harm or grief. And to some extent that is true. They feel no pain, no emotion other than battle-lust and an abnormal form of heightened joy. Hence when they are wounded or when they die, they laugh. Their companions take up their bodies and return them to Yxon, who imbues them once more with life. That is the totality of their existence.'

Shadd gave this some thought. 'Brutishness and enslavement are abominations in themselves, but the idea of a life without pain, free of the torments and desires that plague normal men is not one to be lightly dismissed.'

'When I was a Blue Knight I did not complain, it is true,' replied Thufor. 'I lived in a state of sustained elation. I knew nothing other and would have preferred nothing other. Then I was captured by Yxon's enemy, who returned me to the human state. I perceived upon the instant the emotional and spiritual impoverishment of the Laughing Blue Knight, for all its lack of pain. They are golems, nothing more; mere adjuncts of the Enchanter. Once I had tasted the fullness of being a man, of having my own thoughts, emotions, will, I would not relinquish it, for all its travails.'

Shadd nodded. Turning, he said, 'You say that it is someone else's magic that keeps you free of Yxon's design.'

Thufor rotated his heel discomfitedly into the floor. 'Aye.'

'Then whose thrall are you now?'

The blood rushed to Thufor's cheeks. He sat forward, glaring. 'I am no one's thrall!'

'Are you saying there was no price for your "freedom"?'

The fire passed from Thufor's eyes. His shoulders sagged; he stared at the flames. 'It is as you have surely already surmised. The Drear-hag is my employer. I perform occasional tasks for her – such as guiding you, sometimes spying on her enemies, acquiring things she desires. She asks nothing more, and in return for these services I am able to remain as I am. There is no other way for me, other than to slay Yxon – an impossible task.'

'The advantages would appear to lean predominantly in your employer's favour,' said Shadd.

'What would you have?' cried Thufor bitterly. 'That I be returned to Yxon to become his mindless adjunct again?'

Shadd, his features gaunt in the flames, shook his head wearily. 'Not that, no. But with such a thought hanging over him a man could be persuaded to do many things that he would not normally contemplate.'

Thufor stabbed in silence at the earth with his knife.

'Your instructions regarding myself,' said Shadd. 'What were they?'

'They were as I told you, nothing more. I am to deliver you safely, with your cargo, to the entrance of the tunnel through the Gro'd f'ho Ib.'

Shadd nodded, and made no more of the subject. We three now ate, more or less in silence, for none was inclined to further discussion. Near-exhaustion was upon each of us, but it was necessary that a vigil be maintained throughout the night as protection against the approach of our enemies. I volunteered for first duty, with Shadd taking second and Thufor last. Thufor lay down and within minutes his deep and rhythmic breathing told us that he was asleep.

Despite his fatigue Shadd deferred sleep so that he and I might converse, utilising the silence of our minds so that there was no possibility of our words being overheard. What a joy it was to speak again with a human being – albeit without the usual agency of air over vocal membranes. Suddenly I was closer than I had been for many months to my former self and the life I had lost as Ronbas Dinbig, Grand Merchant Adventurer of Khimmur.

As I recounted my story Shadd heeded with few interruptions. Those interjections he did make revealed, unsurprisingly, that his knowledge of what was happening within Khimmur and its burgeoning empire was much greater than mine. Nonetheless it was far from complete.

He became animated at the news of my encounter with Shimeril in the woods of Mystoph, then sombre as I told of the vast army I had witnessed there, of the occupation of Virland and the troop movements I had spied in Chol. As my tale drew towards its conclusion and I came again to the massacre of the vhazz by Yxon's Laughing Blue Knights, Shadd adopted an intense inward stare. Guilt over the death of my last three vhazz companions, I realised, weighed heavily upon his mind.

Shadd faced me, his pale lips taut and quivering. He shook his head wretchedly and his words sounded disconnected and remorseful in my mind. *'If I had known, Dinbig. If only I had known.'*

I was reminded forcefully of our last meeting, two years earlier in Twalinieh in Kemahamek, though it seemed a lifetime ago now. Shadd had been cruelly manipulated by both Khimmur and Kemahamek. He had just been named the assassin of the woman he believed he loved, Kemahamek's Holy Wonasina, Seruhli. The citizens of Twalinieh howled for his blood, while his countrymen, the warriors and citizens of Khimmur, believed him a coward and traitor to his half-brother the King. The two of us had found temporary refuge in a small wooded park below the walls of Twalinieh's Sacred Citadel. Shadd had revealed to me events that had just transpired. His soul had been tortured then over circumstances in which he had had no real control, yet for which he believed he was responsible.

*'You could not have known,'* I said. *'Vhazz and human have been enemies for as long as the two have existed. Even under the extraordinary circumstances that prevailed today, little could have been changed. It was a fight for survival. It could have been nothing other.'*

I moved away from the subject, for I too was deeply affected. *'Tell me now of your escapades since we last met. I can barely contain my impatience.'*

Now I learned of Shadd's escape from Twalinieh as the Vulpasmage's troops sacked the city; of the terrible loss of his paladins, and his subsequent decision, overwhelmed as he was with sorrow, guilt and revulsion at all that he had witnessed, to exile himself from the world. He told me of his harsh life in the wilds of Drurn March. I saw a spark in his eyes, a ghost of a smile upon his lips as he related this latter episode. Evidently, notwithstanding its privations, that period in Shadd's life had brought its own rewards. Knowing him as I did, I could not help wonder whether in solitude and contemplation of the natural world he had discovered a measure of peace.

Now he came to his 'capture' by Odus, the Commander of Drurn March fortress, and of the arrival of Chol's defeated Prince Regent, Fhir Oube. Shadd revealed to me much of what he had learned from Fhir Oube in regard to recent and current events. Perplexedly, and with mounting anger, he questioned the fall of Twalinieh, the mysterious pact that had been somehow struck between Khimmur and the Simbissikim, and the subsequent deployment of Kemahamek troops to supplement Khimmur's occupying forces elsewhere.

'It defies belief, Dinbig, yet I know it to be true. And now you bring further confirmation. The Vulpasmage, as always, displays brilliance and uncanny foresight. He achieves the impossible, and remains several steps ahead of anyone.'

Lastly Shadd told me of the visit to his cell of the woman Elore, who had announced herself as the sister of Fhir Oube, of the news she had brought, of his escape and the journey that followed into Qotolr and Mesmia's tower, and of what had befallen him since.

'Ah, and now, while Sleen and Thufor sleep, I may introduce you to two other companions – boon allies who have travelled in secret with me these past days, and without whom I would not have survived this journey.'

From somewhere in the rafters of the hut fluttered a tiny creature which alighted upon Shadd's shoulder. I found myself gazing upon an exquisitely-formed winged female, no larger than a hummingbird, who stood smiling at me, her delicate wings shimmering, reflecting hues of rose, gold and orange from the subdued embers of the fire. She was clothed in a light garment of grey, silky material, and held a slender silvered rod in one hand.

'This is Temminee, of the Gwynad. And this . . .' from a pouch at his waist Shadd brought forth a rough lump of stone which he laid upon the palm of his hand ' . . . is a hylozote.'

To my astonishment the stone then spoke. It greeted me in polite and cordial tones. I gaped, then laughed – something I had done little of in recent weeks, and which I had scarcely been aware a vhazz was capable of. Then quickly I apologised for my poor manners.

'Think nothing of it,' said the hylozote evenly. 'I understand perfectly your reaction. Indeed, I find myself commonly of the same astonished frame of mind, for I am as much an enigma to myself as I am to you.'

Shadd smiled and said, speaking so that we all three might hear, 'This sedimentary fellow has given me much to think about. He lacks vocal apparatus, yet he speaks; he is without ears and eyes, yet he hears and sees; he has no brain, yet he uses intellect to good and impressive effect. He is, truly, an enigma.'

I gazed a moment longer upon the hylozote, then shook my vhazz head. *'The Blue Knight was right, though he did not know the half of it: we are a motley company indeed!'*

Shadd became grave once more. Whispering so that Temminee and the hylozote might hear, he said, 'Dinbig, there is yet something else, something I had forgotten to mention earlier. It may be of extreme relevance to you. Only a few nights ago I saw you. That is, I saw my old friend, Ronbas Dinbig, in the flesh, here in Qotolr.'

*'You are mistaken, surely? How can that be?'*

'I do not know, but it is not a mistake. At the time I half-thought I dreamed, yet the following day

402

the hylozote assured me that it had been no dream, for he has seen you on other occasions. But, though it was you, you were undeniably different. One arm was merely a stump, and – I hesitate to say it, old friend – you were not your old self. Your behaviour was eccentric, and the hylozote has attested to the fact that when he has seen you you have been in a state of unusual distraction.'

This news brought a thrill of excitement, as well as deep disquiet and foreboding to my heart. *'If it is true – and I do not know how it can be, for I myself witnessed my death – but if it is, then the only explanation, surely, is that my corporeal self is possessed. It has become a Wanderer.'*

This was a far from happy prospect. The Wanderer is a sorry but perfidious thing, the body of a human adept who has failed to return from a journey to the Realms of Non-Being. Motivated by the Custodian entity which guarded it when its rightful occupant was lost, the Wanderer traipses the land in a confusion of identities. The Custodian's natural bent is to endeavour to exert its full personality upon the flesh, but the Custodian, having formerly manifested in the physical world in animal form, half believes itself to be an animal.

From Shadd's account, endorsed by the hylozote's own experience, I could hardly doubt that this was what they had witnessed. And yet, in Twalinieh, I had seen my death, felt the cruel severance of the ethereal cord that bound me to corporeality. I considered Yo, my former Custodian. Was it possible that my flesh had somehow survived, and was now in Yo's charge? Throughout his service to me he had made plain his ambition to one day experience life from the human vantage. His unintentional mischief in this regard had caused inconvenience on a number of occasions. Most latterly a flagrant disregard for the conditions of his service had resulted in certain grotesque violations, for which I had not had the time or opportunity to mete out appropriate punishment. In the final event, it had been Yo who had purloined my body and brought me to grief.

Yes, that was surely the answer! My flesh was a Wanderer, possessed by my former Custodian. This being so, it would without doubt be succumbing to dementia, assuming characteristics of both Yo and his bestial 'worldly' manifestation (in this instance a Wide-Faced Bear — and one that was itself chronically enraged, as I recalled), whilst still imbued with a vestigial sense of its former identity, which is to say, *my* self.

For some moments I was gripped by a feeling of helpless shock. When I at last returned to a consciousness of my surroundings it was to find Shadd still before me, silently observing.

'What will you do?' he asked softly.

I gave a stupefied shake of my head. '*I suppose I must search myself out, if that is possible. Moban, but this is strange beyond telling!*'

'Qotolr is a land strange beyond telling,' muttered Shadd. 'Perhaps your fleshly existence here may be somehow connected with its uncommon properties. I have had experiences and witnessed things here that defy explanation. And more, I realised soon after entering this land that my abilities had been depleted, as if by dint of the excess of magic innate to this place. In Drurn March I had greatly enhanced my strengths, learning to listen ever closer to the whispered words of nature, of the trees, the air, the land beneath our feet. Yet here I am able to perceive nothing. It is as though nature holds her breath, does not communicate between her myriad parts for risk of exciting or disturbing another presence which abides in Enchantery.'

*'Still, you are able to enter my mind, to communicate at length with a clarity I do not recall from before,'* I pointed out.

'I have been fortunate, as I have said, in the friends I have met along the way.' Shadd touched the crystal at his neck. 'This is the Soul Crystal, a sacred object of the Gwynad. Through this, and with Temminee's aid, I have been granted abilities. Without it I believe I would have been lost.'

I regarded the blue-white crystal with its fiery heart. *'Then conceivably when you leave this land your powers will be further increased through its agency.'*

'It is possible,' mused Shadd. 'But my hope is that I may return it to its rightful owners, the Gwynad, from whom it was stolen.'

The embers cast their low light upon Shadd's face and I saw the heaviness of his gaze. I was depriving him of much needed sleep. In a few short hours I would be waking him that he might take over the watch. There were other questions I had wished to put to him: certain things I had heard today had given me cause for concern. But I put them temporarily in abeyance. They could wait until morning.

# 15

## I

The morning brought a sullen light and further heavy cloud which threw down abrupt showers of cold, sweeping rain. There had been no sign of the Laughing Blue Knights during the night. Sleen, though weak and still a touch feverish, was fit enough to ride, and eager, as were we all, to be away and out of Yxon's domain without delay.

We rode cautiously, keeping to the woods and avoiding areas of habitation. Conversation was held to a minimum, partly out of prudence, partly mood. Thufor rode lead, hunched in the saddle. Sleen, his shoulder and arm bound with linen, came behind. Shadd was last, with I for the most part trotting on all fours beside him. We saw no one.

Late in the morning we came up beside an ancient way, and Sleen announced his intention to leave our party. 'My home lies an hour away over yonder hill. There I can take my ease and recuperate in grand style and contemplation of my good fortune and the manifold pleasures the future now holds.' With his good hand he patted the sack of booty strapped behind his saddle and produced a smile that would have been roguish had he not looked so weak and sickly. The effort of twisting, furthermore, caused him to stiffen and wince with pain. He sat still for a moment until the sensation had passed, then said, 'Thufor, it has been a successful venture. I trust we will meet again.'

Thufor nodded, stony-faced, and said nothing. Sleen

turned to Shadd. 'And you, sir, I have found a worthy, if somewhat mysterious companion. I thank you for your attention to my wound. Though sore, it appears to be healing with remarkable speed.'

Lastly he glanced dubiously in my direction, clicked his tongue several times, but made no comment.

'One thing before you part,' said Shadd. 'I would like to know, for I have suspected since we met, was it your intention to betray me or do me ill?'

'Betray? No,' said Sleen, and added with candour, 'Had you proven a hindrance I would have slain or abandoned you, whichever came the easier. And I will admit, had you brought out valuables that might have fitted better in my pockets I might well have taken them from your charge when your usefulness was done, and taken your life had you resisted. As it happened you brought out nothing of value or use to me. And more, you had already shown yourself to be a man of formidable talents, one with whom I quickly resolved not to meddle. I am many things, sir, but a fool is not one of them. Now, I salute you, and bid you all farewell.'

He doffed his hat with a flourish, wincing again, then turned his horse and rode away at a walking pace through the trees.

'Come,' said Thufor, moving off. 'We can be beyond Yxon's domain by nightfall. The way will be safer from thereon.'

As we travelled my thoughts were largely taken up with the matter of my itinerant flesh. I was bound to attempt to seek it out. A confrontation was demanded, and a reckoning. Perhaps even . . . I tried not to build my hopes, but it was impossible not to dwell upon the concept of my reclaiming my corporeal form.

To become once more the Ronbas Dinbig of old!

The notion thrilled and tormented me. Could it be done? I knew of no precedent.

I considered the physical facts. Shadd had seen my flesh less than a week ago, somewhere in this vicinity, upon this very road. The hylozote told of an enchanted glade beyond the mountains where my wandering self had tarried. But by now it could be anywhere, near or far. What real chance had I of locating it?

The odds did not appear to be in my favour, yet I had been delivered here, in this form, by some strange and imponderable quirk of Fate. It was Fate, surely, that had brought me to Shadd, and the knowledge that my flesh had not perished? Everything now lent support to the notion that I should pursue my corporeal form. Why, it might even now be somewhere close by, watching me from the trees, or roaming just out of sight, ahead of me around the next corner or over the next rise!

The thought caused me to pause a moment in my step and scrutinise the landscape. Nothing did I see. I trotted on alongside Shadd.


I was hesitant to part company with Shadd. The terrible vhazz fear of being alone was gathering itself, compounded further by my human longing to remain in the company of my fellow men. Were I to seek out my corporeal self I would inevitably have to do it alone. Shadd would take his leave of Qotolr as soon as the opportunity provided. His own tasks and burdens precluded his delaying to help me with mine.

But my hesitation did not stem entirely out of self-centredness. I was also concerned for Shadd himself. I could not help but be aware of how much he had changed since we had last seen each other. He had matured, yes, but aged also. Ever prone to melancholic turns and periods of profound self-examination, Shadd struck me now as having become significantly more withdrawn and inwardly focused. I knew that his uncertain heritage troubled him. A weight of responsibility and, more recently, self-recrimination, hung upon him, becoming ever more difficult to bear. I observed now an added sense of bewilderment about him; he seemed on the verge of desperation, evinced qualities both gloomy and wild in his mien. The unfathomable, always a part of him, had taken on a new dimension. I was afraid for him – and perhaps even *of* him, though in the latter instance I could not say precisely why. I felt a certain responsibility for him, and wished to be on hand to proffer any assistance I could. And assistance, or at least sound advice, he was going to have need of, I was certain of that.

Furthermore, a sense of deepest disquiet was aroused in me by a certain element of the quest Shadd was engaged upon and the end he hoped so fervidly to achieve. I had as yet no certain corroboration, and needed to communicate further with him, but from the details I had so far gleaned I suspected that far more might be bound up in Shadd's venture than he could possibly be aware of. A fantastical and chilling scenario had suggested itself to my mind. If it proved to have any substance then Shadd was engaged upon a task more dangerous and many-faceted than he could possibly conceive. The consequences now, should he actually succeed, might turn out to be far-reaching and catastrophic beyond imagining.


II


How might I tell him?

I pondered this over and over throughout the remainder of that day as we moved out of Yxon's domain. My most immediate fear was for Shadd's state of mind. The terrible events that had ended in the fall of Twalinieh had taken an incalculable toll from him. He had been deceived, manipulated, duped. Through no fault of his own his actions had helped bring about Kemahamek's downfall, and the deaths of many of its citizens. He had been falsely arraigned for cowardice and treachery, then for the murder of the Wonasina, Seruhli, the woman he loved. By this means he had gained infamy. His name, I did not doubt, was spoken of with anger and loathing by uncountable thousands who knew nothing of the true facts. Now history appeared to be repeating itself. Shadd strove to make amends for wrongs committed in his name, and was in danger, if my suspicions proved founded, of setting off another chain of events that could result in further carnage and suffering. But what a dilemma faced him if I was correct, for if he chose now to abandon his task Seruhli would be lost, as would Kemahamek. The Beast of Rull would continue to grow and devour, unhindered.

I sensed that Shadd had suspicions of his own, but I was sure he could not have grasped the scope or gravity of the situation as I perceived it. What was evident to me was that he was in an emotionally perilous state, to the extent that I was not certain whether he was capable of coping with what I had to say. If my suspicions were grounded, it might prove sufficient to push him that last fateful step beyond the bounds of sanity. I dared not leave the issue; before I could say anything I had to ascertain the truth.

We camped that night in a hollow on the edge of a barren and inhospitable plain of weird, tortured black rock. Shadd said that we were now only hours from his destination. There was a growing restlessness in him as he anticipated the encounter which he expected on the following day.

The guard rota of the previous night was agreed. After we had eaten, Thufor settled down to sleep. Shadd and I sat together some yards away, and I tentatively broached the matter that preyed upon my thoughts.

'You mentioned that the object of your quest into Ciracar's Warren was to obtain a certain scroll. The scroll is said to contain the formula for the antidote for the Semblance of Death, of which Seruhli is a victim.'

'That is so.'

'Do you have it with you?'

Shadd withdrew an engraved ivory tube from within his tunic. This he had attached by a ribbon to his belt. He untied the ribbon, removed a plug which sealed one end of the tube, and drew out a roll of several leaves of parchment. The musty scent of ages rose into my nostrils. I carefully unfurled the leaves, noting their unfamiliar texture. I ran my eyes over them, and what I saw there brought a sudden chill to my heart.

I could make no sense of the inscriptions that filled each page. The language itself was ancient, and, so I believed, couched in a particularly cryptic form. But though I could not decipher the arcane signs and symbols that confronted me, I recognised their origin. Zan-Chassin schooling had been comprehensive and thorough; and particular emphasis had been laid on this specific form, that it might be instantly recognised by any adept. This was an ancient Qotol script. Over and over had been drummed into me the possible significance of such writing. I had never thought to hold in my hands what I was holding now. I was awed and frightened, so much so that I found I had begun to tremble.

*'Dinbig, are you all right?'* said Shadd's voice within my thoughts.

I tore my eyes from the parchment. For a moment I could not face him; I could not predict his reaction to what I now was compelled to reveal to him. Softly, endeavouring to conceal much of my own feelings, I said, *'Do you know anything more than what you have told me about this scroll?'*

But Shadd was within my mind, listening and sensing. He was aware of my emotion. He swallowed, and a haunted look came like a shadow upon his visage. *'Is it not what I was told?'*

*'Quite possibly the formula for the antidote to the Semblance of Death is here,'* I said. *'I cannot decrypt these ciphers, so it is impossible for me to say. What I can say is that there is more here, much more.'* I sifted through the pages. *'One of these may be the formula. But the others, what are they?'*

Shadd stared with wide glazed eyes at the parchments, but said nothing. I carefully weighed my next words, though for what end I cannot say, for the blow I was about to deliver could not be softened. In the end I could only ask outright, *'Are you familiar with the tale of Yshcopthe's Ruse?'*

A shudder passed through Shadd's body. His features sagged with shock. His eyes met mine; they were disbelieving, then fierce, then afraid. The light passed suddenly out of them. He turned away. He was sitting against the bole of a tree, and his head tipped back now to fall against the bark. He breathed as though winded by a physical blow. He let out a low, anguished groan.

*'It brought about the end of the Enchanter Wars which threatened to destroy Firstworld,'* I said, still

speaking directly into Shadd's mind. *'Yshcopthe tricked her adversaries into placing much of their arcane knowledge into a great Pandect, then took the Pandect and vanished. The Pandect was lost, then believed destroyed. But fragments survived, so it was said, though none have ever been found.'*

Shadd whispered out loud. 'Until now.'

I nodded. *'Until now.'*

The tiny winged female, the Gwynad, Temminee, alighted on Shadd's shoulder. I heard her voice, a mellifluous whisper, as she spoke into his ear. 'Duke Shadd, is something wrong?'

'Something is wrong, Temminee,' breathed Shadd. 'Something is terribly, terribly wrong.' He turned back to me. *'I don't understand. This was foreseen. Ciracar knew me. He guarded the warren through eons, knowing that I, or one who answered in all respects to my description, would come for this scroll. He even called me Savor.'* He put his hands to his head. *'What does it mean, Dinbig! What does it mean! What am I to do?'*

At that point I did not know. I absorbed this latest revelation, which added yet another sinister dimension to this affair. What *could* it mean? That Shadd was some unwitting bearer of destiny, of doom? I quickly shifted this thought, knowing that Shadd could perceive it. *'I must ask you more. The Drear-hag whom yesterday Thufor confessed is his employer – can she be the same Mesmia who has sent you on this mission to recover the scroll?'*

Shadd nodded, with fearful reluctance, so concerned was he for what this answer might mean. I closed my eyes, for he had confirmed the worst. I said, *'Drear-hag is a name oft-times applied to one of the enchantresses of yore. She was known by many names and utilised many guises. At the time of the Enchanter Wars she*

413

was known most commonly as Strymnia. She was the arch-enemy of Yshcopthe, and it is widely held that she outlived her. It is possible that she is one of the five surviving Enchanters who rule Qotolr.'

'And I am bringing to her pages from the Pandect which will provide her with the power to dominate the other four.'

I nodded. These leaves of parchment might contain anything. One page, certainly, could hold the formula needed to save the Wonasina, Seruhli. But the other seven . . . I shuddered to think what secrets might be contained thereon, and to what lengths certain persons might go to get their hands upon these pages.

'The Drear-hag claims to be able to read what is written upon these pages,' said Shadd. 'That was the bargain, that I return the scroll to her so that she might translate it in order to save Seruhli.'

'If she is Strymnia – and almost certainly that is who she is – then undoubtedly she will know this language.'

'She claims to be an enemy of the Vulpasmage. Perhaps she will keep her end of the bargain.'

'Perhaps. But once she holds the formula she may intend to blackmail you further. I cannot doubt that her ultimate aim is power, and with these other pages in her possession . . .'

I examined the parchment. The leaves were of an uncommon substance and were said to be indestructible. We could not attempt to separate them, for the Drear-hag was almost certainly aware that the ivory tube contained more than a single page of the fabled Pandect. And besides, we had no way of knowing which was the page we sought.

We sat in silence, and after some time had passed Shadd got up and walked away into the darkness of nearby trees. He seated himself upon a low earth bank, his back to me, and stared brooding into the depths of the encroaching night. Throughout my period of watch he remained there, and when the time came for him to relieve me he still did not stir. Nor did I attempt to disturb him, though from the way he shook his head from time to time or lifted his hands as though conducting some internal dialogue with himself, I knew that he was wakeful. Later I roused Thufor, who took over from me and allowed me to get some sleep. When morning came Shadd was as I had left him, and when I went to speak to him seemed hardly aware that the night had passed.

He rose, his face etched with fatigue, and muttered words of apology for having neglected his watch. I waved the apology away. Shadd stared disconsolately towards the rocky plain with an unfocused gaze. I became aware of his words in my mind. *'All night I have racked my mind without cease. I have consulted with Temminee, who in another form spent years as the Drear-hag's prisoner. She has offered me advice, as has the hylozote, but essentially we are no closer to a solution. I considered an attempt to escape Qotolr. Though I know of no other route that avoids Mesmia's tower, one surely exists, for your fleshly form has been seen on both sides of the mountain, and he surely did not come via the tower.'*

This was something I had not thought of. I knew only of the route by which I had entered Qotolr with Yaoww. For a human it would prove a difficult and arduous way, though Shadd would probably have been capable of negotiating it.

*'But escape is not feasible,'* Shadd went on. *'A shadow dogged my footsteps at an earlier phase of this journey. The hylozote believes it is still with us, and now I am drawn to conclude that this shadow is Mesmia's servant. Surely, then, she knows that I am*

here, in which case she will follow and intercept me if I attempt to avoid her. Probably she is aware that the scroll is in my possession. What she does not yet know — and I thank Moban that we communicated last night in silence — is that I am aware of her ploy. How much that awareness can aid me I do not know.'

Distractedly he nudged a clod of dry earth with his foot. 'Another idea that came to mind was to make a copy of the fragments. That way, should Mesmia fail to keep her side of the bargain, I might at least have ensured that the means still existed to save Seruhli, if somehow the formula could be deciphered. I have no writing materials with me, but as I considered this possibility I idly attempted to copy a part of the inscription with a twig upon the earth. Observe, Dinbig.'

He took the scroll from its tube and unrolled it. With a sharpened twig he commenced transcribing the initial characters from the ancient writing onto the earth. Even as he wrote the earthen characters faded before my eyes.

'The Pandect defies replication,' Shadd declared. 'It is also resistant to flame, for in a moment of sheer despair I placed a page in the embers of our campfire. As you can see, the parchment is unaffected.'

He re-rolled the leaves and returned them to the tube. 'There exists, then, only one possible course. I must proceed as with the original agreement, and confront Mesmia. I cannot predict the outcome. Perhaps I will be destroyed, but I must try. If she is indeed the enchantress Strymnia it may yet be that she is disquieted at the ascendancy of the Vulpasmage. If that is so, perhaps a bargain can still be struck.'

'It is a slim and fragile hope. And a precipitous one.'

*'I cannot see that I have any real choice. And listen, Dinbig, Temminee has given me certain advice which may prove to have effect.'* He proceeded to outline what could scarcely be termed a plan, nor even a realistic notion. It was, at best, a hope. But knowing so little of the Drear-hag, her true motives, or the extent of the powers at her command, it was hardly one that inspired confidence.

Still, I could only accept as I considered the situation, that Shadd was right: he had little choice. The damage, in effect, had been done: the fragment from Yshcopthe's Pandect had been released from its secret vault in Ciracar's Warren. The longer Shadd remained in Qotolr the greater was the possibility that others might come to learn of this fact. For all the consequences that might yet ensue, he was bound to take the scroll to Mesmia's tower and attempt, somehow, to bargain.

Clouds obscured the peaks to the east. Through them filtered a low, watery morning light. *'We should make way, then,'* I said.

Shadd raised a hand as if to bid me be silent. He stepped past me and across to where Thufor, some yards away, was preparing a breakfast of griddle-cakes. Shadd lowered himself onto his heels beside him. For some moments the two spoke in undertones. Thufor raised his eyes once or twice to cast morose glances in my direction. At length Shadd straightened and returned to face me.

'You will not accompany me, Dinbig.'

I started to protest; he cut me short. *'What aid can you possibly give me against this woman? Were you in your human form, possessed of your former abilities and faculties, then yes, perhaps by rapture and deft manoeuvre we might together have faced her. But now, by your own admission, you are without strength*

417

or magic: a *vhazz*, albeit with human thoughts, human emotions. I have spoken with Thufor. I told him about you and enquired as to whether he had knowledge of the "lunatic" who has been seen by both myself and the hylozote. Apparently your corporeal form is not an unfamiliar sight in these parts. Thufor informs me that for a year or more a chucklehead answering to its description has travelled the same road, back and forth. Though previously Thufor led me to believe there was no other way through these mountains, he has now, faced with what I know, admitted the existence of another route. It is a circuitous but navigable way. It lies some thirty miles south of here.'

'But you have already said you will not take another road.'

'And I have not changed in my resolve. But you will. Don't you see, Dinbig! It is upon that road that you are most likely to encounter the Wanderer that is your rightful form. It may take days, or weeks of waiting, and even then you have no guarantee that you will be able to reclaim your flesh. But you must try. If you succeed you can then make your way back to Khimmur and the Zan-Chassin. Hopefully we will be reunited there, but if that cannot be, then at least you can tell my tale, and let all know what has transpired in this land.'

I protested ever more vehemently, but Shadd would not be swayed, and gradually the logic of his argument wore through and my resistance lost its fervour.

We parted, then. Not without emotion. Again I was reminded of Twalinieh, when we had last taken leave of one another. As now, we had been engaged upon hazardous and consequential tasks. As now we had not known what the outcome might be, or whether we would ever set eyes on one another again.

Shadd gave me coins and food from his rations, reasoning that my corporeal form would most probably be without money or the means to easily sustain itself. He relayed further details concerning the road and region along which the chucklehead wandered. Then, with Thufor, he rode away onto the plain of jagged rock. I watched as their forms slowly diminished into the distance. A light movement touched my shoulder, and a voice spoke quietly in my ear: 'Don't be afraid for him, good Dinbig. I owe him much and will help him all I can.'

A tiny form flew away from me, gliding swiftly over the slivered stones towards Shadd's back. I did not doubt Temminee's sincerity, nor her courage or resolve. But I wondered what possible aid she could give against an enchantress both potent and vengeful.

I remained where I was until they passed beyond sight, then turned with a heavy heart and began the journey south.

# 16

They stood upon the plateau at the foot of the rock face where Shadd had first emerged from the mountain tunnel and met Thufor. Before them, amidst a tumble of rock and undergrowth, was an opening.

'The way is unbarred,' said Thufor. 'Evidently you are expected.'

'Do you accompany me now?' Shadd asked.

Thufor shook his head. 'My friend, here we part. My job is done. I go to enjoy what I can of the existence I have been granted – greatly enlivened, I would now hope, by the wealth that I have newly acquired.'

'Then I wish you well.'

'And I you. We are kindred spirits, it seems to me. Both compelled by forces greater than we to follow roads we would not ordinarily pursue. I would hope that one day we might meet again under easier circumstances.'

'And in another land!' added Shadd. 'I will not by choice return to this place.'

Thufor gave a shrug. 'It is the country of my birth, and I know nothing other.'

'Aye, and I apologise. I did not mean to cast insult. I recognise that it is your home, and as such is dear to you. But for a foreigner like myself it is strange beyond comprehension.'

'Might that not be said of life anywhere?'

'It might, and often is! Nevertheless, Enchantery is unique in my experience. Its principles and laws of existence seem to lack correspondence with those of the world beyond its borders.'

Temminee's voice sounded in Shadd's ear. 'I have been in the tunnel. There is a presence there. I am unable to properly identify it. But as I entered it seemed that something entered with me. I glimpsed a movement upon the ground, like a shadow. It might have been cast by a bird, or perhaps a small cloud, but there is no sun to cast such a shadow. And it seemed to move of its own volition, swiftly and with purpose.'

Shadd became instantly alert. 'And once inside the tunnel, what then?'

'The shadow was lost to my sight, but as I say, I had awareness of an uncertain presence in the dark.'

Shadd peered uneasily at the tunnel entrance.

'You look troubled, my friend,' said Thufor.

Shadd glanced aside at him. As if casually he moved away, so as to put space between the two of them. There was a movement within the tunnel mouth. Out of the gloom a figure materialised, a woman, young and of striking appearance, garbed in a dark purple cape beneath which could be seen a long dress of deepest crimson.

She smiled as she stepped into the light, showing bright, even white teeth. Long russet-toned hair fell about her slim shoulders, and her eyes flashed, deep blue, almost violet, vivid against smooth ivory skin. Her gaze, somehow limpid yet sparked with a smouldering heat, rested lingeringly upon Shadd, inquisitive, assessing and provoking.

From the side Shadd heard Thufor draw a deep and involuntary breath. Shadd himself was not unaffected by the woman's unusual beauty, but he returned her gaze, unabashed.

The woman spoke. 'Good day, Duke Shadd. So you have returned. And, I understand, with some success.'

Temminee's voice: *'Beware, Duke Shadd!'*

Shadd nodded to himself. He glanced briefly beyond the woman to the tunnel entrance, then back. 'Good day, Elore. I had wondered when we would meet again.' Archly, he added, 'How fares your brother? Is he here with you?'

'He is not. I left him at Drurn March soon after you escaped the fortress. All is not well there. Most recently his troops have suffered another major defeat. The Vulpasmage's army has broken through into the south of Chol. It is likely that Fhir Oube's whereabouts are now known to the enemy.'

Shadd assessed this, scrutinising Elore the while. She in turn seemed poised. He had the impression that she was searching, appraising him keenly, apprehensive of his response. Was she connected with the shadow thing that had followed him so far? She had stepped from the tunnel into which it had entered. Almost certainly, then, some form of communication had passed between them. And she worked with Mesmia, of this Shadd could be assured. What was her precise role?

Her information, he reasoned, might well be correct – in fact he sensed within himself that this was so. It was dispiriting news, but not wholly surprising.

Shadd made as if to move towards the tunnel entrance. 'Please forgive me if I appear brusque, Elore. I must with all urgency now return to Mesmia's tower.'

Elore held up a hand. 'A moment. I am here at Mesmia's behest. She has requested, before you enter the tunnel, that you relinquish certain articles which she furnished you with upon your departure. I have need of them.'

'What articles are these?'

'A Stepforth and the dual-crystal which you wear on

422

a chain about your neck.' Elore held out her hand. 'Perhaps you would give them to me now.'

'I intend no disrespect, but I would prefer to discuss the relinquishment of these articles with Mesmia herself.'

A flicker of some fiery emotion seemed to mar for an instant the beauty of Elore's face, then was gone. She spoke again, her voice level. 'Mesmia's instructions were precise: I am to recover the articles from you prior to your entering the tunnel. I have need of them for purposes of my own. The scroll you may deliver to Mesmia herself.'

Shadd detected the concealed urgency behind her apparent calm. *She speaks only part-truths!* he thought. *It is plain. I am to be dissuaded from returning to Mesmia's tower whilst in possession of the Crystal.*

He wondered at the clarity of his thoughts; he perceived Elore's dissemblance with certainty. He sensed the Soul Crystal at his breast. He said, 'Alas, I am unable to comply with Mesmia's directive. I no longer have the Stepforth in my possession.'

A flash of wrathful fire in Elore's eyes. 'You have lost it?'

*There!* thought Shadd. *The verification. It is in her face, her voice, her posture.*

'Not lost, no. But I feel it is improper to speak further of this matter, except to Mesmia herself.'

Now Elore's anger rose unmistakably to cloud her features. She strove to contain it. She extended her hand again. 'The Crystal, then.'

'Again, with respect, I can speak of this only to Mesmia herself.'

A minatory tone now as Elore replied, 'And again, Duke Shadd, I reiterate Mesmia's directive, which was precise and unequivocal: before proceeding to the tower you are to hand to me those articles belonging to Mesmia: the Crystal and the Stepforth, or any remnant or altered form of the Stepforth that you carry.'

*Ah! Now she truly gives herself away! She reveals her knowledge of the Stepforth's provenance.*

Warily he phrased his next words. 'In the course of my journey here I learned that the Stepforth was not, as I had believed, an inanimate object. It was a living being, transformed and cruelly imprisoned against its will. I therefore chose to liberate it. It is now free of the evil restraint that held it, and is no longer an object to be owned. Hence, I cannot relinquish it to you.'

'You liberated the Gwynad?'

'That is so.'

Elore's features were transformed. First, a look of shocked disbelief, then apprehension, quickly obliterated by fury.

'Fool!' she spat. 'You do not know with what you meddle! Where is the Gwynad now?'

Shadd shrugged. 'I imposed no restrictions upon her, nor did I question her as to her intention or destination. I simply set her free to do as she wished.'

Elore's entire frame seemed to tremble with emotion. Her eyes blazed, and her voice shook as she spoke again. 'But you still have the Crystal.'

'That is so, but it is not mine to give, nor yours to receive. I am pledged to do all in my power to return it to its rightful owners, the Gwynad race.'

Elore absorbed this, then her emotion seemed to melt away. Her face became composed and beautiful once more, though in her eyes remained a glow of almost supernatural intensity. Shadd was acutely conscious of the seething tension behind the serenity of the mask.

'Duke Shadd, I will say a final time: give me the Crystal. You may then proceed with the scroll to

Mesmia's tower. If you persist in your refusal I regret that your life will be immediately forfeit. Your obstinacy will have gained you nothing: I will simply take the Crystal and the scroll from your corpse, which will lie here to be devoured by scavenging beasts.'

'That is not a prospect I would relish. Yet, I cannot comply. The crystal is not mine to give, other than to its rightful owners.'

'Thufor, you may kill him,' said Elore.

Shadd took two steps backwards, distancing himself from the two of them while keeping both easily within his field of view. His hands went to his weapons.

Elore made a contemptuous sound. 'Your swords are useless here. They will avail you nothing. Thufor, why do you hesitate? Kill him now!'

Thufor stood with a troubled expression, his hands grasping the helve of his axe. He glanced at Shadd, then at Elore. 'Mistress, don't ask this of me.'

*Mistress!* thought Shadd. *Yet I believed him to be in Mesmia's employ.*

'I do not ask it, Thufor.' Elore's voice, menacing and low, rose to a guttural bark. 'I order it. Slay him, now!'

Thufor advanced a half-step, then hesitated. 'I cannot.'

'Cannot? What? Are you afraid? Surely you know you have more to be afraid of if you disobey me?'

'I do not fear him, Mistress, though I have seen him in combat and know him to be my equal at least. But more, I am reluctant to take the life of a man whom I have come to respect and feel liking for. Mistress, I beg of you, do not ask this of me.'

Elore beheld him with a withering stare. 'Kill him, Thufor, or know the consequences.'

Thufor settled his eyes upon Shadd. He widened his stance. 'My friend, I am sorry. I must do this.'

He lifted his axe. Shadd crouched slightly, poised to spring.

'Pah!' screamed Elore. 'What use is a man who fights without spirit? Already you are beaten, Thufor. You are useless to me!'

Thufor turned a stricken glance towards her. She raised a hand, made a complex gesture, mouthed incomprehensible words. Something of reddish-hue formed in the air before her. It shot across the glade at Thufor, who staggered back with a scream. He dropped his axe and fell backwards, clawing at his face, which had become a pullulating mass of wriggling, wormlike things.

Instantly Shadd sprang. His twin swords drove at Elore. As they met her flesh they were stayed, as if meeting stone. The shock of their impact sent a spasm of pain up Shadd's arms.

Elore turned upon him with an expression of grim wrath. Her hand flickered. Temminee flew, diving straight at Elore's eyes, her silvered rod held before her. Like Shadd she failed to penetrate the magical armour protecting Elore's flesh, but she was successful in distracting her. Elore's hands flew up to swat at her. Temminee darted away. Elore struck her with the tip of a finger, sent her spinning to the earth.

Elore spat words which became bubbles of fiery substance. The bubbles sped towards Temminee, who lay stunned upon the grass. Elore turned back to Shadd, her fingers moving. A stream of blue energy materialised, drove towards Shadd. In a reflex motion he dived to the side. The energy stream zipped past where he had stood. He leapt forward, feet high, slamming into Elore and kicking hard.

Protected from the impact of his blow by her magical armour, she was nevertheless knocked from her feet under its force. Shadd sprang at her again. With a snarl

426

Elore raised her hands, spitting words. Shadd felt himself lifted, carried over her and hurled with jarring force against a rock. At the last instant he managed to swivel his body aside. He avoided the rock but slammed hard into the earth.

Elore had risen to one knee. Shadd spun to face her again. A searing pain erupted upon his skin, making him cry out. Elore uttered new words. As he writhed in agony Shadd found suddenly that he could not move from the spot.

In the air before Elore a second cloud of pullulating red wormy-stuff began to form. Elore gave a triumphal smile. The cloud rushed towards Shadd. Into his mind came a clear thought: *Return her power!* He had a vision of something glowing fiery red pulsating within a shimmering field of darting blue motes. He felt the energy of the Soul-Crystal charging his own. Fear vanished, and with it went all thought. As the worm-cloud fell upon him he spoke with a voice that came unbidden, out of the depths of his unknown self.

'Back! To your Maker!'

The worm-cloud left him, reversing its path to bear straight down upon Elore. Her head was engulfed before she could respond. She fell back with a shrill shriek.

Writhing upon the ground, Elore gibbered words of magic. The worm-cloud dissolved. She raised herself, half-supine, supported on one elbow. Her hair fell in disarray over her face; her body was angled and stiff. She glared at Shadd in a paroxysm of fury, her unblemished features now a mass of mottled red.

Shadd advanced towards her, free of pain, his limbs no longer bound by her spell. With a scream of frustrated wrath Elore seemed to shrivel upon herself. Her form diminished, to become nothing more than a dark shadowy thing which streaked across the grass and disappeared into the tunnel mouth.

Shadd turned, to find Temminee hovering close by. The flaming bubbles had not touched her. Diverted from Elore's control they had flown wild and dissolved into the air. Shadd strode to where Thufor lay. The worms had gone, but Thufor's features were a welter of blood and ruined flesh.

Kneeling, Shadd spread his hands above Thufor's face, murmuring an invocation.

Thufor opened his eyes. 'What tongue is that?'

'Aphesuk. It is a healing mantra taught me long ago. It will stimulate your own energies and help the flesh to restore itself. Now, are you well? You must come with us!'

Thufor sat erect. 'You know I cannot. I must remain here and take my chances.'

'And be returned to Yxon?'

'If that is the way of it. If I accompany you I will surely find myself bound to attempt to destroy you.'

Temminee cried out, 'Duke Shadd, the way is closing!'

Shadd glanced behind him. The rock about the tunnel was advancing, inwards over the entrance, rapidly sealing the opening.

'Go, my friend, and go well,' urged Thufor. He pushed him away.

Shadd reached out and squeezed his shoulder. He rose, turning, and dashed for the tunnel mouth. He dived through the narrowing gap, rolling on the dark earth floor, and rose to turn again. Thufor stood in the glade, his face bloodied and deformed, one hand raised in farewell.

'Thufor! Your lamp!' cried Shadd.

Thufor ran to the edge of the glade where their horses were tethered. He wrestled with his pack, drew out a lamp. As the rock closed before him Shadd watched as Thufor rushed back. He made to hurl the lamp, but before it had left his hand the entrance had sealed itself, and Shadd was embraced by chill darkness.

## II

'I will be your eyes,' said Temminee.

'And I,' added the hylozote from its pouch at Shadd's belt.

Shadd nodded. 'So it must be. But I will be vulnerable. The shadow entered the tunnel. Do you detect its presence, Temminee?'

'It is not close by,' replied the Gwynad. 'My guess is that it has fled deeper into the mountain, or more likely, has returned to Mesmia. After all, she knows you are in the tunnel now, and can go nowhere except onwards to her tower. She has no further need of the shadow.'

'Are Elore and Mesmia one and the same, then?' said Shadd, half to himself.

'It would appear that Mesmia may manifest in any form she chooses, via the shadow-form,' Temminee said. 'What manifests is, of course, a projection, and not the enchantress herself, though it would seem to have flesh and reality. A fabulous thing. Nevertheless, Elore was bested, for much of the enchantress's power would be channelled into creating and directing the projection. Mesmia herself will not be as easily beaten. But she will be cautious, for she has learned the worst: that you have control of the Soul Crystal. She does not know its full power, of that I am positive. Nor will she have knowledge of the power you may command through its agency.'

'It gives me scant advantage,' murmured Shadd, 'for I am similarly ignorant.'

'The advantage is already proven. Had you not had the Crystal we would both now be dead.'

Shadd considered the notion of the projection. If Elore was a manifestation, given temporary substance and directed by the enchantress, what of Seruhli, whose ghostly form he had encountered upon the shore of the Lake of Clouds? Had that too been Mesmia's contrivance? He had allowed himself to hope, and through hope had come almost to believe, that the encounter had been genuine. But he recalled the hylozote's claim that it thought it had spied the shadow upon the shingle at the lakeside. Was Shadd now to accept that what he had encountered had been another of Mesmia's conjurations, that Seruhli had not tried to enlist his aid, that she was in fact wholly unaware of his actions? Was she, indeed, alive, held in the Semblance of Death, or had she truly relinquished her life at Twalinieh? Had he, Shadd, been duped and manipulated yet again, fooled into serving only the ends of an evil Qotol enchantress?

A weight descended upon him, a gloom so intense as to blot from his consciousness all hope or thought of continuing. Enveloped in the cold blackness of the tunnel, the longing came upon him for death, for release from the turmoil and darkness that gripped his soul.

'Duke Shadd,' came the voice of the hylozote after some moments, 'it is possible that the enchantress works more subtle magic upon you, poisoning your mind against itself.'

'Is there no end?' implored Shadd. 'Can I never know the reality, the truth?'

'You have seen truth, and recognized it,' said the hylozote. 'Recall when you stood with me in the enchanted glade. At first you saw only illusion, the

430

enchantment. Then I told you of the existence of another reality, and you found it within yourself to perceive that. You saw the truth, even if only for a moment. It was dismal, unwelcome, barely acceptable, yet you recognised it for what it was.'

'It is not the same thing,' Shadd replied.

'Is it not? In my experience men live their lives and pass beyond without knowing anything of the world behind the veil of appearances. You have at least glimpsed what lies beyond the veil. You saw through the enchantment, but only when you knew an enchantment to exist. Similarly now, you know that you are confronted by appearance and deceit. Within you, I do not doubt, is the ability to probe beyond it and perceive what is real and actual.'

'I wonder whether the illusion is preferable.'

'That you must discover. But whether the truth be good or not is scarcely of relevance. You are close to *knowing it*, and that is the important thing. You cannot turn back when you have come this far.'

'Come,' interposed Temminee gently. 'It is cold here, and we have a long way to go.'

They moved on into the mountain. Progress was painfully slow; even with his two friends to aid him Shadd found the going arduous. At least the effort of groping his way forward under such difficult circumstances was a distraction, but he could not entirely shake off his feeling of wretchedness. It sapped his energy and prohibited clear thought or reasoning.

Temminee, for the most part, hovered close by so that Shadd might avail himself of her view of the path ahead. Even so, guiding his body with eyes that were not his own proved irksome and unsettling after a short time. Frequently he stumbled or slipped. Sudden attacks of vertigo obliged him to cease walking, to reach out with his hands for the rock wall that he might regain his sense of balance and orientation. On occasion the vertigo was accompanied by a petrifying terror which demanded all his wits and resources to dispel. Spectral visions assailed him: demons and other unnatural creatures forming out of nothingness to rush upon him; gaping chasms yawning suddenly at his feet. All turned out to be phantoms, conjured perhaps by his own inner fears, or by Mesmia, who hoped by such means to destroy his will before he arrived at her tower.

Every fifty paces or so Shadd would find it necessary to halt while Temminee flew ahead to reconnoitre the next section of the tunnel. Alone in the engulfing dark his terror and disorientation were merciless. The visions were of greater intensity; he distracted himself by talking to the hylozote, or observing Temminee's progress through her eyes until she returned, having adjudged the way safe, and they resumed their journey.

The strain grew. Shadd sat and applied meditative techniques to clear his mind of its fears and phantoms, and restore his waning strength. Hours passed; they agreed a break while Shadd and Temminee ate from Shadd's rations. They moved on again. When later he began to feel hunger once more he calculated that evening must be falling upon the landscape outside the mountain. They found an even shelf of rock at the side of the tunnel, free of damp, and while Temminee and the hylozote maintained a vigil, Shadd slept.

It was a deep, dreamless sleep, the sleep of utter exhaustion. When he awoke, and had shaken off his grogginess, he felt stronger, though scarcely more certain of himself. He swallowed a few mouthfuls of food and drank clear water from his sack, then moved on once more.

A period of some hours passed; progress was no easier than before, but in due course Temminee announced that they were approaching the end of the tunnel where a short flight of stone stairs led up to the trapdoor which was the entrance to Mesmia's tower.

'Now comes the true test,' muttered Shadd.

'Focus at all times upon the Crystal,' Temminee breathed.

He arrived at the foot of the stairs. Above his head the trapdoor sprang abruptly open and a flood of greenish light slanted in to illuminate the uppermost steps and grimy rock wall. Shadd gazed up into the interior of the small chamber. From somewhere overhead came the sound of Mesmia's voice: 'Enter, Duke Shadd of Mystoph, without fear. It is discussion I have in mind. You will suffer no harm.'

Gingerly Shadd ascended and entered the small chamber.


III


His skin tingled under the subtle thrill of magic in the air. Before him the panel through which he had entered from Mesmia's tower was open. He waited while his eyes adjusted to the brightness then stepped through into Mesmia's gallery of erotica.

Nothing appeared to have changed. The precious statues, figurines and other sculpted works still disported themselves in lifeless play, as did the subjects of the paintings set around the circular wall. And Mesmia sat at her table of dark green serpentine, her blubbery legs splayed beneath. She wore the same shapeless garment of black and orange, her aubergine hair flying out in all directions. Her arms rested heavily upon the table. At Shadd's entrance she displayed a toothless leer and a fleshy hand moved, to indicate a gold pitcher and goblets upon a salver before her, alongside a platter containing gingerbread and small custard tarts.

'Sit, relax, and refresh yourself after your long and arduous journey. You look weary. Here is good spiced wine, blended to my own recipe. You will find it reviving.'

'I require neither food nor wine, and prefer to remain standing,' replied Shadd curtly.

The Drear-hag gave a gesture of indifference. 'As you wish.'

Shadd attuned himself to the atmosphere within the gallery. Magic was certainly here, as was to be expected, but he detected nothing that he had not been aware of when he had last stood in this place. No traps or magical devices. His senses were heightened; he sensed the energy of the Soul Crystal mingling with his own. Even so, he knew there might be much that was too cunningly-laid for him to detect.

Mesmia herself was a different matter. He sensed her power, tempered by her apprehension. *She is uncertain of me!* he thought. *This I must play upon.*

'I apologise for the behaviour of my servitor, Elore,' Mesmia said. 'Her actions did not meet with my approval.'

'Apologise?' Shadd raised his eyebrows in mock-surprise. 'Are not Mesmia and Elore one and the same; her actions yours?'

'Ah, if only that were so! It is true, she is my projection. But with time and repeated use these creations gain greater substance and a sense of self. They begin to realise a yearning for independent existence, and become less tractable and subject to whims and fancies of their own. I have expected such a development from Elore for some time, but your encounter

434

with her was the first instance in which she has
conducted herself in direct contravention to my own
wishes. My instructions to her were simple: that she
meet you and request the return of the Stepforth and
twin-crystal. Nothing more. That she acted as she
did is a certain indication that she has outgrown her
usefulness to me. Hence she is no more. Now, please,
do sit and take your ease.'

*Part truths, always part truths! Never with Mesmia
is it possible to know how much is real, how much
chaff.* Shadd studied the old woman with care. 'I am
at ease standing.'

A gimlet stare from behind the folds of heavy facial
flesh. 'Duke Shadd, if I wished to do you harm or take
your life I could do so with scant effort. You defeated
Elore, but she was a mere adjunct, possessed of little
power. Mesmia is something other.'

'And what of Strymnia?' enquired Shadd. 'Is she
something other again?'

The Drear-hag's mouth stretched into a gummy
smile and her little eyes glittered. 'That is a name
by which I was known long ago, it is true. Your little
Gwynad taught you well.'

'It is not she who told me.'

'No matter. Where is the flittering thing, by the
way?'

Shadd shrugged. 'I gave her her liberty, without
conditions.'

Mesmia briefly scanned the gallery. 'She accompanied you to the tunnel. I suspect therefore that
she is here now. It was foolish of you to release
her, Duke Shadd. The Gwynad are a malign and
mischievous race. Still, she is of no consequence to
me.'

Clear in Shadd's mind was the certainty that
Mesmia was not as easy about this matter as she

strove to appear. She spoke on: 'You still have the twin-crystal about your person?'

'I do.'

'Good. We will discuss that presently. Of first importance, of course, is the scroll.' She extended a fleshy arm. 'Perhaps you would permit me to see it.'

The moment was charged. Despite himself, Shadd became tense. He spoke in an even voice. 'Before I do, there are certain matters I wish to clarify in regard to our agreement.'

A flicker of displeasure on Mesmia's face. She dropped her arm and pushed her weight back in her chair. 'Speak, then.'

'I have examined the scroll,' said Shadd. 'It is in fact more than a single document, and it is plain that it contains more than a single formula.'

Mesmia's eyes shone. She could not conceal her anticipation. 'What of it?'

'I would wish to know what else is inscribed upon these leaves of uncommon parchment.'

Again she lifted her hand. 'Pass the tube to me and I will examine its contents and endeavour to tell you.'

Again the unmistakable feeling of tension. So much rested here; Shadd sensed it, and wondered: *Does she really not know what is written on these fragments?* He felt that this was so. Mesmia had no knowledge of what the fragments contained. Unlike him, however, she had the ability to decipher the cryptic formulae once she had them in her hands. His spirits fell. He experienced a sense of betrayal and loss, and great foreboding. *She does not even know whether the formula for the Antidote to the Semblance of Death is written here! I have been deceived. Does she, then, as she professed, know anything at all of Seruhli?*

He spoke again. 'I know these leaves to be fragments from the fabled Pandect, wrought in a past age by the enchantress Yshcopthe to bring an end to the Enchanter Wars.'

At this Mesmia stiffened slightly. Her expression became foxy. 'I have not seen them. I cannot say.'

'I believe you can. I believe you know these to be pages from the Pandect.'

Mesmia assumed an unconvincing geniality. 'And if they are, Duke Shadd, what of it? Written upon them is the formula which will save your love, the Wonasina. Surely that is your one concern?'

'You contradict yourself. A moment ago you intimated ignorance in regard to the contents of the manuscripts.'

Mesmia grew agitated. 'I do not know everything that is written there. I do know that one of these fragments contains the formula.'

*She's lying!* Attuned to the Soul Crystal his heightened perceptions told him this without doubt. But what was the lie: that the formula was written here? Or that she knew nothing at all of what the fragments held? Shadd felt the weight of unbearable pressure upon him. So much rested here, so much depended on the outcome of events within this chamber.

'It is said that whoever holds a fragment of Yshcopthe's Pandect, and has deciphered its text, holds power untold,' he said.

Mesmia affected a smile of condescension. 'A single fragment can contain but a scintilla of the knowledge contained in the original Pandect.'

'Eight fragments, eight or more scintillae. Conceivably sufficient arcane knowledge to bestow great advantage upon its possessor.'

Shadd was deprived of her immediate response, for there came a sudden commotion from outside the tower. Shadd recognised the savage baying of the two great curs chained at Mesmia's gateway. With a grimace of annoyance Mesmia swivelled heavily in her chair. She heaved herself to standing and lumbered to a window to peer through. Muttering a curse she moved to a small portal set further along the curving wall. This she opened, and stepped onto a balcony which overlooked the forecourt and approach to the tower. She leaned over the balcony and scrutinised the landscape, then with a word silenced the two hounds.

She returned to her seat. 'A rabbit, a fox; I do not know. They make a hubbub at the slightest thing.'

Despite her words she seemed edgy. She fixed her beady eyes again upon Shadd.

'Now, Duke Shadd, you have allowed yourself to be diverted from the essential point. The full contents of the pages are of secondary consequence. What is important is that therein lies the possible means of combating and destroying our arch-foe, the Vulpasmage.'

'"Our" foe? My reasons for wanting to end the Vulpasmage's reign are obvious and well known. But yours . . . they are less than clear.'

'The Vulpasmage is my enemy too,' declared Mesmia. 'You are aware of that, surely?'

Shadd gave a brief shake of his head. 'Are the mighty Enchanters of Qotolr threatened by this Being? Your land is generally considered impregnable.'

The Drear-hag smiled an unattractive smile. 'Evidently you do not know. The Vulpasmage is itself of Qotolr. The Beast of Rull is one of us.'

Shadd could not conceal his surprise. 'One of you? How? That cannot be so!'

There was a glow of satisfaction in Mesmia's eyes. She settled her mass more comfortably in her chair. 'You and your kind meddle compulsively, in total ignorance. You never consider with what you fool.' She reached for the pitcher of spiced wine and poured the heavy golden liquid into a goblet. 'All this talking has brought a dryness to my throat. Are you sure I cannot tempt you?'

Impatiently Shadd signalled in the negative. Mesmia chuckled. She raised her goblet to her fleshy lips and drank a leisurely draught, savouring the liquid as it passed down her gullet. She smacked her lips and let out a sigh of pleasure. 'Truly it is a rare elixir! You should sample it. I have given it a certain treatment. It is like no wine you will ever have known.'

She regarded him for a moment more, amused at his discomposure, then said, 'I will explain; perhaps then you will be done with your preciousness in regard to the fragments you carry. Listen well:

'During the First Era of your history there existed upon this continent twenty-four Enchanters, as you term them. We were virtual deities upon this world, and we waged war, for it was true that we were jealous of one another, and we each sought ascendancy over the others. During the course of our conflict – which you call the Enchanter Wars – four of our number were beaten, and perished. But of course, we are immortal, and do not die as such. We discard, or are deprived of, physical form and are obliged to depart this domain, to reside in altered form in otherwheres. These four, then, existed beyond the world of matter, space and time, and to all intents and purposes were never heard of again.

'Then came the Great Pooling, in which the archdeceiver Yshcopthe played her infamous Ruse and made off with the Pandect. Through her treachery, those of us who remained behind were reduced in our powers and abilities. We struggled on over the years, eventually to become five in number. The five – of which I, as you have rightly deduced, am one – exist here still.

'But now, let me return to the four who perished. Who were they? Well, two were comparative weaklings, of negligible consequence. Another had been a beneficent fellow of some stature. But the fourth was a creature of evil, who had been one of the most formidable of the twenty-four original Enchanters. This being, had it not been prevented through the combined efforts of several of our number, could well have risen to dominate us all, for it was evincing signs of having gained access to potent forces as yet unmastered by any other.

'But as I have said, these four were no longer of any concern, being effectively trapped beyond the physical domain. And there they would have remained, kept forever from Firstworld in their banished form, had it not been for the tampering of a certain race of men, and in particular, of a certain mystery-oriented sect within that race.

'These persons chose to delve into the arcane reach, seeking knowledge, power, "wisdom". They discovered worlds and modes of existence beyond the physical – Realms of Non-Corporeality, as they called them. They learned to enter and explore the most accessible of these realms, and to tame certain of the denizens there. This sect – I see by your expression that you are perhaps already ahead of me, Duke Shadd – this sect called itself "Zan-Chassin", the sorcerers-elite of Khimmur.'

Mesmia allowed herself to pause a moment. She took another gulp of wine, and nodded in grim affirmation. 'Yes, it is true. And have you deduced the rest?'

Shadd stared at the Drear-hag in dismay, struggling to grasp the import of what she was telling him. Mesmia smiled a contemptuous smile. Her voice rose. 'At a certain point in their explorations these Zan-Chassin meddlers came across four entities of greater power than any they had previously encountered. These entities, it became evident, could greatly enhance men's capacities to interact with the Spirit Realms, and in addition held limited influence over certain aspects of the physical domain. The Zan-Chassin named them the Four Sovereign Entities, and decreed that they be accorded great respect. It was further declared that the Four Sovereign Entities might be tamed and bound only by one designated to become a king of Khimmur. By such means, a true Test of Strength, might the king-designate demonstrate his worthiness to rule. And thus was established a long-standing tradition, which has endured until the present time. Successive kings would announce their choice of spiritual ally from the Four Sovereign Entities. The Entity would be summoned, combat would ensue. If the king-designate survived, the Entity would be bound to his service, to guide and influence his rule.

'Do you require me to tell you the names that the Zan-Chassin gave to these four, Duke Shadd? I see that you do not. Nevertheless, I choose to do so, that there be no possibility of miscomprehension on your part. They were the Mordfar, who it was learned held limited domain over apes, cats, wolves and bears; the Sith's'th, who influenced slithering creatures – snakes, lizards and some insects; the Hul-Banno, who was a thing of the water. And lastly there was the most powerful Entity of all, the Vulpasmage, whose domain took in elements of each of the other three, but whose full scope was unknown, for it had proven too powerful to be bound to the service of men.

'Is it clear, then? Your half-brother has unleashed upon this world one of the original Firstworld Enchanters, a being of immense cunning and unsurpassed evil. It is

441

a vengeful creature, possessed of immeasurable power – for remember, it was undiminished by Yshcopthe's Great Pooling. Potentially it is far stronger than any of we five who still rule Qotolr. It allowed Oshalan to become its human host – not the contrary, as Oshalan believed. It took advantage of his arrogance, his pride, his ruthlessness and ambition. It is true, Oshalan himself was a rare human being. The Vulpasmage waited long ages for a man with the qualities and strengths to bear it, for it was too great a force to be contained in the physical form of an ordinary man. It bided its time and developed its powers, awaiting its chance. Now, through Oshalan, it is incarnate; though it has yet to attain its fullest height of manifestation and mastery upon this plane. Even so, it is stronger than anything the races of men have known. When it achieves its full strength it will launch itself against its former adversaries, the remaining Qotol Enchanters. It will attempt to destroy us, and probably succeed. In the meantime it eats up the lesser nations of Rull. Thus, you see, we are allies, like it or not. We share a common foe.'

## IV

Mesmia let a silence descend upon her gallery. This time she had not lied, Shadd perceived that. Indeed, her tale had an all-too-convincing logic to it.

'There is a way to prevent this happening,' Mesmia said presently. 'Though already it may be too late.'

'Give you the pages from the Pandect?' asked Shadd bluntly.

'The Vulpasmage is wary of the power of the Twin Wona Souls of Kemahamek. That is why it has destroyed the one and trapped the other in the Semblance of Death.'

'Then it is true, what you have told me of Seruhli?'

'It is. If she is freed she may – I stress *may* – have access to the power to combat this evil. She will not be able to do it alone, but she could become the figurehead behind which others will unite.'

Now there was prevarication. There was something not quite true behind her words. But Shadd could not focus upon it. He was taking in too much. His thoughts were becoming fogged.

'But you are not certain that the formula for the Antidote is contained upon these pages.'

'I believe that it is. I cannot be positive until I have studied the fragments.'

'And when you have the fragments you too have access to forgotten secrets and formidable powers.'

Mesmia made an irritated gesture. 'No matter their contents, the fragments will not give me the power possessed by our foe. We have wrangled enough, Duke Shadd. You must make your choice. Give me the fragments that I may apply myself to the decipherment of the Old Script. Then, with fortune on our side, you will gain the key to free Seruhli. Or refuse, and permit the Beast of Rull to continue unopposed. Remember, the Old Script is known to none but myself and the remaining four Enchanters – and of them you know less than you do of me. There is little time. The Beast grows stronger with every passing day.'

*She makes no attempt to take the fragments by force,* thought Shadd. *Though she claims she can do so without effort. What stays her? I am nothing to her. Is it the Crystal? What if I refuse to give her the fragments? Will she use force now? Ah, but what choice do I have? What choice?*

He was torn, divided in himself, unable to know which course he should choose. He felt himself giving way to despair.

As if reading something of his thoughts, Mesmia said, 'Truly you have no choice, Duke Shadd. You will give me the fragments. You know that you can do nothing other.'

There was a shift of emphasis in her tone. She held a benign smile – something that did not sit naturally on a face like hers – but the voice betrayed her. It was harshly vibrant with unwholesome desire, and something was held back. She gloated, yet there was just the faintest edge of uncertainty. As she finished speaking her eyes left his face, dropping to rest fleetingly upon the place below his throat where, beneath his tunic, the Soul Crystal hung on its chain.

*It is the Crystal!* Shadd's thoughts raced. Was there a way to take advantage of this? It seemed scarcely relevant in the light of what they were discussing. And he could not think clearly. He could not think.

Mesmia spoke on, and now she left him in no doubt as to the value she placed upon the Soul Crystal. 'And you may return to me that other article which I gave you on loan to aid you upon your quest. The Stepforth is lost, which vexes me. But the twin-stone you still have.'

'The Soul Crystal is the property of the Gwynad race,' said Shadd, struggling, for he felt suddenly disconcerted. Perhaps he had misjudged Mesmia? Why was he resisting her? She was offering help.

He was confused. The issue seemed to have become so blurred. He said, 'It is to them . . . that I will return it.'

'It is mine!' snapped the Drear-hag. 'You withhold property that is mine.'

Her anger allowed him a glimpse of clarity. 'My information is that it was stolen from the Gwynad, for whom it is an object of reverence.'

'You have been seduced by that little flitting

fairykin. Give the Gwynad that stone and they will rise to make mischief again. That is why I keep it here. You are not of this land, Duke Shadd, yet you insist upon meddling in its affairs. Beware. I will not permit a manling to interfere in matters of which he has no comprehension.'

Was there truth in that? Were the Gwynad not to be trusted? Shadd shook his head to clear the growing fog that befuddled his thoughts. He focused upon Mesmia. 'You brought me here, and had me interfere in matters that suited you.'

'To avert catastrophe!'

'I require proof. You have told me tales, persuasive but unsupported. Before I can act further I must have proof.'

Mesmia lifted her hands in exasperation, crying, 'The Vulpasmage ascends! What more do you need?'

'What of Seruhli? How do I know that what you tell me of her is true? How do I know, even if she can be freed, that she has the power to combat the Vulpasmage?'

'What would you have me show you? Your proof lies in taking the deciphered formula to those who tend her now. She will be revived. After that, I cannot say. All depends on fortune and fate.'

'You do know then, where she is?'

Mesmia threw him a haughty look. 'I told you that when you first came here. Once I have deciphered the formula, you will be shown where to find her.'

*Shown where to find her!* It was what he wished more than anything. But Mesmia knew that too. She dangled it before him, expecting him to leap gladly forward to take it. But did it matter? Let her have the fragments. All that mattered was that Seruhli be returned to life.

Through his confusion came the awareness that he

445

was under attack. Subliminal energies worked upon his mind. Mesmia had prepared her trap well, he had not detected her ploy. She had allowed him to detect certain magics, to divert him from the true danger. He had resisted so far, aided by the Soul Crystal, but she had worked beneath his thoughts and perceptions. Testing him, baiting him, testing the Crystal to assess the measure of his control of it. And now she was intensifying the pressure.

He could not see clearly, was suddenly unsure as to what it was he had come here to achieve, or avert. He could think only of Seruhli. Seruhli, who was helpless, who depended upon him. Seruhli. Seruhli.

He became conscious of frantic baying. Mesmia swore, and cocked her head with an angry grimace. She listened, then pushed herself up and quickly crossed the room to the portal. From the balcony she peered out for some moments, then silenced the din of the two hounds. She remained there a while longer, observing the landscape.

Eyeing her back, Shadd thought to notice a movement, a flicker in the shadows cast by sculptures and artefacts upon the curve of the wall slightly to his right. He peered into the shadows. For a second he thought he saw something outlined there: a crouching form, vaguely defined, possibly human. He blinked and peered again, but it seemed he had been deceived. Where he had thought there was something he could now see only wall and shadows. A thought came: an echo from the past. He stared hard, then was interrupted by Mesmia who wheeled from the balcony, closing the portal, and strode with sudden deliberation towards him.

Her eyes pierced him. 'Duke Shadd, we waste time. I will have the twin-stone and the fragments, *now*!'

The final word struck Shadd with unexpected force.

He was caught off-guard. The Drear-hag had chosen her moment well. He was distracted and confused. Into the word she had placed the pitch and timbre of irresistible command. Her hand was held open before her, and Shadd, scarcely aware of what he did or why, found himself stepping towards her, reaching into his tunic to withdraw the ivory tube.

He jerked the tube free of the ribbon which secured it to his belt. His inner voice screamed at him to withhold, to resist, but he was hypnotised, powerless under the Drear-hag's command. As if in a dream he placed the tube into the palm of her outstretched hand.

'And now the stone,' commanded Mesmia, her eyes boring into him, the voice permitting no denial.

Shadd lifted his arms to take the silver chain from around his neck.

'*No!*' From the rafters overhead shot Temminee, darting in with her rod before her.

Mesmia was prepared. She whispered a single word. Temminee dropped to the floor like a stone, and did not move.

The Drear-hag smiled. '*The stone!*'

Shadd bowed his head, raising the chain to loop it free. He knew, so certainly, that what he was doing was wrong, but he could not help himself. He pulled the Soul Crystal from within his tunic.

At that instant something came at speed from between the statues. A blur of movement from the side of the gallery to Shadd's right. It came in low, rolling across the floor. As it reached the two of them it came erect: a slight, human-ish form. Without ceasing its motion it reached out, snatched the ivory tube from Mesmia's open hand, and sped between them, spinning beyond reach.

Mesmia stepped back in shocked disbelief, uttering a sharp cry. As she tried to focus upon the fast-moving figure the portal which let onto the balcony flew open with a loud crash. A second figure leapt into the room, two small metallic discs in its hands. These it flicked at the confounded Drear-hag. The discs whizzed through the air and bit into her flaccid bulk before she could protect herself. Her own magical defences saved her from grave injury, but she staggered back, a mask of terrible startlement and tumult upon her face.

The first figure, holding the ivory tube, raced back along the gallery, weaving and spinning at incredible speed. It darted through the portal onto the balcony, and was gone. The second now made to follow.

Mesmia recovered herself. She vented a great shriek. Quite suddenly the chamber came to life. The sculptures moved, discarding their frozen erotic play. Myriad creatures, mythical beasts, men, women, in sizes ranging from tiny to life-sized, closed upon the figure before the balcony.

Shadd was momentarily forgotten. The power of Mesmia's command over him dissolved. The figure that had cast the discs was at the balcony, leaping out. The living sculptures crowded after it. Mesmia rushed with great ululations of anger and woe towards the balcony, yanking the two discs from her flesh as she went.

Outside the two curs, which had resumed their commotion, fell suddenly silent. Shadd, clutching the Soul Crystal in one hand, knelt and gently lifted the still form of Temminee. He moved quietly to the door at the head of the stairway which led down to the ground floor of the tower. This he opened and slipped through, to depart the gallery.

Downstairs he moved cautiously across the dingy chamber towards the entrance. The thump of heavy footsteps overhead told him of Mesmia's approach. Quickly he melted into the shadows. Mesmia pounded

448

down the stairs and rushed across the chamber, her face pallid with shock, her great robe flapping behind her. She disappeared through the doorway to the fore-court outside.

Shadd came from hiding and moved into the lobby before the outer door. Across the forecourt Mesmia's bizarre servants loped, hopped, ran, flew in frenzied pursuit of the two mysterious figures, which were nowhere to be seen. Mesmia's two great curs lay sprawled upon the ground between the gate posts, their life's blood spilling out onto the rubbly soil. Mesmia herself tore at her hair, staring down the trail. Then she dashed, first one way, then the other across the trail. In a delirium of shock she bellowed and shrieked and waved her corpulent arms.

Shadd slipped unobserved through the doorway and ran along the base of the tower wall, to an outhouse situated beneath the cliff.

# 17

I

In the cover of the outhouse he turned his attention
to Temminee. At first she gave no indication of life,
but he placed his hands over her and silently directed
a healing energy upon her. She stirred and opened her
eyes.

'What has happened?'

'The tube containing the fragments has been taken.
Neither I nor Mesmia now hold it. Are you hurt?'

Temminee sat up and gingerly tested her various
parts. 'I will perhaps be stiff for some time, and sport
some uncomely bruises, but little else. But tell me,
who has taken the fragments, and to where?'

Shadd peered between the wooden slats of the outhouse door. Mesmia was leaving the gate to stride
back towards the tower, cursing maniacally, her face
that of a thwarted demon.

'Mesmia at this point would give anything to know
the answers to those questions. Her bizarre acolytes
scour the trail and surrounding forest for the thieves.
My guess is that she repairs now to her workroom
to effect some dire magic to further aid her in her
search. The theft was masterfully wrought. Without
it I would not have escaped.'

'But the fragments?'

Shadd cast her a wan glance. 'They are safe for the
present from the Drear-hag's clutches, and I suppose
that is the main thing. Now, we will remain here
a while longer. I would prefer that her minions

put more distance between us before I take to the woods.'

Close in Shadd's ear a voice hissed: 'Pay greater heed to your Blending, or you will not get far!'

He jerked his head around, stared into the shadows. Not until there was a movement did he see the young woman who crouched against the dark stone of the tower base, though she was scarcely more than an arm's length away. So total was her concealment, so perfectly did she seem to blend into the stone, the wood, the earth and the shadows that she had to tilt her head and blink to give her presence away.

Shadd's lips spread suddenly into a warm smile. 'Kekhi!'

The young woman moved, unshrouding herself from a cloak similar to Shadd's own. She made a sign with her hands.

'Jhoso, brother!' said she, and stepped forward to embrace him.

Shadd clasped her. 'Jhoso, Kekhi! Jhoso! It is good to see you!'

She stepped back and he gazed upon her. Her skin was clear and dusky olive; her eyes deep brown, wide and slightly slanted. Their gaze was alert and inquisitive, and, at this moment, warm. Short hair the colour of ebony framed her face. She looked scarcely more than a girl, though Shadd knew this to be an illusion. They had been companions in childhood and early youth. He had trained alongside Kekhi, and at times had been pitched against her. Young she might be; slight in stature and feminine in her character and appearance. But he knew her, and knew what she was capable of.

'Your entrance was timely,' said Shadd. 'The Drear-hag had tricked me. I was lost. I glimpsed you hidden against the wall, but – '

451

Kekhi interrupted him with a wry smile. 'I *allowed* you to glimpse me, brother. I thought it would give you heart. As it happened, it was a mistake, for it distracted you further, and she chose that very moment to strike.'

'She had defeated me. She had worn down my resistance in ways I had not detected. She had control of my will.'

'You acted well,' said Kekhi. 'But she is powerful. We had hoped not to have to intervene, but in the end she left us no choice.'

Shadd cast his eyes around. 'Where is Rin? It was he who accompanied you, wasn't it?'

Kekhi nodded. 'Outside the gallery I transferred the ivory tube to him. Now he leads the Drear-hag's minions a merry chase.'

'She is desperate to gain those pages. She will not give up easily. It is a dangerous flight.'

'I know, as does he. The woods are also filled with traps. Some of them we disarmed on the way here, so he has a route of escape. Rin is accomplished. He will not be easily caught.'

Shadd made to rise. 'Even so, we should go. He will need our help.'

Kekhi stayed him with her hand. 'If he is caught it will avail the Drear-hag nothing.'

'But he has the fragments!'

'I said he has the ivory tube.' Kekhi patted her tunic below her small breasts. 'I carry the pages from the Pandect. Now come, we should leave here before our presence is detected. And concentrate, Shadd. You blend like a camel in a herd of goats!'

They left the outhouse and crept around the base of the tower to where the cliff rose sheer behind. Without pausing Kekhi proceeded to ascend, moving lithely up a rock face that would have daunted the most experienced cragsman not equipped with ropes, pitons and other climbing aids. Shadd watched with admiration. Even as she climbed Kekhi seemed to merge into the cliff, so that within seconds he was hard put to spot her.

Shadd followed, utilising scaling techniques that he had learned as a child in the mountains of the Endless Desert. As he climbed the gruelling tests of his youth were brought suddenly to mind, and he thought briefly of those who had failed. In the Desert the strong and capable survived. The Aphesuk had adapted themselves to its harsh and merciless terrain. Their regimen of training reflected the character of the land itself. Those who could not adapt were doomed to perish. This was the Way of the Tribe, and hard though it was, it was the only way of survival.

Even so Shadd's ascent was laboured and erratic in comparison to the young female who had preceded him. When he arrived at the head of the cliff Kekhi was seated upon the grass, chewing a stalk, waiting. She grinned as he hauled himself up over the lip of the bluff, then gazed upon him warmly. 'You are lumbering and ham-handed, but you have not forgotten everything.'

'It is a pleasure to be the butt of your insults once more.'

Kekhi put her hand to her mouth to stifle a giggle. Then she grew more serious. 'I have scouted this area while I waited for you. A monitor-eye is set in the branches of yonder fir. It will not spot us if we slide on our bellies. Beyond those rocks we will be safe from its scrying. There will be other traps and scrying devices, but fewer than on the other side of the tower. Once we are in the valley below I think we will be safer. Now, this is yours to bear.' She reached inside her tunic and withdrew a small, flat satchel of soft leather. This she opened, to reveal inside the pages from Yshcopthe's Pandect. 'In Mesmia's gallery I took them out of necessity, but it is right and fitting that you should carry them as long as you are able.'

Shadd accepted them with a melancholy stare, but kept his thoughts to himself.

On their bellies they wriggled across the grass until they were beyond the scry of Mesmia's monitor. They descended as silently as shadows through harsh scrub and rocky woodland, choosing a difficult route where there was less risk of discovery or snares. Twice Kekhi pointed out areas in their path in which she suspected magical traps lay concealed, and which Shadd, with his heightened senses, was able to confirm to be so. Temminee flew on ahead, spying the woods from on high to ensure that they did not inadvertently blunder into the path of Mesmia's servants.

They arrived at last in the valley, followed its course for a short distance, then ascended once more. Skirting a bare ridge they emerged eventually at the edge of an olive grove upon a grassy slope. Far below them to their southeast lay the grey-white pall of the Lake of Clouds.

Overhead the Qotol sky was a brooding grey. A chill breeze scurried out of the snow-clad heights, racing over the grass and rippling the leaves on the trees. Shadd and Kekhi, with Temminee close by, made their way along the upper side of the grove, and Shadd voiced something of what troubled his mind.

'Do you believe it true, what Mesmia told me of the origin of the Vulpasmage?'

'It has a ring of authenticity. More than that I lack the qualifications to say.'

'And of Seruhli?'

Kekhi ceased walking and turned to gaze up at him with sympathy. 'Again, Shadd, I do not know.

There have been rumours that she did not die at Twalinieh, that she does in fact exist in that state called Semblance of Death.'

'Then I have failed her. I brought the fragment, but have not put it to use.'

'Nothing has been confirmed, Shadd. And we do not know what any of the fragments contain.'

'And we will not know, for there is no one but Mesmia who can translate that secret language.'

'Perhaps. But we cannot permit documents as critical as these to fall into the hands of the Drear-hag.'

'We might have struck a bargain. You heard what she said, the Vulpasmage is her enemy.'

'She also said that she intended you no harm, yet she tricked and overpowered you. A creature like that keeps no bargains. She is an enchantress and she seeks power. We must not be the ones who permit her to gain it.'

'Then who will fight the Vulpasmage? And with what?'

Kekhi gave no answer. They walked on. A short while later Shadd became aware, quite suddenly, of another presence behind him. He turned, to see Kekhi's Aphesuk companion, Rin.

Rin gave a curt smile and a nod, and formed a sign with his hands. 'Jhoso, brother!'

Shadd returned the greeting. 'Jhoso!', and for the moment no further words were exchanged.

Dusk approached. They found a secluded hollow protected by dense undergrowth and ancient boulders. Kekhi and Rin produced bread, dried meat and fruit from their packs, which they shared with Shadd's depleted stock of rations. As they ate Rin briefly recounted his adventures as he led Mesmia's minions away from her tower.

'They seemed fierce but dim-witted things,' he said.

'I experienced no great difficulty in eluding them. A pair of flying creatures, swifter than the others, came upon me at one point. Foolishly, they attacked. Had they bided their time and followed me, while allowing the others to catch up, I might have been overcome. As it was I dispatched them with little trouble. Later I found myself close to the lakeshore, pursued by a dozen or so gibbering things. Again, had they had the benefit of intelligence, they could have caught and killed me. But I broke cover and ran to the water's edge. There I took the ivory tube and hurled it as far as I could into the mists that cover the lake. The creatures ran into the water like crazed things, ignoring me. Few of them seemed able to swim. They simply disappeared beneath the surface. The others swam out into the mist and were lost to sight.' Rin shrugged matter-of-factly. 'An interesting exercise.'

'There will be others,' said Shadd.

Kekhi nodded. 'But tomorrow we will enter the domain of Urch-Malmain. Mesmia will think twice about sending her minions there.'

'She will not give up. She will search high and low for these fragments.'

'I don't doubt it. But beyond Qotolr her abilities will be reduced. The five draw much of their strength from the strange magical properties that have lingered within this land since the Enchanter Wars. Beyond its borders they are unable to manifest their full powers, other than in a handful of isolated powerpoints dotted across Rull. That is one reason why the races of men are rarely seriously troubled by the attentions of Enchanters.

'Furthermore, a great deal of their energies are expended upon one another, maintaining defences and ploys to protect themselves against the intrusions of the other four.'

'She manifested her projection, Elore, in Drurn

March,' Shadd pointed out. 'I believed her real; her scent, her touch: she was a perfect simulacrum.'

'Then beware of beautiful strangers!' smiled Kekhi. She shook her head. 'Mesmia will search for the fragments, and will find ways of manifesting beyond her borders. But we have an advantage. She does not know who we are, or from where we have come. Nor does she know that we are connected with you. She perceived the fragments snatched from both you and herself by thieves unknown. Likely she will suspect us to be servants of another Enchanter, and will direct her first efforts at the other four.'

Shadd observed a silence for two or three minutes. Presently he enquired, 'How long had you been waiting at Mesmia's tower?'

'Our arrival was fortuitous,' replied Kekhi. 'Shimeril received information that you had been in Chol, at Drurn March. In secret we made our way there, then took up your trail. We arrived at Mesmia's tower only hours before your return.'

'And Mesmia had no notion of your coming?'

'She was greatly distracted, otherwise she would almost certainly have detected us, despite our stealth. It seems that the prospect of your return fully claimed her attention. At first we could not guess what had become of you. Your trail ended at the tower, yet you were not within. We knew nothing of the tunnel in the mountain. But we concealed ourselves and observed Mesmia. In her excitement she told us everything, for she communed feverishly, if fitfully, with herself and all manner of imaginary presences. Thus it was merely a matter of waiting.'

Shadd took the leather satchel which contained the precious pages from Yshcopthe's lost Pandect. He held it in his hands with a forlorn expression. When he spoke an edge of bitterness tinged his voice. 'What now? We have kept the fragments from the Drear-hag. Where do we take them? Where do we go?'

'First, to Khimmur,' Kekhi said. 'There, among friends, we will consider further. The pages must be placed under the aegis of those best qualified to guard them. They must be hidden where no Enchanter can find them. And the fact of their existence must forever be kept secret.'

'You will entrust them to the Tribe?'

Kekhi shrugged. 'That is one possibility. The decision will not be mine to make.'

'Nor mine?'

She fixed him with a veiled stare. 'You are their bearer.'

'For as long as I do what is considered right.'

Kekhi made no reply.

Presently he asked, with deliberate emphasis, 'Why did you come after me?'

Kekhi raised her eyes to his. 'You know why. We are assigned to you, unto death.'

'Unto death . . .' He lifted his gaze to the dark blot of trees rising above them, and the stars in the far cold heavens overhead. 'You could have killed me after Twalinieh, before I escaped you.'

'You had infringed none of our Laws.' Kekhi spoke flatly. 'And do not fool yourself, Shadd. You did not escape us. You were permitted to go. It was necessary for you. You had become a shell, or less. You would surface again, we knew that. Then would be the time for reassessment.'

'And now . . . you have saved me from Mesmia, perhaps from myself. Yet, you are still, perhaps, my executioners.'

'You know the Law,' said Kekhi with chilling gravity.

'I know the Law, and I have held it sacred at all times.'

Kekhi and Rin exchanged glances. 'We have seen nothing so far to indicate otherwise. And truly it makes me happy that it should be so.'

'Nonetheless, you will be watching, for signs.'

Kekhi leaned across and put her hand upon his cheek. He found himself looking deeply into her clear dark eyes. She said, 'Shadd, my brother, you are dear to me, as you are to the Tribe. But the Tribe is the Way; its secrets are sacrosanct. The Law applies to every one of us.'

'Ah, but I am not truly of the Tribe, nor even of the Desert. I am one who does not truly belong. I must be watched more closely than most, for I may perhaps entertain a conflict of loyalties.'

'Is that the way of it?'

Shadd averted his gaze. 'I am unclear within myself on many things, yet never have I questioned the Way of the Tribe, nor thought to betray its secrets. The Tribe saved me from the Desert. It adopted me and brought me up as one of its own – though that I can never truly be. I would die before I betrayed its faith in me.'

'That is as I had believed.' Kekhi tenderly withdrew her hand.

Shadd sat in brooding silence for some time. When eventually he made up his litter upon the earth and lay down, Kekhi remained where she was, her chin resting upon her knees, her look troubled. As he slept she watched him for a long time into the night.

II

They arose early, before the first pale pink fingers of dawn had touched the eastern sky. The morning was chill, the cloud high, in broken strands. A light

459

breeze played down from the mountains, shifting the reluctant mist which hung in the dark hollows. As they prepared to leave Shadd spoke to his two Qotol companions, Temminee and the hylozote.

To Temminee he said, 'My journey takes me now to lands far from here. We have been good companions, but you are of the Gwynad, and Qotolr is their home and yours. It is time to part.'

From around his neck he took the Soul Crystal on its chain. 'This is yours. I wish to return it to you, and to your people. Yet you cannot carry it alone, and I for the present at least am not able to divert myself in a search for survivors of your race.'

'I have said before that I do not know if any of my race have survived,' replied Temminee. 'Until I do I would wish that the Soul Crystal be held by one who will not misuse it, nor give it to others who would. You have proven yourself worthy of it, Duke Shadd, and it is my hope that it may continue to be of use to you until a day comes when it can be returned to where it belongs. I would ask, then, that you keep it, though that is a great responsibility and I will understand if you feel it is not one you wish to undertake. As for myself, I have no desire to remain here alone. Survivors of my kind may be anywhere, as likely scattered across the nations of this world as here. I do not know where to begin to search. Rather, if you will permit me, I would accompany you still — at least for the present time.'

'Gladly!' said Shadd. 'I will admit, I have been saddened by the anticipation of our parting. And what of you, friend hylozote? What is your preference?'

'There is hardly a choice to be made,' said the hylozote. 'I have no desire to be dumped upon the wayside for another eon, no matter how pretty the view. I have seen more than enough of this Enchantery. If you can bear my company I would become a traveller with you. I have a yen to experience more of this strange world.'

'Then let it be so!'

Kekhi and Rin meticulously erased all traces of their campsite. As they worked Shadd climbed from the hollow and mounted a nearby knoll to gaze back in the direction from which they had come.

The first light filtered over the jagged horizon, though the land lay in near-darkness still. Far away a low pall of mist, almost luminous, showed in the gloom where the dawn could not penetrate: the Lake of Clouds. The dark heights rose forbiddingly all around, defiant as ever of the focusing eye. Into Shadd's mind came a vision of the ghostly maiden he had met upon the lakeshore.

'Seruhli, was it truly you?' He felt a weight of sorrow upon him, and a heart too full to bear. 'I have failed you, though truly I could do nothing other. Is it true that you exist in the Semblance of Death, or are you gone from this world, to be reborn as another? I will discover, this I swear. And if it proves to be that you have indeed been betrayed, and are held in the Semblance of Death, then I swear this also: if a way exists by which you may be freed, I will find it. I will search to the ends of this world if I must, but I will not falter. I will find you and will bring you back. This is my solemn and sacred pledge to you.'

He gazed forlornly into the middle-distance. For a moment it seemed that something stirred in the deep shadow of junipers close by. Shadd caught his breath. Before him was the frailest apparition, softly white; a ghostly, hovering shape. He started forward, but it faded before his eyes, dissolved into fragile wisps, and was gone; a wraith of mist dispersed by the breeze snaking down from the mountains.

Shadd looked once more towards the distant lake. A bird called from somewhere far overhead. He turned away and strode back down the slope to where his companions waited.

# 18

## I

A journey of a relatively few miles can, under certain circumstances, seem like an endless road. Such was my experience as I travelled south to link up with the route which Thufor had described to Shadd. My head was filled with clamouring anxieties. I was beset by an abysmal loneliness. Huwoorsk, his vhazz nature assailed by the knowledge that he was totally alone, had been transformed into a pathetic, cringing thing. So overpowering was his sense of purposelessness, his desolation, his growing, almost pathological urge towards death, that at times I could barely keep his body moving.

And Dinbig of Khimmur, who lacked the comforting swaddle of his own flesh, was plagued by doubts and dire misgivings. Had I, realistically, a hope of finding the Wanderer? If I did, what then? How would I communicate with Yo and assert my identity? How would I persuade him to relinquish control of my corporeal self? It would require guile, perhaps cajolery, and more, and I had no guarantee of success. Yo would

---

It is a fact that the first bound entity, the Custodian, is often the least tractable, frequently making the First Realm Initiation and subsequent experience more testing than is the case with other spirit allies. This is generally considered to be due to the Custodian's having access to corporeal flesh, and thus being subject to fleshly temptations and worldly pleasures. Many and varied are the tales of Zan-Chassin practitioners who have had difficulties with their Custodian.

likely be stronger than I; quite able to resist force. I knew his character: he could be wilful, stubborn, downright obdurate. Now he could well be demented, and perhaps hostile. And would he even be capable of recognising me?˙

Accompanying these thoughts came hopes and yearnings that I hardly dared entertain. To return to my homeland in my own body. To be with Rohse and little Eroniss. Ah, but even if it were possible, what would I find there? I was dispossessed, a traitorous pariah. My trading empire was gone, my wealth and assets seized. Tyranny ruled. I would be obliged to live the life of a fugitive and outlaw, hiding in the woods, fighting my own people.

Frequently as I padded south I wondered as to Shadd's fate. The urge was strong to turn around, to retrace my steps and rejoin him. But I forced myself onward, for it was true, I could be of little use in my present form. Dinbig of Khimmur I had once been, and Dinbig of Khimmur I must become again if I was to play a role in the liberation of our land and peoples.

Early in the evening on the day after parting with Shadd and Thufor I came upon a rough intersection of ways. A dirt track, rutted by the wheels of carts and wagons, but little-used, snaked westwards. Along this I now proceeded. The way led into lonely mountain passes, through a region barely inhabited but for weird creatures and isolated bands of brigands, both of which I had little difficulty in avoiding.

My anticipation mounted. Along this trail the Wanderer plied its solitary path, back and forth for a year or more. Surely, then, the chances were that we would, after all, meet? I recalled that Shadd had spied the Wanderer in the dead of night. The hylozote's account, supported by Thufor, indicated that the Wanderer moved in both daylight and dark.

It appeared to follow its road without particular aim, faring forth at whim or by sudden impulse, unconcerned with time or destination. To be certain of intercepting it I would needs be alert at all times.

Through these days of waiting I worked upon the vital development of my psychic self. I focused upon one ability, that in which I already had a limited proficiency: the leaving of the flesh. This was going to prove the decisive factor in dealing with Yo. I could not communicate with him directly as long as I occupied the vhazz form; I would have to leave my vhazz body and summon him, master to servant, as had been my practice of old.

Thus I passed long hours of each day immersed in Zan-Chassin meditations, concealed close beside the road where I might simultaneously be aware of the passage of any wayfarer. I focused deeply upon the physical world around me, absorbing every detail; then switched my attention to my corporeal person, concentrating on every muscle, every sinew, every organ, every nerve. I consolidated and familiarised, anchored my flesh so that I might dissolve the world and pass beyond the objective plane.

Previously I had managed to remain free of the vhazz body for a minute or a minute-and-a-half, scarcely more. Now I placed special emphasis on basic preparations before endeavouring to float free. Even so the effort was immense and progress negligible. I wandered that trail for more than two weeks and scarcely noted any change as I strove to liberate my soul from the clasp of the gross world.

After each meditation I would trudge dispiritedly on, covering a few more lonely miles, ever alert, ever hoping and fearing. I passed isolated villages and, once or twice, a remote castle or fort. These I did not enter, but remained close by and observed them over the course of a day or so in case the Wanderer was within. He wasn't; I moved on. The road ascended, looping into the mountains, then winding its way into hilly country beyond. I became discouraged. I found myself giving up all hope of ever meeting my chuckleheaded flesh, or of finding my way back to Khimmur.

Then one afternoon, as I sat upon an earth bank overlooking the trail and tore into the meat of a freshly-caught yearling, a solitary figure traipsed into view. I sat for some moments transfixed. He was some distance away. I could not make out many visual details and he was down-wind of me, so no trace of his scent reached my nostrils. But I was excited. I slipped into the cover of bracken.

The traveller came closer. He walked with a slight limp, and an erratic gait. I could hear him mumbling to himself, then realised that he was singing, some lurching doggerel. His appearance was shabby, his hair long, grey and matted with filth. A thick shaggy beard covered most of his face. His clothing, a simple loose robe, was threadbare, and his feet were naked.

Now I caught his scent, and a tremor ran down my spine.

He was within yards of where I crouched. He skipped and gave a twirl in the road as he sang. Then he stopped for a moment and gazed about him. He appeared suddenly dazed and wretched. He lifted his arms to put his hands to his head. The left limb had been severed above the wrist, leaving a stump bound in soiled rags. The fellow shook his head and his voice became a whimper of dismal despair. I experienced a sudden trembling empathy for the poor creature.

The Wanderer limped on. I stared at that tortured face as it passed. There was no mistake. I knew that man, that shambling ruin of a man. I knew him intimately. He and I had been the same flesh, the same person.

My gullet went dry. My vhazz heart beat so thunderously against my ribcage that I thought it must surely give me away.

This was it at last.

The time was at hand for the reckoning.


## II


I allowed the Wanderer to pass. I was not yet ready to make my presence known. He moved onwards with a tipsy gait, babbling, and I followed unseen, keeping pace a short distance behind him off the trail.

I was reasonably fresh, having rested only an hour earlier. But the Wanderer's abrupt arrival had pitched me into a state of heightened dismay. I was close to panic; reticent, frightened, overcome with absurd diffidence. I could not yet entertain the idea of confronting my erstwhile Custodian.

A half-mile or so down the trail the Wanderer stopped beside a meadow spotted with wild flowers and encircled by a low drystone wall. In the meadow grew a number of plum trees. The Wanderer left the road to clamber over the wall, then crossed to the nearest tree. With his good arm he plucked a fruit from the branches and stuffed it into his mouth. Chomping gluttonously, he followed immediately with another, then another, although to my eyes the plums looked hardly ripe.

Beyond him was a steep shrubby bank, at the foot of which coursed a wide stream. Cheeks bulging, the Wanderer now walked to the head of this bank, spitting out plum-stones as he went. He stared down towards the water, then scrambled over the lip and was lost to sight.

I loped across the meadow and crept to the bank. A small shingle beach lay below me. The Wanderer had crossed this and stood knee-deep in the stream. He was inclined over the water, peering into it with an intent, acquisitive expression. His good hand he held poised at the level of his head. At first I took him to be peering at his reflection, then I noticed that his head made small darting motions. He seemed to be following the movement of something I could not see. His raised hand was formed as if to jab or strike.

He bent lower, until his nose and dense beard came almost into contact with the surface of the stream. Then he lunged. The hand plunged into the water. There was a great deal of splashing and thrashing; the Wanderer staggered around a bit, his hand submerged, his head tilted sideways. He straightened. He shook his head and muttered disconsolately to himself.

Only now did it dawn on me that he was fishing. He was fishing in the manner of the creature whose physical form Yo had occupied during the period of his service to me: the Wide-Faced Bear. This was a difficult task for any man – for a man with only one hand it was surely impossible. Yet he persevered, gamely repeating the operation over and over, and landing nothing.

His anger mounted. Several times he slapped the water violently and cried out in frustration. Then, unexpectedly, he succeeded in scooping a handsome brown trout out of the shallows. Now his handicap became fully evident. The trout flapped wildly. The Wanderer could not gain a hold on it. The fish flew from his grasp, did a lateral flop into the water an arm's length away, and was gone. The Wanderer swore and beat the water hard.

I crept down the bank to conceal myself behind the bole of a river birch. For the first time I became aware of how emaciated the flesh of Ronbas Dinbig had become. Though not massively muscled in my former life, I had always prided myself in a body maintained in robust good health. The figure that splashed in the water before me now was a pathetic sight, a veritable starveling, and judging by its efforts among the lazy trout it was not hard to see why. I wondered that Yo had not considered fashioning a crude fishing-spear from the nearby bushes. It would have greatly facilitated his task. Had he come to identify so strongly with the character of the Wide-Faced Bear as to lose all human ingenuity? By what means had he managed to sustain my flesh during these past two years?

The Wanderer fished on for some further time, caught nothing and eventually turned and waded back to the little beach, his face pale and despondent. I took a deep breath. I had seen enough. This, then, was the moment I chose to confront the squatter in my flesh. I rose to my full height and stepped from behind the tree.

At the sight of me the Wanderer stopped still. He showed no fear or alarm, nor even surprise. He was defenceless, standing but three paces from a well-armed vhazz, yet he merely blinked blankly, then produced a small enquiring smile. His expression was genial, if a touch vacant. He seemed to be waiting, as if for some expression of greeting, or perhaps an explanation from me.

For my own part, I cannot describe the sensation of looking into that haggard face. *My face!* I found myself mute and rooted to the spot, unable to tear my gaze away.

He looked so tired, and confused, as though reduced in mental stature by a life that made no sense nor offered comfort in any form. But it struck me, oddly, that the face had altered its physical form. The cheeks were broader than I recalled. The brow, also. The features had an unfamiliar bluntness, and the entire face, despite its gauntness, seemed rounder.

Then there was the beard . . . I had always sported whiskers, but.they were not profuse, and I kept them respectably trimmed. Now I stared upon a veritable jungle of dense yellow-brown growth which covered almost all of the cheeks and extended beneath the chin and down the neck.

What I was witnessing, of course, were bestial effects. The tormented flesh of the Wanderer was succumbing to the influence of its Custodian, Yo, and his belief in himself as a Wide-Faced Bear. My flesh was assuming ursine attributes.

The Wanderer, evidently tiring of my silence, mumbled something in a low half-whisper. A greeting, or an enquiry as to the nature of my business. Or perhaps pure babble – I did not catch the words. But the sound – my own voice, oddly contorted and throatier than I remembered – brought me back to my senses. I strove to recompose myself, reminded of my purpose here. This was the moment! It had to be seized!

Directing my focus within I suppressed the vhazz consciousness, reaching for the inner stillness so necessary to the success of this crucial endeavour. I entered trance.

There came the welcome sensation of being no longer anchored; the physical held no lordship over me. The gross world dissolved. I ascended, coming to rest slightly above and to the left of my vhazz body.

'Yo!'

Into that word I put all the force and command I could muster. The result was gratifying. The Wanderer – the bewildered flesh of Ronbas Dinbig – gave an almighty jerk and leapt back two paces in fright. An involuntary cry came from its mouth. Into its widened eyes sprang a look of unease and perplexity. Its head shook and it gibbered something unintelligible. I addressed Yo once more.

'Yo, make no mistake. It is I, your Master. I have returned to reclaim what is mine.'

The Wanderer did a little dance of agitation at the water's edge. The eyes darted this way and that, then narrowed. The head came forward to peer at me. 'Master Dinbig?'

Already my stratagem was faltering. Yo had not responded as I had intended to the summons. He remained in my flesh.

It was vital that he leave my body, for as long as he was its occupant I could not hope to reclaim it. Ordinarily, of course, I could have forced him out; but the ordinary did not apply to these circumstances. I lacked the strength and resources to do battle with Yo – as had been the case when he first assumed control of my corporeal form in Twalinieh. My gamble, and one hope, was that he was not aware of this. If he was, or if for reasons of his own he chose not to rise out of my flesh, I was lost.

I spoke again, once more with authority, and again addressing the psychic entity, the non-corporeal Yo, rather than the imbecilic flesh.

'It is I. You may vacate my form. You have served me well in my enforced absence, for which I thank you. You have guarded my flesh to the best of your abilities. You have kept it safe from danger, as is your sacred duty. Now your task is done. You may depart.'

The fleshly Ronbas Dinbig gaped, its confoundment written plainly upon its features. But Yo remained in the flesh, and it was through the flesh that he spoke.

'I'm confused. I thought you were gone.'

I gathered myself, permitting cold displeasure to tinge my next words. 'What possible cause have you for confusion? The situation is unequivocal. I have returned. Your service is done. You are dismissed.'

My flesh quailed before me, yet still Yo remained corporeally bound. I put menace into my address. 'Servant, do you defy me?'

'No! No!' uttered my corporeal form. 'It is just that I– I–'

Suddenly I saw tears forming in the Wanderer's eyes. It made small flapping motions with its arms, became distraught, began to gibber, to blubber.

I could afford no pity. This was an encouraging indication of Yo's state of mind, yet already I felt my psychic strength beginning to wane. I considered my next words. I required a balance between direct command and the camaraderie that Yo and I had enjoyed in happier days. I wished him to be persuaded that nothing had changed. Too much authority on my part might prove over-intimidating, causing him to either fall back upon his obstinacy and wilfully defy me, or take fright and embed himself ever more firmly in my fleshly form.

But equally if he detected my own uncertainty or desperation he might perceive himself master of the situation, in which case I could give up all hope of evicting him.

I did have a trick up my sleeve, but it was a dangerous one to play. Mismanaged, it could precipitate the encounter into one of those areas beyond the conditions of our normal relationship, where anything might occur. But my dwindling strength left me in no doubt that my time was short.

The Wanderer ceased its gibbering and spoke clear words.

'Master, I don't understand. Where have you *been*?'

Ah! A development! Small but significant! The single word: Master!

Encouraged, I reasserted myself. I spoke with the authority tempered by affection that one might use to correct an errant child. Then, hopefully without direct threat, I threw in my ace.

'Where have I been? That is for myself alone to know, and not for you to ask. But what is this? I have thanked you for your service and dismissed you. Yet you remain there, within my fleshly self, while I wait here, without. Is this deliberate insubordination, Yo? I will have none of it. Vacate my form, now! Or must I invoke the Rapture of Banishment?'

I was bluffing. It is no mean feat to successfully banish a bound entity from the physical realm. Skill, and the expenditure of considerable psychic energy, are required in its accomplishment, moreso when that entity is resident in flesh. The Zan-Chassin Master that was my former self could have done it, though the effort might have left me weakened for some time. But in my present state I had no hope. But to Yo, who I gambled was unaware of this, the implication was real: to be cast from this world, naked and in shame, without ability and with his true name broadcast at large . . .

More suddenly than I could have hoped Yo had discarded my flesh. We beheld one another in the intangible fabric between realities. I was taken aback and did not immediately seize the advantage and return to my bodily self.

'Master, it was never my intention to cause you harm!' Yo cried.

I steeled myself to contain my feelings. A whole catalogue of misdemeanours rose before me, for each and every one of which Yo was deserving of sound punishment. But now was not the time.

'Perhaps not, Yo. We will discuss it at a later time.'

I moved towards my body, but Yo still hovered there. I realised that the battle was not yet won. Right of possession might still be disputed, for the Wanderer which now stood vacant and lost below us possibly had a greater attachment to Yo than to myself. If Yo should choose to fight it out he could yet emerge the victor.

'Where am I to go now?' enquired Yo plaintively, and I allowed myself a moment of relief, for his tone informed me that he had accepted the situation.

I considered for a moment. 'Can you not return to your Bear, Yo?'

'He is not here, nor near here.'

'Physical distance is of no relevance in this matter. You know that.'

'But I do not know his whereabouts, nor even if he still exists. And if he does, I will not return to him. Master, you know how I suffered with that Bear!'

'Yes, I recall. Well, perhaps another physical form would suit you.'

With undisguised distaste Yo said, 'You mean this thing, don't you?'

I turned my attention to the place he indicated. With my absence the body of Huwoorsk had withdrawn a pace or two. It now sat on its haunches upon the shingle, bereft of vigour, wearing a hangdog expression. I felt a sudden spasm of sympathy. The creature was as sorry a sight as the feeble-minded Wanderer that stood before me: its ribcage and spine protruded; its fur had come out in large tufts; it was scarred and scabbed; its ears were low, its tail curled to its belly, and its snout was matted with the blood of the yearling it had recently feasted upon.

'For now, take the vhazz form, if you will, Yo,' I replied. 'If it proves to be unsuitable I will endeavour to provide you with another.'

'It is not handsome.'

'No, it is not.'

'Does it know the meaning of joy or pleasure?'

'At the moment it does not, Yo. You are perceptive in this regard. Recently it has known great suffering, and at the best of times its lot is an arduous one.'

'I will be miserable, then.'

I declined to respond.

'Must I take this form, Master?'

'If you wish to remain in the physical, yes. At least for the present.' I made to move towards my own flesh, but again was interrupted.

'You are ingenious, but cruel, Master, to visit such a terrible punishment upon me for my transgressions.'

I suppressed a non-corporeal sigh. 'Yo, this is not a punishment. It is simply all that I have to offer at the present time.'

'Then am I to be punished even further, Master?'

I could not prolong this exchange. My strength was almost gone. The vhazz body exerted its drag upon me, inciting me to return. I said, quickly, 'Yo, there are many things to be reviewed and discussed. Your transgressions number prominently among them. For the nonce, however, such matters will be put in abeyance. I have journeyed, I am tired. I will return to my body. The vhazz is yours if you want it. Now, I thank you again for your service. You are dismissed.'

'I am your servant, Master.'

I sank down and re-entered my flesh.

# III

It lies beyond my powers of description to adequately relate the full experience of finding myself once more in my own body. Liken it to returning to one's home to sit before a glowing hearth after weeks spent wandering in a frozen wasteland, discarding damp and uncomfortable clothing to don an old and favoured robe and slip into warm fleece-lined slippers. Liken it to returning to good and vigorous health after a prolonged, debilitating illness; to climbing into your lover's bed to be clasped in her warm embrace after months of enforced separation. Liken it to the most comforting and pleasurable experiences your mind can imagine. It was like all of these things, and more. Much, much more. I had achieved my goal. The nightmare had ended. I had returned. Ronbas Dinbig was himself again!

There were changes, certainly. A swift examination revealed unfamiliar stiffnesses in joints and muscles. Mild gout, which I had suffered intermittently in one toe, had become severe; the toe was huge and red and extremely tender – hence the limp. But these were minor irritations. My response was one of elation – though I sensed that this was not entirely as a result of my success. I perceived a feeling of wildness, of unpredictability in this fellow that I had become. His mood was complex and intense, his perplexity profound, his exuberance charged with unfathomable discomfiture. Underlying these feelings I sensed an unstated anger, a violent heat that threatened to surge to the surface, something quite alien to my former self. The exigencies of the last two years had taken their toll. Clearly it was going to be no simple task to achieve mastery of myself.

But I was famished!

This urgency overcame all other considerations as I grew alert to the grumbling demands of my belly and the weakness of my frame. Immediately I set to remedying the situation. The plums, it appeared, had done little to appease my hunger. Judging from the noises that now thundered in my gut I could expect grim reprisals for having inflicted such a quantity of unsuitable sustenance upon it.

I limped up the beach to a nearby hazel at the base of the slope. I would break off a branch and fashion a spear, then catch myself a trout, though I lacked a blade to either cut the spear or sharpen its prongs. Choosing a suitable straight branch I leaned forward to grasp it with both hands – and discovered that only one hand existed for the task. Extraordinary, for to my mind it was as if the hand had never been struck from my body. I could feel it quite definitely, in its proper place on the terminus of my arm. So certain had I been of the existence of this hand that I had not even noticed its absence in my examination of myself. Yet the physical evidence was before my eyes. A severed stump. No hand.

Over the ensuing hours a second effect of my limblessness was to become apparent. My sense of balance was disturbed. Unconsciously I walked with a pronounced rightward list as my body tried to compensate for the missing weight which its senses yet informed it was there. What with this and the torrent of confused impressions flooding my brain, I was to find myself to be a difficult fellow, clumsy and daft, subject to irrational outbursts and quite uncoordinated in my movements.

But for now nothing mattered but my belly. Stumped, literally, by my limblessness, I recalled the small pack of rations which Shadd, with foresight, had provided me with when we parted. Huwoorsk carried it. Furthermore, Huwoorsk was possessed of both a blade and his full quota of functioning limbs. He could cut and fashion a fishing-spear; either of us, whichever proved most adept, might then apply our talents to the trout-stream.

I relieved him of the pack and tore it open. Inside was hardtack, cheese, raw bacon and bread. I devoured it all – barring the bacon – upon the instant, then sat back upon the shingle, greatly relieved.

My gut rumbled and pumped, grateful for the food yet seemingly uncertain of how to deal with it. I belched, farted, shifted my position to ease numberless gaseous bubbles which pressed rudely upon my innards. I noticed that Huwoorsk was observing me with a reproachful eye, but chose to pay him no heed for the present. No doubt Yo had something he wished to say, but I was in no mood to engage in further discussion just now.

Not content to be ignored, Huwoorsk emitted a series of small yaps and whines. I glanced his way. Seeing he had my attention he slid onto his belly and edged towards me, to press his cold wet snout against my leg. A pathetic sight. Still I ignored him. He nudged me more insistently, and for a moment I felt a twinge of compassion. Then I reminded myself that this was not Huwoorsk. Huwoorsk was long dead. His fleeing soul I had encountered an instant before I had been sucked from blissful lightness into his torn and bleeding body. There was no Huwoorsk. There was Yo.

So I let him whinge and whine a while longer. I could not just then summon up any great feelings of love for Yo, nor had I any wish to give an ear to his complaints. Nonetheless, there was a lot I needed to learn from him in regard to past incidents, and in truth it was greatly to my advantage for he and I to remain on good working terms. In due course, then, I relented.

I closed my eyes and entered trance. Ah, how simple, how natural, to rise from the corporeal world now that I was no longer vhazz!

I summoned Yo forth from his unhappy prison of flesh.

The action was unnecessary, of course. He was there before me upon the instant.

'Master, this is not a comfortable beast to be!'

'I am acutely aware of that, Yo! I have had long and intimate acquaintance with the sufferings of the vhazz. There is nothing you can tell me about this creature that I do not already know.'

'But he – '

'I know it.'

'And he has – '

'Quite so. You need say no more. My only advice at this time is that you try to learn something from your predicament. It is an education, though I accept that it is not easy to look upon it as such when you are so stricken with its pains.'

'You are sarcastic.'

'Not so. With the benefit now of hindsight, I am able to say truthfully that I have learned much from my existence as a vhazz. My understanding of the world has undergone a profound change. I have been forced to consider again fixed ideas and preconceived notions which I would previously never have thought to question. Much appears in a new light. In short, I find I am entertaining a significantly amended world view, and am therefore thankful for the experience.'

Yo was highly dubious. I added, 'And of course, it is you I truly have to thank.'

'Me, Master?'

'Yes, Yo. You. Come now, do not pretend innocence. You committed a monstrous crime against me – '

'I thought you were dead!'

'A moment, Yo. You appear to be suffering a some-what convenient and selective memory loss. Let me remind you of certain facts. You thought I was dead after I had been thrust from Holdikor's Bridge. I can accept that you speak truth in this instance, for that was also my interpretation of the event. But we will discuss this presently. Firstly there is the matter of your having blatantly and purposefully purloined my living body prior to the unfortunate events upon the Bridge. You took it with the intention of using it for your own ends. You became an illegal occupant, a squatter, acting in direct defiance of the conditions of your service to me.'

'Your body demanded exercise, Master.'

'Under the circumstances I recall I find that some-what hard to believe. Even if it were so, it did not demand to go wandering like a mooncalf along the streets of a city ravaged by war, straight into the arms of the enemy.'

'I did not know they were the enemy!'

'Precisely, Yo! You knew nothing of my world! Yet you took my body abroad, without permission, into dangers untold. You transgressed. You perpetrated a vile and indefensible crime against me, your Master. You violated in the most flagitious terms the condi-tions of your service. And not for the first time, I might add!'

'But I intended you no harm!'

'Then why, when I returned and demanded my body back did you wilfully disobey me?'

'It was the Bear, Master! It was the Bear!' Yo whim-pered. 'You know how I begged you to free me of him. He afflicted me so, yet you did nothing. I could not go back to him.'

There was a measure of truth in this, I could not deny it. I perceived, too, that this matter was not going to be quickly or simply resolved. Yo had a knack of turning the simplest exchange into a tortuous debate; and we were straying from the issue I wished more immediately to address.

I said, 'Yo, this is not the time or the place to contend this matter. Other urgencies claim my more immediate attention. For now I simply wish to make plain how gravely I view your actions. We will discuss it again later, and in the meantime I will consider suitable penance. Do not think I have forgotten; I have not. Do you understand?'

'Yes, Master.' A sheepish tone.

'Now, I am mystified and intrigued by your survival, and the survival of my corporeal form. When my body pitched from the bridge into Death's Deep I felt the severance of the ethereal cord. I perceived death to have occurred. So how is it that my flesh stands before me now, quite alive, if somewhat the worse for wear?'

'Ah, Master, it was a strange thing. I too believed your body dead. Its terror at the prospect of the watery grave towards which it plunged was sufficient in itself to frighten its life away before ever it met the waves. When it smashed into the dark water the shock deprived it of sentience. I was bludgeoned forth, spiralling out of the body. I felt the severing of your cord; I understood it to be the end. Master, in all honesty I believed that for a period of some moments your body did die, or came so close to death as to make no matter.'

I endeavoured to recall my precise impressions at the time. I had been so weak then, both psychically and physically. Could it have happened that the cord had actually been severed, visiting momentary 'death' upon my flesh, and that somehow, after I had departed, the body had returned to life? In the light of subsequent experience I could hardly deny this as a possibility.

'Then what saved me, Yo? What brought me back to life? For I should have drowned. I cannot swim; my dread of water is overwhelming. I stood no chance in those wet depths.'

As I spoke these words it struck me that only minutes ago I had observed my flesh wading knee-deep in the stream — something I could never have brought myself to do. Furthermore, I had only just been planning to make a fishing-spear, with the intention of returning to that water to fish for dinner. No notion of fear at the prospect had entered my mind, yet for the Ronbas Dinbig of old the mere act of sitting here upon this little beach, in such close proximity to the water's edge, would have been a cause of acute unease and an urge to be elsewhere.

'Your flesh went down, down into the gurgling depths,' said Yo, with a certain relish. 'It did not struggle, it did not thrash. It was without sensation or life-vigour. Currents hurled and swirled it like a plaything. Again and again it was thrown towards dreadful rocks, to be smashed and ruined, yet each time it was dragged back unbloodied, and sucked deeper into the dark watery chasm.'

'You remained, then, as witness to its ordeal?'

'Out of loyalty, and concern for it in its plight,' declared Yo in earnest. 'In the hope that I might somehow render it aid.'

'Mmmh.'

'As yet your flesh had made no attempt to breathe, had not drawn into its lungs the foul water. It had been dragged deep into the chasm, and was taken quite suddenly in the grip of a current which thrust it upwards. And it seems that at that moment a quiver of consciousness returned. It began to thresh and kick. I sensed its terrible panic. Fortuitously it broke the surface of the water and was able to take in air. But its mindless thrashings and the swirling of the waters forced it back under. Your body was its own worst enemy, Master. It made no attempt to swim. It acted like a crazed thing.'

'It could not swim, Yo. It was crazed with terror.'

'This I perceived to be the case. Fortunate, then, that I was at hand.'

A pregnant pause, which I sensed I was expected to fill with some appreciative word. I could not. I said, 'Greater fortune would have been mine had you conducted yourself properly from the beginning.'

In hardly chastened tones Yo resumed. 'Immediately, then, with life returned, I re-entered your flesh. For though your corporeal form was as frightened as a tiny lamb surrounded by ravening wolves, though it was as helpless as a newborn babe, though it would have squealed if it could like a pig on a pyre – '

'Yes, yes, Yo. I have confessed my failing. It is unnecessary to draw closer attention to it. Please keep to the point.'

'Well, although, as I say, you were pathetic in water, such did not apply in my case. I had been a Wide-Faced Bear, and the Wide-Faced Bear enjoys a pleasing relationship with water. It is a most capable swimmer.'

It is a not uncommon mistake for bound Entities to identify too closely with the physical form they occupy. In extreme cases their belief that they are their host beast – rather than merely occupants provided with that animal form in order that they may experience and interact with the physical world – can have undesirable consequences. To all intents and purposes they do actually become that creature, and their usefulness as servant-allies is lost. In the past I had pointed this out many times to Yo, yet he had failed to grasp the reality of it, as was evidenced now by my vaguely bearish appearance. For the present, though, I chose to ignore the solecism.

'So I resumed custodianship of your body,' he continued. 'It was not easy. It struggled so, and its mind would not be calmed. Moreover, it was terribly weak. I exerted my best efforts, and had it tread water, though it could not find the strength to swim. I somehow succeeded in keeping its head above water for the most part, and gradually its panic began to abate. The currents still played mercilessly with it, the waves tossed it this way and that. As though angry that I had taken control and wrested it from them they tried to hurl it upon the cruel rocks that bounded the cavern.'

'Cavern? What cavern?'

'Did I not mention it? The currents had dragged you into a large cavern deep within the rock.'

'Intriguing,' I said.

'A row of lamps illuminated a narrow causeway which traversed the cavern at its far end,' said Yo. 'And towards these I endeavoured to guide your flesh. But you were weak beyond telling. The blood pumped from your poor severed arm, and I began to fear that you would die, despite all my efforts. The waves dashed you against the rocks, which were smooth here, and slippery and denied me a handhold. I sensed your life-force ebbing, ebbing. I felt again that I was about to be expelled from your body, that this was, at last, the end for you.'

Another irritating pause, this time for dramatic effect. I prompted him to continue. 'Quite plainly it was not the end, Yo. Please go on.'

'You were on the point of expiring,' said Yo. 'And then suddenly you were plucked limp and lifeless from the water.'

'Plucked? By whom? By what?'

'By hands, Master. From a portal in the rock at one end of the causeway a group of persons had emerged.

484

One of them spied your body which floated close beneath the causeway, and cried out. Immediately they rushed forward, and two pairs of hands reached down to pull you from the water.'

'Ever more fascinating. Who were my rescuers, then?'

'They were humans, about twenty strong. The majority were soldiers, liveried in yellow and green.'

'Yellow and green?'

These were the colours of Kemahamek's crack Eternal Guard, whose duty it was to protect the lives and welfare of the Holy Wonas and Wonasina. There was a mystery here.

'And the others?'

'Most wore long robes of ochre-yellow. It was these who brought your body back from death, for I confess, I had done all I could. It could not have survived without their immediate aid.'


IV


'These are Simbissikim priests that you describe,' I said, absorbing this new revelation with growing suspense. 'This cavern, then, would be situated beneath the city of Twalinieh itself?'

'That would be my own assessment, certainly.'

'And this party of priests and soldiers, had they descended there from the city?'

'As I was later to ascertain, yes.'

'Where were they bound, then? Did they say anything that might enlighten you as to their purpose there?'

'Their destination was not revealed, but certainly their purpose was to escape from the city with the litter which four of them transported with such care.'

'Litter? Yet again you introduce a new factor. What was this litter? What was its cargo?'

'I don't know, Master. It was a long bundle, draped in rich cloth. Four of the women carried it with great care.'

'You have done it again, Yo! You say women, yet you did not include any women in your account a moment ago.'

'Those in the ochre-robes, Master; they were women, seven of them.'

My thoughts raced. He was describing Simbissikim priestesses.

Blessed Intimates? Was it possible?

'Yo, think back, please. Describe this bundle.'

'It was a long, shrouded bundle, of no little mass. I cannot tell you more.'

'Borne on a litter, with great care, you say?'

'That's so.'

My mind leapt four paces ahead of me. Incredulously I said, 'Yo, is it possible that this bundle might have contained the body of a human being?'

'It is possible, Master. In fact, from what I saw of it, and from the concern which all in the party lavished upon it, that is the conclusion I would be drawn to. The body of a person greatly loved and accorded much respect.'

*Great Moban!* Could it be? Surely, it was the only explanation? This bundle was the lifeless form of the Wonasina of Kemahamek, the Holy Royal Princess Seruhli! What Yo had witnessed were the efforts of her loyal Intimates and Guard to remove her from the city, out of the clutches of the invading Khimmurians. By sheer happenstance, then, my near-dead corporeal form had been dragged by the currents of Death's Deep to some secret place beneath Twalinieh, there to be found by this party in its flight. But Seruhli . . . was it her corpse that they were spiriting away, or was she truly held, as Shadd had been told by the Drear-hag Mesmia, in the Semblance of Death?

'What happened next, Yo? You seem to be telling me that these people saved my life, yet they believed I was their enemy.'

'Upon this point there was animated discussion. When they laid your body upon the causeway one of them immediately cried out, "It is the Khimmurian Foreign Minister!". Two of the priestesses bent over you and swiftly bound your severed arm and ministered to you, singing mysterious chants in low voices as they worked. The others argued over what was to be done with you. Your precise status, it seemed, was uncertain. Some called you a vile cur, a low, slimy creature which should be left to perish, a purulent – '

'Yo, keep your account precise and a little less colourful, if you will. That is all that I require.'

'Yes, Master. Others were less sure. These people were all highly agitated, very nervous and anxious to be away, but all were agreed that the situation in their city was confused. Much was said in your favour. More than one of them was inclined to the belief that you had tried to save their city and their Holy Leader. Eventually agreement was reached: You would be taken with them for a certain distance, and left at some unnamed place with persons who could nurse you back to health. If you survived – for it was still not certain that you had the strength to live – you would be questioned, and a final decision then made as to your fate.'

'Then where was I taken?' I asked, with mounting excitement. Was I about to learn the true fate and whereabouts of the Holy Wonasina?

'Master, I truly recall little of the journey,' said Yo.

'You must remember that, just as your body was without consciousness, so were my perceptions greatly diminished. For weeks, until you eventually recovered, I could not gain a full impression of everything that occurred.'

'But you must remember something!'

'They took you with them, leaving the cavern through a narrow passage which led into the rock. Along this they marched for some time, emerging eventually into forest. It was night. I remember that in the distance fires burned, revealing the location of the city we had left. We marched on, the city at our backs. Further in the forest horses awaited us. We rode until light, then took refuge in the home of an ochre-robe and his family. Here you were laid upon a pallet in a barred and shuttered room. When evening came the party moved on once more. You were left behind to be tended by the priest and his helpers. And that is where you remained until your physical health was restored.'

'And when I had recovered, what then?'

'You were allowed to leave.'

'Leave? Just like that?'

'Throughout your convalescence you were visited frequently by two other ochre-robes, both female and plainly senior to the priest who tended you. On one occasion they were accompanied by another person who wore no priestly robes. They came with an armed guard, and subjected you to careful interrogation. I will not go into details, but suffice to say that you – which is to say, I – could give no proper answers to their questions, for I knew nothing of what had occurred in the city, or of what had happened to you prior to that time. Furthermore, I was beginning to discover something of the difficulties of occupying and controlling your corporeal form. Many were the pressures upon me. I found your world exceedingly strange and utterly incomprehensible, and did not know whether I was myself, or yourself, or indeed some other self not yet realised. Master, I have had a most exacting time being you.'

'I have not always found it easy myself. So, then, you were unable to provide satisfactory answers. Did the ochre-robes accept this?'

'At first they were suspicious. But with time, having observed you closely, they adjudged you to be irretrievably addled, your mind damaged beyond hope and left with less intelligence than a ball of dog-spit. You were quite evidently of no use to them, nor did you represent a danger. So you were blindfolded one day and taken on a long journey. When after some hours the blindfold was removed, you stood at a roadside with a man unknown to you. He pointed along the road. "Go that way," said he. "Do not return, if you value your life."

'With that,' concluded Yo, 'he mounted his horse and galloped away.'

'And where had I been left?'

'I do not know, Master. You were lost. I was lost. I began a life of forlorn wandering.'

'Extraordinary,' mused I. 'And now we both end up here, beside this stream. Can this be a quirk of Fate, or sheer haphazard?'

'This is simply where I find myself,' said Yo.

'But why here, in this Enchanted Land, so far from your starting point?'

'I don't know, Master. I roamed aimlessly for many weeks. With every passing day I found that my capacity to come to terms with your human existence was diminishing. I knew distress; I did not understand how your fleshly form could continue to live on while you had, as I perceived it, perished. I found myself shunned

489

by other humans, or made a figure of ridicule. On occasion I was beaten, or stoned, and forced to run to save myself from your kind. I became lonely and unhappy and greatly confused. But in this land in which we now find ourselves I have discovered that at times my suffering is lessened. Certain locations here seem to benefit my senses – that is, your senses. The mental burdens upon me are to a degree lifted; I see things a little more clearly, find my existence less clouded and my mind somewhat eased. Hence I have remained here, wandering back and forth until this very day, when lo! – by wondrous happenstance I find, to my inexpressible joy and pleasure, that my beloved Master has returned!'

'Yes. Quite.'

I had heard sufficient to occupy me for some time, and my body was calling me. I therefore thanked Yo and dismissed him, ordering him back to his vhazz body, and returned to my own flesh to reaccustom myself to myself.

My flesh was in fact demanding my return with some urgency. I found it in a state of extreme discomfort. The sour plums had done their work, exacerbated no doubt by the rations I had gluttonised only minutes earlier. My gut griped, almost doubling me over in pain. I rushed my flesh to the bushes, crouched and delivered a long and painful voiding.

This done I removed my rags and tatters and took myself to the stream, for I was filthy and stank like a mire. I bathed in the chill water, and as I bathed I marvelled, for my former dread of the stuff was entirely gone. It was, I could only assume, the product of Yo's part-belief in himself as a Wide-Faced Bear. But what other aspects of my former self might I yet find altered as a result of my two-year absence?

I came from the stream refreshed and clean, though

with a lingering uncertainty in my bowels. My only clothes were the stinking rags I had met myself in, and into these I had no choice but to climb once more. I had coin, thanks to Shadd: sufficient to purchase more respectable garments. I recalled passing a small township earlier in the day, and with this in mind I clambered up the bank, foregoing the prospect of trout, and crossed the meadow to the roadside. With Yo at my side I set off back down the trail.

## V

The settlement was a sprawling clutter of dank dwellings built of wood and mouldering boulder-rubble, set in a swale with high tree-covered slopes rising all around. At its heart was a small, almost lifeless square in which were situated one or two taverns, a few poor traders' booths and a handful of lowly shops. As we approached I cautioned Yo.

'Better that you do not accompany me. Your presence will almost certainly excite alarm and perhaps hostility. Rather, rest here on the outskirts. Conceal yourself, and be alert for my summons. I may have need of your service later.'

Yo slunk away with sulky growls. I think he still held the opinion that my visiting of the tormented vhazz body upon him was a calculated act of requital. Well, let him think it. It was all one in the end.

I wandered on into the centre of the township.

It was a cheerless place. Few people ventured out onto the streets. Those who did moved quickly, wearing expressions taut and intent. They gave the impression of being anxious to be about their business. None gave me greeting; they hurried past with eyes downcast or, at best, fleeting nervous glances.

In the square I discovered a clothier's. Within its dim interior a lean, long-faced fellow with a broken nose was seated before a wooden bench, working with needle and thread. As I entered he looked up and fixed me with an unwelcoming stare, but at the sight of my coins he discovered a new mood, and readily displayed his wares.

The choice was not excessive; the garments were functional and drab, made to withstand time and toil. I purchased a complete outfit, from tough stockings and undergarments to woollen shirt, tunic, coarse baggy breeches, a cloth cap and cloak. When I left, the proprietor had been transformed. His eyes shone and a smile lit his countenance, in a way which suggested it was something of a rare augmentation.

Still barefoot, I repaired to a cobbler's next-door-but-one and purchased a pair of strong leather boots. Outside clouds had gathered overhead. There was a rumble of thunder as I stepped back onto the little square, and the sky threw down a sudden lashing of cold rain. I made for a ramshackle inn across the square, whose sign, faded and cracked, depicted a Red Ram. Outfitted and feeling a little more like the Ronbas Dinbig of old, I had discovered quite suddenly a desire to re-acquaint myself with an old and greatly-missed friend. I marched up to the bar of the common room.

'Landlord, a pitcher of your most distinguished red wine, if you please!'

The landlord arched an eyebrow and looked at me askance as though my request exceeded the bounds of reason, then slowly moved off to fill a pitcher. I took a seat within the common room. There were only two other customers: a pair of Qotol travellers who sat glumly on the other side. I had no yen for conversation at that moment, and doubtless they would have proven dull companions. Instead I listened to the beat of the rain upon the roof and on the stones outside, and reflected upon the gloomy nature of the Qotol and their extraordinary land.

The wine came, delivered with ill-grace by a flat-footed serving girl who did nothing to warm me to her country. When she had gone I filled the dented tin goblet she had provided and sampled the ruby liquid. It was hardly distinguished, lacking character and attack, though in its favour was a surprisingly discreet smoky nose. I swilled it around my palate, and swallowed. It was young and not well-balanced, but quite long in the mouth; gravelly, harsh, oaky, with a trace of hawthorn and violets. I had tasted better.

Nevertheless, it was a joy to quaff. I rested there in that dreary inn and revelled in the sensation of the wine's essences suffusing my veins and charging my spirit. I emptied the goblet, replenished it, and giggled. Embarrassed, I looked around, but no one seemed to have noticed. Still, I was reminded again that I might yet suffer something of the dementia my poor vacant self had known in its existence as a Wanderer. There was much to be watched for, and perhaps guarded against. I drank sparingly of the remaining wine.

A blackboard above the bar included fish soup upon its menu, and this I now ordered, along with a loaf of bread, feeling that such bland and innocuous food would make no great demands upon my sensitive innards. I enquired as to the availability of a chamber for the night, and was furnished with a small room overlooking the square. Thus, when my meal was done, I went immediately to my bed.

In the early hours before the dawn I awoke and sat up in bed. I performed the preparations usual for one about to depart the corporeal plane, then closed my eyes and entered trance.

I summoned Yo.

'Yo, I must journey. Briefly, I hope. You will guard my body.'

'I am your servant, Master.'

I wondered. My future relationship with Yo hung somewhat in the balance here. Though it was true that I needed to undertake this journey, I was also viewing the exercise as a test. My psychic strength was high; if Yo planned mischief I was confident that I could confront and expel him upon my return. But I hoped this would not prove to be the case. It would sadden me to have to banish Yo. For all his faults and misdemeanours, I still, at bottom, felt a strong affection for him. And I did not relish the prospect of having to find and bind another Custodian.

I said, 'Take care while I am absent, Yo. I am still not strong. I may be vulnerable to influence.'

'I will not fail you, Master.'

I pronounced the ritual incantation: 'Custodian, enter this form and guard it until my return. Keep it as though it is your own. If it thirsts, let it drink; if it requires sustenance, let it feed. If it is endangered, protect it and recall its rightful occupant. Ensure that none severs the cord between this body and its rightful occupant. Guard it well, for this is your sacred duty. Fail, and your true name will be broadcast to your enemies. You will be cast out of this world in shame, naked and without ability, forever.'

'It shall be as you command, Master.'

So saying, Yo entered the corporeal me. I soared high. Above the world I gently probed the fabric between this world and First Realm. I sensed no immediate danger. I rent the fabric and entered First Realm. I sent forth a summons to my Guardian Entity, Gaskh.

'I am here, Master.'

'Gaskh! You have survived!' I was overjoyed. I had known nothing of the fate of my Guardian during my absence, nor even whether his loyalty to me had faltered.

'I have survived, Master. And I am the bearer of an urgent message for you.'

'A message? From whom?'

'From the female whom you call Chariness. She summoned me and expressed great concern for you. She advised me that you had contacted her, but did not know of your subsequent fate. She instructed me to pass on her words, should I ever be called to your service again. They are: "There is great danger in the Realms. Make no journeys, nor any attempt to contact us. Return if you can to Khimmur. We will know of your coming."'

I considered this, then said, 'Gaskh, do you know of the whereabouts of the Chariness?'

'I do not. It is a secret. But if I make my presence known she has said that she, or others, will contact me.'

'And are you able to journey without risk?'

'Not without risk, Master. But with precautions I can avoid those who would do me harm. Master, I would respectfully advise that you return now to your body. It is unsafe.'

'I will do so. Should you at any time find yourself able to communicate with the Chariness or others of the Zan-Chassin, give them my reply: *I am returning!*'

'That I will do.'

'One further word, Gaskh: can you tell me anything of Flitzel?'

'Of Flitzel there is nothing to tell, Master. You know her fate. She is no more.'

'Aye. But I had hoped . . .'

Gaskh said, 'Master, you must go.'

I thanked and dismissed him and withdrew from the Realms to re-enter once more the corporeal world.

I chose not to announce myself immediately to Yo. Rather, I hovered in a corner of that small Qotol chamber where my corporeal form rested, and observed. My flesh was precisely as I had left it. Not a finger had moved; not even a hair. Pleased, I revealed my presence, thanked Yo for his service, and dismissed him. I slid back into my flesh and slept the remaining hours till morning.

At first light I was up. I took breakfast in the common room, had the landlord prepare a small pack of provisions to sustain me on the road ahead, settled my account and departed.

Yesterday's storm had passed, clearing the air. The sun rose over the mountains in a golden haze, climbing into a sky of pale azure and high white puffs of cloud. Cold morning shadow still held the land, a patina of silvery dew covering the grass and dripping from the trees. My toe pained me, and I regretted that I had not enough money to purchase a horse.

I wandered out of that dreary town, and about a mile or so along the way my attention was caught by a rustling in the bushes close by. The foliage parted and a vhazz stepped out onto the road. I took note of its forlorn appearance, its scarred hide and reproachful eye.

'Yo, remain close. We have far to go, and it is a dangerous road.'

The vhazz nodded and took his place at my side. Together we turned our faces to the west and began the long journey home.